THE
LAST WINDWITCH

Also by Jennifer Adam:

Lark and the Wild Hunt

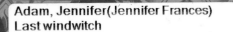

THE
LAST
WINDWITCH

JENNIFER
ADAM

HARPER

An Imprint of HarperCollinsPublishers

Library of Congress Cataloging-in-Publication Data
Names: Adam, Jennifer (Jennifer Frances), author.
Title: The last windwitch / Jennifer Adam.
Description: First edition. | New York : Harper, [2021] | Audience:
    Ages 8–12. | Audience: Grades 4–6. | Summary: Twelve-year-
    old Brida, an apprentice hedgewitch, discovers she is the key to
    saving her kingdom and must journey far from tiny Oak Hollow to
    confront the wicked Queen of Crows.
Identifiers: LCCN 2020034596 | ISBN 9780062981318
Subjects: CYAC: Magic—Fiction. | Witches—Fiction. | Apprentices—
    Fiction. | Adventure and adventurers—Fiction. | Kings, queens,
    rulers, etc.—Fiction. | Fantasy.
Classification: LCC PZ7.1.A2285 Las 2021 | DDC [Fic]—dc23
LC record available at https://lccn.loc.gov/2020034596

Typography by Alice Wang
22 23 24 25 26   PC/BRR   10 9 8 7 6 5 4 3 2 1

First paperback edition, 2022

— This book is dedicated to —

my husband, who made me believe in the
power of dreams (and true love!) when he sold
his motorcycle to buy me my first horse

my children, who gave me a second chance to
experience the wonder and magic of the world as
they discovered it for the first time

— and to —

any reader who likes to choose the biggest book
on the shelf and hide under the covers with a
flashlight to read past bedtime

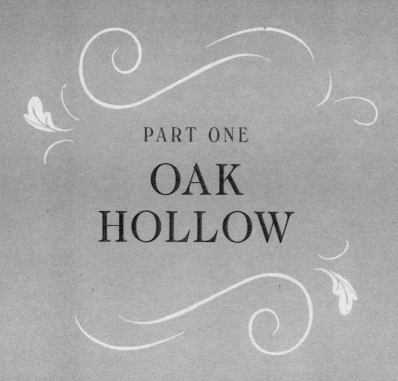

PART ONE

OAK
HOLLOW

— ONE —

Remembering

A BREEZE TUGGED dark strands of Brida's hair across her eyes and tangled them around the rosebud she'd stuck behind her ear. With a sharp, impatient yank, she shoved the hair out of her face and dashed down the road, following the murmur of voices.

She'd never been allowed to participate in the Day of Remembering because Mother Magdi said it was too dangerous, but the hedgewitch had gone to nurse a child with lung fever, so Brida seized the opportunity to satisfy her curiosity.

She knew, of course, that the Day of Remembering was also forbidden by Queen's Law, but Oak Hollow was in a forgotten corner near the farthest rim of Fenwood Reach, so what did it matter? Mother Magdi and the town goodwives might whisper about the queen's spies, but *everyone* in town would be heading for the crossroads.

Brida swallowed the lemon-sour pucker of guilt and

promised herself she'd make up for it later by sweeping the barn or cleaning Mother Magdi's saddle.

Right now, she needed to hear the stories for herself. Twelve summers—nearly thirteen!—was old enough.

Clenching her fists, she raced through a tunnel of arching trees and past Wayfarers' Well, where tired and thirsty farmers or traders could pause in the shade to sip cool water from a battered tin cup. Today a handful of unfamiliar people clustered around it, cheeks gaunt with hunger and eyes dull.

Brida's feet slowed. The women looked old enough to be goodwives—one even bounced a babe on her hip—but they didn't wear the red shawls customary in Oak Hollow. Instead, black vests laced across their ribs before flaring slightly at their hips. Though their skirts were drab and dust colored, frayed remnants of rich embroidery swirled from their tattered hems to their waists.

The men's trousers were tucked into their scuffed knee-high boots, and they wore battered high-crowned hats with feathers in the brim rather than the simple flat caps Brida was used to seeing. Like the women's skirts, their faded shirts displayed intricate embroidery at collars and cuffs.

Brida's fingers twitched at the thought of how much time and needle skill it must have taken for each garment. Her own stitches—practiced only when Mother Magdi absolutely insisted—would look unbearably clumsy in comparison.

She wondered where these travelers came from, what

4

stories they carried. The valley that held Oak Hollow was an isolated wrinkle of land tucked between forbidding hills and dense forests. It wasn't the sort of place people stumbled across by accident, and these strangers had clearly endured a difficult journey to reach it.

According to Mother Magdi, visitors used to be a rare occasion, but for the last couple of years they'd become more common. She called them refugees, people fleeing famine and hard times from across the queen's realm. A few settled in the valley, but most stayed only a day or two before drifting farther away, eyes haunted and lips whispering nightmares.

Brida smiled at the travelers by the well. She could hardly imagine how terrible things must have been to make them leave their homelands with nothing but the packs they could carry. Perhaps they'd find comfort in sharing their experiences, though they didn't return her smile and simply huddled closer together.

But before she could welcome them and explain the Day of Remembering, a burst of familiar laughter from behind the trees sent her skimming past. Dev, the butcher's boy. She was in no mood for his trouble, especially when the Voice's stories awaited her. When she glanced over her shoulder, the travelers had already turned away.

Maybe she and Mother Magdi could look out for them later.

Dodging past the blacksmith's yard, she hurried down

Trade Row, where the craftspeople and shopkeepers lived. Oak Hollow was a small, circular village of stone cottages springing like thatched-roof toadstools from the rich earth, but it boasted some of the best crafters in the region. Their wooden signs swung proudly in the wind: a stack of painted bowls for Goodman Potter; baskets for Goody Withy and her widowed sister; and a needle and thread for Goody Thimblewicket and her son, who sewed clothing so fine it was sent to manor houses for lords and ladies far outside the valley in wealthy cities across Fenwood Reach.

Brida glanced in the empty shop windows as she passed. Everyone had already headed to the crossroads.

She'd heard that in years past, blue streamers and white banners would have fluttered from roof to roof, with garlands of ivy, wild rose, and wisdomflower hanging over every door and window to celebrate this day. She wished she could have seen the traditional decorations before the queen's edicts outlawed them, but even so Brida glimpsed scraps of festive blue silk tied to a gate here and there.

And as she approached a small knot of people, she noticed stems of ivy slipped in the goodmen's pockets or rosebuds bound in the goodwives' braids. Blue ribbon peeked beneath kerchiefs and vests, pinned in brave defiance of Queen's Law.

Brida dragged her steps, letting the group round the corner ahead. She wasn't *hiding*, precisely, but she wasn't all that eager to draw attention to herself, either. Wishing she'd thought to wear her cloak despite the warmth of the day, she pinched the hem of her tunic and hoped she could reach the crossroads without anyone deciding they needed to tell Mother Magdi where she'd been.

Trade Row ended across from Goodman Hooper's workshop, barrels stacked beside his doorway. Here the town green spread like a mother's apron. Brida and Magdi often came to the weekly market to exchange fruit, vegetables, goat's milk or cheese, and magical remedies for things they needed, but today the grassy square was empty and silent.

The inn across the way was doing a brisk business, though, and laughter spilled from the open doorway. "Tell us another and I'll buy you a pitcher of ale!" someone roared cheerfully. Voices rose and fell in the ebb and flow of conversation.

The Day of Remembering was a day for stories. Small ones, secret ones, sad ones, spooky ones.

True ones.

Brida's heart swooped like a chimney swift and she hurried past the inn toward the bakery. The air held a warm cloud of sugar, spice, yeast, and cream and she couldn't resist following a young couple through the door.

Despite the queen's prohibitions, Brida had heard that the baker still observed the old traditions. On the Day of Remembering, he gave away storycakes free to anyone with a tale to tell. Brida wasn't sure what story she could offer, but her stomach rumbled and her mouth watered. She'd begged Mother Magdi to let her taste a storycake for *ages*. And there they were: a row of golden, flaky triangles steaming on a wooden tray beside the baker's elbow.

The young woman ahead of her at the counter—could it be Lilibet? No, wait, it must be Nan, who spun the smoothest, finest woolen yarn anywhere—adjusted her new red shawl and said, "I remember when I first met Mikel, one year ago this Midsummer Eve. He wore a plaid vest in a style I'd not seen before and starvation pinched his cheeks. He offered my father work in exchange for a meal and a night's sleep in our sheep barn . . . and then he stayed. I remember the sparkle in his eyes when he learned my name and the way his hands closed around mine when I showed him my favorite spot to count the stars. I remember how my heart soared when he asked me to be his wife and the feel of the silk binding ribbons as they flowed around our wrists like colored water when we spoke our love oaths. I remember wearing my grandmother's lace to walk beneath the blessing arches on the day I left my old life behind and began my new one, not as a girl but as a goodwife."

The baker leaned across the gleaming counter and handed her one of the triangular biscuits wrapped in waxed paper. "Your story is a good one. May you have a long and happy telling of it."

Mikel, standing beside Nan, ears pink, cleared his throat and said, "I come from the Meadowlands, near the western border of Fenwood Reach. I remember when winter ate the sun and froze our fields. We waited for a thaw that never came, until we grew so desperate we sent the elders out to find food and help. We waited, and shivered, and starved. At last they returned with baskets of withered fruit and parched grain, and tales of a land where summer never ended. The sun's heat sounded more promising than being slowly buried by ice and snow, so we gathered up all that we could carry—all that we had left—and began a trek across a blinding white wasteland. I remember the fallen, the lost. I remember lurching into a blazing desert where dust clouds rose to meet the sky and even the rocks cracked for want of water. I remember my parents—"

His voice broke and the baker made a sympathetic noise. "I remember being alone then," he went on, "and desperate. I wandered until I had no strength left, and that was when I stumbled into Oak Hollow and met Nan. She felt like waking up from a nightmare."

The baker handed him a storycake, grasping his elbow and giving his arm a gentle shake. "It's a hard tale but a good turning. I wish you a long and happy telling of the stories that come next."

The couple left, heads tilted toward each other as they murmured softly.

Brida swallowed and stepped up to the counter.

"Ah! Brida!" the baker exclaimed. "I wondered when you'd come to beg a storycake. Let's have it, then. What's your story?"

Brida's tongue stuck to the roof of her mouth. What *was* her story? She didn't know where she'd come from, who her parents were. She'd been left on Mother Magdi's porch like a squash no one wanted. The hedgewitch had cared for her as a baby, raised her as a child, and taken her as an apprentice. All her memories felt like borrowed ones.

The baker, Goodman Wittin, smiled gently. "It doesn't have to be a long one. It just has to be yours. And it has to be true."

Brida chewed her lip. She'd been coming to the bakery with Mother Magdi since she was a tot barely tall enough to see into the glass case beneath the counter. Wil Wittin used to save scraps of dough for her, rolling them into twists dusted with cinnamon and sugar. He knew her past as well as she did.

After a minute, she said, "I don't know where I come from. I was left in a basket on Mother Magdi's porch. She was lonely and decided to—"

He held up a hand. "That's not your story, lass. Your true story isn't just facts someone else has told you. It's how you *feel*, who you *are*."

"But—"

"Try again."

Brida's stomach growled and her cheeks flushed. "I remember . . ." she started.

And then she had her story.

"I remember when Mother Magdi introduced me to

Burdock. My pony. He'd been left in an empty barn by himself too long. He was hungry and tried to kick his way out, and that's when a neighboring farmer finally heard the racket. Burdock had hurt himself, but he was too upset, too scared and angry, to let the farmer near him. Someone fetched Mother Magdi. When she opened the barn doors, he tried to run away, only he couldn't because his back legs were injured and swollen. Eventually he let her put a rope around his neck and he hobbled home with her.

"I remember how sad he looked when I first saw him. I could count his ribs and his coat was covered in burrs. There were dark scabs on his back legs. Mother Magdi made a salve to heal him, but he wouldn't let her get close enough to apply it.

"I stared at him and he stared at me, and I felt like he could see right through my skin into all the loneliness inside my bones. He snorted in my face and I started to cry and laugh at the same time, and then he let me put that ointment all over his scrapes and scabs. I fed him and brushed him every day, and when he got better Mother Magdi showed me how to ride him. I remember the way it felt the first time we galloped, the way the wind sang in my face. It was like flying."

Brida smiled. "And I'm still the only one who can touch his back legs."

The baker chuckled, blue eyes crinkling and a dimple flashing in one rosy-apple cheek. "Now *that* is a marvelous story. I wish you joy in the growing of it." He handed her a warm storycake. "Now you'd best hurry to the crossroads. The Voice will be there soon and you don't want to miss her."

A sudden thought struck her. "If Mother Magdi asks—"

Grinning, he laid a finger alongside his nose. "Ah. That's how it is, eh? Well, lass, I've seen a whole crowd of folks at my counter today and I can't be expected to remember all of them, now can I?" He winked. "Go on, then. Quick!"

Brida laughed. "Thank you, Goodman Wittin!"

Plunging through the door, she raced to the crossroads near the edge of the village. The afternoon had quickly ripened into evening and rich golden light emptied from the sky. Not much longer to wait.

She found a place behind a large family from Maple Hill, just to the north—she didn't know them, but the men had orange maple leaves embroidered on their jackets. Then she carefully unfolded the waxed wrapper around her storycake. The biscuit was rich and flaky with butter, sprinkled with salt and rosemary for remembrance. Her mouth watered at the savory, herbal fragrance and she nibbled a corner.

Delicious. She licked the soft cheese filling from her lips and took a bigger bite.

"Used to be that every town had its own Voice," a man in front of Brida said to his son. "Only a scattered few left now to hold all that history."

"Remember the procession, when all the girls and boys would hold flickering lanterns in the darkness to escort the Voice through the village and out to the crossroads? I couldn't wait until I was old enough to join them," a woman commented. "It's a pity the queen outlawed the Parade of Light the year I could finally participate."

Someone in the crowd nearby clicked her tongue. "Aye, and now I keep my own children home. It's one thing for me to stand out here. What would the queen want with me? But my girls . . . ah, now I've heard stories, and—"

Ssshhh. Husssshhhh. Shhh.

The sound hissed through the crowd, and Brida stood on her tiptoes, craning her neck to see, straining her eyes in the cooling purple shadows of dusk. . . .

Yes, there! Hunched over her cane, a crone, bent and gnarled with the weight of long years and heavy memories, slowly hobbled through a respectful gap until she stood in the center of the crossroads.

She planted her cane on the ground with a firm thump! and cleared her throat.

A deep silence fell as the crowd collectively held its breath.

The last remaining Voice of the valley—the old woman who gathered songs and stories as if they were grapes from a vine or berries from a bush, pressing them between her teeth until she recited words as rich and sweet as summer syrup—shrugged off her blue hood. She squared her shoulders, took a length of woven strands and colored beads from a pouch at her hip. Brida knew these beads and strings were a code recording history in fiber and glass rather than ink and paper.

The Voice cleared her throat again . . .

And began a forbidden tale.

"When the world was still newly woven of sea winds and starlight, these lands belonged to the Silver Fae. They ruled the Five Realms—from the Northern Reach to the Southern Sands, the Western Woodlands to the Eastern Ridges, even the Blue Isles in the ocean.

"In those days, the young world was so steeped in power it gave rise to magical creatures like wyverns and kelpies, river sprites and forest boggles, hearth gnomes and stone goblins."

A couple of men around Brida shuffled their feet. She heard one of them mumble something about fireside tales for children, but another smacked his arm to keep him quiet.

The Voice stroked her fingers down the knotted cord she held and raised it so the crowd could get a closer look. In the fading light, a faint gleam seemed to chase along the strands.

"The most powerful creatures were the stormhorses, wrought from elemental energies and summoned by the Silver Fae," the Voice said. "The stormhorses carried the magic of wind and sun, rain and thunder, bitter snow. They raced from one end of the Realms to another, dragging chaos behind them.

"The Silver Fae ruled the land but never quite tamed these wild horses. The best they could do was direct the storm damage and hope the herd eventually chose a place to settle far from the crystal palaces and moonlit manors of the royal Fae court.

"And so it was, for centuries.

"But"—here the Voice pointed to a polished blue stone bead—"the stormhorses couldn't swim the seas, so the Blue Isles never suffered the destruction of these elemental storms. The island folk grew strong despite the slow decline of their own magic. They built cities from the rock and learned to chart the paths of stars. They built rafts, then boats, then mighty ships.

"One day, long after they'd mostly forgotten the feel of magic, they sailed from their harbors and landed on the rugged coast of the Western Woodlands. They drove the Silver Fae away, not with magic or power but with salt and iron. They chased the stormhorses beyond the borders of—"

Lightning split the sky, pouring waves of rolling thunder across the horizon. It startled Brida and made a small child scream. Another streak of lightning and crack of thunder sent sizzling goose bumps chasing along Brida's arms and frizzed the hair at the nape of her neck.

Restlessness swept the fringes of the crowd and heads tilted up, waiting for raindrops that didn't fall.

"Maybe if we had stormhorses our weather would cooperate and we wouldn't be starving," said a barrel-chested man.

A woman spun around to glare at him. "You don't know how lucky you are, Jackon Everet, living here in the valley. Things may be hard, but out there you'd know *real* hunger."

"I'm just saying—"

The Voice scowled and flung up a hand. "No!" she growled. "Stormhorses are not plow horses, to be tamed and set to work. They're not cart ponies or pleasure horses. They are the embodiment of the very elements themselves. They are beautiful, yes, and powerful, but also wild and dangerous. You see—"

But she was interrupted again. "The stormhorses also aren't *real*." A man's voice ripped through her words. "We came here to listen to true stories, not nursery fables and old legends."

Grumbling discord swelled. Some listeners agreed, while others protested his rudeness toward the Voice.

Someone else yelled, "We don't need stormhorses. We need a Windwitch. Tell us about the last one. Tell us the story of the three feathers." He was met with cheers of agreement.

The Voice frowned. She twisted the knotted strands in her crooked fingers and tapped each bead with a long nail. After a moment, she thunked her cane on the ground three times. "So be it," she said, and thrust the cord back inside her pouch. She withdrew another, braided from black, white, and brown thread and tied with three feathers.

Brida leaned forward, curiosity singing in her ears.

"Some years ago, there was a lady—Melianna of Idlewild—who wanted nothing so much as a babe of her own, so she went to the Windwitch on the Veiled Cliffs to beg a spell." The Voice's words were soft now and colored with sorrow.

"The Windwitch warned her that such a spell might not turn out quite as she hoped, but the lady insisted. So the Windwitch reached into the pocket of her cloak and pulled out three feathers: one from a sparrow, one from a dove, and one from a crow. She cast them on the wind so it could carry the lady's wishes to the ears of the Great Mother.

"The lady did not have a baby.

"Nine months later, she had *three*—sisters born just seconds apart.

"The first had eyes like the sky and hair so fair they called it silver. The second had rich chestnut hair and eyes the color of sun-warmed earth. And the third . . . her eyes were as green and dark as jealous secrets, her hair like midnight shadows.

"Oh, how the lord and lady celebrated! They called their daughters Morning, Noon, and Night and loved them dearly.

"But not everyone in the manor shared their joy. The nurse left before the babes had seen their third summer.

'It's the clever one with eyes the color of clover,' she said. 'There's something not quite . . . Ach, I can't find words to shape it. Only it's time for me to be leaving, is all.'"

The Voice's tone changed as she bent forward, fingers twisting through the length of thread and feathers she held.

"The lady loved her daughters and closed her eyes to ugly truths. But the servants saw, and whispered. Some of them left and never returned.

"When the girls were nine years old, the lady took them back to the Windwitch on the Veiled Cliffs to have their futures read, as was the custom at the time. They'd left their hair unbound and unbrushed for three days so that the wind, breath of the Great Mother, could tangle their destinies into the long and messy strands for the Windwitch to decipher.

"'My daughters,' the lady announced, tipping her head respectfully.

"The Windwitch beckoned the girls forward so she could examine the knots in their hair. But the green-eyed daughter pulled a silver knife with a bone handle from the pocket of her skirt. Quick as a scorpion sting, she cut a hank of her hair while chanting words of smoke and shadow and threw a binding spell at the Windwitch.

"The Windwitch reached for the sky, but she had no time to call a storm in her defense. The young girl's powers were already dark and strong.

"So the Windwitch did the only thing she could think to do in that moment. She flung herself from the cliffs, turning into a great eagle that was never seen again."

The Voice let her words sink to a murmur, a breath, a memory.

"Without the Windwitch to weave the winds of spring, summer, fall, and winter, the seasons snarled in disarray. We told ourselves it was only fair, that it was just the wheel of the year finding a new balance. After all, we'd had the blessings of a Windwitch for a long time, while other communities across Fenwood Reach had never been so lucky. We told ourselves that we could adapt, that we could learn the rhythms of the weather even without the Windwitch's magic to guide us just as the rest of the queen's realm had to.

"But without the Windwitch to braid the clouds into ribbons of rain across the land, to unravel storm knots and snow snags, the weather turned fierce and unreliable, growing worse year by year. Crops withered and died, flooded and died, or froze and died. People shivered, drowned, burned. They were struck by lightning or caught in wind twists.

"Without the Windwitch to read the breath of destiny, chaos cast its hand over the country."

The Voice clutched the feathers in a tight fist. "And it is only growing worse. People are starving, and the Queen of Crows—"

The crowd pressed closer, jostling Brida as everyone strained to hear what was coming.

"What do you think you're doing?" Mother Magdi's sudden question sliced through the story like a sharp blade. She stalked toward the crossroads, cloak fluttering around her ankles. The three green leaves of the hedgewitch emblem embroidered on her chest seemed to catch the flickering glow of the lantern light around her.

Brida spun on her heel, looking for a place to hide, but there was no way to duck through the crowd. They were packed in too tightly.

"Bertram! Adalyn! Grigor! You sit on the Council of Wisdoms. One would presume that means you at least have enough sense not to break Queen's Law like this!"

Brida wedged her elbow in between two women and tried to squeeze her way past. One scowled at her and the other stepped on her toes.

"Peace, Mother Magdi," Wisdom Grigor said. "They're only stories."

"You are a *Wisdom*. You should know better! They aren't just stories. The Queen of Crows has forbidden them, and—"

"The castle is days away, and the queen doesn't care about our little corner of the Reach here. Let us all have some fun, can't you?"

A chorus of agreement echoed his words.

"It's only one day," someone called. "There's no harm in—"

"I recognize you, Mitchum Fletcher. You're from Hollygate, past the bend in the river, aren't you?"

"That's right, and I've come all this way with my family just to hear—"

She spread her arms. "Tell us, Mitchum, why you traveled *here* for the Day of Remembering. Hollygate is a large town, isn't it? You've got your own river barge, three inns, and a carriage service. And yet you had to come *all this way*, through the valley—what did it take, six hours? Seven?"

He shuffled his feet. Scratched the rough black beard on his chin. "Nine. Got caught in a hailstorm."

"So, why did you make the trip? Where is *your* Voice?" Mother Magdi pressed.

"Gone," he grudgingly admitted. "Captured by the queen's men four—no, five?—years ago."

"And what of those who were listening when she was taken?"

"Arrested as well. Beyond that I can't say. No one knows." His voice held resignation, regret.

Mother Magdi turned in a slow circle, brows lowering when her gaze landed on Brida. "Can't you all understand I'm only looking after you? It's my responsibility to keep you safe! I *encourage* you to seek our Voice, to ask for her stories and share your own. But not like this. Find her in the market square or beside the well—not at the crossroads. If the queen notices, if she realizes how loosely her laws apply out here . . . well, there could be worse trouble than any of you imagine."

Brida heard disgruntled mutters about Magdi's sour-milk attitude spoiling the Day of Remembering. She was disappointed, too, but Mother Magdi had dedicated her life to caring for the valley communities and wouldn't ruin a holiday unless she truly feared the risk. A guilty flush burned in Brida's cheeks as Wisdom Adalyn raised her chin and called, "Hold your tongues! We are fortunate to have a hedgewitch protecting us. How many other villages can say the same? Show respect!"

The grumbles dwindled to resigned sighs, sheepish shuffles, and mumbled apologies.

The Voice said, "Mother Magdi is right. It grows late, anyway." She cleared her throat and shook the cord of feathers. "But hold this in your minds: the Queen of Crows can forbid our Day of Remembering, but even she cannot erase our memories. She can burn books and scrolls on blazing pyres in her great stone courtyards, but ink and parchment only hold the shape of stories. As long as there are those to tell them, no flames can burn our tales away. The queen can send snakes to snatch our voices, but words aren't always necessary."

She thumped her cane in the dust of the crossroads and

Brida jumped at the unexpected emphasis. "You can't kill truth," the Voice declared.

Murmuring assent, the crowd scattered like fallen leaves. Brida seized her chance to dart away, hoping she could make it home with a plausible excuse before Mother Magdi got there.

She wasn't quick enough.

The hedgewitch caught her by the wrist. "Hold a moment, Brida, and we will walk back together." To the Voice she said, "I wish you wouldn't encourage them. My protection only extends so far, and the queen's attention is bound to wander this way sooner rather than later."

"I understand your concern, Mother Magdi. But I am the Voice. Who would I be if I did not mark the Day of Remembering?" She patted Magdi's shoulder and hobbled back toward the village, humming softly to herself as she shoved the feathers and string back in her pouch.

Brida stared at her own worn leather boots and wriggled her toes. The weight of Magdi's dismay pressed her chin to her chest. "I'm sorry. I just wanted to hear the stories for myself."

"It's not the stories that trouble me. It's the *danger*. How many times have I warned you against drawing the queen's notice?" Magdi waved a hand at the departing villagers. "The Day of Remembering, this gathering, all of it is against the law. And when the queen discovers it's still going on here—and she will, eventually, realize—I don't want you caught in the consequences. Can't you see that?"

Brida nodded miserably as they turned toward home. She'd heard this lecture a thousand times before. And even though Brida understood that the hedgewitch's worry meant she cared, it didn't ease the ache of *wanting* in her chest.

Mother Magdi sighed. "Curiosity is—"

"A trap to catch the cat, I know. But I'm not a cat. I'm careful. I just want to *know*."

"And aren't you my apprentice? It's my job to teach you what you want to know. All you have to do is ask."

Brida's tongue curled in her cheek. She *did* ask, but that didn't mean Mother Magdi always answered her questions. Still, if the door was open . . . She thought about the starving refugees by the well, about Mikel and Nan, about failing crops and the unpredictable seasons. She blurted, "Where did the stormhorses go?"

Mother Magdi was silent as they left the lantern-lit road in town and followed a curving path through the trees. Their footsteps shuffled a soft counterpoint to the rustle of leaves overhead and the song of crickets in the underbrush. After Brida had decided Magdi was ignoring the question, the hedgewitch finally answered. "None of the stories say for sure, but they all agree that the stormhorses followed the Silver Fae to other lands. Far, far away."

"But they *are* real?"

"I believe they once existed, yes. Do they still?" She spread her hands and shrugged.

Brida replayed the Voice's story in her mind and asked, "Why hasn't the Windwitch come back to weave the weather right again?"

"No one knows where she went, either. Some say she will return when we need her most. Others say she was killed. Maybe she simply chose an aerie that suited her better than the Veiled Cliffs."

"Those aren't really answers," Brida complained.

"Many questions don't *have* answers, but they're still worth asking." Magdi waved away the cloud of fireflies and nightmoths following her.

"Why hasn't another Windwitch come, then?"

"Windwitches are not like hedgewitches, child. The power to work hedgemagic is rare enough, and sometimes those with the talent are too afraid to even use it. But Windwitches . . . if one is born, it is a blessing from the Great Mother. We may not see another in our lifetimes."

They followed a fork in the path to the clearing that held their cottage. Rich golden-red light flickered in the windows from the embers on the hearth and a twist of smoke curled against the starry sky.

"I'll see to the fire and fix us a kettle of tea before bed while you tend to the animals," Magdi said.

But Brida had one last question. "What about the boy with lung fever? Did you heal him?"

Magdi untied her cloak as she climbed the porch steps. "An herbal steam to ease his breathing, a warm compress for his chest. He'll be right as summer roses in a day or so, if the fool boy doesn't try swimming somersaults in a cold pond before he's fully recovered. Go on to the barn now and hurry with the feeding. Tomorrow will be a long day. . . . To make up for your disobedience, I expect the green room cleaned and restocked with herbs. I'll leave you a list."

Brida sighed, but at least the punishment was worth the chance to hear the Voice and to taste her first storycake.

TWO

A Wingnote

"BRAMBLES AND THORNS," Brida cursed and scuffed the toe of her boot across the mucked-up earth. There were starflowers here three days ago, she was sure, but something had torn them out. The only other patch she knew was half a league farther into the forest—assuming it was still there.

Grumbling, she hiked up the hill and headed deeper into the trees. The gathering basket banged against her hip with every step, so she switched hands and adjusted her grip, muttering as she ducked to avoid a low-hanging branch.

Instead, she walked right into a cobweb, which did not improve her mood.

Dumping the basket on the mossy ground, Brida swiped at her face with both hands. Spider silk clung to her eyelashes even after she tried to claw it away.

"Ugh!" She flung herself to the ground beside the half-full basket.

A white dove flashed through the dappled shadows and

Brida's gaze traced it past a hickory tree. She recognized the bird as one that frequently visited the woods near the cottage. Brida had a knack with birds, though the first time she'd talked a hawk out of catching a rabbit, Mother Magdi had scolded her for interfering in the natural cycle. But this dove, despite Brida's attempts to speak to it, often seemed to ignore her.

Just another in a long list of failures.

Brida rubbed her neck. Her right ankle itched from a bug bite and her left wrist burned from a regrettable encounter with a patch of stinging nettles. She had a blister on her heel and another on her little toe, and sweat trickled uncomfortably down her back.

It had not been a very good morning, and she still hadn't collected half the plants on Mother Magdi's list.

So much trouble for only a couple of stories.

She leaned back against a fallen log and closed her eyes, letting the leaf-damp breeze lift tangled hair away from her face. Birds sang in the oak branches laced above and somewhere nearby a woodpecker knocked for bugs.

It was the perfect day for a pony ride, but instead she'd spent hours grubbing about in the dirt for weeds.

She shouldn't complain, she knew, not after all that Mother Magdi had done for her. And as punishment, it was a fair price to pay for sneaking off to the crossroads. She just wished . . .

A sudden silence descended as the forest held its breath,

distracting Brida from her self-pity. The birds went still in midsong and a prickle of alarm drew tension along her spine. She sat up slowly and turned her head.

A twig cracked behind her, breaking beneath the weight of a step too clumsy to be anything but human.

Oh, brambles, Brida thought. She didn't feel like speaking to anyone, but she shifted her weight and prepared to stand anyway.

Too late. A voice she wished she didn't recognize was already bellowing out that irritating song.

"Little witchling, sitting in the road,
Crossing her eyes and scratching her nose,
Trying to remember how her spell goes.
One blink, two blinks, three blinks, woe!
She's turned herself into a toad!"

Brida rose to face him, folding her arms and frowning in her best imitation of Mother Magdi on a bad day. "Well, Dev Druse, at least you've got *something* in your head, even if it's just a nursery song."

The butcher's boy flushed and shifted his grip on a curved bow. He stood a head taller than her, with pale hair the color of stale porridge and skin like curdled milk.

The stain of old blood on his leather vest turned Brida's stomach. She and Mother Magdi ate no meat; and even though Magdi said they should not hold an honest job against honest men, Brida would never call Dev honest. He was a brute, pure and simple, and he liked killing things.

"What are you saying, witchling?" he growled.

"Oh, did I use words that were too big for you? Don't fret. You'll catch on eventually."

He reached for the quiver over his shoulder and plucked an arrow, his eyes as dark and hard as river rocks. "Think you're so smart, do you, witchling?"

Brida took an involuntary step backward, thrusting a hand in the pocket of her tunic. She clutched the charm Mother Magdi made her carry: a linen pouch containing two pebbles—a polished bit of agate with a dark band around the center and a smooth, black stone from the mountains of the north—as well as a small white feather. Protective energy buzzed beneath her fingers and gave her a measure of courage, but she also knew what Mother Magdi would say: "If you poke an angry badger you'll end up getting bitten."

But Brida wasn't in the best temper, either, and she was tired of Dev and his stupid songs.

"I'm not a witchling," she spat. *And I'm smarter than you!* she added silently, but even she wasn't foolish enough to say that aloud.

He grinned, but it wasn't a friendly expression. "Right. You're just a foundling nobody else wanted. Lucky for you the hedgewitch can't turn away a stray, eh?"

Every word was as sharp as broken glass, and Brida forced herself not to flinch.

Striding forward, he stroked the fletching of the arrow, and a snake tongue of real fear flickered in Brida's chest. Dev was a bad apple, that was certain, but he wouldn't really hurt her, would he?

She stared at his jack-o'-lantern smile and suddenly wasn't sure.

With a sigh, she said, "Listen, Dev. I'm not looking for trouble. Let's just go our separate ways."

That jack-o'-lantern grin rotted and collapsed in on itself as he opened his mouth to say something, but a chill wind suddenly screamed through the woods, tearing away his words. It thrashed the trees, breaking branches and tossing shredded leaves and pine needles in green showers. It spun dirt and twigs in the air, howling as it ripped past them.

Dev huddled against the trunk of a massive old oak, cowering from the wind's terrible power.

But Brida watched the storm, shivering and hugging her elbows. Clouds the color of bruised plums boiled overhead and a flash of lightning sizzled through the trees to her right. It left a purple-gold streak seared across her vision. She tried to blink it away as crashing thunder rolled around her, shaking the earth beneath her feet.

"What are you doing? Make it stop!" Dev cried, staring at Brida as he lurched toward a pine tree a few paces farther away. He stumbled and fell, cursing as he clambered back to his feet.

"It's not me! I can't call storms!"

Another gust of wind brought a glitter of snowflakes dancing from the sky like stardust. Frost glazed the tattered leaves still clinging to their branches and glistened on soft patches of moss. Brida's teeth chattered.

Dev gripped his bow and twisted wildly. "What's happening?"

"I don't know!" Though the weather had become increasingly unpredictable over the last few years, this squall was far worse than anything she could have imagined. It felt as if the seasons had tangled themselves together all at once, and the resulting tempest carried the tingle of strong, wild magic. But where had it come from?

Brida tried to sense the spellweave the way Mother Magdi had taught her, but there were too many conflicting energies swirling around and she couldn't trace any of them.

Who was powerful enough to cast a weave like this?

Lightning flashed again, but the crack of thunder sounded farther away this time. The clouds burst, sending curtains of cold rain to lash the forest. Dev dropped his bow and covered his head, moaning.

The wind howled—and then it blew away, taking the rain with it.

The sun came out and the sky cleared. The frost melted and steam rose in a swirling mist from the damp ground.

Brida and Dev stared at each other for one shocked heartbeat, and then he spun away. "I don't care what you say. I'm going to tell the Council of Wisdoms you did this on purpose!" he shouted over his shoulder, before plunging through the dripping underbrush.

"I didn't do anything!" she cried. "Dev, wait! You forgot your bow—" But he was already out of sight. "Fine. Be that way."

She kicked the bow into a patch of poison ivy—let Dev have a little fun finding it later—and turned to retrieve her gathering basket, anxious to get home so she could tell Mother Magdi what had happened.

"Oh, brambles and thorns," she muttered as she picked up her basket. The storm had dumped it over, scattering the stems, leaves, and flowers she'd worked so hard to collect. What hadn't been blown clean away was frost blackened or crushed into the mud, but it was too late to start again.

She was going to be in even more trouble now.

Brida's anger at Dev and anxiety about the strange storm started to dissipate as she neared the peaceful sanctuary of home.

Mother Magdi's cottage crouched at the edge of the forest like a friendly turtle. It was old and gray and rather squat shaped, but the surrounding gardens gave it a rugged beauty that made up for the occasional leak in the roof.

A small grove of apple trees—the crispest, sweetest, reddest apples in the country—grew in the southeast corner of the clearing near several beehives and a bed of purple clover. A circular herb garden took up the center of the yard and a vegetable patch sprawled along the western edge. Blackberry bushes, wild strawberries, and a crooked wooden trellis holding up a grapevine bordered the eastern side.

Flowers grew in every other available space. Bluebells and dragonbane, heartsease and lady's slippers and wishlilies. Moonflowers and sunflowers. Honeysuckle and fairydrops.

And roses. Roses *everywhere*.

All the plants in Mother Magdi's yard could be used in remedies and charms, but not all the plants the hedgewitch needed could be cultivated. Some of them only worked if they were left wild and gathered as necessary, much to Brida's dismay. She frowned and rubbed a smudge of dirt off her wrist.

Her pony, Burdock, grazed in a grass pasture behind the gardens with Velvet, Mother Magdi's elegant chestnut mare. The two bumped noses and chewed side by side, tails swishing in the late afternoon sunlight.

Brida dropped the empty basket near her feet and hooked her elbows over the top of the gate, resting her cheek on her arms as water droplets trickled from her chin-length hair. She was tempted to stay and watch the horses, waiting for the sun to dry her rain-soaked clothes. Or, better yet, to simply ride off on Burdock until Mother Magdi forgot the punishment she'd given.

But the hedgewitch never forgot *anything*. She had to be

faced sooner or later. Brida would just have to promise to try harder tomorrow.

Besides, Mother Magdi needed to know about the magic storm.

Snatching up her basket once more, Brida headed toward the cottage with a sigh.

A rustle in the lilac bushes near the porch revealed Nettle, the goat, with a mouthful of leaves. Brida paused to scratch Nettle's head before climbing the crooked steps to the door.

She toed her soft leather boots off and left them under the porch bench, setting the gathering basket on top. Nearly a whole day wasted.

"Mother Magdi, I . . ." she started to say, stepping inside the cottage.

But the hedgewitch stood in front of the window facing the back woods, murmuring to a pearl-gray pigeon. The bird bobbed her head and lifted a leg with a tiny cylinder attached. As Brida watched in surprise, Magdi gently removed the cylinder. She pulled a string to break the wax seal and unrolled a slip of ribbon-thin paper.

A messenger pigeon!

Wingnotes were forbidden by Queen's Law and anyone keeping a coop faced punishment if they were caught, but it didn't stop desperate or daring people from trying. Brida saw messenger pigeons flying through the woods on rare

35

occasion, carrying little leather tubes on their banded legs. She'd even tended one with a broken wing, though she had to care for it in secret. But Brida had never known Mother Magdi to receive a wingnote before. What sort of message was so important—so confidential—it had to be carried to the hedgewitch by an outlawed pigeon? Who could afford the danger?

Magdi slammed a hand down on the windowsill, startling the bird. The pigeon clicked her beak and ruffled her wings before settling again, bright eyes fixed warily on the hedgewitch. "Bloody bones," Magdi cursed. "Hold a moment. I'll have an answer."

Brida couldn't believe her ears. Mother Magdi *never* cursed.

Whatever was in that note must mean trouble.

Magdi glanced over her shoulder, noticing Brida for the first time. "Why are you so wet?" She shook her head. "Never mind. Fetch a dish of water and some of the seed mix in the tin on the highest shelf and then change your clothes." Concern creased her face and her words were clipped and brisk, as if she had to bite them from the air. The small scar beneath Magdi's right eye—the result of a childhood accident she refused to speak about—stood out in livid scarlet the way it did when she was upset.

Something was terribly wrong.

Questions bubbled on Brida's tongue but she pressed her lips together and hurried to do as Magdi asked.

As she tipped a little birdseed into a clay dish, Brida watched Mother Magdi from the corner of her eye. Magdi had lived in Oak Hollow for as long as anyone could remember and seemed to have no family. Twice a year she visited Ivy Sorin, the hedgewitch who lived across the bay in Granite Cove. But Mother Ivy would never send a wingnote—hedgewitches had to be careful not to draw too much attention, and she wouldn't take the risk.

So what was this about?

The pigeon gave a coo of satisfaction when Brida handed her the birdseed, happily pecking out her favorite bits.

Before Brida could even glance at the note Magdi was scrawling in return, the hedgewitch rolled the paper slip up tight. With a frown, she tucked it into the leather cylinder and held it out to the pigeon.

The bird lifted her leg with a resigned click of her beak and let Magdi fasten the carrier tube. Magdi said, "No hurry, friend. Finish your seed and water first."

"What's the matter?" Brida asked, unable to contain her curiosity any longer.

"Nothing that need concern you yet," Magdi answered, passing a weary hand over her eyes.

"But—"

"Go change into something dry and hang your clothes out on the line. Did you find—" Magdi was interrupted by a heavy pounding at the door. "You'd better hurry. Someone needs our help."

Brida sighed. Someone *always* needed help. While Magdi sent the pigeon on her way, Brida flung a clean tunic over her head and finished pulling on soft leggings. She rushed back down the ladder from the loft as Magdi threw the door open.

"Oh, Mother Magdi, come quick! My wife . . . I think the babe is coming! Linna's screaming!" Jon Irons, the blacksmith, danced from foot to foot, twisting his cap in his large hands and practically panting with anxiety.

Brida lifted the satchels from the hooks on the wall while Magdi clucked and laid a gentle palm on his arm. "Easy, now, Jon. I've been expecting this. Linna will do just fine, and so will the babe. We're coming."

He grabbed both satchels from Brida and half dragged, half led her and the hedgewitch to the cart at the end of the lane. His shaggy brown mare switched her tail and nickered when she saw Brida—Brida usually brought extra apples to share whenever she took her own pony in for his shoes—but there was no time for pats and scritches because Jon had already leaped into the driver's seat and twitched the reins.

As they rattled past Burdock and Velvet, the pony whinnied and kicked up his heels.

"I'll be back soon!" Brida called to him, hoping it was true.

Bringing babes into the world was supposed to be a marvelous miracle, but to her it seemed a long, tedious, squalling mess. She sighed and knotted her hands in her lap.

It had been such a strange day of storms and secrets. She'd wanted to spend her evening in front of the fire, sipping tea and talking with Mother Magdi—*not* attending a delivery.

Hopefully it would go quickly and there would still be time for quiet conversation later.

Brida chewed her lip, feeling selfish. Sometimes she very much feared she would never learn to be a proper hedgewitch.

— THREE —

Stormhorses

BRIDA AWOKE THE next day with a muzzy head and the sense that time had done something strange while she dreamed. She blinked and scrubbed a hand over her gritty eyes, then sat up with a start.

The light pouring through the windows was the rich, clear gold of late morning. She'd overslept.

Why hadn't Mother Magdi woken her? She had chores to do and the animals would be impatient.

She scrambled to her feet and flung the woven coverlet across her pallet, yanked her sleeping gown over her head, and pulled on a clean tunic and leggings. "I'm awake!" she hollered, clattering down the ladder from the loft. "I'm coming!"

But the cottage held the hollow sense of *waiting* that meant Mother Magdi had already stepped out for the day.

Brida frowned. They'd been over at the Irons' homestead well into the night—the birth had not been an easy one—and Brida hadn't slept well once they'd returned home. But Magdi shouldn't have let her lie abed for hours when there was work to do and a scruffy pony to ride.

She hurried to the bucket of water by the hearth and splashed her face, rinsing away the residue of troubled dreams. Then she looked around, trying to get her bearings back in the waking world.

A wire basket, full of brown speckled eggs, sat on the scarred wooden table beside a stoneware crock of fresh goat's milk. Mother Magdi had already tended the animals, and guilt pricked Brida's skin. Magdi was the one who'd called Linna's exhausted spirit back from the realm of shadows to save her life after her babe was born, and the hedgewitch needed sleep, too.

Brida lifted the crock of milk from the table and prepared to put it in the springhouse where it would stay cool, but a folded note had been stuck in the egg basket with her name written in large, firm letters.

> Brida, dear, I've been called away but will return later this evening. While I'm gone, please sweep the floor and clear the cobwebs from the springhouse. The window glass needs wiping and you might turn the potatoes in the root cellar, too. Some of them smell musty. Also, did you find the wild herbs on my list? I didn't see them in the green room. Stay safe and enjoy your day. I'll be home in time for supper.

She'd signed it with a heart and a scrawled *M*, but Brida blew hair out of her eyes and dropped the note with a flicker of irritation. Wasn't she old enough to know what needed doing without a list of reminders? She could manage the cottage by herself for a bit.

If she hurried with the chores, though, she would have time to take Burdock for a ride *and* collect Magdi's herbs. Cheered, she headed for the springhouse with the milk.

On her way back to the cottage, as she stepped along the winding stone path between the barn and the henhouse, a pigeon cooed and she suddenly remembered the message Magdi had received the day before. Though the drama of Linna's birthing labor had sent her questions flying, they now came home to roost, pecking the edges of her mind with curious insistence.

Magdi was hiding a mystery, and Brida was determined to puzzle it out. If she only knew what the message had said. . . .

She turned questions over in her head as she turned the potatoes, and considered all the reasons Magdi might be keeping secrets from her as she wiped down the window glass. And then, as she swept the floor, she spotted a tiny scrap of paper forgotten in the corner. Brida pounced on it, unrolling it with eager hands. It wasn't right to pry, she knew, but Magdi had dropped it, so . . .

She squinted at the tiny writing, surprised to see only two words: *She suspects.*

That was it. No greeting, no signature. No details. Just two maddening words.

She suspects.

"Who suspects? Suspects what? And why does it matter to Magdi?" Brida wondered aloud.

She didn't expect an answer, of course, but she got one nonetheless when a snort punctuated her questions. Brida turned to see Burdock's soft whiskery nose sticking through the open cottage door.

She laughed and held up a hand. "Don't you dare step in here! I've been sweeping!" She hurried over to scratch the white star beneath his messy forelock. "Do you want to help me find some herbs for Mother Magdi?"

He flipped his nose and whickered.

"I'll take that as a yes. So, how did you get out this time?" She patted Burdock's neck as she stepped out of the cottage.

He raised his upper lip in a silly pony grin and nudged her shoulder. It was his favorite game: finding clever new ways to sneak out of his paddock and then waiting for her to guess how he'd done it.

Brida hurried to the paddock gate—still latched—and walked the perimeter of the split-rail fence. No broken gaps, so he hadn't gone through. And she didn't think he'd gone over, either—he'd jumped out almost a fortnight ago and didn't like to repeat his tricks too often.

Burdock pranced along behind her, pleased with his

success, as she studied the paddock. Then she spotted a skid mark near the corner of the fence, where the ground dipped low. A streak of mud and crushed clover stems, a telltale hoofprint . . .

"Burdock, did you wriggle *under* the fence?" She pointed to the spot. He nickered and tossed his head, making her laugh. "You're a lot more agile than you look, pony."

Brida led him back to the barn and tied him in the aisle. He stood patiently while she brushed his coat and picked mud and pebbles from his hooves, and he didn't flinch when she set a wool blanket and leather saddle on his back. But when she lugged out the saddlebags, Burdock stomped a front hoof and swished his tail.

"I know," she told him. "But we can help Mother Magdi and have fun, too, I promise."

Snorting skeptically, he lowered his head for the bridle. Brida scratched his chin and blew softly in his nose. "We always have a good time, don't we?" she said, leading him outside.

But just as Brida prepared to climb into the saddle, a terrible clatter came from the barn. "What now?" she grumbled, marching back inside with her hands on her hips.

She should have guessed. Nettle the goat, disgruntled by the lack of attention, had climbed into the hayloft and head butted two bales of hay over the edge. They'd tumbled onto the rack of shovels and pitchforks, which in turn had fallen across the barrel of oats and two empty buckets.

And now Nettle peered down at the dusty chaos, eyes glittering with mischievous glee.

Brida frowned up at her. "This is the reason we can't trust you, you know. If you'd behave decently, you wouldn't have to stay in the barn while we go out on adventures."

"*Mehhhh?*" Nettle bleated, scrambling out of the hayloft.

"Sorry, but no. You never stay with Burdock like I ask and then I have to waste all day rounding you up again. And last time I took you gathering with me, you ate all the chicory and dandelions I was supposed to bring back to Mother Magdi. I'd leave you outside, but"—Brida cast a sharp look around the mess in the barn—"you'd just cause trouble. You'll have to wait here until we get back."

She sighed and patted the goat on the neck. "If you're good while I'm gone, I'll bring you extra flowers to nibble."

Brida closed the barn doors and hurried back to Burdock. She would have to sort out the mess once they returned.

Hopping into the saddle, she gave her pony a nudge with her heels. He walked out of the yard and threaded his way through the trees, ears pricked cheerfully and tail gently swishing. His skin twitched away the occasional fly and Brida relaxed with the swinging rhythm of his gait. Now and then she pressed her calf against his side or lay the reins against his neck to direct him, but mostly she let him pick his own way along the narrow deer track winding into the hills.

As he stepped into the bright sunshine of a high meadow, Brida leaned forward to peer at the ground they passed. A trail of broken grass stems and crushed clover blossoms looped through the meadow, an occasional hoofprint pressed into the dirt. Mother Magdi and Velvet wouldn't have ridden this way, would they? The wind whispered through the grass, and Brida frowned, straightening in the saddle. Something tickled her mind. . . .

She tried turning Burdock off the trampled path and toward the shelter of the tree line, but he snorted and tossed his head, nearly yanking the reins from her hands. She squeezed a knee against his side and gathered the reins more firmly, but he clamped his teeth on the bit, pulled her half out of the saddle with a sudden lunge, and took off trotting along the trail of hoofprints.

"Burdock!" she cried, shifting her weight for better balance and trying to gain stronger control of his steering.

He tipped his head to one side, fixed a warm brown eye on her, and flicked his ears in mock apology—but he neither slowed nor changed his course.

"Fine," she huffed. "Where are you taking us?"

He blew out his breath and slowed to a smooth, easy jog, dropping his nose to the ground as if following a scent like a dog. Brida rolled her eyes. In spite of all the gentle, sturdy ponies in the valley, she'd ended up with *Burdock*.

While her stubborn pony picked his way through the grass, she studied the meadow for anything Mother Magdi might need. The wheel of seasons had spun lopsided and uneven for so many years now, it was getting harder to collect the plants they used for magic and remedies. Some wildflowers had grown so scarce, Brida wasn't sure they could even be found in the valley anymore.

Of course, it was also possible she was just overlooking them. Even after all her years of study with the hedgewitch, Brida still had trouble identifying plants. Oh, she knew the easy, obvious ones: starflowers and blood drops, bruisewort and feverfew, thistles and nettles and loverbane. She knew wild thyme and spice grass by scent, and most of the time she managed to guess right just by paying attention to the tingle in her fingertips and the whisper in her ears.

But she still made mistakes. Too many mistakes.

Brida's cheeks prickled as she recalled the pain salve she'd tried to mix last week. She *thought* she'd followed Mother Magdi's instructions precisely, and yet the pungent goop had raised purple blisters on Goody Candler's hands instead of soothing her swollen joints. Magdi had managed to salvage the situation with a quick distraction and a hasty counterspell, but the memory still carried a flush of shame.

And she *still* didn't know what she'd done wrong.

Although Magdi never held Brida's failures over her head, she couldn't help feeling like an endless frustration.

Despite all her studying, practice, and effort, Brida hadn't earned the Greenleaf rank of a qualified hedgewitch candidate yet. She hadn't passed the last two tests, and if she couldn't recognize flowers and plants with more accuracy than her current fumbling, she'd *never* become eligible for initiation as a hedgewitch.

She could copy runes and draw the magic phases of the moon. She could recite the uses of potions, purgatives, poultices, teas, and tisanes. She could even manage simple candle charms and basic knot spells.

But the last time Mother Ivy had visited to test her plant lore, Brida couldn't correctly name the herb samples and stem cuttings. And when she was asked to coax a pink rosebud to bloom, it burst in a cloud of sickeningly sweet mist that nearly drove them from the room instead.

Brida had offered, once, to apply for an apprenticeship to someone else. Maybe, with enough practice, she might learn to bake bread that didn't fall flat or sew seams that didn't wander. Or maybe she could carry messages for the Council of Wisdoms. How could she mess that up? She could read better than most in the village, thanks to Magdi's secret library of forbidden books.

But the hedgewitch said Brida was where she was meant to be, and that was that. "Do you remember the day your magic awoke?" she'd ask. "You were eight years old and we were in the meadow gathering clover blossoms. You picked a dandelion bud, and there in your palm it opened into a sunny yellow flower and then turned to a white puff of seeds before blowing away. You made that happen, Brida. Your magic did. You have all the power you need," she promised.

Only . . . what if Mother Magdi was mistaken? What if Brida *never* learned proper hedgemagic?

A purple and white flower shaped like a bell swayed as Burdock stepped around it, jarring Brida out of her dark thoughts.

"Whoa, pony! Stop!" Brida cried, tugging on his reins.

This time he listened, coming to a perfect halt so she could jump down and pluck one of the blooms.

Brida studied it, twisting the stem in her fingers and trying to remember what it was called—why hadn't she thought to bring her book of plant sketches?—but she was certain it was something important.

As she tucked it gently into one of the saddlebags, Burdock suddenly raised his head and snorted. His muscles quivered and he flattened his ears.

"What is it?" she asked, stroking his neck. "What's wrong?"

He nudged her knee with his nose and gave a low, urgent nicker.

An ember of worry kindled in her chest. He'd been acting strange all morning. What did he sense?

Brida lifted her chin, letting the wind toss her hair as she scanned the meadow. She didn't see a fox or coyote or anything that might warrant his concern. . . .

Burdock shoved his muzzle against her belly. She blinked and frowned at him, but he wasn't trying to be funny. Fear rimmed his eyes in white and his nostrils flared.

Danger?

He sidled nervously as she climbed in the saddle, his head swiveling from side to side. She kept her hands light and steady on the reins, letting him canter to the edge of the trees.

Burdock ducked beneath a series of low-hanging branches and slowed finally to a trot. When the meadow was almost out of sight, he shuffled to a stop and pricked his ears.

Brida's heart thumped her breastbone unevenly, but she fixed her gaze in the direction of her pony's attention and waited.

She didn't have to wait long.

A sudden shiver of wind spun across the meadow, flattening the grass and lacing it with a rime of winter frost. A blade of bitter cold sliced through the trees, casting Brida's breath in clouds as goose bumps rose along her skin. Currents of magic, swift and strange, chased around her, making her head spin with the dizzying surges of energy.

Slipping out of the saddle, she tugged Burdock farther in the trees to hide and peered around the brush.

Something drummed at the edge of hearing, a sound she felt through the very bones of her feet. Burdock tensed his muscles.

And then she saw the horses.

A white mare galloped in the lead, mane and tail streaming like tattered ribbons behind her. Shrieking wind cast dirt and debris in twisting spirals, and gusts roared past the trees, stealing the air from Brida's lungs.

A blue roan mare followed, dragging ribbons of rain that hammered the grass and collected in puddles across the meadow. Brida chewed her lip as they veered away from the trees and raced out of sight, chased by a bay mare with white spots sprinkled across her rump.

As the bay mare galloped closer, Brida saw snow flurries sparkling in the air. Frost trailed from the horse's hooves, leaving white scars behind her.

A heartbeat later, a jagged bolt of lightning and an explosion of thunder startled Brida so badly she bit her tongue, distracting her from the snowflake mare. But here was another horse—this one a black stallion with a crooked white blaze down his nose—galloping after the others. Sparks gathered in his mane and tail until a bolt of lightning sizzled from the sky down to his hooves, rolling thunder along with it. The ground shook and the air filled with the scent of scorched, metallic earth.

Rivers of magic poured through Brida. Tingles of fire and ice swept her skin, like the time she'd lost control of a spellweave and almost blew Mother Magdi's cottage away with the backlash instead of repairing the thatched roof.

Brida clenched her teeth to keep them from chattering and wrapped her hands in Burdock's mane. Suddenly, brilliant sunbeams burst from the clouds. A palomino raced along the edge of the meadow, her golden coat gleaming in shimmering heat waves as the air around her warmed. Her hooves glowed like hot coals, scorching the stems they touched.

She caught up with the rest of her herd and disappeared, leaving the meadow a ragged, wind-tossed, frost-blighted, rain-soaked, sun-scorched mess.

Mingled exhilaration and terror sent Brida's pulse leaping wildly. *So much power . . .*

It took her breath away and left her trembling.

"The stormhorses," she breathed, leaning against Burdock's sturdy shoulder. "The stormhorses are *real*."

They were also terrifying. Beautiful, but terrifying.

Where were they going? Where had they come from? Why were they *here*?

Mingled disbelief and curiosity coursed like a tide through her blood and she swung a leg over Burdock's back. "Follow them!" she cried. She had to *know*.

Burdock kicked up his heels and plunged into a gallop.

The wind sang in Brida's ears and her pulse skipped. *Stormhorses.* How was it even possible?

They belonged between the leather covers and gilt-edged pages of old, forbidden faerie stories . . . the books Mother Magdi let her borrow from the locked cabinet at the back of the cottage. They belonged in myth and legend, in whispered tales told across evening fires. In stories recited at the crossroads.

Maybe you imagined them because the Voice's words are

still too fresh in your head, she told herself. *Maybe all you saw was a farmer's herd escaping their corrals.*

But the condition of the meadow proved otherwise, and Burdock had certainly seen them, too. If they'd been ordinary horses, he would have simply nickered a friendly acknowledgment and then ignored them.

Magic buzzed across Brida's skin and hummed along the wind, and she felt the tension in Burdock's muscles as he chased a trail of snowflakes and lightning.

The herd of stormhorses *had* to be real.

"Faster!" she urged, and Burdock stretched his neck and sped up, hooves almost skimming the earth.

Brida's hair whipped her face, stinging her eyes. She caught glimpses up ahead of the stormhorses, but they were so much swifter than her own pony there was no way he could catch them. Worried he might hurt himself, she reluctantly sat deeper in the saddle and shortened the reins to slow him. "Never mind!" she called. "Let them go!"

Burdock *wanted* to keep running, Brida knew, but sweat darkened his coat and flecks of foam speckled his lips. She could tell he hated that he wasn't fast enough to catch them, but after a few strides he grudgingly slowed to a canter, then a trot. And then, with a deep snort, he lowered his head and walked.

"It was a brave chase." Brida patted his neck. "At least we saw them, right?" Besides, she wasn't sure how close she actually wanted to get to those lightning bolts.

In the distance, the stormhorses slowed and circled to face her and Burdock. For one startled moment Brida stared at them, a thread of connection unspooling between her and the white mare.

"Why have you come?" Brida whispered, feeling the wind lift her words and carry them to the white mare. "What brought you here?"

The white mare took a single step forward and raised her head, her mane and tail streaming like cirrus clouds.

The other stormhorses sidled anxiously, but the white mare fixed her gaze on Brida across the stretch of wind-tossed grass separating them. It was almost as if she wanted Brida to understand something, but before Brida could figure out what was going on, a crow croaked from the trees and a dog barked. The stormhorses scattered.

Brida watched the herd gallop away, mouth dry and hands shaking on her pony's reins. Would she ever see them again?

Did she want to?

Dimly she heard the sounds of a rider approaching: hoofbeats; the creak of a leather saddle; the clink of buckles, spurs, and bit. She glanced over her shoulder, a polite greeting perched on her lips ready to fly, but at first all she saw was a dark horse emerging from the trees. He wore a saddle and bridle, so he couldn't be one of the stormhorses, but where had he come from?

Burdock flung his head around and stomped a hoof, agitated.

The dark horse hesitated, ears flat, and then a sudden gust of wind sent colors shifting over his back and Brida finally spotted his rider. The man wore a cloak so finely woven in shades of green, brown, gray, and blue that he nearly vanished into his surroundings.

A flurry of barking and baying erupted in the trees and a hare bounded away, zigzagging through the grass at Burdock's feet, startling him. Something about its panic kicked Brida's own instincts into high alert.

Run! Run before he notices you!

She squeezed her calves against Burdock's sides, and with a wild kick of his heels he galloped for home.

— FOUR —

Forgiveness

VELVET AND NETTLE were both in the pasture when Brida and Burdock returned. Mother Magdi was home, then. She must have let the goat out, but the mess in the barn would have to wait just a while longer. Brida yanked off her pony's tack and turned him out to graze before running toward the cottage, scattering chickens as she dashed up the porch steps.

"Mother Magdi! Mother Magdi! You'll never believe what I—"

Skidding to a stop, Brida swallowed her words and flushed. She should have guessed Magdi wouldn't be alone. The hedgewitch was busy most afternoons, but Brida hadn't seen a horse or cart so she'd assumed . . .

Magdi stared at her, brow puckered sternly.

The other woman, wearing a brown dress and the red shawl of a goodwife, turned to face her.

Brida resisted the urge to tug at her tunic. "Happy

afternoon, Goody Weaver," she said in a rush. "Please forgive me for interrupting."

Daise Weaver smiled and waved away the apology. "It's no concern, child."

"Did you fetch the plants on my list?" Mother Magdi asked.

"No, because I saw—"

Magdi frowned and opened her mouth, but a sharp peck at the window surprised all of them.

A pigeon perched on the ledge.

Brida gaped as the hedgewitch lifted the latch and opened the window. Two messenger pigeons in as many days!

This one was in rough shape, though, with rumpled feathers and a leg that looked sore. As a light breeze drifted through the window and rippled across the bird's wings, images suddenly filtered through Brida's mind. She collected an impression of an attack in the sky: dark wings, sharp beak, a tumble from the clouds, and an ugly crawk.

"She was attacked by a crow!" Brida blurted.

Magdi's shoulders stiffened but she didn't respond, gently cradling the pigeon in her palms as she took the message from the carrier tube. "Brida, water and seed, please."

Brida didn't need to be told, but she watched the hedgewitch's face curiously as she carried birdseed to the window.

Magdi shoved the note into her apron pocket and said to the bird, "Rest here awhile, friend." To Daise Weaver, she said, "Please excuse us just one moment. I need a word with my apprentice."

Daise knotted her fingers together. "Certainly."

Magdi tugged Brida by the elbow into the green room at the back of the cottage, where crowded shelves held her books and bottles, jars of powders and dried berries, and piles of assorted oddments. Bundles of dried herbs hung from the rafters, perfuming the air with a pleasing spicy scent. A heavy worktable took up the center of the space, stained with ink and berry juice.

"Brida, I've been summoned away and I don't know how long I'll be gone. I need you to take care of things here."

"What is it? What's happened?"

"Just something requiring my attention. Nothing for you to fret about."

"But I saw—"

"I'm afraid I must leave immediately," Magdi went on, "which means you will have to help Goody Weaver. She needs a potion to rekindle love in her marriage. We've practiced this for months. Do you remember the remedy for repairing romance?"

"Of course." She wasn't lying—not exactly. After all, she *did* remember endless afternoons, reciting ingredients and instructions while Magdi barked corrections.

"Good. It isn't complicated, fortunately, and the recipe is in my grimoire. Just follow it exactly and things will turn out fine. I know you can handle it, can't you?"

Brida nodded uncertainly. "Of course," she repeated. "But—"

"Very well, then." And, taking a breath, Magdi sailed back into the main room. "I'm so sorry, Daise, but I must see to something. My apprentice is adept, though, so you needn't worry. She will prepare your remedy right away. There'll be no charge for this one."

Daise wrung her hands and frowned. "I can come back tomorrow, if you—"

"This is what Brida has been trained to do. She knows exactly what you need," Magdi told her firmly. But the look she sent Brida said as clearly as words, *I am counting on you. Don't make a mistake.*

Brida swallowed her nerves and tried to appear capable and confident.

Magdi continued, "Now, Daise, why don't you have a seat there and put your feet up for a bit. Here's some cool cider. . . . Just relax while Brida gets to work. I'll see you when I return." With a quick hug—and one last warning look—for Brida, Magdi cupped the wounded pigeon in one hand, grabbed her cloak from the hook by the door with the other, and bustled out.

Brida cleared her throat awkwardly and shifted her weight from foot to foot.

Goody Weaver took a sip of cider, watching Brida over the rim of the pewter cup. She seemed nervous—which wasn't unexpected. Most folks were when they came to see Mother Magdi. Everyone knew that those with magical abilities were oath bound to use their powers in service to their neighbors, but magic could be a tricky business and people feared what they couldn't explain.

Of course, trusting an apprentice with magic was an entirely different thing than trusting the valley's own hedgewitch.

Brida twisted her hands. "I'll just go start that remedy."

"Thank you," Goody Weaver said. "I do need to get back soon."

Ducking into the green room—which wasn't green at all but got its name from the work they did in it—Brida grabbed the heavy grimoire and set it on the table with a thump. Magdi's grimoire was the biggest, oldest book Brida had ever seen. The pages were stained with age, the ink faded, the handwriting nearly illegible in places. Magdi said it had been her grandmother's book and then her mother's, filled with the recipes and wisdom they'd gathered over the courses of their lives.

When Brida opened the leather covers, the scents of cedar and lemon verbena rose from the pages. She carefully flipped to the section for love spells and dragged her finger down a page with remedies: tonic for a broken heart, tea for patience, remedy for jealousy. The next page had potions for opening the heart, for binding loyalty, for recognizing love when it appeared. . . . Ah, there it was. The remedy for repairing a broken romance.

Brida marked the page with a ribbon and hurried to the shelves to gather the ingredients she needed. Crumbled rose petals, three. Dried apple blossoms, three. Dewdrops collected on the morning of the spring equinox, three. (Careful not to spill!) Honeysuckle nectar, a splash. Clover, one stem. Vanilla bean, half, crushed. Grated nutmeg, one pinch . . .

These were all easy enough. The jars and bottles were neatly marked with Magdi's precise lettering.

But the rest of the ingredients involved dried herbs.

Brida eyed the bundles of leaves, stems, and flowers hanging from the rafters. They were tied with colored thread and swayed slightly in a draft of air. She squinted. Was that peacewort? And that one, tied in yellow. Vervain or verbena? Where was the fennel?

Panic perched on the back of her neck and dug sharp claws into her chest. How could she help Goody Weaver if she couldn't identify the correct herbs? And how could she face Mother Magdi with yet another failure?

I'll never be a hedgewitch, she thought miserably.

But she could feel different threads of magic strung across the room, tangled among the rustling herb bundles. If she could figure out which strands of energy she needed for the remedy she was making, it wouldn't matter if she couldn't name the herbs giving off the magic.

It might be a bit backward, but Magdi never had to know.

Closing her eyes, she held her palms up and fingers spread, sensing each wisp of magic in the air currents sifting through the room. Goody Weaver wanted a remedy for her marriage . . . something to rekindle the romance she thought she'd lost. . . .

Brida let different threads slip through her hands until something tingled in her fingers. There! She opened her eyes and grasped the stems hanging before her, gently separating one from the bundle.

It took her a few minutes, but at last she had everything spread across the table. Worried that Goody Weaver might wonder at the delay, Brida hurried through the ritual to bind and blend the magic.

When it was done, the little glass bottle she'd filled glowed softly with swirls of pink and blue light that faded as she stared. Was it supposed to do that?

She carried it out to Goody Weaver and carefully placed it in the woman's hands. "Sprinkle a pinch under your pillows and at the foot of the bed. Let the rest steep in a kettle of water heated just to boiling for five minutes. Then strain and cool. Drink before supper. It should take effect quickly."

Daise Weaver nodded, thanked her, and left the cottage with the bottle tucked safely in her pocket. She seemed satisfied, so why did Brida's stomach hurt?

Brida tidied up the mess she'd made in the green room, sweeping up bits of leaves and stems and wiping the table.

She washed the mortar and pestle in spring water, wiped them with a soft cloth, and put them away. Her eye fell on the open grimoire and she started to close it when the words caught her attention.

Her heart sank. She'd made a mistake. Again.

The directions clearly said, *Steep in a kettle of water heated just to boiling for five minutes. Strain and cool, and give to your beloved to drink before the evening meal.*

Goody Weaver wasn't supposed to drink it—her *husband* was!

Brida darted from the room with a stifled cry. Flinging herself through the front door, she raced down the path, praying she might somehow catch Goody Weaver, but it was already growing dark and there was no time to ride to Daise's home in Maple Hill.

She was too late.

Brida heard Magdi return in the middle of the night. She'd been tossing and turning, too fretful to sleep. What would the hedgewitch say when she discovered the error Brida had made with Goody Weaver's romance remedy?

When the sun rose, Brida rushed through her morning chores, trying to decide how to tell Magdi what she had done. But she never had the chance.

By the time she finished feeding the horses, chickens, and the goat, Goody Weaver was already walking up the path to the cottage. Brida's heart twisted. She wished, for one impulsive second, that she could simply hide in the barn. But that wasn't the way she'd been taught, so she made herself head inside, prepared to accept the blame she'd earned.

What she wasn't prepared for was the bone-crushing hug that squeezed the breath from her ribs the instant she closed the door behind her. "Oof," she grunted.

Daise Weaver's face glowed. "I'll admit," she said, "that I was skeptical at first. I shouldn't have doubted you, though. Mother Magdi was right. You are certainly adept! I know she said there was no charge, but I can't thank you enough. Hallen and I spent all night talking in bed, and . . ."

Her cheeks bloomed like summer roses. "And I'll just say our problems are behind us. Here . . . I want you to have this as a token of my gratitude, in payment for the potion." She thrust a length of lovely blue fabric at Brida.

Too surprised to respond, Brida caught the cloth by reflex. Did this mean her mistake hadn't mattered? Did the potion work after all? Relief, huge and overwhelming, crashed over her.

Daise turned to Magdi, offering the empty bottle. "You've trained her well, Mother Magdi. She did a marvelous job. I'm only sorry I waited so long to ask for help."

She patted Brida's shoulder as she brushed past, on her way back to the door. "I think that cloth would make a perfect dress for you, dear. You can't run around in tunics and leggings forever, can you?" And, still beaming, she breezed out.

Magdi wore a bemused smile. "I'm so proud of you, Brida," she said. "And Daise is right. That periwinkle color will be beautiful with your eyes, but if you'd like another tunic I don't see why you can't—"

Her nose twitched. Her expression stiffened. Her eyes flicked from the bottle in her hand to Brida's face and back again. Raising the bottle slowly to her nose, she inhaled.

"What," she said in a voice like midnight, "did you put in here?"

"I followed the recipe," Brida stammered. "Except . . ."

"Except *what?*"

"Except I accidentally told her to swallow the steeping instead of her husband," Brida admitted, twisting the blue cloth in her hands. "But it didn't matter, right? I mean, Goody Weaver said it worked, so . . ."

Magdi frowned and sniffed the bottle again. "What herbs did you use?"

Brida gulped. "The ones in the recipe." The magic wouldn't lie, would it?

"No, you didn't. There's something different. . . ." And then Magdi pressed a hand to her stomach. "Oh, brambles and thorns! You couldn't identify the herbs, could you? Even after all this time?" She groaned and closed her eyes. "You could have poisoned Daise Weaver."

"No!" Brida cried. Her magic wouldn't do that. It was meant to help people, not hurt them. Wasn't it? Her stomach twisted like a water snake in a muddy creek.

"Show me what you used."

Trembling, Brida led the way into the green room and started toward the shelves of jars and bottles.

"No," said Magdi. "The herbs."

Brida caught her bottom lip in her teeth and closed her eyes, feeling out the currents of air and magic again. She pointed to the first bundle of herbs. When Magdi said nothing, she pointed one by one to each of the others.

Silence stretched . . . and stretched . . . and stretched until the urge to break it rose in the back of Brida's throat like a scream.

"Forgiveness," Magdi said at last, and Brida blinked. Was it being offered, or . . . ?

"I'm sorry?" said Brida.

"You didn't make a remedy for romance. You made a potion for forgiveness, and it was—apparently—precisely what Daise Weaver and her husband required. How did you know? What made you choose those herbs?"

"But the recipe—"

Magdi clucked her tongue. "Had nothing to do with what you added."

"That can't be right. I . . ." Brida swallowed. The magic didn't care about the recipe, that was clear. It only cared about what was necessary. With a reluctant sigh, Brida explained how she'd let the magic guide her choices. "I tried to pick the right ones, Mother Magdi. I did. But they all look so similar, and the magic was there. . . ."

"Oh, yes," Magdi said thoughtfully. "The magic is there, all right. It's just not what I expected."

"You aren't . . . you aren't angry with me?"

"No, child. I'm not angry. I should have realized—"

But what she should have realized was lost in a heavy thumping on the door.

Magdi flew to answer it, but Brida hung back.

A curl of paper had fluttered from the hedgewitch's pocket. It drifted to the floor at Brida's feet, a tiny, tempting scrap of secret. She knew she shouldn't look, but curiosity drummed against her rib cage, and she couldn't resist. Swiftly bending down, she plucked it from the ground and read, *The circle of thistles grows in the stony hills.*

What on earth did that mean? And why would Mother Magdi wish to keep it from her?

Brida let the paper fall and nudged it with her foot under the worktable so Magdi wouldn't suspect she'd found it.

Shaking off a needle prick of guilt, Brida hurried toward the door and the voices now filling the cottage.

Goodman Druse, the butcher, stood on the front porch, face twisted with fear or fury—Brida couldn't tell which. "It's Dev," he choked. "He's hurt bad. Please, come quick!"

Brida tried not to look at the fresh blood staining the butcher's boots. She disliked Dev, that was certain, but poison ivy vengeance was not the same as wanting to see him injured.

"What happened?" Magdi asked, her voice steady and cool as she took her satchel from the hook.

"Not sure. He was taking a wagon to the boneyard"—Brida winced—"and when he didn't come back, I got worried. Took Danil with me to go looking, and we found him." His voice broke, and he passed a hand over his eyes. "Blood everywhere . . . I left Danil sitting with him, but . . ."

Magdi flung a light cloak over her shoulders and settled the satchel on her back. "Wait outside. I'll be right there, and you can take me to him." As soon as he'd stepped out she said, "Brida, Dusty and Elspeth Hooper asked for a fertility charm. I've arranged all the ingredients on the table and marked the place in the book. Would you finish it, please? Then wait for me."

Brida fidgeted with the hem of her tunic and watched Mother Magdi ride away in the butcher's cart. A chill oozed through her bones, and the wind whispered dark warnings in her ears, but she bravely lifted her chin and firmly closed the door.

I'm just afraid of making another mistake, she told herself. *But this time I'll get everything right.*

She had to.

Magic thrummed in the air and shivered across Brida's skin as she stood at the table in the green room. Mother Magdi had left various stems and flowers lined up neatly, waiting to be worked into a charm.

Brida's heart twisted like a wrung rag as she skimmed the recipe in the grimoire. The Hoopers must want a baby badly, and yet her own parents had left her on Magdi's doorstep.

She blinked back tears and stiffened her spine. She was too old to cry about shadows in the past, and Mother Magdi had been as kind and caring as any mother.

Brida began weaving the herb stems into the figure of a leaf baby. She'd practiced this charm before, and at first the threads of magic settled smoothly into the shape she fashioned.

It was a good time for this sort of magic. The moon was new—perfect for planting seeds and starting things. And yet . . .

Random wind gusts rattled the windows, threatening her concentration as the magic began to resist her control. She tried to wrestle it into place, but she kept losing hold.

This was not going to work.

Stumbling twice over the words to seal the charm, she finally stepped away from the table and let her hands guide her as she had before. She followed a strand of magic toward the shelves. Mother Magdi would not be pleased to know she'd altered the charm, but she had to do *something* or the Hoopers would get no help at all.

Chewing her bottom lip and reluctantly following the tug of magic, Brida added three juniper berries to the center of the green felt, a handful of spruce needles, and one small acorn. This time, when she recited the words of the spell, they flowed freely off her tongue and tasted sweet as honey.

As she wrapped up the pouch and tied it with red string, she felt the magic take effect. This was a strong charm. It might not be what they'd asked for, but Brida knew—she *knew*—it was the charm the Hoopers needed.

— FIVE —

The Boneyard

AS THE SUN slipped below the rim of the world, Brida went outside to do the evening chores. She tidied the barn, settled Velvet and Burdock in their stalls with an armload of sweet-smelling hay and buckets of clean water, then took care of Nettle.

She left a bowl of goat milk behind the barn for the wandering cats and scattered stale bread crumbs for the birds. While she looked around for the white dove, a robin landed atop the low stone garden wall, hopping from one crumb to another. Brida watched for a moment, wondering if she might gather an image or impression from the red-breasted bird. Maybe the robin had seen the dove? Or another messenger pigeon? But nothing floated through her mind, so she wished the robin a pleasant evening and stepped away.

The air turned silver blue and fireflies flickered in the shadows as she locked the chickens in their coop for the night, but Magdi did not return. A seed of worry dropped roots through Brida's stomach and sent slow vines climbing up her throat.

Magdi was the only hedgewitch in the whole valley and there was always someone in Oak Hollow, or nearby Maple Hill or Walnut Creektown, who needed her skills. Perhaps she had been called away to help another and hadn't had time to stop home first.

Brida prepared a pot of lentils and roasted vegetables, but when Mother Magdi still didn't come home, she ate her bowl standing by the window. She squinted her eyes, watching for a bobbing lantern light along the road, and desperately strained to hear the crunch of wagon wheels, the clop of heavy hooves, the rusty jingle of an old harness.

But the night remained still, dark, and silent.

Her worry grew.

She reminded herself that it wasn't unusual for Mother Magdi to miss supper, to come late to bed. But Brida couldn't shake the sense of dread.

What if something had gone wrong?

She grabbed her cloak and her own healer's satchel, then hesitated by the door.

Mother Magdi often chided her for recklessness, urging her to learn patience and caution. But she'd been patient all afternoon, hadn't she?

Where are you, Mother Magdi?

Suddenly wind screamed across the yard and rattled the wavy panes of glass in the cottage windows. The thunder of distant hoofbeats rumbled in her chest.

Brida's shoulders stiffened as recognition crashed upon her.

The stormhorses.

She'd sensed their agitation in the meadow with Burdock, but this was a thousand times worse. Their fear, fury, and desperation burned in Brida's own muscles as if she shared their danger. Her body trembled with the need to *run*, to race the night—and yet she knew she wasn't safe if she left the shelter of the cottage.

But Mother Magdi was out in that darkness, too. If something threatened the stormhorses, the hedgewitch was at risk as well.

Hiding inside might be the prudent thing, but Brida knew what it was to be abandoned, didn't she? She wasn't about to leave Mother Magdi alone on a night like this.

She flung open the door.

The sense of wrongness was stronger once Brida stepped outside. It wrapped her in a cold embrace that chattered her teeth, though the dusk air should have felt pleasant.

Gathering a ball of wind in her palm, Brida blew warm breath into her cupped hand until the ball glowed blue. It was a trick she'd discovered by accident, but now it proved more useful than she'd ever expected.

Letting the light float a few feet before her, she hurried to the barn and woke Burdock. He grunted and rolled his eyes, but when she slipped the bridle over his ears he didn't shake his head in protest. She didn't bother saddling him, so it took her two tries to jump on his back and throw a leg over.

Velvet nickered. "I'll find her," Brida promised.

She tossed a couple clover stems to Nettle. "There'll be more of that if you stay out of trouble," she told the goat, trotting out of the barn.

Nettle bleated once and curled back up in her pile of straw, eyes glinting when Brida glanced back.

Burdock pricked his ears and arched his neck, sensing Brida's nerves. When they rounded the curve and reached the road leading into town, Brida didn't have to ask him to stretch into a canter.

As they sped away, Brida waved her glow-globe from one side to another, searching the shadows. She wasn't even sure what she was looking for; she just knew she should be watchful.

The butcher had said Dev was injured on his way to the boneyard. Brida had been there once, years ago, when Dev and his older brothers grabbed her and dragged her to the edge of the great pit. She'd had nightmares for months afterward. Mother Magdi made the boys chop firewood, repair the barn, and build new fences as punishment.

The thought of going back there in the dark tied Brida's insides into queasy knots and squeezed the breath from her throat, but she needed to find Mother Magdi, and that was the only clue she had.

At least the boneyard wasn't hard to locate.

Nudging Burdock into a gallop, she wrapped her legs around his barrel, lifted her seat off his back, and leaned over his neck as the night wind whipped her hair. Her satchel of herbs and remedies thumped her back with every stride like a drumbeat of terror.

They raced through the center of the village, leaped the brush at the back side of the green, and turned down the path leading through the outer hills. Brida's eyes blurred as her glow-globe flashed over the dew-coated grass.

Burdock reached the first of the hills rising out of the valley and slowed for the climb.

Brida bent forward, letting her blue light play over the ground as she looked for any clues: wagon wheel marks, hoofprints, footprints, anything.

A snatch of sound caught her attention.

"Hello?" she called. "Mother Magdi?" She reined Burdock to a stop and listened, breath rasping in her ears. "Hello?"

There was no response and, with a sigh, she lifted the reins. Just before she asked Burdock to trot, another scrap of murmured words snagged in the wind.

The boneyard was off to the left, in a hollow tucked between two hills. To the right, a ridge climbed to a stony outcrop crowned by a copse of twisted cedar trees. Brida closed her eyes and listened. Which direction . . . ?

There. A voice in distress.

Her eyes flew open. Brida turned Burdock to the right

and they trotted toward the cedars. As they neared the crest of the ridge, she let her blue glow-globe fade.

Burdock slowed, picking his way cautiously past the stones. He stepped around a boulder and marched up a narrow track, easing through the shadows.

Brida heard wood snapping from somewhere up the trail and a crackling burst of orange embers swirled into the air. She urged Burdock around a bend and saw the dancing flames. "Mother Magdi?" she called.

This time she was answered. "Brida? Oh, Mother bless us. Brida, I need your help!"

Someone screamed.

Brida jumped off Burdock's back and looped the reins in a loose twist around his neck, high enough not to tangle his legs if he dropped his head but not so tight as to choke him. "Wait here, pony, please," she whispered, scrambling toward the firelight.

"Mother Magdi? What's happened? What's wrong?"

As she came closer, she caught the metallic tang of blood on the air and her stomach heaved. A hunched shape on the ground moaned, and Brida heard a rough voice—the butcher's?—mumbling prayers.

Magdi lurched for her, yanking the satchel off her shoulder and gripping her elbow so hard her fingers tingled. "How did you know to find me?"

"I waited and waited, but something felt wrong, so—"

Dev's scream interrupted her, peeling the words she'd

been about to say right off her tongue as she stared at him, aghast.

He might be a simpleminded bully, but the pain echoing in his cries . . . Brida wouldn't wish that on anyone.

As Mother Magdi rummaged through Brida's satchel for more herbs, she clicked her tongue. "The boneyard. How many times have I told these fools that leaving all their bones in one pit is a fierce attraction for predators best left alone? Is it the wolf's fault he thinks he'll find his food here? The bear's? No. But they carry the blame when witless men do dangerous, stupid things."

Magdi knelt beside the crumpled figure on the ground, casting a quick glance at Brida over her shoulder. "It was reckless, racing after me in the dark, but, oh, am I relieved to see you. This is worse than I'd thought."

"What happened?"

"Animal attack."

Brida frowned, studying Dev more carefully. Firelight played with the shadows across his still body, revealing a series of gaping lacerations torn across his shoulders and stomach.

The worst was across his neck.

Brida swallowed a scream of her own—a hedgewitch must never, *never* show her horror—and stumbled backward a step or three. Once she'd caught her breath and forced herself closer, she shook her head. Dev's injuries certainly looked like they'd been caused by teeth and claws, but as the night wind tossed wisps of ash and embers into the air,

Brida sensed a lingering undercurrent of some dark power she'd never felt before.

It certainly wasn't the residue of Magdi's hedgemagic, nor did it feel like the wild rush of the stormhorses, that surge of elemental power. No, this was . . . different. Colder. Harder. More brutal.

But . . . what was it?

"Do you feel that?" she whispered. Not even a bear defending her cubs would have mauled him so badly and left such a . . . *taint* . . . behind.

"Feel what?" Magdi replied, distracted.

"I don't think any ordinary animal did this." The words left her mouth louder than she'd intended.

Dev's father heard and let out another moan.

"It's her fault!" he cried, pointing a shaking finger at Brida. "Dev told me how she called the storm and nearly froze them both in the forest the other day. She must have summoned a beast to attack my poor boy!"

"Called the storm?" Magdi echoed.

"I didn't! I can't! It was the—"

Dev wailed, fresh blood spilling from his body.

Magdi crushed a handful of fragrant leaves between her palms and pressed them lightly against Dev's wounds. The butcher continued spluttering incoherent rage behind them.

"Give me your hands," she said to Brida.

"No!" the butcher protested.

Magdi scowled at him, the flickering firelight turning

her expression fierce. "If you want your boy to live, I need her help."

Brida stretched her arms so Magdi could grab her hands, setting them above Dev's throat. Chanting under her breath, the hedgewitch began layering another woven healing spell over the ones Brida could already feel in place. She drew energy through Brida's fingers, borrowing strength. They'd only practiced this once or twice before, when working on badly wounded animals, but Brida felt Magdi's exhaustion like a gray haze.

It was like trying to roll a boulder uphill or fill a leaky bucket. The magical balance was all wrong. Each spellweave sucked away too much power, but Brida couldn't understand why.

Unless it had something to do with that strange evil taint.

Beneath Brida's palms, Dev's heartbeat limped weakly. His breath sounded faint and gasping as his spirit seeped slowly into the damp ground beneath her knees.

Mother Magdi twisted the spellweave into place and started another.

Brida sensed the darkness contaminating his injuries start to coalesce. Like black pearls in a bone shell. Like beads of poison.

Magdi looked up, startled, and met her eyes. "Do you—?"

Brida nodded. Yes, she saw the congealed bits of darkness—and wished she hadn't. "What are they? What could have done this?"

But Mother Magdi didn't answer. Frowning in concentration, she changed the weave of her magic to pluck the pearls from each wound, one by one. When she cast them out, they burst like beads of barely visible smoke and vanished. Dev's tissues began to knit together, silvery scars the only marks to trace where his body had been torn.

He took a deep, shuddering breath and his heart skipped into a steady rhythm. He took another breath, and another, and then his eyes fluttered open, and he coughed. "Da?"

The butcher shouldered Brida and Mother Magdi aside. "Dev? Oh, my boy!"

At that moment Danil crashed out of the shadows and lurched toward the fire. "I looked, Da, but there's no sign of the horse. The wagon he was driving is wrecked about nine paces north of here. Looks like it dropped a wheel off the track and— Dev!" He dropped beside his father when he realized his brother was awake, patting Dev gingerly on the knees.

Magdi rocked back on her heels, pinching the bridge of her nose. "Easy on the lad. He'll live, but he'll need time to regain his strength."

The butcher and his oldest son ignored her, hurriedly lifting Dev and setting him in the back of the cart. As they fumbled with blankets, Brida caught a faint sound on the wind—a whimper of pain that seemed to drag echoes of loneliness and fear through the darkness, stinging her eyes with unexpected tears. There was no choice but to follow it.

SIX

A Hound and a Monster

BRIDA SLIPPED AWAY in a quiet, careful crouch, wrapped in the shadows past the rim of the fire's light. She almost cast another glow-globe to help her see before deciding darkness might be safer until she knew what she faced. She had no desire to draw the attention of whatever had attacked Dev, but if someone else was injured, she needed to help.

Holding her breath, she eased past a tumble of boulders. Something could be hiding in the rocks, waiting to pounce. Her shoulders ached with knotted tension and the nape of her neck prickled, but nothing moved or made a noise.

Brida considered turning back. If she were attacked next, Mother Magdi wouldn't have enough strength left to save her. But when another muffled whine broke the silence, she knew she couldn't just leave.

Straining her ears, Brida waited. . . . There. Again. A soft whimper.

Creeping forward one step, then another, she followed

the trail of low sounds until she heard a heavy panting that proved she was getting closer. When the wind shifted, the metallic tang of blood scented the air, and her heart tried to leave her throat.

She took two more steps and almost stumbled into a shaggy shape lying in the grass. Though it was dark, she could make out a mound of black fur almost as big as her pony. It had a long tail that thumped the ground once at her approach and paws the size of her hands. With a whine, it lifted its head and stared straight at her.

Her gaze traced the outline of a dog's muzzle, sharp teeth, a long tongue . . . and eyes that looked nearly human, except for the way they reflected the dim starlight.

Startled, she fell back, bruising her elbow on a half-buried stone. No dog she'd ever seen looked like this. But he didn't look like a wolf, either.

And he wasn't wild. A wide leather collar studded with metal thorns encircled his neck.

Fear breathed goose bumps across her skin. Was this the creature that had so savagely attacked Dev? She didn't sense any violence or hatred, but if Dev had provoked him . . .

The creature whined again and licked her hand. She jerked away in surprise, and then regretted it. He hadn't tried to hurt her, after all.

"Who do you belong to?" she murmured. "Where do you come from?" *What are you?*

Cautiously petting his head, she sent her awareness

drifting across his body, looking for the source of his pain.

He collected himself to stand, but when he tried to put weight on his back leg, it folded beneath him. He nudged her hand with his nose and then bumped his leg to show her where he'd been hurt.

"I'm not a real hedgewitch," she whispered. "I'm only an apprentice."

He flopped his tail.

He didn't *seem* dangerous. . . .

"Very well, then." Brida wrapped her hands around his leg, but something resisted her magic. It was as if he wore a shield of some sort.

The giant wolf-dog-thing whimpered again.

Narrowing her focus as the night breezes ruffled his fur, she fought to send threads of magic deep beneath his skin, twisting them below or through the strange cloak of resistance around him. Sure enough, she discovered a crack in his leg bone. Letting each strand of magic work its way into the bone and tendon and muscle, she wove healing through his leg. It wasn't as quick or neat as Mother Magdi could have done, but Brida didn't think she'd made any mistakes, at least.

The wolf-hound-beast-whatever-he-was sighed in deep relief, but when he tried to stand, she rested a firm hand on his shoulder. He had other hurts that needed tending: a shallow gash across his chest, another along his flank, and a deeper tear near his belly.

Working as fast as she could manage, she tried pulling magic from the rock, the grass, the dew like Magdi had taught her, but the strands slipped through her fingers. She was tired and having trouble concentrating. Despair threatened to swallow her.

Was Mother Magdi too worn out to work one more healing? Should Brida call for help?

The wolf-hound-whatever licked her hand, and Brida clutched at one last burst of magical energy as the wind sighed around her, managing to cast healing nets over each of his bleeding cuts.

When she was finally finished, the hound-beast shuffled to his feet and grinned at her in relief, teeth catching the starlight.

Brida couldn't help grinning back, as fearsome as he looked. She'd sensed only gentleness in him, though something about that strange shield of resistance around him troubled her. It felt like magic, but where it had come from she couldn't guess.

"You mustn't go around attacking people, you know that, right?" She didn't think he'd been responsible for Dev's wounds, but . . . he was *huge*, and those teeth . . .

He shook his head and growled low in his throat. It didn't sound like a warning, more like . . . a disagreement.

"You didn't hurt that boy?" she guessed.

He licked his nose and wagged his tail.

"Do you know who—what—did?"

He sat on his haunches, head as high as her chest, and whined.

"The same thing that injured you?"

He thumped his tail.

"Will it be back?" she whispered.

The hound-beast gave a soft whuff! and then jerked to his feet, head snapping over his shoulder.

The wind rose, carrying a braided chorus of howls. The wolf-hound-beast turned toward her, pressing his head into her chest until she had to back away or let herself be flattened.

His message was clear. Time to go.

Brida turned and ran, scraping her palms against rough stone as she stumbled in the dark. Barks and growls echoed in the distance as she flung herself down a small rise.

She skidded to a stop just as the ground in front of her heaved and burst open like a slow bubble in a pot of thick, lumpy porridge. Something sharp and pale thrust from the broken earth, emerging bit by horrifying bit: a clawed, skeletal hand attached to an arm that almost looked human; then a long, oddly jointed neck; a hinged jaw with sharp teeth and a beak-like nose; gaping eye sockets. . . .

Brida's blood ran cold.

The collection of mismatched bones stretched itself to its full, awkward height—and turned those blank eyeholes in her direction.

Even in the dim starlight, from where she stood, Brida

could see dark stains on the creature's snapping jaw and on its grasping, talon-like fingers. She smelled blood and felt the ooze of chill, dank magic seeping from the monster like a poison. Whatever this nightmare was, this was certainly the beast that had attacked Dev, its evil, unnatural magic contaminating his wounds.

It started to move toward her, scraping and rattling across the rocky ground. Ill-fitting joints clicked and clattered as it shuffled forward, reaching out. . . .

She was too scared to scream—too scared to *think*—but her feet were already carrying her away before her mind had even processed what she'd seen. She bounded back to the copse of cedars, breath rasping in her throat and teeth chattering.

"Where did you go haring off to?" Mother Magdi scolded. She was crouched on the ground, stirring leaves in a battered tin kettle. "It's dangerous out there and we need help putting out the flames." Then she took a closer look at Brida, and alarm tightened her face. "What happened, child? Are you all right?"

"Quick! There's a—" Brida swallowed. What could she call it? A patchwork skeleton?

A howl rose at her back, chased by echoes.

Magdi smiled reassuringly. "The pack of wolves won't bother us tonight, but it's best we head home as fast as we can. Finish putting out the fire and I'll see to Dev. Boy needs to drink this before we can move him." She poured the brew into a cup and straightened.

"No! You don't understand! That's not a pack of wolves, and anyway, I don't think they're the ones who hurt Dev. I saw a—a bone monster! It crawled from the ground and . . ." She panted, fear squeezing breath from her lungs, and pointed vaguely behind her. "We have to *run*!"

Magdi's brows lifted. "A bone monster?"

"Yes! A thing made of all sorts of bones. Part bird, part . . . horse, or something. Part bog lizard, part human." She retched on the word, wishing she could scrub the terrible sight from her mind.

"From the boneyard . . ." Magdi hissed between her teeth. "Has her reach already spread so far?"

"What? Whose reach? What are you talking about?"

"Douse the fire. Hurry!" Magdi carried the cup to the cart and urged Dev to take a sip.

"Burdock!" Brida called, kicking dirt over the dwindling fire. What if the bone monster went after *him* next?

But as the last embers smoked out, she heard Burdock's familiar nicker and the comforting rhythm of his steady hoofbeats. He trotted into view, snorting and swishing his tail.

"Come on, Dev! You *must* drink this, and quickly!" Mother Magdi said from beside the cart.

"It smells foul," the butcher said. "What's in it?"

We just brought his good-for-nothing lackwit son back from the realm of shadows and he has the nerve to question Mother

Magdi? If Brida wasn't so terrified, she'd be outraged.

Magdi held Dev's head as he spluttered the brew down his chin. "Just herbs to help him sleep on the way home," she said, "else every bump in the road will slow his recovery."

"But you healed him. He's—"

"Still weak, as I keep trying to explain." The hedgewitch poured the last dregs of brew on the ground and tucked the cup inside her apron pocket. Then she hefted both satchels over her shoulder and climbed in the cart, settling herself beside a heavy-eyed Dev.

Magdi looked down at Brida. "You and Burdock need to stay close. If there are wolves and . . . *other things* . . . out roaming, it will take both of us to drive them away."

There was a tremble at the edges of her voice. Exhaustion laced with worry—and a whisper of fear.

"Dev said it weren't a wolf that tore him up. Said it was something *magic*." The butcher's lips twisted on the last word, and he scowled at Brida.

"I assure you I will get to the bottom of this tomorrow morning. In the daylight," Mother Magdi told him sternly.

Goodman Druse grunted, but he flipped his reins and the old plow horse lurched forward, dragging the creaking cart along.

Brida unlooped her reins and climbed on Burdock's back, but the butcher pointed his whip at her feet and scowled.

"I don't care what the hedgewitch says. You keep your distance, girl," he snarled. "We won't be needing any more of your interference."

"Quiet!" Mother Magdi held up a hand.

In the distance, an eerie screech dragged along the wind. It sounded like iron scratching stone, or . . . bone scraping bone.

Brida's stomach lurched, and Burdock's muscles quivered. She stroked his neck to steady both of them.

"My strength is all but spent," Magdi admitted. "If you call the beast's attention, Goodman Druse, we will all regret it. Please, hold your tongue until we are safe and can discuss matters like sensible people."

He snorted and snapped the reins again, urging the horse to a slightly faster version of his usual amble. "Fine," he growled. "But *she* stays out of my sight, and away from my boy. She may be your apprentice, but I don't trust her."

Magdi sighed, but Brida wasn't in the mood to fight with the butcher. She didn't care to stay any closer to Dev Druse than she absolutely had to anyway. She held her pony back, letting the cart roll slightly ahead.

Burdock jigged and tossed his head, begging Brida to let him run for home. She was tempted, but she couldn't leave Magdi to defend herself alone, not when the hedgewitch was so clearly worn out. And she *really* didn't want to face another bone monster by herself.

Brida shivered and wrapped a hand in Burdock's thick

mane, reaching for courage. Bone monsters and giant hounds . . . what dark power could have called them? She'd felt magic tonight that she hadn't even guessed existed, had seen creatures she never could have imagined. And yesterday—had it really been just a day ago?—she'd seen *stormhorses*, legends come to life!

She glanced at the back of the cart, where Mother Magdi was cradling Dev's head on her knees and talking quietly to his brother, Danil. There hadn't been a chance to tell Magdi about the stormhorses and the secret buzzed in her mouth like a hive of bees. But it wasn't something Brida could just blurt out in front of the butcher and his boys, either.

A cold fear pressed an ache through her head. In the stories, myths and nightmares always seemed to be linked . . . but what did that mean for Oak Hollow?

SEVEN

The Council of Wisdoms

BRIDA AWOKE TO the enticing smells of fried griddle cakes and warm honey. Her stomach growled as she sat up, blinking the gritty sands of sleep from her eyes.

She and Mother Magdi hadn't reached home until dawn. She'd fed the animals an early breakfast and stumbled to bed without changing her clothes, and now it was past midday. She couldn't let any more hours slip by.

Hurriedly dressing and dragging a comb through her tangled hair, she'd just managed to make herself feel awake and respectable when Mother Magdi called, "Brida? Are you hungry?"

"Starving!" She rushed to the table, surprised to find it was only set with one plate.

"I've already eaten," Mother Magdi explained. "I didn't want to wake you too soon, but I need your help today. Join me in the green room as soon as you're finished?"

Brida nodded, greedily forking griddle cakes onto her plate. "I'll be there as quick as I can." She smothered the cakes in honey and shoved the first sweet bite in her mouth.

"Don't make yourself sick! You have time to chew, at least," Magdi said wryly, turning to go.

But when Brida finished eating and began wiping the dishes, someone tapped gently on the door. Drying her hands on an old apron, she hurried to open it.

Elspeth Hooper stood on the porch, smiling nervously.

"Happy morning . . . er, afternoon?" Brida said. "Is there something I can do for you?"

"Well, I've come to return the charm I asked for."

"What went wrong?" Mother Magdi asked sharply, appearing over Brida's shoulder.

Brida winced.

"Nothing!" Goody Hooper said. "It's just . . ." She held out the green felt square, balanced in the palm of her hand. "I realized I don't actually need it."

"You're already with child?" Magdi asked, eyes misting out of focus as she scanned the other woman's belly.

"No," she said. "You see . . . well, the truth of it is, I don't honestly *want* a child. And last night I finally had the courage to tell my husband. He was . . . disappointed, I suppose, but we'll work it out someway. We still intend to pay you for your trouble. You'll have a new barrel for rainwater before the moon turns, but I'm sorry I wasted your time. Perhaps you can use the charm again for someone else?"

Brida reached for it—hoping Mother Magdi wouldn't notice she'd changed it—but Magdi scooped it up before her fingers could so much as brush the green felt.

"I just wish for you to be happy," Magdi said. "All the better that you didn't need magic to find your peace and contentment."

"Would you like tea?" Brida offered, hoping to prove her manners despite her flimsy hedgemagic.

Goody Hooper smiled and shook her head. "No, but thank you. I'm heading into Walnut Creektown to see about selling the lace I've made. Have a lovely day." With a quick wave, she skipped off the porch and down the path to a polished carriage and two matched black horses.

Brida closed the door with a soft click, and slowly turned to face Mother Magdi. "Thank you for the griddle cakes," she said, still hoping to distract her. "They were delicious."

But the hedgewitch curled her fingers around the charm. "What have you done, child?"

"I . . . I was only following the—"

Magdi interrupted before she could say *magic*. "You didn't follow the directions, did you? I laid all the ingredients on the table. All you had to do was place them in the green felt and recite the ritual words." She closed her eyes and pinched the bridge of her nose. "Such a simple thing, and I *know* you have the power to manage it!"

"Mother Magdi, I did follow the grimoire's instructions. But the spell didn't seem to *take*. Then the magic tingled in my fingers, and I had to see where it led. It *wanted* me to add the other herbs. I . . . I think it knew that Goody Hooper did not want a fertility charm. Not in her true heart."

Magdi's spine stiffened. "What do you mean? Explain how the magic feels to you."

"I can't. It's . . . like a breath of air on my skin, a buzzing in my fingers."

"And this leads you to the herbs?"

"Yes, but—" Brida was interrupted by the ringing of a bell. She groaned, "We never get a moment's peace! Someone is forever banging on the door or—"

"Silence, child! Don't you know the bell? The Voice has come. Show respect!" Magdi hissed.

But when Mother Magdi opened the door, a grubby child stood on the porch, balancing on one leg like a lake crane. Brida recognized Dev's youngest cousin, poised to run away. He clutched a pewter bell on a leather cord in one hand.

When he saw Brida peeking over the hedgewitch's shoulder, he tapped three fingers against his forehead in the sign against hexing. Then, realizing he'd been rude, he flushed red as a pickled beet and pretended he was adjusting his grimy cap instead.

Brida stared at him, confused. Had something happened to Dev again?

"Yes?" Magdi said, and Brida blinked at the fury humming in that single word.

The boy rang the bell again, with enough enthusiasm to call every cow in three leagues, and announced, "You are summoned to the Council of Wisdoms immediately."

"We'll fetch our cloaks and be there." Magdi shut the door firmly.

Brida wouldn't say Magdi *slammed* the door, because a hedgewitch would never *slam* a door, but . . . the timbers did creak with the force of it.

"I can't believe they sent Tevin—the same urchin I had to pull from the dry well behind Goodman Fletcher's place not four days ago!—to summon us. The Voice should have come herself," Magdi fumed, brushing dust from her cloak before settling it over her shoulders.

"Don't dawdle, Brida. Tidy your hair—no, not like that; pin it back—and then let's be on our way. I can only imagine what nonsense the Wisdoms have been told. The sooner we can set the fools straight, the better."

Brida's heart twisted. Dev had said he was going to tell the Council that she'd called a storm and tried to hurt him, but surely they would never think *she* had the power or the cruelty to do such a thing! They'd known her since she was born and . . .

No, she thought. That wasn't true. They'd only known her since she'd been left on Magdi's doorstep. She was a babe at the time, but still.

If no one knew where she'd come from, who she really was, why would they trust her word over Dev's? His family had been in the valley since before the great trees had been cut and cleared for farmland.

Brida smacked a hand against her thigh. "Mother Magdi," she said, "before we go, I need to tell you about the storm the other day. The sudden strange one? Dev thinks I called it just to scare him or . . . or to hurt him, but I—"

"Oh, child, no one is going to think you were responsible for *that*. Don't worry. The Council will ask, of course, because they must. But it's only a formality. Everyone knows the seasons have run amok. Hurry now." Magdi laced up her boots and straightened the hem of her skirt before marching down the porch steps.

Burdock stuck his nose over the pasture gate and nickered, but Brida was distracted as she rushed after the hedgewitch. "But, Mother Magdi," she tried again, "the truth is, I saw . . ." She stopped, fumbled for words. How could she describe the stormhorses, the most incredible creatures she'd ever encountered? She knew they must have been responsible for the squall that caught her and Dev— she'd recognized the feel of their wild magic in the meadow with her pony later. But how could she explain that dizzying rush of energy, the sheer *power* of the storm?

Magdi wasn't listening, though. She grumbled, "If they think we'll take blame for Dev's attack, I'll thrash the lot of them. They may be *called* Wisdoms, but I'm a hedgewitch, and I don't answer to simple village elders, no matter how important they think themselves. There's only so much we can do. . . . Come along, Brida. And when we get there? Don't say a word about the bone monster. Just let me handle it."

Brida jogged beside the hedgewitch, struggling to keep up. This was maybe not the best time to tell Mother Magdi she'd seen a story come to life. They had enough to worry about.

What if Dev tried to blame her for the bone monster, too?

Surely everyone who knew him also knew what a toad-wart he could be, right? As she and Magdi rounded the curve in the road and headed for town, Brida kicked a stone and tried to ignore the gnawing doubt in her chest.

It didn't matter what Dev thought. Brida had never sensed power like that before, and she certainly couldn't work it. Just the memory of those dark smoke-pearls of poison in Dev's wounds, the *evil* she'd felt seeping from the bone monster, was enough to make her sick. And the fact that giant hound-beasts had appeared the same night, stormhorses the day before . . . Strange magics must be stirring in the valley. But why? Where did they come from? How were they connected?

The Council met in a round stone building with a tiled roof and doors made of ironwood. It stood sentinel on a hill just past the crossroads, visible from all three valley towns it represented: Oak Hollow, Maple Hill, and Walnut Creektown. The squat tower wasn't meant to look sinister, Brida knew, but as she and Magdi stepped beneath its shadow she couldn't help a nervous shudder.

Magdi didn't wait for the bell boy to open the doors or announce their arrival. She brushed past him, shoving her way in without apology.

Brida cast a startled glance at Tevin and hurried to follow, a sick wobble in her stomach.

"You send a *boy* to summon me, as though I were an apprentice lacking enthusiasm for work or a goodman too fond of strong whiskey? I am your *hedgewitch*!" Magdi growled, marching to the center of the room.

Brida fluttered by the door, clutching the hem of her tunic. The entire Council was sitting today, ranged along a curving half-moon table in high-backed chairs that looked like thrones. To the right sat four men in black robes, to the left four women in white robes. And in the center, the Head of the Wisdoms in a gray hood.

Just in front of the table, off to one side, the Voice sat with baskets of beads at her feet and balls of colored string scattered about her lap. Her age-gnarled hands were still— this particular exchange would not be woven into the public record.

"Peace, Mother Magdi," the Voice said with a trace of laughter behind her words. "It was not a mark of disrespect. The child owes a debt and this was his service for the day."

Tevin cleared his throat, rang the bell three times, and quavered, "Wisdoms, I present Mother Magdi and"—his eyes darted to Brida—"and her apprentice, Brida Greenleaf."

Brida flinched. She was no Greenleaf yet. Was he mocking her for failing her exams, or did he just assume she had to have passed by now? Either way, the name stung her pride like a poisonous barb.

She stared at her feet, a hot flush of shame blooming in her cheeks.

"Step forward," the Head ordered her.

Magdi clicked her tongue and Brida shuffled closer to the center of the room.

"Brida *Greenleaf*, is it now, child?" the Head asked.

Now the Voice's hands flew, fingers weaving patterns into colored thread as she prepared to record Brida's responses.

Brida swallowed, choked, spluttered out a nervous cough. All the Wisdoms watched her, faces blank and still.

"No, Honored Council," she finally managed to croak without lifting her eyes. "I haven't yet passed the last two exams."

Her face burned in the heat of the Council's scrutiny.

"Does she study? Is she a satisfactory apprentice?" the Head asked Mother Magdi.

"Oh, yes, Honored Council," Magdi answered without hesitation. "She is a good girl. Honest, hardworking, helpful. It isn't a lack of effort holding her back."

"Does she have any power?" one of the men in black asked, steepling his fingers with a slight frown. The Council was generally uncomfortable with matters of magic, being more accustomed to resolving mundane issues like fence disputes and stolen pigs. But Queen Moira had destroyed the Temples that used to regulate such things and now they had no choice.

"Yes. Yes, there is clearly magic in her. It just needs more time to ripen."

Brida chewed her lip. Was she in trouble?

"We have heard," a woman in white said, "of a strange storm."

The Head leaned forward, hands pressed to the table, and murmured, "Tell us what happened, child, and leave nothing out."

"It wasn't me, I swear it by bud, bough, and bloom!" Brida cried.

Mother Magdi made a sound, but Brida was afraid to look at her. *They have to believe me!*

"Just tell us what happened," the Head said in a thorny voice.

Brida rocked back on her heels. "I was in the woods, gathering plants for Mother Magdi. Dev came by to tease me, and the next thing I knew, a storm was howling around us. I could feel the magic in it, but it wasn't like anything I'd ever experienced before. It wasn't dark, but it was . . . wild. Dev got scared and ran away, but I—"

A Wisdom interrupted. "Mother Magdi, did you sense anything while this was happening?"

"I was in the middle of a tricky bit of work requiring all my concentration, but things have been unsettled for some time. Hard to say when a particular anomaly occurs."

"Do you know anyone capable of calling a storm?"

Magdi snorted. "You don't have to ask your questions sideways, Wisdom. I know what you mean. Dev and his father are superstitious fools who understand the workings of magic as well as they understand the movement of stars. Brida did nothing but help me save Dev's life after he'd been mauled near the boneyard."

"We will speak of that in a moment," the Head said. "What of Ivy Sorin? Could she have called such a storm?"

"No. And I happen to know that Hedgewitch Ivy has been in Middlebury this past fortnight visiting her sister's children—far outside the scope of a weather weave. I will ask if she has any suspicions, but it has been many years since anyone had the power to—"

"But it wasn't a witch," Brida blurted.

The sudden weight of all their stares pressed the voice from her throat and she shifted from foot to foot, wishing she could run back out the door. And maybe never stop running.

"Do you mean to say that you know who was responsible?" the Head asked.

"Yes. I mean, I didn't at first. But when Burdock—he's my pony—and I went looking for starflowers, something bothered him. While we hid in the trees, the same kind of magic storm that caught me and Dev blew in. Only this time I saw the stormhorses."

There was a snort. "Stormhorses? Familiarity with folklore and myth is not the same as an education, Mother Magdi. If the girl can't pass her exams, perhaps the fault lies in her training. Perhaps she has spent too much time listening to stories at the crossroads." He flicked a glance at the Voice, but she kept her eyes fixed on the quick working of her fingers and ignored him.

"You may be a Wisdom now, Bertram Carver, but I'm the one that brought your bare bottom into this world!" Mother Magdi snapped.

Brida held her breath. She'd never heard anyone speak to a Wisdom that way—then again, she'd never heard anyone speak so rudely to Mother Magdi, either.

The Head raised a hand for silence, glaring equally at both Wisdom Carver and the hedgewitch. "Go on, child. Tell us more."

Brida chewed her thumbnail, sifting through her confused impressions. She tried to describe what it felt like to see the stormhorses, to be swept up in their elemental magic.

"I think a man on a black horse was chasing them," she tried to explain. "He was hunting with a pack of giant dogs. . . ."

"You can't expect us to believe—!"

The Head rapped sharply on the table. "Be still, Wisdom Carver."

"But this is no place for nursery tales and night stories!"

"If Brida says she saw the stormhorses, then she saw them. *Rare* does not mean *unreal*," Magdi said, hands on her hips.

A warm glow suffused Brida's chest and she raised her chin. This wasn't the way she'd intended to tell Mother Magdi about the stormhorses, but knowing the hedgewitch believed her was such a relief.

The Voice's fingers fell still as she paused her record weaving. "I must consult the knots and beads to say for sure, but I believe the last mention of the stormhorses in this area was in the Year of Three Winters, when King Otis negotiated a pact with the Silver Fae to drive them away and save the crops."

Brida sucked in a sharp breath. The Voice had talked about the Fae on the Day of Remembering, but she hadn't mentioned a pact with them. Mother Magdi's contraband books described the Silver Fae and their magical creatures—shadowcats, stormhorses, firedrakes—but only said that the clans of the Twilight Court didn't get along. They commanded elemental beasts as weapons against each other in their struggles for status and power until the people of the Blue Isles brought war to the shores of the Five Realms.

According to the stories, the Great Mother herself appeared and banished the Fae as punishment. The island people were allowed to remain so long as they agreed that any who developed magical abilities would swear an oath to use them only for the greater good.

No one had seen the Silver Fae for generations, though there were said to be artifacts—a suit of armor as light as silk, made of solid sunlight; a sword of ice; musical instruments that played ribbons of color—in Queen Moira's private collection.

Wisdom Carver folded his arms across his chest and glowered into his beard. "The Silver Fae? Pah. And the Year of Three Winters would have been nine or ten generations ago, if it were true."

"Do you dispute the record?" the Voice demanded.

"Council, hold your peace," the Head ordered. "Mother Magdi, do you think it possible these weather events were, in fact, caused by stormhorses?"

"I think it certain."

Murmurs and rustlings swept the Council until the Head rapped the table again.

"We'll set that aside for the moment. What about the beast that attacked Dev Druse?" he asked, leaning forward slightly. "His father mentioned seeing giant hounds or wolves in the vicinity. It is no secret that Brida has an affinity for certain animals."

Horror dropped Brida's stomach to her knees and her neck tried to shrink into her shoulders. How could they even *think* she would have anything to do with hurting the butcher's boy? She hated Dev's stinging taunts and cruel tricks, but wishing him a nasty case of poison ivy was a far cry from seeing his throat all but torn out and the flesh peeled from his muscles.

And besides, her ability to connect with animals was mostly limited to birds, hares, horses, deer—maybe cats and dogs. Not wolves. Not creatures fierce enough to rip a boy to shreds.

"I told you there was a man with a pack of great big dogs chasing the stormhorses!" She tried to protest, though her voice came out an appalled squeak. "Those hounds must have been his!"

The Council ignored her, concentrating entirely on Magdi.

Mother Magdi frowned. "Completely unrelated, and not Brida's fault in the slightest. The fool boy was at the boneyard. I've told you before that such a place is bound to draw predators. And it's thanks to her help that I was able to heal the boy at all."

Brida waited for Magdi to mention the black poison-pearls they had drawn out of Dev's wounds, the bone monster that had burst from the ground, but the hedgewitch did not offer further details, and Brida was too nervous to bring them up herself, especially after she'd been told not to say anything.

The Head finally nodded. "Very well, then. Brida, do you swear upon the waters of life, the breath of thought, the bones of the earth, and the sacred fires of justice that you were not involved with or responsible for the attack on Dev Druse last evening?"

"*Yes!*"

The Head rang a bell three times. "This Council declares you cleared of any charges. The Voice will weave your innocence into the public record."

"But we haven't—" one of the Wisdoms started to argue.

The Head interrupted. "The discussion is not closed, but it's clear whatever happened to the butcher's boy was not her fault. She is dismissed."

An attendant indicated that Brida should follow him out of the chamber, but she dragged her steps as slowly as possible so she could continue listening.

"Now, Mother Magdi, if the stormhorses have been seen once again, what does that mean? Several days ago you notified us of a strong summoning spell. Is it connected? Are you still confident that the one you suspect is responsible for the recent disruptions?" the Head asked.

The attendant gripped Brida's elbow and gave a tug, tearing her attention from the Council and propelling her toward the door.

Which wasn't fair, since she was the one who had seen the stormhorses in the first place. Maybe she couldn't add much information—she didn't understand where the magic horses came from, why they had suddenly appeared, or where they had gone—but didn't she deserve to be included in the conversation, at least?

She twisted her arm away from the attendant and turned back to the Wisdoms. Sucking in a deep, shaky breath, she blurted, "Wait! I want to hear what you know about the stormhorses. Who do you suspect is responsible? *What is going on?*"

There was a moment of shocked silence. Brida felt their dismay land on her like a heavy bale of prickly hay and she avoided glancing at Mother Magdi. She didn't want to see the shame and disappointment in the hedgewitch's eyes. There were rules about how to behave before the Council—when to speak—and she'd just broken them.

But she wouldn't apologize for her questions.

"You know the procedures of the Council, child!" one of the Wisdoms said in an angry splutter. "You have been *dismissed*. The rest of this conversation does not concern you! Now go, before we assign you a week's punishment to reinforce your manners!"

"Actually, Honored Council, my apprentice"—Magdi gave the words weight, as if to remind the Wisdoms that Brida wasn't just a village girl—"has a fair point. She *is* the only one to see the stormhorses."

Brida fought to keep a grin off her lips, but then Magdi continued, "Unfortunately, Brida, until we know for certain what we're dealing with, allowing you to listen to our speculation would be too risky. The Council has your best interests in mind, as do I. Return home, and I will meet you there soon."

Brida's smile slipped. She'd been so close. It was hard to swallow her frustration.

The Head, fingers steepled, nodded once. "Mother Magdi is right. We recognize your role in bringing the stormhorses to our attention, but now we face some difficult decisions. We are already struggling with broken seasons. . . . If the stormhorses bring elemental weather magic into the valley, the chaos could ruin all of us. This Council must consider heavy questions, matters that are not meant for a young girl—even if she is our hedgewitch's apprentice." The Head glanced at Mother Magdi with a twitch of eyebrows. "So, again I say, you are dismissed."

The note of finality in the Head's voice and Mother Magdi's curt nod indicated that further arguing would be futile, so Brida let the attendant lead her out of the chamber.

But as the heavy ironwood door thudded closed, she fought the urge to kick it. She hated to be dismissed. Disregarded. Excluded.

Especially if something terrible threatened her valley.

— EIGHT —

Scrying

A SUDDEN BREEZE sent a skirl of leaves across the path as Brida made her way home from the Council. She froze, scanning the shadows between the trees for any sign of the stormhorses.

A cloud drifted across the face of the sun and a busy squirrel darted from one branch to another. She waited for the rush and tingle, the flash and chill, of wild magic that never came. After a moment, she resumed walking, kicking pebbles as she went.

It should have been a relief to be released from the scrutiny of the Wisdoms' disapproving stares, but knowing the Council would continue discussing the stormhorses and magic without her was nerve-racking.

Would she have been allowed to stay if she'd already been promoted to Greenleaf status?

The thought brought a prickle of unease. If the Wisdoms pressed Magdi for a more detailed progress report on Brida's hedgemagic, what would she say? And how much time would they give Brida to pass the Greenleaf exams?

If she failed again, would they let her petition some-one else for a new apprenticeship, or would they name her Wanderer and send her to seek her future in one of the neighboring towns?

Brida thrust a hand in her pocket and clutched the stone and feather charm from Mother Magdi. She'd already been abandoned once . . . it would break her heart to be cast out again.

The last time the Council of Wisdoms had named someone Wanderer, Brida had just started learning to work hedgemagic. As she remembered it, a miller's apprentice named Amory was caught shorting flour from families he didn't like. He claimed it was a mistake at first, but when it happened again the miller terminated his position.

The Council gave the boy a purse of coins, supplies for the road, and a charm for luck, but there weren't many towns that would welcome a Wanderer who hadn't finished training in some sort of trade. Especially a Wanderer with a reputation for deceit.

Brida chewed her bottom lip. She was honest and hardworking, at least. And whenever she doubted herself, Mother Magdi assured her she was where she belonged. But her magic never worked the way it was supposed to, and she was running out of time to learn.

What she needed, Brida thought, was a way to prove her

abilities to the Council of Wisdoms, Mother Magdi, and . . . herself.

She crossed the creaky wooden bridge over Picklefrog Creek—hopping on one foot three times for luck, as tradition dictated—and climbed the last hill before the woods closed in.

The seed of an idea took root as she entered a tunnel of trees and green shade that swallowed her in cool, mossy silence.

What if she could find the stormhorses again, figure out who was chasing them and why?

If she could solve the mystery of the stormhorses, if she could discover what evil power threatened the valley, she could prove to everyone that her magic wasn't a mistake. That she wasn't a failure. That she could be useful.

That she belonged.

And she knew how to do it, too.

Back at home, Brida closed her eyes.

She wasn't supposed to do this.

She had stumbled across the ability to scry by accident, simply staring at a bucket of water in an absentminded daze. At first she assumed the images she saw were figments of her imagination, but then she glimpsed Goody Turner hurrying up the lane with a wounded lamb in a basket. A moment later the shepherd's wife herself knocked on the cottage door, startling Brida so badly she'd spilled the entire bucket of water on her boots.

After experimenting for several months, Brida started figuring out how to make the pictures clearer, sharper. She'd found this silver bowl in the cabinet and realized it worked even better than a wooden bucket—and then Mother Magdi caught her and said that scrying wasn't allowed. When Brida demanded an explanation, Magdi only said it was dangerous.

Brida tried not to disobey on purpose . . . usually. But this time she didn't see the harm in it. There were things she needed to know.

Letting all the tension drain from her body, she counted to three.

Three was the magic number, she had discovered. If she opened her eyes too soon, she would only see a silver bowl of clear water. Nothing would rise to the surface. But if she waited too long, the scrying bowl would be filled with muddy images blurred in meaningless swirls. A soup of melted color.

She took a breath and opened her eyes.

Perfect.

Sparkles danced beneath the water, fracturing the reflection of the candle flame on the table in front of her. The glittering light in the antique bowl coalesced as she watched, slowly gathering form.

Brida leaned forward, shoving her dark, messy hair

behind her ears and blinking impatiently.

There.

An image rose from the bottom of the bowl and floated before her: the soft curl of a nostril. Whiskers and a velvet muzzle. A deep, warm eye fringed with lashes. The curve of a cheek, the gleaming sweep of a long, white satin neck.

The horse shook her mane, scattering glints of silver light as a draft of air ruffled the water in the bowl.

Brida's heart pounded. She needed to see more. Lifting a feather from the table—hawk, for clear vision—she gently stirred the water with it.

The white mare dissolved so another image could form.

This time the horse she saw was a blue roan, with a head as black as night and a body the speckled blue-gray of a sky painted with summer storms. The roan whinnied and pawed the ground, sending up a spray of magic raindrops.

Nearby a black horse with a jagged white blaze reared and lightning flashed from his hooves.

But where *were* they?

Brida brushed the hawk feather through the water again.

When the colors stopped spinning, a distant scene appeared, framed by a low stone wall and a palisade of dark pines. Two horses now: a golden palomino and a brown horse with white spots on her rump, held captive in a grass enclosure.

Brida carefully breathed a gentle sigh across the water and the image lurched as if she'd leaped across time and space. It took her eyes a moment to settle; the dizzying effect was almost sickening.

The horses sharpened in closer focus. Brida could see that the two in the pasture wore elegant silver halters, but their flattened ears, white-rimmed eyes, wrinkled lips, and quivering muscles indicated pain and misery.

Brida frowned. She hadn't entirely mastered the art of seeking specific answers from the scrying bowl, and she hadn't had much opportunity to practice. Squinting at the shimmer of water in the bowl, she willed it to reveal the details she sought.

The stormhorses vanished as other images flashed: a massive dog, teeth bared in a ferocious snarl; a silver whip cracking through dark shadows; steam curling from a cast-iron cauldron. A white dove.

Brida stared so hard her eyes burned. How did all these puzzle pieces fit together? What did they mean?

Then a beautiful, dark-haired woman strode into view. Rich skirts in iridescent purple and bruise blue trailed behind her as she stalked across a flagstone courtyard.

A man in a brown leather vest and green tunic met her, coiling a whip in his palm. He bowed his head and said something Brida couldn't hear.

Brida pressed her hands to her ears and chanted the words to a charm she'd found in Mother Magdi's grimoire. A chill tingled through her scalp and curled like ice inside her ears.

Then voices, soft and indistinct, drifted above the water in the bowl. Brida strained to catch the words, missing a few.

"Two, *mumble*," the man in brown leather said.

"I need all five." Even distorted by magic, the woman's voice sounded cold.

Her frown bleached the color from his face and the lines of his jaw tightened. "The others may come to join their herd. They should be easier to catch now, *mumble*."

"Your delays and excuses weary me, Darius. You're my Huntsman. You're supposed to be able to handle a few wild ponies. Time is growing short. *Mumble mumble* remind you of your promises?"

"With all due respect, *mumble*." He cleared his throat nervously and continued, "If the stormhorses were simple to catch, I would have already—"

"If the stormhorses were simple to catch, I would have no need for you." Dismissing him with a gesture, she added, "You have a week and a day to capture the last three horses and bring the entire herd to me, or our bargain is forfeit."

He touched two fingers to his forehead and bowed, but the lady had already turned away.

Brida's head throbbed from the strain of concentration and fear squirmed in her stomach. But before she could break the spell in the scrying bowl, the lady's back stiffened and she tossed a glance over her shoulder.

Her moss-green eyes seemed to catch and hold Brida's

gaze even through the water. Laughter boiled from her throat and the candle on Brida's table guttered and smoked out.

Brida blinked. The sensation of being *seen* was strong enough to give her goose bumps, even though she knew it wasn't possible. A scrying bowl was more like a mirror than a window, and yet . . .

The woman reached into a fold of her gown and threw something into the air.

Brida couldn't resist leaning closer to see what it was. A scrap of black velvet ribbon? A piece of lace? A . . . *feather*.

The feather twisted, sparked, grew. . . .

An instant later, a crow appeared to fill the bowl and furious squawking clawed Brida's ears. The image suddenly burst in a storm of feathers and talons as the bird's wings shredded the surface of the water.

Brida flung herself backward, panting as the crow thrashed in the bowl.

Just as the bird righted itself and prepared to launch at her face, she was shoved roughly aside.

"Get away!" Mother Magdi shrieked. She tossed something—a coin, a polished stone?—at the crow with a sharp exclamation that sounded like a magical curse. It hit the bottom of the bowl with a clink.

The crow gave one last angry *crawwwwwk!* and was gone in a swirl of smoke, leaving the bowl teetering on the edge of the table.

Brida was still trying to catch her breath when Mother Magdi rounded on her, eyes blazing.

"What in the name of all the sacred stars did you think you were doing? Have I taught you *nothing*?"

Mother Magdi swept the scrying bowl off the table, dropping the coin or pebble or whatever it was in one of her pockets again. She poured the remaining water out, hands shaking. "Didn't I tell you never to do this?" she cried, shoving the silver bowl back in the cabinet and slamming the doors shut.

"I'm sorry! I only wanted to see if I could find the stormhorses. . . ." Brida let her voice trail away. She had never seen Mother Magdi so angry. The scar beneath her eye practically glowed with her fury.

True, Brida had been forbidden to scry, but it was one of the only magical exercises that had ever come easily to her. It had always seemed harmless enough, at least until that crow flew out of the bowl.

"Did you touch a crow feather?" Mother Magdi grabbed her by the elbow, spun her around.

"What?"

"*Did you touch a crow feather?* Did one brush your skin?"

Brida frowned. "I . . . I don't think so."

How was she supposed to know? She'd been too busy trying to avoid a snapping beak and scratching talons. "Why?"

The hedgewitch waved a hand and the cool tingle of magic brushed Brida's skin.

She recognized the weaving of a seeking spell, but she couldn't guess what Mother Magdi was looking for.

"I'm fine!" she huffed, jerking backward. "What is going on?"

"Not a summons, then. Just a warning. Hopefully she didn't get a clear look at your face."

"I don't understand!"

Mother Magdi's scowl sharpened. "Haven't I told you that I am trying to keep you *safe*? I can't protect you if you deliberately disobey me! First you sneak off to the crossroads for the Day of Remembering, and now I catch you doing *this*!"

"I only wanted to help." Brida's voice cracked. "I thought if I could find the stormhorses, maybe figure out what brought them here . . . if I could find the link between the bone monster and the giant hounds and . . . and everything, then maybe I could prove that I'm not useless and the Council wouldn't name me a Wanderer."

"A Wanderer? Why on earth would you worry about that? You're my apprentice, child. Everyone knows that. And you certainly aren't useless. I couldn't have healed Dev without you."

"I keep failing the tests. I should have been named Greenleaf ages ago, but I can't get anything right and the Wisdoms know it. If the Council trusted my magic, they would have let me stay and talk about the stormhorses with you." Brida swallowed a lump of tears. "Scrying is the only thing I'm good at. Why won't you let me practice?"

Mother Magdi sighed. "Oh, child." She wrapped Brida in a hug. "You have strong magic in you, but all magic carries risk and using it requires caution." She patted Brida's back, rubbed soothing circles along her shoulders.

How can my magic be strong if I always make mistakes? Brida wanted to say, but Magdi wasn't finished speaking.

"You *are* exceptionally gifted at scrying," she continued, "and I did not wish your practice to attract the wrong sort of attention. There are those with the power to sense and trace the use of certain magics, and scrying them is like opening a door to their awareness. The shields I've placed around this valley can't protect against that possibility."

Brida blinked. Snuffled. Stepped out of the embrace and wiped her eyes with the heels of her hands. "What do you mean? Whose awareness?"

Mother Magdi smoothed her skirt and turned to the hearth. "What did you see in the bowl?"

Although Brida wanted to repeat her questions, the memory of Magdi's anger still crackled in the air so she let them go—for the moment. But how could she explain what she'd seen? So much of it had been a mystery. . . .

The sudden appearance of the crow in the scrying bowl had thrown Brida's thoughts into confusion. She closed her eyes to concentrate.

"I saw two stormhorses," she said slowly, "wearing silver halters that hurt them somehow, that held their power in check. And then there was a woman. . . ."

As she tried to describe what she'd seen, she realized what had first disturbed her about the image of the lady.

There'd been something too familiar about her face. The arch of her brows, the shape of her nose, the angle of her chin . . .

She looked too much like Mother Magdi.

NINE

Walking the Valley

"DO YOU KNOW who I saw in the scrying bowl?" Brida asked.

Mother Magdi's face had gone pinched and pale after Brida told her about the lady and the hunter she'd seen. What Brida *really* wanted to know was why the lady looked like Magdi, but the fierce expression in Magdi's eyes twisted the question on her tongue and she had to find different words.

Instead of answering, Mother Magdi bustled into the green room, beckoning Brida to follow.

"Who did I see?" Brida repeated, hurrying after her.

Magdi pulled drawers open, started grabbing things from the cabinet. "Hard to say for certain," she said, "but if she could get even a glimpse of you through the veil of scrying, she is dangerous. That's all that matters right now."

Brida knew Magdi was hiding something, but the hedgewitch's frantic scramble distracted her. "What are you doing?" she asked.

Magdi tossed a clatter of polished rocks on the table, followed by spools of colored thread and a handful of feathers. "Do you have your protection stones? Your dove feather?"

Brida patted her pocket. "Yes, like always."

"Good. Grab that bundle of rowan twigs, would you, please?"

Brida handed her the sticks and frowned at the supplies Magdi was now tucking into her satchel.

Before she could ask, Magdi said, "I promised the Council we would walk the valley. We need to leave as soon as we can. Bring the lantern and traveling kettle."

"We're walking the valley *today*?" Brida asked.

"Yes," Mother Magdi answered, preoccupied.

Walking the valley was something they ordinarily did once each year, on the winter solstice when the longest night also marked the slow return of the sun. They would travel through each town—even the tiny, unnamed hamlets—of the valley to check the protective charms Magdi had woven around the borders. It was a chance to renew the magic, strengthen the wards, and patrol the paths. Though the seasons might be scrambled, she and Mother Magdi tried their best to observe the regular rhythms of the year's cycle. But the winter solstice had been just months ago. Why were they doing it again? Brida set the lantern and a small tin kettle down and eyed the growing collection of herbs, bottled distillations, and oddments spread across the table.

Something else had been tickling the back of her mind.

She asked, "Did you mention your wingnotes to the Council?" After all, they were against Queen's Law so whoever sent them must have had a compelling reason—and something important to say.

The hedgewitch cast a sharp glance at her and then turned back to the satchel she was packing. "No. I didn't consider it necessary."

Brida waited, hoping for a hint about what the messages meant, but Magdi continued filling the satchel. So Brida asked instead, "Why does the Council want us to walk the valley again?"

"The Wisdoms want proof of the stormhorses, and they are worried about the pack of giant hounds—or wolves, or whatever they were—that Dev said he saw. They asked me to check the valley boundaries and look for signs of the beasts. Given everything we've seen, I agreed it was a prudent idea."

"You didn't tell them about the bone monster? Dev wasn't attacked by those giant hounds!"

Magdi pressed her fingertips to the table and frowned. "You heard them, Brida. It was hard enough for them to accept the possibility that the stormhorses have returned. Do you think they would believe that a creature cobbled out of bone attacked the butcher's boy? And if they *did*, how do you think they would react? They already mistrust magic."

"But Dev will tell them he wasn't injured by a wolf or hound."

Shaking her head, Magdi said, "While we were returning in the cart I convinced him his impressions of bones, teeth, and claws were the result of shock and blood loss before I arrived. He now believes he must have been attacked by a wolf."

"That's hardly fair to the wolves." Then Brida chewed her lip. "What are we going to do about the bone monster? It's still out there, isn't it?"

"We need to send it back into the ground where it belongs, and ensure that no others rise. We're strengthening the protections around the valley to guard against it, just as we do for any other threat."

"What about the giant hounds?" Brida asked.

"We'll deal with them, too, if we have to."

"And the stormhorses? They've been captured and—"

"One thing at a time, Brida."

Magdi poked a finger in a dusty glass jar and scowled. "Out of dragonbreath poppyseeds. I haven't seen a living plant in two years, and none of the peddlers have had any to sell, either." She set the jar back on the nearest shelf and sighed. "Fetch me the bottle of sundew sap. It will have to do instead."

Brida crossed the room to the back shelves and scanned the labels until she found the bottle marked Sundew Sap. "What if a bone monster manages to injure one of us?" she asked. "Or . . . what if there are different monsters? Worse ones?" If the stormhorses were real, what other creatures might surprise them?

"I don't know. But it's our job, isn't it? To do whatever we must in order to protect this valley and all the people in it. It's the pledge we make in exchange for our powers—to serve and defend."

Her face darkened with an expression Brida couldn't read. "I hate bringing you close to possible danger. If I could leave you home and know that you'd remain safe I would, but I have a feeling you're better off staying with me. In any case, I'm afraid I simply can't do this without your assistance."

A rush of pride lifted Brida's chin. Mother Magdi *needed* her! And then her stomach twisted.

"But . . . we need to protect the entire valley and I'm not yet a Greenleaf. I may not be enough help. Maybe you should wait for Mother Ivy."

Magdi stepped around the table to rest her hands on Brida's shoulders. Her eyes—hazel pools swimming with flecks of gold and brown—stared deep into Brida's own. "There's no time to wait. You have worked with me for years. Together we have delivered babes, healed broken bones, patched up injuries, and worked charms for all sorts of ailments. Your strength helped heal Dev. And all on your own you made a remedy for forgiveness that proved to be precisely what Daise Weaver needed. I know you are capable of great things, Brida. You just need to trust yourself. Trust your magic."

Then she gave a gentle squeeze and released her grip. "But keep your protection stones with you and stay close to me."

Magdi tied her satchel closed and handed another to Brida. "See how that feels. Is it too heavy?"

Brida hefted it over her shoulder. "No, I can manage."

"Good. The rest should fit in our saddlebags."

Brida slipped the satchel off and peeked inside. In addition to spools of thread and a jar of glass beads, Mother Magdi had also packed a spare lantern, two pairs of socks, a round of cheese wrapped in grape leaves and waxed paper, several apples, a loaf of bread in a linen cloth, a tin of tea, and a packet of nuts.

It was difficult to judge the rations. Usually walking the valley took three days, but they stopped frequently for midwinter celebrations and ate at the houses they visited. "How long do you think we'll be gone?" Brida asked.

"Hard to say. Two days if we're lucky, longer if we're not. Grab your extra cloak in case we're caught in a storm."

Brida was less concerned about a storm than she was about Magdi's secrets and the woman in the scrying bowl, but she put on her pack and followed Magdi outside.

They rode in silence for a time, Mother Magdi leading the way on her elegant mare. Velvet had a quick, swinging walk that forced Burdock to break into a jog now and then to keep up. Brida left her reins loose and let her thoughts drift until they reached Wayfarers' Well.

If this were a traditional winter solstice walk, the well would have been surrounded by villagers in their most festive clothes. While they sang to the sun and rang bells for luck, Mother Magdi would have hung a sprig of holly and a twist of red and green ribbon by the well to bring health and good fortune to all who sipped its waters.

Today, however, she and Brida were alone. They dismounted, Brida holding both Velvet and Burdock by their reins while Magdi struck the well's stone rim three times with a rowan twig. After shoving the stick in the soft ground nearby, Magdi hung a pigeon feather and a small pebble with a hole through the middle of it from a cleft in the sturdy twig.

As she then whispered a chant of protection and earth wisdom, power thrummed in the ground. Brida felt it like a hum against the bottom of her feet, rising at Mother Magdi's call. Magdi anchored it with the rowan charm, building a beacon of safety for the people of Oak Hollow.

Brida had grown up with the hedgewitch. For twelve years she'd been watching, learning, practicing—but she'd never seen Mother Magdi work green magic quite like this.

This was more than a winter blessing. More than a luck charm.

This was deep earth magic . . . which meant Mother

Magdi was even more concerned than she had let on.

Brida glanced over her shoulder, but no one approached the well. The road appeared deserted.

"Where is everyone?" she murmured.

Mother Magdi dusted her hands and adjusted her satchel before climbing back in Velvet's saddle. "I imagine Goodman Druse and his sons have scared everyone with tales of Dev's attack." She turned her mare away from the well, heading down the cobbled road to the blacksmith's yard.

The ring of hammer on anvil stopped when Jon Irons spotted them. He stepped away from his forge, face reddened by heat and arms slick with sweat. "Mother Magdi, young Brida, what can I do for you?" Sudden worry creased his forehead. "Is something amiss with Linna and the babe? Did someone call you?"

Magdi smiled at him. "No, Jon, it's nothing wrong. I just came by to beg a favor, if you can spare the time."

"Certainly! What do you need?" he asked, rubbing Burdock's shoulder.

"Brida and I have rounds to make through the valley and may be gone for a couple of days. Would you mind checking in on our goat and feeding the chickens while we're away?" Magdi asked.

"And don't forget to leave milk for the cats! There's a ginger tom and a small black cat that often stop by," Brida told him. "Oh, and you might see a white dove. There's a container of birdseed by the springhouse and—"

He laughed and patted her foot in the stirrup. "Don't worry, Brida. I'll take good care of them all until you get back."

Magdi said, "Thank you, Jon. I'll make certain Linna has a fresh stock of sleep-soothe remedy for the new babe as soon as I return."

He grinned. "Well, now, we'll all be grateful for that! Safe travels, then."

Riding away from his yard, Magdi led the way toward a small white gate hung across a narrow, rocky path that skirted the edge of Oak Hollow.

Brida followed on Burdock, though she was puzzled. Ordinarily they went through the center of town, where they'd share hot cider or rich warm cinnamon milk and sweet buns with friends and neighbors. They'd hang small charms on doorways and everyone would join in the ritual chants.

Mother Magdi clearly had a different route in mind this time.

"Keep your eyes open," Magdi said in a low voice as they slipped through the gate and latched it behind them again. "If anything catches your attention, strikes you as strange— no matter how small or insignificant—let me know."

Brida nodded, remembering the way the ground burst open to expel the bone monster. She was afraid to ask what Magdi expected them to find—she *never* wanted to see that again.

The rest of the afternoon passed peacefully, to Brida's relief. Although Mother Magdi politely declined offers of company from friendly neighbors, explaining that she and Brida were on important Council business, they hardly traveled alone. They were joined by the occasional curious rabbit or squirrel, a couple of toads, even a shy fox. For a few minutes a small turtle with a colorful shell plodded along behind them. Birds sang from the trees and once or twice Brida thought she glimpsed the white dove.

She could almost convince herself this was just a pleasant ride, though Burdock's ears flicked nervously, and she felt the tension in his back.

But then, as they left the border of Oak Hollow behind and crossed into the woods near the less secluded north end of the valley, toward Maple Hill, they started noticing signs of blight. Mottled yellow and brown leaves hung limply from tree branches. Pale spots scarred clumps of otherwise green, velvety moss. Wild roses bloomed black with rot, and flies buzzed around mold-furred berries.

The farther they rode, the worse things looked. Brida's skin started to itch and a creeping lethargy weighted her arms. Velvet and Burdock slowed to a dull plod, snorting occasionally as though they caught foul odors on the air.

The edge of Maple Hill was marked by three boulders beside an old maple tree. Brida's heart twisted when she realized that the proud tree was clearly dying. Curls of bark hung like peeling skin from its trunk and brown leaves had fallen in drifts beneath its branches.

"Did the changing weather do this?" Brida whispered. "The broken seasons?"

Mother Magdi's face was stricken, the red scar beneath her eye a livid mark. "I was here just a fortnight ago, and the tree was thriving. No . . . this looks like . . . an infection."

Still in the saddle, Magdi opened her pack and began crafting a charm. But when she hung it on the lowest branch the thread unraveled, the feather decayed, and the stone crumbled to dust.

Brida crossed her arms over her chest and hugged her elbows. Magdi's charms *never* failed. Sensing her distress, Burdock shook his head and tried to back away.

"I need your help." Magdi tied another charm and let it dangle from the fingers of one hand. She dismounted and reached out to Brida, clasping her palm as Brida slid out of the saddle.

"This is no different from the protection charms we hang around the cottage or the barn—it's just bigger. Once we've anchored the earth's energies to this"—she gave the feather and stone a small shake—"we'll send our magic out like a protective bubble around this entire area. After that's done, we will see about healing the damage to this tree."

Brida nodded and closed her eyes. She had never been able to call deep earth power by herself, but she'd had practice weaving the energies Magdi drew upon. Of course, she'd only done it on a small scale: helping Magdi call groundwater up to nourish the roots of sun-parched trees and bushes in their garden when the rains failed, casting rocks aside to help new trees thrive, or warming the soil to melt frost that stayed too long. This would be more difficult, but with Magdi's strength . . .

Right away Brida could tell something was wrong, though. Instead of feeling energy rising from the rocks and the soil, spilling from the sunlight and the leaves, Brida's own power drained away. The air grew still and heavy.

There was no balance of magic, no equilibrium. She was used to the natural ebb and flow of energy when she and Mother Magdi worked together, shifting power from one thing, one place, to another. It's what preserved the harmony of the living world. But now . . . something had disrupted that cycle.

She staggered and nearly fell, her vision blurring as the air in her lungs was squeezed out. Her pulse thundered in her ears and dizziness buzzed through her head.

The maple tree creaked and groaned, dead leaves rattling without a breeze.

A moment later the brittle grass surrounding the tree's roots swayed and rustled and a snake slithered into view. Its scales were dull and mottled, scabbed with patches of gray and brown. "Stay away from it!" Mother Magdi cried, breaking the magic connection and tugging Brida backward.

Brida wasn't afraid of snakes, but she had to admit

something about this one *was* a little unnerving. It writhed and twisted, and she realized it was shedding.

No wonder it looked so . . . diseased.

But when its old skin flaked away, she was dismayed to see that the new scales underneath were in even worse shape. The snake flicked a forked tongue at them and slithered back out of view, leaving a dusty husk behind.

"Something is very, very wrong," Mother Magdi muttered.

Brida sank to the ground. She felt cold and clammy, her stomach sick and sloshy. "What is going on?" she gasped.

Magdi frowned and dropped the charm into her satchel. "This is worse than I thought." She helped Brida into the saddle, mounted Velvet, and led the way down the road toward Maple Hill's town square.

Brida was still weak and shaky. She clutched Burdock's mane and tried to catch her breath. "I'm sorry I couldn't help you. The harder I reached for the magic, the faster it poured away." It had felt like trying to hold smoke or water.

"You don't have to apologize, Brida. It wasn't your fault. Something has poisoned the land, leaching away its vital energy and our power."

Poison . . . "The same influence that created the bone monster?"

Magdi nodded and waved a fly off Velvet's neck. "The same contamination that caused the bone monster to rise must be responsible for this blight, yes. Anything more than that I can't say yet." She squinted, scanning the sky.

Burdock shuffled sideways to snatch a bite of grass from the verge and Brida nudged him back onto the road with her knees. She was afraid it wasn't safe to eat.

Her thoughts circled the lady she'd seen in the scrying bowl. There'd been something cruel and hard in the woman's expression, and Mother Magdi had said she was dangerous. Clearly the silver halters she forced upon the captive stormhorses caused them pain. But why did she want to catch all five stormhorses? To contain their power before it caused more damage? Or to *use* that power?

"Mother Magdi, could the stormhorses fix the broken seasons? If they were captured?" Brida asked. The idea of catching them stung like a wasp—every instinct she possessed told her they were meant to be free—but if the weather continued to worsen, maybe drastic measures were necessary?

Magdi slowed Velvet. "You know we work within the proper balance of things. We don't *possess* magic. In order to call it, contain it, or control it, we must also *surrender* to it. The ability to weave magic and work with it requires an understanding of the energy in everything around us. Because we have an affinity in our blood that allows us to sense the threads of magic in all the natural world, we can use the power according to our needs."

Brida nodded. This was a familiar lesson.

"The stormhorses . . . they aren't part of the natural

order anymore. If they ever were. The Great Mother banished them to another realm because she knew their power was too wild to be contained in these lands. That sort of elemental energy . . . it's too much to hold, too much to direct. None of us is strong enough to surrender to it without being destroyed in the process. Brida, you must understand how dangerous they are, despite the wonder of their beauty."

"But the lady in the scrying bowl—" Brida's voice cracked on a shard of cold fear and she couldn't finish the question. If the mysterious woman was willing to go to such lengths to capture creatures of legend, what power did she already wield and what did she hope to achieve? Could she be responsible for this darkness?

"Right now we must focus on our own valley. When our friends and neighbors are safe, we will consider our next steps. I'll have to consult with other hedgewitches before we decide how to deal with the stormhorses, and— Blood and thorns! Get down!"

Magdi jumped off Velvet and half pulled, half helped Brida down from Burdock. They led the horses behind a hedge and then Magdi shoved Brida beneath a cluster of large ferns.

"What—" Brida tried to protest, but Magdi clapped a hand over her lips.

A bee buzzed in a nearby bellflower and a beetle clicked its way over a carpet of pine needles, but otherwise silence fell around them. Brida's ankle tingled and she tried to twist into a more comfortable position, but Mother Magdi gripped her arm and hissed, "Be still and don't make a sound!"

A muscle in Magdi's jaw quivered and a bead of sweat collected above her lip. Brida froze, cold fear spider-webbing across her skin. What could be so bad that Mother Magdi would feel the need to *hide*? Hadn't she just been saying that it was their job to protect the valley?

In the distance, a crow let out a loud *crawwwwk!* and was answered by another to the west. A tremor ran through Magdi's body.

Brida's stomach tightened. What did Mother Magdi perceive?

Another crow called much closer and Brida suddenly thought of the bird that had burst from her scrying bowl, its thrashing wings and sharp talons launched at her face. Dread squeezed the breath from her lungs. It hadn't seemed quite like an ordinary crow, but she'd been too startled for clear perceptions. . . .

No. She was letting terror cloud her thinking. Crows were clever and curious, though for some reason she rarely saw them around Oak Hollow. Perhaps they could show her what Magdi sensed so she could be prepared.

Collecting her courage, Brida closed her eyes and cast her awareness out toward the birds. After seeing storm-horses, giant hounds, and a monster made of bone she would *not* let herself be scared by a flock of crows. Especially not when she could feel Mother Magdi's fright. She needed to know what they saw. Anxious to connect, she stretched her senses . . .

And frowned. It could be difficult to communicate with birds—they were vague and distractible—but usually she'd feel at least a tickle at the edge of her mind, a swift impression if nothing else. Now, though, she felt . . . nothing.

Perhaps she was just tired. Brida tried again, *reaching* with her mind. This time, however, she only caught quick flickers of something dark and oppressive. It reminded her, oddly, of the magic she'd sensed enveloping the giant hound she healed by the boneyard.

It reminded her of the instantaneous flash of *wrongness* she'd felt from the crow in the scrying bowl. Maybe she hadn't just imagined it. Maybe there was something wicked about these birds.

"They're coming. Don't draw their attention!" Mother Magdi whispered in Brida's ear, barely louder than a breath.

Brida gasped and scooted farther under the ferns, trembling as she finally understood that the unnatural crows were the cause of Magdi's fear. And if she *had* managed to communicate, she would have given away their hiding place.

The thought made her sick.

She felt the hedgewitch spin a delicate thread of magic to keep the horses quiet and calm. Velvet let out a sigh and folded her knees, settling to the ground. Burdock flared his nostrils and did the same a second later.

Huddling beside Brida, Magdi eased her cloak over both of them as the air filled with the rush of wings and a cacophony of cawing and croaking. Dozens of crows swept through the air, circling and diving between the trees.

From a gap beneath the edge of the cloak Brida watched them, chilled by the methodical way the birds seemed to be searching. They were far larger than any crows she'd seen before and that vague sense of dark magic grew stronger.

Several long minutes later, they gave up hunting whatever they were after and flew away. Mother Magdi remained still, eyes closed. "They're gone," she finally murmured. She stood up slowly, scanning the forest.

"What were they looking for?"

"There's a reason Moira is called the Queen of Crows. Those birds"—Magdi gestured at the sky—"those were her spies."

"I thought that was just a story to keep us from breaking rules!"

"Well, it's a true one," Magdi said. "Hurry—there's no time to waste. We are lucky they didn't see our horses. Next time we might not be so fortunate." She grabbed Velvet's reins, coaxing the mare back up and praising her for staying still.

Brida rubbed Burdock's neck as he scrambled to his feet, and then she climbed in the saddle again. "If they were spies, what were they looking for?"

If they were spies, did that mean the crow in her scrying

bowl had been seeking something, too? The possibility sent her pulse racing.

"Lawbreakers. Dissidents. Troublemakers. Magic."

"Magic?" Brida brushed a leaf from her hair and straightened her tunic, hands shaking. "But *hedgemagic* isn't against the law, only white magic is. We aren't doing anything wrong."

"No . . . but the queen is hungry for power, and she won't hesitate to use another's magic when she can. If her *Crows*"—the word was weighted with emphasis—"are in the area, our job has suddenly gotten much more difficult." Magdi sounded grim.

"What should we do?"

"We'll have to wait until dark, when the Crows have returned to their roost." But she showed no signs of slowing down, so Brida wasn't sure what *waiting* Mother Magdi intended to do.

Just before sundown they came to a thicket of hemlock, spruce, and yew trees. The tang of pine sharpened the cool evening air and shadows puddled the ground. The horses quickened their pace, anxious to pass the grim trees. Brida had to agree there was something forbidding about them.

They looked like the perfect place for crows to nest.

But to her surprise Mother Magdi and Velvet veered off the narrow dirt trail they had been following and headed straight for the copse. Brida and Burdock reluctantly followed. Surely they weren't going to spend the night *here*? During their midwinter valley walks they usually stayed at an inn a few leagues away.

Velvet plunged into the deep stillness of the evergreen thicket without hesitation, Magdi turning in the saddle and beckoning Brida to keep up. Low limbs snagged their cloaks and tugged at Brida's sleeves. Needles caught in her hair and scratched her arms.

And then, suddenly, they burst into a clearing with a small timber-frame cottage. Its whitewashed walls almost glowed in the fading light and the white roses climbing the porch filled the air with sweet perfume.

A dog barked inside the cottage. When the door opened a moment later, he came barreling out in a blur of black-and-white fur and lolling tongue. He circled the horses, tail wagging and ears flopping.

Brida dismounted when Magdi did, laughing and kneeling down to pet him. "Aren't you a marvelous fellow?" Brida said, scratching his chin.

"His name is Rooster, because he's a noisy mess and too proud of himself by half," a lovely voice said. The dog gave a gleeful bark and spun away from Brida to fling himself at the young woman who had just stepped down from the porch. "Still, I love him anyway, don't I?" And she rubbed his ears with a fond smile.

She straightened, resting one hand on her dog's head. "Happy evening, Mother Magdi. I am glad to see you.

And . . ." She turned to Brida, dark eyes measuring. Her gaze flicked back to the hedgewitch, one brow curving in a question. "This is her?"

"Rissi, this is my apprentice, Brida. Brida, this is Rissi," Magdi said, as if that answered everything.

"I am most glad to meet you," Brida answered politely, trying—and, she suspected, failing—to keep the surprise off her face. She didn't travel as often as Magdi, it was true, but she thought she knew almost everyone in the valley. And yet she'd never even heard of Rissi.

How did Mother Magdi know her?

Could Rissi be the one sending wingnotes? No . . . Brida cast a quick glance around the small yard but didn't see a pigeon coop.

Magdi said, "Rissi moved here several years ago. I was good friends with her mother."

Her explanation only raised more questions, but asking them might prod painful memories, so Brida simply nodded and smiled. She could discreetly press Magdi for details later.

Rissi smiled back, brushing thick straight hair the color of polished walnut over her shoulder. Her skin was burnished copper and she wore a long, simple dress the color of the lake at dawn. She exuded grace and something Brida couldn't quite name—a charisma or energy that felt both strange and familiar at the same time.

She made Brida feel young and grubby.

"It's my joy to meet you," Rissi said kindly. "Please, be welcome in my home. There's a pen out back for your horses and a water pump with a couple of buckets. It's late and I imagine you're hungry. Shall I fix some supper? Hot tea?"

"That would be nice, thank you," Magdi said. "Brida, would you please get the horses settled for the night? You'll find grain in my saddlebags and you can leave all our things by the back door. Join us when you're finished."

As Magdi and Rissi disappeared inside, Brida led Velvet and Burdock to the pen Rissi had mentioned. It was a sturdy enclosure, small but containing enough sweet grass to keep the horses happy. "Burdock, please stay inside. I'm afraid it isn't safe to play games tonight, do you understand?"

She found two buckets by the water pump and filled them both, wobbling with the weight as she carried them into the pen. "Here you go," Brida told the horses. She removed their bridles, lifted off their saddles, and poured some grain onto the ground—in two separate piles, because Burdock didn't like to share—and then lugged all the tack to the covered deck by the back door.

Just as she raised her hand to tap on the door, voices drifted through a small open window above her head.

"Did you see the *Crows*?" Rissi asked, giving the word the same emphasis Magdi had used.

"Yes. We had to hide in the hedge like bandits." There was a wry twist to Magdi's words, but the humor sounded forced.

A cabinet door opened and closed, dishes rattled. "I've noticed one or two before, but never so many. Is it because of the girl?"

What girl? Brida wondered. She knew she shouldn't be listening, but Magdi had been so secretive lately. Brida couldn't resist the chance to get some answers.

"Hard to say. Could be the magic I tried to work earlier at the waymarker near Maple Hill—I didn't realize the blight had come this far. The queen's reach is obviously growing stronger. But the silly child was scrying and drew attention—"

Brida's arm jerked when she realized they were talking about *her* and her elbow knocked the doorframe.

"Come on in!" Rissi called, her voice suddenly strong and clear as though she hadn't been whispering about Brida a moment before. The next thing Brida knew she was being ushered into a tidy kitchen and shown to a bench piled with soft cushions. The dog flopped at her feet, yawning and thumping his tail.

Rissi set a kettle on a small cast-iron stove and took a tin of tea leaves from a cupboard. "Did you get your horses settled?"

"Yes, thank you," Brida answered, but she wanted to ask: *What were you talking about? What do I have to do with anything?* If they knew she'd been listening, though, it might be even harder to glean more information later, so she held her tongue.

Rissi tied an apron around her waist and began chopping vegetables, dumping them in a large pot. "So, what brings you out here?"

Magdi told her about the giant hounds and the bone creature that had attacked Dev, surprising Brida with her candor. Evidently she trusted Rissi even more than the Council of Wisdoms. "And Brida has seen stormhorses," Magdi finished.

"Stormhorses! Truly? They're real? What do they look like? Are they as magnificent as the stories say?"

Brida nodded. "They're beautiful, and each one is different." While Rissi finished preparing the meal—fresh bread with a spicy vegetable and rice dish—Brida described the golden palomino and the warm light that surrounded her, the blue roan and her raindrops, the spotted bay and the snowflakes, and the black stallion with his lightning blaze and thunder hooves. "The mare that leads the herd is white, and she brings a wind like nothing I've felt before," Brida said.

"Oh, now that's a sight I'd love to see," Rissi breathed, passing bowls around the table.

Magdi poured the tea, clicking her tongue. "From a distance, I'd hope. The storms they could bring would destroy everything you own. They aren't meant for this land."

"Then why are they here? Why now?"

Brida blurted, "Someone is pursuing them, trying to capture them."

144

Rissi dropped her spoon. "For what purpose? The stormhorses should be free!"

"I agree," Magdi said, lifting a hand. "But right now this spreading blight is our most pressing concern, especially if—as I suspect—it's linked to whatever force awakened the bone monster. I told the Council of Wisdoms I would walk the valley, but the charm I tried to hang by Maple Hill's waymarker crumbled. In order to protect our borders, Brida and I need your magic."

So *that* was the strange charisma Brida had sensed! Rissi had magical ability, too. "You're a hedgewitch?" Brida asked.

"No . . . my affinity is with white magic," Rissi said, bending down to offer her dog a cooked carrot.

"White magic! But I thought—"

"That we should all be in Temples? Yes. We should. I'm supposed to be a priestess in the Temple of the Salt Winds, like my mother. My grandmother helped establish the Temple of Stars. But the queen broke the Temples, outlawed sacred magic, and killed my family. *You*, of all people, should know why I cannot help, Mother Magdi," Rissi said, eyes shimmering with tears.

Magdi stood, bracing her hands on the table. "Yes, I of all people know what you have been through. I *know* what was lost. I know the risk! But do you think I would be here with *this girl* if I did not think it absolutely necessary?"

This girl? Brida took a breath to tell them she knew they

were talking about her when Magdi cast her a stern look and shook her head.

Rissi also glanced at Brida and then away. She sighed and covered her face in her hands. "Mother Magdi, you know I never completed my training. I only learned the basic songs."

"That's more than we have now. It may be enough."

After a long moment, Rissi nodded. "I promise only that I will try."

"That's all I ask. We'll head out at moonrise."

— TEN —

Magic

AT TWILIGHT, BRIDA followed Mother Magdi and Rissi to a rocky hillside hidden by pine trees and towering white oaks. A faint glow from a thin sliver of moon filtered through the branches, but Rissi had given them lanterns to carry before they'd left her cottage. The dancing flames cast wavering splashes of golden light as they walked.

Mother Magdi and Rissi spoke quietly just ahead of Brida, heads tilted toward each other. She could hear the grim cadence of their voices but couldn't make out what they were saying.

She had a feeling they were talking about her. Why did it seem as if Rissi—only a few years older—knew her, even though they'd never met?

Rissi had changed into a simple white robe tied at the waist with a pale blue ribbon. A silver band with a crescent moon amid a row of stars perched above her forehead, holding back her hair. She looked elegant, mysterious, *powerful*. But there had been dark circles under her eyes when they set out, and when she told her dog farewell Brida had noticed the shine of tears on her cheek.

Was she afraid, too?

Something rustled in the leaves overhead and they all froze, hands covering their lanterns. In the swallowing darkness, an owl asked *Who? Whoooo who who?*

"Not a Crow," Rissi murmured. "Just a great horned owl."

"How much farther?" Magdi asked.

"A few more paces. Nearly there," Rissi said.

Brida's heart stuttered. She wasn't certain what Mother Magdi had in mind, but it was going to involve white magic and that was something she'd never expected to witness.

Sacred magic—also called white magic—had been banned by the queen for as long as Brida could remember. She knew it had once been practiced by both men and women, that the power came from the Great Mother and the Sky Father and all the lesser gods and spirits. It was the traditional magic of the old Temples, used in rituals to protect and replenish the land, to forecast the future and predict the tides of time. Though Queen Moira's soldiers had destroyed all the Temples when Brida was a baby, Mother Magdi had always told her that some of the priests and priestesses escaped and still recited the spellsongs in exile.

Brida had never dreamed she would meet someone who knew white magic so close to home. She watched Rissi climb a mossy hill speckled with glowworms and brushed a mosquito off her wrist, scurrying to keep up.

Priestesses were supposed to wear a silver cuff on their left wrists with a triple moon design: a waxing crescent, a full circle, and a waning crescent. Rissi hadn't finished her initiation so she only wore a thin silver bracelet with a small circle in the center.

A wasp sting of shame pricked Brida's heart. The only reason Rissi hadn't completed her training was because there weren't any Temples left and all the priestesses had been killed or sent into hiding. She had no one to teach her, and just studying the *history* of sacred magic was against Queen's Law.

But Brida didn't have any excuses.

Hedgemagic—sometimes known as green magic—was the most common form of power, though still unusual enough. It was generally worked by women. Since it often only manifested as a knack for gardening, the queen didn't consider it a threat and had never forbidden the practice. It was drawn from nature, from stones and shells and feathers, from growing things. Brida spent her days *surrounded* by sources of hedgemagic. Mother Magdi was a powerful hedgewitch and an excellent teacher, and yet Brida still couldn't pass her Greenleaf exams.

And lately, not even Magdi's magic seemed capable of stopping the spread of whatever had poisoned the world.

Brida chewed her lip because there was another magic,

wasn't there? One she didn't like to think about. Black magic—sorcery. The power of shadows and darkness, illusion and secrets. It was forbidden—not by Queen's Law but by the natural order.

If this blight had been caused by dark sorcery, would green and white magic together be enough to overcome it?

"Watch your step," Rissi warned, snapping Brida out of her grim thoughts. They had finally arrived at a rock overhang and, in the fitful flicker of their lanterns, Brida spotted what looked like a cave opening.

Her throat closed around a lump of cold fear. She *hated* small spaces and the thought of stepping inside—or under?—all that stone made her head ache. Surely there was somewhere else they could do this? Somewhere higher up, in the open, beneath the wide, starry sky?

But then the risk of getting caught would make this magic far too dangerous. She sighed and tried to gather courage. It was just a cave, and hiding under rock was far better than being chased by giant hounds or attacked by creatures made of bone.

As Brida tilted her chin back for a last glimpse of the sky, a flash of distant lightning crackled across the horizon. Even from where she stood she sensed the flare of wild magic.

The stormhorses were out there.

A moment later the distant baying and barking of hounds floated on the evening air and she clenched her teeth. The stormhorses were still being chased.

"This way," Rissi whispered, ducking beneath a curtain of ivy and disappearing.

"Come along, child," Mother Magdi said over her shoulder to Brida. "We have work to do tonight."

Brida swallowed her objection and reluctantly followed the others into the cave. She *really* hated small, tight, dark—

"Oh!" she gasped, stepping under a natural arch of stone and into a vast cavern. Part of the rock ceiling had collapsed ages ago, leaving the center of the space open to the sky. Beneath the vaulted fissure a giant tree grew, spreading its branches as if in welcome.

Small niches along the cavern walls held fat beeswax candles, and when Rissi sang a short phrase they burst into flame, filling the cavern with light.

"Beautiful," Brida whispered.

Rissi flashed her a smile. "It is my favorite place. I've never showed it to anyone else."

"How did you find it?"

A rustle near her feet sent Brida scuttling backward and Rissi chuckled. "*She* showed me." Rissi pointed to the ground.

Brida's gaze traced the other girl's finger and landed on a massive snake as long as two men and as thick as a sapling tree trunk. The snake lazily uncoiled herself to show off iridescent scales of black, emerald green, and deep blue glinting in the light. She was beautiful and vibrant—unlike the diseased snake Brida had seen beneath the blighted maple tree earlier.

"Her name is Mystery," Rissi offered. "You don't have to be scared. I promise she won't hurt you."

But Brida wasn't scared. She was in awe. "She's magnificent!"

Mystery raised her head, forked tongue flickering as her gem-bright eyes met Brida's.

"I think she likes you," Rissi said with a smile, reaching out to stroke the snake's wedge-shaped head.

"Girls, there's no time to waste." Mother Magdi hefted her satchel as if to remind them.

Rissi stepped away from the snake and led them toward the base of the huge tree. As they approached, Brida heard the gurgle of water and realized there was a spring trickling up from the ground between the tree's gnarled roots.

"Ahhhh," Mother Magdi breathed. "You have found a deeply sacred place, indeed. Well done."

Rissi ducked her head, candlelight casting warm gold across her cheeks and forehead. "As I said, Mystery led me. I never would have discovered it if I hadn't followed her."

"Water, earth, air, and flame," Mother Magdi said, turning in a slow circle. "All four elements, in a space that straddles the border between land and sky, earth and water." She nodded once and set her satchel down, crouching to rummage through it. "This is perfect. We can weave strong magic here."

Magdi took a bundle of herbs from the satchel and glanced up at Rissi. "Your mother would be proud, Rissi."

Rissi's dark brows drew down and she twisted her hands. "I wondered . . . I mean, sometimes I hoped . . . I wished . . ." She swallowed and said in a rush, "Sometimes I thought maybe my mother might have, somehow, sent Mystery to show me the way?"

Magdi considered the snake now watching from a few feet away. "It's entirely possible," she said. "Snakes aren't bound by the same laws of time or place that we are. It's been said they can carry messages from the dead."

A radiant, teary smile bloomed across Rissi's face and she knelt between the snake and the rim of the spring's pool. "That's what I thought," she murmured. Then she looked up at Magdi. "I'm ready. How do you want to do this?"

Magdi drew a circle around the pool by sprinkling the ground with crushed herbs and rose petals. Then she rested a hand on Rissi's shoulder. "If you'll begin a chant—"

Brida cleared her throat, ears burning hot with shame and embarrassment. She felt the power of this place like a cool hum in the center of her chest, felt an aura of waiting magic emanating from Mother Magdi and Rissi. But what could *she* do? Protecting the valley was far too important for her to risk making a mistake. Besides, if Mother Magdi had Rissi to help her, why would she need Brida?

But Magdi reached for Brida's hand before she could protest, tugging her down beside them. The ground around the spring was soft and spongy with moss, but a damp chill seeped through Brida's knees almost immediately. Releasing her hand to grip her shoulder, Magdi said, "Brida, you belong here with us. Besides, three is a sacred number, remember?"

"But what if—"

"Just follow our lead. And trust yourself, child. You are stronger than you know."

The snake—Mystery—hissed as if in agreement, and the knot in Brida's stomach slowly unraveled.

Rissi gave her a crooked smile. "I'm worried, too. I only know the simple spellsongs, and even those . . . Well, I've been singing protection chants and we can all see how well those have gone, hmm? But we're doing our best, and maybe together . . ." She lifted her hands, dropping one on Magdi's shoulder and one on Brida's.

Brida liked the feeling of connection so she put her hands on their shoulders, too, completing the link.

Magdi smiled and nodded. "Yes! This is perfect. Rissi, if you'll sing, Brida and I will tie threads of green magic along the sacred notes of your white magic. . . . You'll understand what I mean when you feel it, but think about weaving harmonies of power rather than sound."

"What if the queen senses what we're doing?" Rissi asked.

"It might be a blessing that there are stormhorses running loose in the valley—their power will mask ours.

Besides, the Crows will be roosting for the night. Now is our best chance."

Rissi pursed her lips, but then, after a moment, she nodded and began to sing.

Brida closed her eyes, surrendering to a rush of power that roared like the wind in her ears.

ELEVEN

Destruction

BRIDA AND MAGDI spent the night at Rissi's after they finished weaving a spell of protection around the entire valley. Before they left the next morning, Rissi caught Brida by the sleeve and tugged her aside.

"I don't know all the ways to forecast the future, but . . . sometimes I catch glimpses. Sometimes I can read a toss of stones and know the shape of things to come. And . . ." She hesitated, then leaned closer and whispered in Brida's ear, "If you want to know the truth about who you are and where you come from, look in a broken Temple. But . . . Brida, when you find out, don't be angry with Mother Magdi. Everything she's done has been to keep you safe."

Brida's entire body jerked in surprise, startling Rooster into a sharp bark. "What do you mean?"

But Magdi's attention had been drawn by the dog, and she marched over, arms wide, to wrap Rissi in a grateful hug. "Thank you for your help and your hospitality. It went even better than I dared to hope, but you know how to reach me if you see anything unusual, so do not hesitate!"

Rissi smiled. "Thank *you* for watching over the valley, Mother Magdi. And, Brida, it was a joy to meet you. You feel like the little sister I never had."

Brida wanted to ask about the broken Temple, but Magdi was already mounting Velvet and there wasn't a chance. "I hope we'll meet again!" Brida cried, climbing in her own saddle. She turned back to wave just before they pushed through the trees and out of sight.

"If we hurry we can reach Walnut Creektown by midday, and then we'll swing by the boneyard on our way back. With any luck, we could be home by dusk," Mother Magdi said, brushing aside a yew limb.

"I wish I never had to see the boneyard again."

"I'm hoping our work last night laid any bone creatures to rest, but we must be certain."

"Mother Magdi, why didn't you tell me about Rissi?" Brida asked, the question sour on her tongue as she thought of lonely afternoons and long evenings by herself while the hedgewitch was busy. Burdock was her best friend, but sometimes she longed for conversation. Rissi understood what it was to be solitary and secluded—and she seemed to know the secret of Brida's past.

"She was a Temple initiate and now she's in hiding. It wasn't safe for either of you to be seen together. Yesterday was a special circumstance."

"Does that mean we'll never see each other again?"

Brida ran her palm along Burdock's neck, blinking away the burn of tears.

Magdi glanced over her shoulder at Brida with an expression full of pity, regret, sorrow . . . and maybe fear. "It just means this is a dangerous time, and you have your own paths to walk."

Brida was the first to notice the hoofprints a couple of hours later.

She and Magdi were riding on the main road between Maple Hill and Walnut Creektown—a flat, stone-paved stretch wide enough for two carts to pass—trying to make up for lost time. Magdi had been keeping watch for Crows, eyes scanning the sky and treetops, while Brida leaned forward and studied the ground.

The first hoofprint was indistinct, just a smudge in the dirt beside the road. But it glimmered in her mind like an echo of magic and she *knew* it had been left by one of the stormhorses.

Two steps farther on she saw a clear set of bare hoofprints—perfect ovals with a triangular impression at their base. She stopped Burdock and slipped off for a closer look. When she crouched down to trace them with a finger, the residue of magic tingled in her skin.

"Mother Magdi, look! Stormhorses!"

The hedgewitch reined Velvet around to see. "Can you tell how many are still free?"

"Not yet. The ground is too rocky. But . . . oh, no. See there . . . that paw print? It's too big to be a dog, isn't it?"

Lightning suddenly crackled across the empty sky, dragging thunder with it. A plume of smoke rose in the distance, and something crashed.

Velvet whinnied and pawed the ground, ears pinned flat and lips pinched. Magdi patted her neck, trying to calm her. Burdock was agitated, too—he crowded close to Brida, nudging her with his whiskered nose as if to say they should *go*.

Brida stood and scratched his chin while she stared in the direction of Walnut Creektown a league away. There was another flash of lightning and then a burst of flame that licked the sky before being swallowed in clouds of billowing smoke.

Velvet whinnied again and Burdock snorted. Brida mounted, gathering his reins in case he decided to run.

Magic practically shimmered in the air—strange currents that left a mint-cold taste in her mouth and made her eyes water.

"The stormhorses are too close to town!" Mother Magdi cried. "All that storm energy in a populated place—people might get hurt!" Holding the reins in one hand and raising her other, she tried to gather magic—and then cursed. "Blood and thorns. We're still too far away." With a gentle squeeze of her legs she sent Velvet ahead in a swift canter.

Brida let Burdock run, buffeted by gusts of wind that

roared in her ears and sang in her head. This was no ordinary wind—it felt like currents of raw magic pouring across her skin and rushing through her blood. Sparks danced at the edges of her vision and her chest ached.

If the black stormhorse was causing the lightning and thunder, the white stormhorse—the wind mare—must be nearby, too.

Brida and Magdi had barely reached the outskirts of town when they started seeing signs of destruction. The walnut grove that had given the town its name was a ruin. Some trees had been uprooted and thrashed by the wind while others bore the dark scars of lightning scorches, branches still smoldering.

They passed a barn surrounded by men with buckets, desperately trying to douse the flames from a lightning strike, and then a nearby cottage with its thatch roof completely blown away.

As Burdock and Velvet stepped through the arch marking the formal entry into Walnut Creektown, a flock of sheep milled around their knees, followed by a shepherd muttering curses as he tried to round them up again. "Apologies, friends," he called to Magdi and Brida. "Wind blew my fences away!"

Someone heard him and shouted, "Wasn't wind, you dozy fool. Was a stormhorse!"

"Who's the dozy fool, Fridrick? In't no such thing as a

stormhorse!" the shepherd yelled back, making a rude gesture with his fist.

"What do you call those, then?" A woman in a green and brown kerchief waved her arms. "I know you saw 'em as well as the rest of us. Wasn't no plow horse bringing lightning with his hooves, was it?"

He ignored her, flapping his hands at the sheep as chaos swirled around them. Dogs barked, chickens clucked and scattered, and children cried. A horse galloped through the town square—not a stormhorse, just a dapple gray taking advantage of the commotion to wreak a little havoc of his own—and a fat sow rooted through an overturned market cart for vegetables.

Burdock jigged and switched his tail, so Brida gently tugged his reins to remind him he had to stay still, no matter how much fun he thought he could have in all the upheaval.

"I'm telling you," the man named Fridrick said to Magdi, "if you'd been here just a few moments sooner you'd have seen them, too. Stormhorses, as real as you and me. I swear it by blood, bones, and breath."

The woman said, "He's telling you true, Mother Magdi. I can't hardly believe it myself, but there were stormhorses here."

"I believe you, Goody Spinner." Magdi glanced around the ruined square, the smoldering buildings. "I can't do anything about the fires, unfortunately, but at least I can tend to anyone who's been burned or injured." To Brida she said, "You're good with animals—why don't you see what you can do about all this?" She waved a hand at the chaos.

Brida nodded, patting the feather and stones in her pocket. While Mother Magdi climbed on top of a table, spreading her arms so the green leaves on her cloak would be clearly visible to any who needed a hedgewitch's help, Brida made her way to the center of the town square.

This sort of magic—impulsive and instinctive and disorganized—she was good at.

Drawing wisps of power, she sent out a blanket of calm. Some animals responded better than others. The dapple-gray horse skidded to a stop, spun, and walked back to her with his head lowered apologetically. The sheep pressed into a tight knot and busied themselves eating bruised clover, but at least they were no longer in danger of running away and getting lost. The chickens cackled and continued pecking bugs and seeds from the ground, but they did seem a little quieter.

The sow ignored Brida entirely, but that was to be expected.

After leaving the animals in the care of the shepherd and several young girls, Brida led Burdock back to Magdi's side to help. Mother Magdi had pulled jars of ointment and salve from her pack and now she tended a line of townspeople with burns, bruises, scrapes, and scratches.

And then someone shouted as a torrent of wind gusted

through the crowd, tossing sparks from the burning roof-tops to neighboring structures and fanning the flames.

The white stormhorse galloped right through town, past Brida, mane and tail streaming like wisps of fog on a cool morning. Foam flecked her mouth and her flared nostrils sucked desperate lungfuls of air.

For one startled heartbeat her eyes met Brida's and a rush of magic shook Brida to her bones.

And then the mare was gone, veering sideways and racing through a gap between two buildings.

From the west, a curtain of rain swept in and helped douse some of the blazes. It flooded the cobbled streets as the blue roan stormhorse galloped past.

For a moment there was stunned silence, and then dozens of voices began speaking at once. "Did you see—!"

"I never dreamed the stormhorses were real!"

"Look at how much they've destroyed!"

"Why are they *here*?"

Brida simply stared after the stormhorses, barely registering the sound of a crow calling overhead until Mother Magdi gripped her elbow and yanked her into the shadows of a damp doorway at the edge of a narrow alley. Burdock's hooves clopped on rain-slick cobblestones as he followed.

"You must not let them see you!" Magdi hissed.

"Who?"

Magdi pointed at six crows—no, they must have been the queen's Crows—flying in a loose formation from one side of the town square to another. Two of them peeled away from the group to follow the stormhorses while another two dove lower for a closer look at the damage.

"We've done all we can here. It's time for us to get home as quickly as possible," Magdi said.

"But what about the bone monster? We haven't finished walking the valley, and if there's more blight—"

"The spell we wove with Rissi should have secured the borders. For now, at least. We must go."

Her words were punctuated by an eerie scream—inhuman, unearthly—as lightning exploded in a single giant ball of brilliant blue-edged white flame that left a stunned, crackling silence in its wake.

The air went still, weather conditions settling back to normal as the elemental magic evaporated. Burdock blew a sigh and shook his mane.

A man in soot-stained clothes gave a ragged cheer when it became clear the stormhorses must have left town. Brida turned on him with a snarl, ready to flay him with her tongue until Magdi gripped her shoulder. "Hold your peace," Magdi said in a low voice. "Some of these people have lost *everything* to the stormhorses' magic."

"But it's not the fault of the stormhorses! You yourself have said wolves and bears are not responsible if men—"

"I do not blame the stormhorses, child. But neither do I blame an exhausted, injured man for his relief when they are gone."

Brida frowned and bit her thumbnail, staring at the devastation around them. Trees uprooted, buildings burned or collapsed, roofs missing . . . The power of the stormhorses was overwhelming enough in the wide-open meadows and deep woods; here, in a settled town full of people and animals, it was a disaster. The disrupted seasons and unpredictable weather patterns had been challenge enough even without the magical tempest the stormhorses had caused.

And this had been just three of them . . . what if all *five* had run through town?

"Mother Magdi! We found a child buried under rubble! Please, come quick! We need your help!" a woman cried.

Magdi stepped forward, then froze as three Crows circled overhead. Pulling the hood of her cloak over her head, she motioned for Brida to wait where she was. "I'll be back to get you. Stay with the horses. We'll speak more of this when we're home and it's safe to talk."

Brida nodded and started to lead the horses farther down the alley to keep them out of sight, but a clatter of hooves whipped her head around. Were the stormhorses back? She didn't feel the tingle of their magic, but—

No. An ordinary black horse galloped across the square. It took her eyes a second to pick out the form of the man in the saddle: a man in a color-shifting cloak that rendered him nearly invisible.

The man she'd spotted in the meadow when she first saw the stormhorses.

The Crows had flown out of sight, and an idea seized Brida's thoughts.

Impulsively, she beckoned a young girl over and handed her Velvet's reins along with a copper coin. "Mother Magdi will be back for her. Just wait here." The girl nodded, eyes shining at the thought of helping the hedgewitch.

Brida jumped on Burdock's back and galloped after the man on the black horse.

TWELVE

The Chase

IT WAS PROBABLY a terrible idea, Brida knew, but it clutched her throat with urgent fingers, and she simply couldn't ignore it.

Magic had shown her the lady and the stormhorses in the scrying bowl for a reason. She felt a connection to them—at least, to the white mare. A link she couldn't explain.

And she was *good* at calming animals . . . usually. If she followed the man on the black horse, she had a feeling he would lead her to the stormhorses. Then perhaps she could keep them from destroying any other towns, using her magic to soothe them. Maybe she could find out why the man was chasing them, why the lady wanted them.

She might be able to *do* something.

She leaned forward, urging Burdock faster with her legs. He snorted and stretched his neck, picking up speed as the black horse left the road and leaped a ditch, veering off across a battered, mostly barren wheat field.

Several leagues ahead, a dark stormy smudge on the

horizon looked like evidence of the stormhorses. They were impossibly fast . . . but if two of the herd had already been captured, Brida guessed the others wouldn't get too far away. They would want to stay near their herd mates.

Burdock snorted and then whickered low in his throat—a warning sound.

"What is it, pony?"

He flicked his ears, tension quivering in his muscles.

"What's wrong?" she repeated.

A sudden howl pierced the late afternoon, puncturing the even rhythm of Burdock's hooves and the pounding of the pulse in her ears.

Burdock's head whipped toward the sound and Brida's heart thumped her ribs like a drum. *It's just a big dog*, she told herself, remembering the giant wolf-hound-beast by the boneyard. But another howl answered, much closer, and then an entire chorus shattered the hazy air. Brida shuddered.

Burdock whinnied in panic, but the black horse was still visible several paces ahead and the pony continued his pursuit. Brida tightened her grip on the reins.

She should have remembered that the man on the black horse had an entire pack of massive hound-beasts, should have realized they probably weren't far off.

Maybe she could use a spellweave to send the giant hound-wolf-whatever creatures away, though the approaching howls now chasing shivers across the back of her neck made that seem unlikely. She considered turning back toward town, but she was *so close* to finding out who this man was, why he was chasing the stormhorses. . . .

Burdock followed the black horse around the curve of a low hill, and a dense pack of the hound-wolf-beasts suddenly spilled from a cleft in a rocky bluff only a few feet away.

One tried to snap at Burdock's heels, but Burdock was fiercer than he looked and the massive creature got a face full of flying hooves instead.

Brida's mouth was so dry she couldn't swallow, couldn't speak, couldn't even scream. She didn't know a spellweave strong enough to deal with *so many*—a dozen at least, though it was impossible to count them in the commotion.

She clung to the saddle as Burdock kicked and bucked and reared, fighting the giant hounds as they growled and lunged at him. And then he set a foot wrong, lost his balance, and stumbled—pitching Brida right over his shoulder.

She screamed—partly in rage, because how dare they attack her pony? and partly in fear, because *those teeth*— rolling to a bruised stop in the weedy grass.

Burdock skidded to a halt and then trotted back to her, neck and flanks dark with sweat and sides heaving. Brida struggled to her feet, leaning on her pony's back for balance. Her ribs ached and a crimson bloom of pain throbbed in her knee through a tear in her leggings.

The hound-beasts circled, hackles raised and lips curled in soundless snarls.

Brida gathered energy and frantically wove a defensive spell, but she wasn't as quick or as strong as Mother Magdi. Praying her magic would work, she flung a net of protection in front of her and Burdock an instant before one of the monstrous hounds lunged. The beast was thrown back—but not far enough. Brida felt the sting as her shield shattered.

Burdock snapped his teeth and stomped the ground, warning the hounds away, but Brida didn't want him to get hurt. "Hold, Burdock! Don't let them get close to you!"

Before Brida could finish the next spellweave, the first hound turned to her with a wicked glare. She tried sending calming thoughts the way she did the summer she and Burdock had startled a mother bear in the woods, but the hound seemed completely oblivious. If anything, he only grew more agitated. His lips peeled back from a mouth of too-sharp teeth, and he snarled.

As a last resort, Brida reached in her pocket for the charm stones and feather she always carried, only to discover they had fallen out during her tumble.

She froze in terror. She couldn't hold off the beasts.

When another hound slipped in front of her, she cried out—until he glanced over his shoulder.

It was the hound from the boneyard. She was sure of it.

Aching betrayal burned in her chest. Had she saved his life just to let him take hers now?

He turned to face the others, growling a warning as he paced back and forth in front of her. He was . . . *protecting* her, Brida realized.

The others snapped their teeth, tails lashing. As they tensed to leap, a man's voice snapped, "At ease!" and all three hounds immediately sank to their bellies while the rest of the pack stilled.

Bloody brambles and thorns. The hunter had found her. Shaking, Brida twisted her hand in Burdock's mane and slowly turned to face the man behind her.

PART TWO

THE
HUNTSMAN

THIRTEEN

The First Feather

"WELL, AREN'T YOU a bright little mouse?" the hunter said, studying Brida.

Mouse? Hardly! Brida stared back, rocking on her heels as anger—and fear—ignited in the pit of her stomach.

His hair was the burnished bronze of autumn leaves and his eyes the color of oak bark. A russet beard covered his chin. He was tall—taller than any man Brida knew—and broad-shouldered, and he wore a brown leather vest over a grass-colored tunic, with a light cloak woven in different shades of green, gray, brown, and pale blue.

When he stood perfectly still he nearly disappeared, blending into the background of grass, trees, shadows, and sky, but she'd recognized him from the scrying bowl, too. She saw the insignia on his chest—an arrow balanced upright between a stag's antlers—when he swept his cloak back over one shoulder. It felt like something she should know, but she was too rattled to think straight.

He gazed at her for a second, and then the stark planes

of his face shifted as his lips curved. But something hardened in his eyes, killing the smile before it reached them.

Brida shivered.

"I'm looking for my lost horses. Two: white and a blue roan. Have you seen them, little mouse girl?"

She bristled. She might be small and slender for her age, but she wasn't a child anymore. She wasn't a mouse, either. She balled her fists, her palms itching with the urge to throw something at him.

"No, I haven't," she told him. *And what about the black lightning horse? Where is he? Has he been captured already?*

He clicked his tongue. "What's your name, little mouse girl? What are you doing out here?"

"Mell Smith," she promptly lied. "And I was on my way to see my sister until your *dogs* tried to attack my pony."

"Are you certain you didn't see which way my horses went? My *Hounds*"—his tone gave the word significance—"seem to have lost the trail."

"No. I was too distracted by your *Hounds*"—she glared at him—"but I can help you look for them. How did you lose them? What sort of horses are they? Where do they belong?"

A muscle in his cheek twitched. Then he lifted his chin to watch a crow—no, it was so big it must be a Crow—circling the sky in the distance. "No time." He started to turn, whistling for his Hounds to follow.

"Wait!" she cried. "I—" But what could she say? How

could she explain why she'd been racing after him? She couldn't let him know that she was following the storm-horses, too, until she knew what his purpose was.

He grunted, glancing back with a scowl. "Little mouse, I am *Queen Moira's Huntsman*. I have more important things to do than minding a girl who shouldn't be out here alone."

The queen's Huntsman? She stared at the arrow-and-antlers emblem on his vest, suddenly understanding what it signified. And if he was the queen's Huntsman, that could only mean that the woman he'd been speaking to in the scrying bowl was . . .

Not just a wealthy, noble lady as Brida had first assumed. No, she must have been the Queen of Crows herself.

Brida's stomach twisted. Why did the *Queen of Crows* want to capture an entire herd of stormhorses? Then she remembered Magdi saying that the queen would use what-ever magic she could find.

Oh, no.

One of the Hounds flattened his ears and growled.

Brida clenched her jaw and started to climb on Burdock's back. This was bigger than she'd expected. She needed to get back to Magdi as quickly as possible.

Suddenly, a *cawwww!* tore through the wind and a heartbeat later a single black feather drifted like a streak of ink toward her.

Before Brida realized what it was, it landed on the back of her hand. The instant it touched her skin, she felt a strange *folding* sensation, a surge of sparkling pain as if her body forgot its own shape and the world melted around her. A scream climbed from her throat.

The Crow feather burst in a little puff of black ash that glittered faintly in the last rays of the dying sun.

"Blood and ashes," the Huntsman swore. "I told you to be on your way."

Confused and oddly disgusted, Brida started to wipe her hand on her tunic. "What was—"

But before she could finish her question, there was a flicker of motion in the corner of her eye and a thin silver whipcord lashed her wrist and pulled tight.

Brida was yanked off-balance and had to flail her free arm to keep from falling. "What in all the brambles and thorns do you think you're doing?" she cried, as the Huntsman pulled her toward him. "Let me go!"

This time, when the Huntsman's eyes skimmed Brida from head to toe, they held a sharp glint of calculation, curiosity, surprise, and something like regret. "So, little girl. Not such a mouse as I first thought." He chuckled, but it sounded like the scraping of rocks. "You've caught the attention of a Crow."

Brida dug her nails under the lash and tried to pry it from her skin, but it only bit tighter. "Let me go!" she cried again.

"Afraid I can't do that. Evidently, they've discovered a seed of magic buried in you and now Her Majesty is inter-ested."

"You're making a mistake. I'm nobody. Just a girl visiting—"

"Her sister. So you said. But you've been feathermarked and now you're coming with me instead." He gave a high, keening whistle and the entire pack of Hounds closed in, surrounding Brida.

Burdock reared, but the Hounds faced him with growls and those sharp, sharp teeth.

"No, Burdock!" Brida cried. "Go back, pony. Go back!" *Please, Burdock. Run to Mother Magdi. Let her know something has gone very, very wrong. Then come find me. Please*, she told him with her eyes, tying her thoughts to wisps of the wind and hoping he could understand.

He whinnied, shook his head, and spun back the way they'd come—galloping faster than he ever had before.

Several Hounds leaped to follow, but the Huntsman barked, "Stay!" Glancing sidelong at Brida, he said, "As long as she comes with us politely, we'll allow the pony to go."

Brida hung her head and let herself be tugged uphill, away from the road. "Why would the queen want—*ooof*!" She stumbled over a root and bit off the end of her question.

The Huntsman said, "Why is the queen interested in a little mouse like you? That's not for me to know. Maybe she just needs a new kitchen girl. Guess you'll have to wait and see."

FOURTEEN

Hunting the Wind

"WEREN'T YOU RIDING a horse?" Brida asked, tripping over a moss-covered rock as the Huntsman pulled her by the wrist.

"She ran away."

"Clever horse," Brida muttered.

"Nearly there. Keep up!"

"I'm trying!" She dragged her toes in scattered leaves and fallen pine needles, scowling at the back of his head.

The Huntsman had pitched his camp in a hollow below a copse of trees, hidden in a wrinkle of hills. He'd laid dead branches for a fire and draped a piece of waxed canvas to make a crude tent. A dogsled on narrow wheels instead of runners stood behind a boulder.

"Where's the black stormhorse? You caught him, didn't you?" she demanded.

His jaw clenched. "Yes. And one of the queen's guards patrolling the road retrieved him, not that it's any concern of yours."

Releasing the lash binding her wrist and coiling his whip again, he said, "Listen, if you try to run—if you cause any trouble at all—my Hounds will hunt you down and drag you back. And then they'll hunt your sister, your family, everyone you've ever cared about and kill them. Including your fat little pony. Understand?"

Brida nodded and rubbed the thin red mark cut into her skin. One look at his bleak eyes, at his snarling Hounds, and she knew he wasn't making an idle threat just to scare her into submission.

She had to cooperate—at least for now.

She just prayed Burdock had returned to Magdi safely.

"Go fetch water from the creek before it gets any darker." The Huntsman thrust a heavy cast-iron cook pot at her. "We'll spend the night here. Jace, Finn, stay with her. Just in case."

There was an edge in his voice, but Brida was more worried about finding a path to the water before the last of the day's light faded. She didn't like the idea of wandering lost in the woods with a couple of Hounds.

Closing her eyes, she tried to weave a seeking spell. She reached for the magic in the ground beneath her feet, in the trees, from the dying sun and the sliver of moon just rising.

Strands of magic swirled just beyond her grasp, slipping through her fingers no matter how hard she tried to hold them. She closed her eyes, concentrated . . . nothing.

I'm just shaken. Too much has happened too fast.

Reciting a quick chant for clarity and calm—one of the first things Mother Magdi had ever taught her—she tried again: calling to the magic, letting it rise, reaching for it. . . .

It tingled in her palms, but when she began to weave the seeking spell, it all dissolved.

The Huntsman had called her feathermarked. Had the Crow feather interfered with her magic somehow? How long would the effects last?

The Hounds whined and scratched the dirt. In the distance, an owl hooted. Soon it would be hard to see.

Fighting panic, Brida forced herself to breathe slowly, to *think*.

Turning in a slow circle, she tried to guess which direction might lead to the creek. She wasn't familiar with this area, but she didn't want to admit that to the Huntsman.

A breath of wind lifted the hair at the nape of her neck, brushed her cheekbone. Brida ignored the Hounds panting at her feet, ignored the snap of the Huntsman's flint striking sparks to start the fire—she held very still and *listened*. Yes . . . there, she caught the trickle of water over pebbles.

The creek. And now that she was paying attention, she could smell cool water on the evening breeze, could practically taste it.

Following the wind, she headed down the hill and through pools of blue shadows. Dusk filled the air with a lavender glow as she walked a narrow deer track to a ribbon of silver rippling in the twilight.

She scrambled to the edge of the water, the Hounds sitting on the bank to watch while she rinsed the blood from her banged-up knee and filled the pot. After she was done they led her back to camp.

The Huntsman grunted when she handed him the pot. "Took you long enough."

"You could have camped closer to the creek," she snapped. One of the Hounds lifted his head and growled, but the Huntsman only laughed.

"The little mouse bites, eh?" He gestured to a brace of rabbits roasting over the fire. "Be done in a minute, if you're hungry."

Brida's stomach growled loud enough to prick the ears of the nearest Hound, but she said in a voice less steady than she intended, "I don't eat meat."

For a second, he just blinked at her. Then he shrugged. "More for me and the Hounds."

Brida chewed her lip. Mother Magdi had taught her— tried to teach her, anyway—how to find roots, berries, nuts, mushrooms, and other edibles in the forest. But it was already too dark to see much beyond the circle of firelight and she couldn't trust her ability not to accidentally poison herself.

Well, she could go hungry, then. Turning away from the fire so she wouldn't have to watch the rabbits roast, she was surprised to see the Huntsman tossing potatoes and carrots in the pot.

"Vegetable stew suit you?" he asked gruffly.

"Um . . . yes."

"It's not a favor. Queen feathermarked you. If you aren't delivered safe and unharmed, my skin's on the line. Suppose that means I'd better keep you fed, little mouse." Then he scowled. "Doesn't mean your family's safe, though, so don't give me any difficulty."

Brida huddled on a dry log, watching sparks dance on curls of smoke twisting above the fire later that evening.

Had Burdock reached Mother Magdi safely? Would she know where to find Brida?

Whispered stories about the Queen of Crows drifted through her mind—scraps of rumor she'd heard over the years.

Stories about the queen's cruelty, about her dark powers.

Even Mother Magdi, the most powerful hedgewitch Brida had ever heard of, was afraid of the queen. *That must be why she reacted so strongly to the Crow and the woman in the scrying bowl*, Brida thought. But why hadn't Magdi just told her it had been the queen?

And—the question that bothered her most—why did the queen look so much like Mother Magdi?

As soon as Brida saw Magdi again, she would demanded answers. She was tired of secrets.

Her hand itched where the Crow feather had landed

and she wiped it on her leggings again with a quiet groan. She hoped its effects—whatever they were—would wear off soon. The thought of not being able to use her magic, as clumsy as it might be, was unbearable.

"Supper's done," the Huntsman grunted, tossing a wooden bowl to her. "Help yourself."

Brida eyed the Hounds, slavering over the scent of roasted rabbit, and hurriedly scooped a portion of stew into her bowl before scurrying back to her seat.

"Tomorrow you hunt your own meat," the Huntsman said to the Hounds, throwing a rabbit in the air. The largest Hounds leaped to catch it, growling and snapping and shoving. Other Hounds darted among them, snatching pieces as they wrestled.

Brida turned away, stomach clenching.

Something nudged her foot and she jerked backward so fast she almost fell off the log. It was the Hound she'd healed, staring at her with a mournful expression—as if he wanted her to know he wasn't like the others. Before she could react, he crept back into the shadows on the opposite side of the fire.

"When you've finished eating, you'll sleep in the tent," the Huntsman told her.

Nervous again, Brida forced herself to spoon up her stew. It tasted better than she'd expected—hunger was a good sauce—but it did little to warm the cold hollow in the pit of her stomach.

Would Magdi find her in time? What did the queen want with her?

After she'd emptied the bowl and returned it to the Huntsman, he gave her a dented tin cup filled with steaming tea. "Drink up."

Surprised by the kindness—she was cold, and thirsty, and scared, and tea was a perfect antidote—she wrapped her fingers around the cup gratefully. But a gust of wind shook her hand and she had to curl her body protectively around the cup to keep from slopping out the tea.

After a cautious sip—it tasted of honey and dark berries and didn't burn her lips—she drank it down to the dregs.

She didn't recognize the flavor until the final swallow. Duskberries and chamomile, lavender and mugwort.

A tea for deep sleep.

Brida frowned. Rubbed her cheeks. Licked her lips with a tongue suddenly fuzzy.

"Why—" The rest of the question crumbled in her mouth.

"For your own good."

At least, that's what his answer sounded like, but her ears felt stuffed with wool and the thoughts in her head were slow and heavy.

The Huntsman took her elbow and led her to the tent. He lifted the flap of canvas and all but shoved her inside.

Brida collapsed on a musty pile of blankets and curled up. The last thought floating on the surface of her mind before sleep swept her under was: *the wind tried to warn me.* Or maybe she was just imagining it. . . .

The last thing she heard was the Huntsman whistling for the Hounds.

Brida's dreams were filled with teeth and terror, worry and wind. She was a horse, running from a pack of wolves—no, Hounds—and then she was a girl, hiding from a Crow that tried to peck shreds of skin from her shoulders. She was made of wind and feathers, soaring over trees and mirrored lakes. . . .

At the edge of sleep, Brida heard the Huntsman call, "Stay with her! I just need to get the queen's magic rope over her neck! Chase her this way!"

Brida awoke in the middle of the night to the sound of canvas ripping, the rattle of dried branches shaking in a sudden gust, the roar of a furious wind. *The white mare*, she thought, scrambling to her knees and wrapping a cloak more tightly around her shoulders. *The Huntsman and his Hounds are trying to catch the white mare!*

She lurched from the tent as another gust tore the canvas off. It was like flinging herself into the heart of a storm.

Ash and smoke billowed from the doused fire and swirls of leaves tore through the camp. Wind lashed tangled hair against her cheeks and whipped away her breath, leaving her gasping for air. She could tell immediately that it wasn't an ordinary wind. It held such intense magic her skin tingled with it, her eyes stung with the force of it.

The white mare plunged and screamed, kicking at the Hounds harrying her heels. Curtains of rain swept the ridge of hills behind her, the blue roan whinnying desperately for her herd mate.

The Huntsman spun a shining silver rope in the air, preparing to toss it at the white mare.

Brida did the only thing she could think of.

She launched herself at his arm, knocking his aim at the last instant so the rope slithered harmlessly to the ground.

"What do you think you're doing?" He shoved her away, grabbing the rope.

Run! she screamed silently to the stormhorse.

But the white mare was surrounded. Everywhere she turned, she faced more Hounds with fierce teeth and heavy paws.

Brida snatched rocks and twigs—whatever she could grab from the ground—and flung them at the Hounds with a furious shriek.

The white mare seized her chance. She reared, pawing the air with hooves that shone silver in the starlight, and raced back to the blue roan on the ridge. Together, they galloped out of sight.

The wind and rain died immediately.

Brida's knees sagged and she gulped air like she'd nearly drowned.

"Bloody bones and ashes! We nearly had her!" the

Huntsman swore, coiling his rope and slinging it over one shoulder. "You shouldn't have interfered!"

He grabbed Brida by the arm and hauled her to her feet, half pushing and half dragging her to the dogsled. With a firm shove, he pushed her down. "Hold on! We have to follow them!"

Mind still dull with shock and the fog of sleep, Brida reached for the rails along the sides of the sled as he hitched the Hounds in teams of two. They barked and fidgeted, but when he raised his arm they all fell silent and waited for the signal.

The instant he whistled they leaped forward and the sled lurched, wheels creaking as it rolled over pebbles and down a mossy slope.

Brida was nearly thrown out, but she clutched the sides and braced herself as the sled gained speed.

The Huntsman jumped on a narrow step behind her and balanced his weight as the Hounds plunged through the trees. Brida's stomach clenched. Dead leaves spun around her, kicked up by the Hound's massive paws.

She could still feel the white mare's fury, her desperation to find the rest of her herd.

I will help you, Brida whispered. *I swear it by bud and bloom, leaf and limb.* She just hoped Burdock and Mother Magdi would be able to help her, too.

And she hoped Mother Magdi wouldn't be too angry with her for riding off. *I was only trying to fix things!* Brida thought. But instead she'd made them worse.

A tumble of wagon wreckage loomed ahead and Brida strained to see through the night shadows. The Hounds veered aside, yanking the sled around it.

A quick gasp of cool wind flung something toward Brida.

Without thinking, she snatched the scrap of cloth and ribbon from a jagged piece of wood as she passed.

The instant her hand closed around it, she felt the residue of Mother Magdi's magic. One of the hedgewitch's charms! It felt like an old one, from an earlier valley walk maybe, but strength and calm seeped through her palm. The itchy, oppressive weight of the feathermark evaporated and her own magic fizzed in her blood in response. Hoping the Huntsman hadn't noticed, Brida quickly tucked the charm away and grabbed the edge of the sled again.

— FIFTEEN —

Escape

BRIDA WASN'T CERTAIN how long the Huntsman and his Hounds pursued the last two stormhorses. She finally fell back asleep before dawn, slumped on the dog-sled.

When she startled awake sometime later, the sled was stopped near the bank of a wide, clear pond. Willows leaned over the water, trailing lacy fronds in the shallows.

She struggled to stand, her legs cramped and clumsy from the awkward position she'd been in for so long.

The Huntsman had loosed his Hounds and the pack now sprawled on their bellies in the shaded grass beneath the trees. He noticed Brida's lurching steps. "The Hounds need rest," he said. "We'll stay here until the sun passes noon. Don't wander off."

Without another glance, he grabbed his bow and arrows and strode away.

Brida blinked and weighed her options. She didn't know where she was, but maybe she could—

As if hearing her thoughts, the closest Hound lifted his head and growled. Brida's mouth went dry as she stared at his long, sharp teeth.

If she tried to run now, the pack would drag her back as the Huntsman had threatened.

But that didn't mean she had to stop watching for an opportunity to escape.

Wiping her mind blank, she took a few deep breaths and forced the tension from her shoulders until the Hound let his head drop back to his paws and closed his eyes.

Brida watched him for a moment and then walked quietly to the edge of the water, glancing at her reflection. So much dust coated her skin she couldn't see her freckles and the wind had snarled knots in her hair.

Kneeling, she splashed cool water on her face. Then she crossed her legs and started tugging her fingertips through her tangled hair as she stared at the shimmering surface of the pond. Bees droned in a patch of clover and the sun warmed the back of her neck, casting flecks of golden glitter across the water. Brida slowly relaxed.

And then her vision blurred.

The reflection in the water shifted, swirled . . . and suddenly she was seeing Mother Magdi's familiar form, standing before the Council of Wisdoms.

Voices hummed above the water, low but clear enough for her to catch the words.

Mother Magdi said, "When we walked the valley we

discovered that the effects of the queen's wicked magic are spreading like an infection. We managed to contain it, but then in Walnut Creektown three stormhorses caused a tempest that nearly destroyed the entire place. Somehow Brida was taken. I tried to follow, but some dark power kept her hidden from me. Last night or early this morning she must have found one of my charms because I felt the chime of recognized magic, but I—"

A stone dropped in the pond with a splash, breaking the image and sending ripples spreading in a wide circle. Brida jerked back, startled.

The Huntsman stood several paces away, watching her. "Time to go, mouse."

Brida reached inside the pocket of her tunic and closed her fingers around the charm she'd found by the wagon wreckage. She hadn't meant to scry, but the lingering traces of Mother Magdi's gentle hedgemagic gave her courage.

She wasn't as alone as she felt.

The Hounds pulled the wheeled dogsled until dusk, the Huntsman occasionally flicking his whip if they started lagging. Signs of weather damage preceded them.

"The horses are heading back toward the rest of their herd," he said at one point, studying a swathe of wind-broken branches. "They seem to be running directly toward the three already in captivity. If we don't catch them on the way, I'll drop you off at the castle and continue on."

It was not a comforting thought.

Brida still didn't know why the queen wanted to see her. She didn't even know how far away the castle was, and when she tried to ask, the Huntsman only grunted.

They made camp that evening at the base of a high ridge. A thicket of poplars and pin oaks offered shelter; and a spring trickled up from between two heavy boulders, spilling down a mossy bank before widening into a deep pool.

"If you're hungry, you'd better hunt while you can," the Huntsman growled at the pack, and the Hounds lifted their heads. The sudden gleam in their eyes, their sharp focus and bared teeth, sent dread spider-walking across Brida's skin. "Go on!" he said, and most of them raced away.

The Hound she'd healed sat near the Huntsman and thumped his tail once.

To Brida's surprise, the Huntsman dropped his hand to the Hound's head and rubbed his ears. "Ach, Bowen. It's a proper mess we're in now, isn't it?" he said so quietly Brida wouldn't have caught the words if a light breeze hadn't carried them to her.

Bowen lifted his nose and howled, then turned his head to stare at Brida.

The Huntsman pounded his fists against his thighs and turned to Brida. "I'm going to fetch wood for the fire. Fill the pot with water after you've finished washing up, little mouse."

Brida watched his back as he strode away, the Hound called Bowen following.

When she was sure they were out of sight, she shifted her attention to the contents of the dogsled. As quickly and quietly as possible, she rifled through the Huntsman's bags until she'd found a potato, an apple, two carrots, a hard roll, and a handful of dried peas.

If she was careful, it would be enough to sustain her until she'd made her way back to Mother Magdi, at least.

Shoving the food in the pockets of her cloak, Brida slipped away from camp. Her heart knocked against her rib cage like a bird struggling to free itself; but she swallowed her fear and ran lightly, balancing on the balls of her feet.

She was going to run out of daylight soon; but with the Hounds out hunting and Bowen and the Huntsman gone, this might be her only chance to escape.

She didn't know how much time she had before they came after her. The pack could see in the dark and trace her scent, of course; but maybe if she kept to the rockiest ground and hurried as fast as she could, her trail would fade before the Hounds and the Huntsman even realized she was missing.

If nothing else, perhaps she could climb a tree and wait them out. After all, it worked for squirrels sometimes, didn't it?

A twig cracked and she dropped to a crouch, holding her breath. In the woods to her right one of the Hounds started barking. Staying low, she hurried toward a stand of birch trees and pressed herself between the trunks. She wished she had a color-shifting cloak like the Huntsman's so she could disappear.

When nothing stirred, she crept out of the birches and ran across a moss-covered stone ledge. Clinging to exposed roots, she heaved herself up a steep bluff and darted through an open glade.

She was distracted by a flash of white in the corner of her eye and stumbled. By the time she'd regained her footing she couldn't tell what it had been. Surely not *her* white dove, all the way out here?

Brida ran for the cover of oak and maple trees, but a howl dragged a finger of fear down her spine. When it was echoed by the rest of the pack she choked on a sob. Had they already discovered she was gone, or were they simply celebrating a successful evening's hunt?

She paused to catch her breath beneath a spreading oak, leaning against the rough trunk. Which way would the Hounds likely run? Should she just climb this tree and wait for them to lose interest and move on?

The tree creaked. Groaned.

Something behind her back shifted and she leaped away from the tree with a startled gasp.

The bark cracked, a seam splitting open from the roots all the way up to the first wide, forked branches. At first Brida blinked, telling herself it was just a trick of the falling evening light. But then she heard another creak, the sound of wood straining past the point of endurance.

Something peeled itself out of the tree and took a step forward. Two gnarled legs with grasping, rootlike toes. A slender torso that bent and writhed like a sapling in strong winds. Two reaching arms like vines, with twiggy fingers tipped in thorn claws. A craggy face with dark pits instead of eyes and a gaping, knothole mouth.

Brida was too stunned to move, until it stretched out an arm to grab her.

She turned to run, but all around her other wooden creatures were stepping from the trees. One of them caught a mouse in its toes and the tiny squeak of death shook something loose in Brida's heart.

She screamed.

Suddenly the pack of Hounds was there, barking and growling and snapping at the tree-things. One of them bit a tree-thing's arm, tearing off a couple twig fingers. Dark sap oozed from the wound, but as Brida watched in horror the injury sealed itself and new fingers grew.

The tree-thing grabbed the Hound by the scruff of the neck and gave it a hard shake. The Hound yelped, dropped in a cringing heap at the tree-thing's feet.

Brida backed away, shuddering. She tried to gather magic, but the chill sensation of something dark and wicked was so strong she couldn't hold any power long enough to weave a spell. She took Mother Magdi's charm from her pocket, gripping it in a trembling hand, but whatever energy had animated these creatures stole the magic from the charm and it fell from her fingers in a frayed twist.

"Mouse!" yelled a voice.

She spun, uncomfortably relieved to see the Huntsman brandishing a flaming torch. He thrust it at the tree-things, driving them back and rounding up his pack of Hounds.

Brida ran to him. "What *are* they?" she cried.

He didn't have time to answer, lunging at the tree-things and leaving one in smoldering flames. "Let's go!" he cried, whistling for the Hounds.

For once, Brida was grateful to be surrounded by giant dogs. She let herself be herded back to the campsite and the reassuring blaze of a crackling fire, flushing as she returned the food she'd taken.

"There are worse things than me and these Hounds out here," the Huntsman told her grimly. "You'd best not try running off again."

SIXTEEN

Red Smoke

SHAKEN AND UNEASY, Brida huddled near the campfire, thoughts spinning like the moths attracted to the red glow.

The Hounds returned and settled around the clearing, licking their muzzles—and their wounds. The one called Bowen lay down near her feet, as if to guard her.

When the Huntsman handed her a hot potato baked in the embers, she wasn't hungry enough to eat it so she gave it to Bowen. He looked like he needed it worse than she did.

"Haven't got another tent," the Huntsman said, "but here's an extra cloak for you. Wrap yourself up and stay near the warmth of the fire."

Brida took the dirty wool cloak he held out, but the idea of sleeping in the open, surrounded by Hounds and whatever else might lurk in the woods, gave her a bad feeling.

Mother Magdi, where are you?

She pulled her own cloak close and tugged the hood

over her head. Crouching near a boulder, she tucked her knees tight to her chest and folded her arms around them.

She couldn't rest, anyway. What if the trees came to life again?

For a while she simply sat and listened to the sounds of the night. The Huntsman kept the flames burning low, the wood crackling and popping every so often. Frogs and crickets chirped until it grew cooler, and then a deep silence settled like a downy blanket.

Brida shivered. She'd thought that she could stay awake until morning—hadn't she spent long nights helping Mother Magdi?—but her eyelids grew heavy and her jaw cracked a yawn.

One of the Hounds raised his head and stared at her across the fire.

Brida looked away, trying to keep fear from showing on her face. She shifted her weight and before she knew it she was lying down.

Paws crunched across dead leaves. A tail thumped the ground. Warm breath tickled her cheek.

If Brida hadn't been so exhausted she would have bolted up, but the Hound called Bowen leaned over and met her terrified gaze. His eyes were kind, and if he'd been a person she would have said he looked worried about her. *You helped me, and now I'll help you,* his face seemed to say.

She was too tired to resist.

He curled up beside her, his body a warm barrier between her and the others. The rhythm of his breath, the gentle thud of his heartbeat, lulled her to sleep.

The Huntsman shook Brida awake a few hours later.

Mist rose from the damp earth like the last breath of dreams and Brida blinked the blur of sleep from her eyes.

"The pack scented the horses. We need to move."

Brida straightened her cloak and frowned up at him. Her body ached from sleeping on the ground, her stomach growled to remind her she'd skipped supper, and her mouth tasted of worry.

He sighed. "Listen, mouse—if I'd had a choice in the matter, I never would . . ." He shook his head. "Doesn't matter now, does it? We need to move."

He helped her up and gestured to the dogsled, but Brida was tired of sitting cramped and stiff in the awkward space. "Let me run alongside for just a little while," she begged. "I need to stretch my legs."

He laughed, but it wasn't a happy sound. "No mouse can keep up with my Hounds. And the queen is waiting. With any luck, I'll have the horses by midday and you'll be at the castle by nightfall."

"Tonight?" Brida's voice squeaked.

He handed her a packet of dried fruit and a round of flatbread without answering.

By midday, it was clear the Hounds had once more lost the trail of the stormhorses. Though it was easy enough to see the swathe of their elemental destruction, they galloped so fast and moved so erratically it was difficult for the Hounds to know precisely where they had gone.

Brida couldn't conceal her relief. "Maybe we need to circle around to the north," she suggested.

"I might," the Huntsman agreed. "But you are wanted by the queen, and she won't wait any longer."

Dread dropped through her belly like a stone in an empty well. She didn't trust the Huntsman or his Hounds, but the queen was even more frightening.

The Huntsman steered the Hounds off the dirt track they'd been following through the woods and onto a wide, flat road. Soon they were passing small cottages, shutters thrown open to the morning light and chickens scratching in the yards.

Other travelers began to join them on the road: farmers driving carts of vegetables to market, men on horseback, and even the occasional child leading a small and stubborn donkey. They all avoided the Huntsman and his pack, eyes skimming past Brida as if they couldn't see her. Or didn't *want* to see her.

Brida's stomach tightened every time she heard the drumbeat of approaching hooves. She hoped the stormhorses would stay far beyond the Huntsman's reach and away from any towns where their destructive power might hurt someone.

As the sun climbed past noon, houses clustered closer together and the road became busier. Brida stretched her neck, peering around. She'd never seen so many people in one place before.

"Bloody fools," the Huntsman cursed. "Wish they'd get out of the way."

The road narrowed ahead, passing through a wooden gate guarded by a sentry in a dented helmet and dirty surcoat. Two wagons blocked the way as a couple of stout men argued with the guard. The merchants finally settled their disagreement and drove through the gate.

The Huntsman called to his Hounds and they picked up speed, never slowing as they loped past the dusty sentry. He bowed his head with respect until they'd passed, but when Brida glanced over her shoulder she saw fear on his face.

"There's an inn nearby where we can get a decent meal and you can clean up properly," the Huntsman said.

But a murmuring crowd filled the town square. They'd gathered in front of a tall stone building with a conspicuous chimney. Everyone seemed to be waiting for something.

"Blood and ashes," the Huntsman muttered. "What now?"

Brida craned her neck to study the building. It was larger than anything she'd seen before, but it didn't look like any castle she had imagined.

Her face must have betrayed her surprise because the Huntsman barked a rough laugh. "That's no palace. It's the town's citadel. This is Edgewood, just one of Queen Moira's outposts. The capital city is a league east, but it looks like I have business here first."

Brida blinked. This was just an outpost?

One of the Hounds howled and it was like a pebble breaking the surface of still water.

People turned to gape at the massive beasts. As ripples of awareness spread, the crowd stepped aside to leave a space for the pack and the strange wheeled sled. Men bowed, women curtsied, and children hid behind their parents' legs.

Ignoring them all, the Huntsman urged his Hounds forward until Brida had a clearer view of the stone building. A black banner stretched above the wooden doors and two guards in black surcoats stood to either side.

"What's this, now?" the Huntsman said.

A man beside him tugged his threadbare cuffs, swallowed, and finally answered, "Trial for treason."

"Oh?"

The man shifted his weight. "You'd best ask them." He tipped his chin toward the guards at the doors.

The Huntsman lifted a hand and gestured to one of the guards, who saluted and hurried over.

"Treason?" the Huntsman asked.

"Aye. Fool was telling stories he should have forgotten. If that weren't bad enough, he was also caught with an unauthorized pigeon coop. Been sending wingnotes but wouldn't say to whom. Her Majesty sent Crows after them, but as far as I know all they found out was that the pigeons went to one of the far valleys."

Brida had to bite the inside of her cheek to stay silent. Mother Magdi had received wingnotes . . . and one of the pigeons had been attacked by a Crow.

The guard rubbed his chin and leaned forward, lowering his voice. "There are even unconfirmed rumors he was once a priest of the Sky Father, but Her Majesty doesn't want people to think the Temples are reorganizing, so we've been told not to mention white magic."

"Are they?" the Huntsman asked. Brida strained her ears to catch the guard's answer.

"Are the Temples reorganizing?" The guard shrugged. "It's not likely—I mean, how many priests and priestesses could be left now? Who would dare the queen's wrath? But . . . he was sending pigeons to *someone*, wasn't he?"

Brida's heart swooped and plunged in her chest. She thought about the way Rissi's white magic had blended with Mother Magdi's green magic to weave stronger shields around the valley. If there were more priests and priestesses willing to come out of hiding, brave enough to risk using their outlawed magic, maybe they could work together to heal the sickness in the land. Maybe they could turn the wheel of seasons back to rights. . . .

"Verdict should be rendered any moment now," the guard continued. "The Council of Wisemen has been cloistered in the citadel all morning."

"Ah," the Huntsman said. "Then we shall wait."

Brida climbed out of the sled, stretched her cramped legs, and cracked her neck. *Please let him be found innocent,* she thought.

The Council of Wisdoms in her village would never hold a treason trial. Drunken fistfights happened on occasion, and there were often disputes over boundary fences and loose cows, missing goats and dry wells. Neighbors sometimes reported each other for skimping on the annual tax collections or letting their dogs run wild, but accusing someone of treason? Just for telling stories and keeping pigeons? For magic? *Never.*

Gnarled fingers gripped Brida's arm and an old man with a toothless grin pointed to the chimney. "Look there," he mumbled. "They've lit the fire."

"What do you mean?"

The man turned his dim eyes from the chimney to Brida with a startled expression. "Don't you know? If the smoke is white, he's innocent. If it's red, he's guilty and they'll hang him."

He gestured toward the edge of the square. Brida stood on her tiptoes and then wished she hadn't when she saw the wooden gallows already erected.

Her stomach tried to flip itself inside out, sick with horror. Hanging a man for telling *stories*? Keeping pigeons?

Now she understood Mother Magdi's warnings on the Day of Remembering.

A hum of anticipation swept the crowd and Brida glanced at the chimney again. A wisp of black smoke curled into the blue sky, a question mark slowly unwinding.

"See? I told you they'd lit the fire." The man chuckled.

Brida heard the clink of coins and saw a few small leather purses changing hands. Were people trading wagers on the outcome of the verdict? Betting on a man's life? She shuddered and looked at the sky again.

Please be white smoke.

Surely this Council would show mercy. . . .

A woman shuffled up to Brida, smoothing a frayed apron with age-worn hands. Her knuckles were red and swollen, the nails broken and dirty. But her eyes were a sharp, glittering blue as she scanned Brida's face. "Do you remember?" she asked.

Brida assumed she was speaking to someone else in the crowd, but the woman plucked Brida's sleeve and repeated, "*Do you remember?*"

"I'm not sure I understand what you mean, Goody."

"I ain't a goodwife." The woman cackled. "And you might not be who I thought you were."

Before Brida could ask for an explanation, the strange

207

woman spotted a boy carrying a tray of small, steaming pies and whistled. "What's the meat today?"

"Rat," he said. "Fresh, with a bit of yesterday's pigeon."

"Want one?" she asked, turning to Brida. "My treat."

Brida shook her head, sick at the thought. "No, but thank you, Good—um . . ."

The old woman laughed and beckoned Brida closer. "I worked in the Temple," she whispered. "Weren't ever a priestess, but I cleaned and cooked and did all the errands. I was called Maid Agathe. Ain't a maid any longer, either, but I reckon my name is still my own."

"It's lovely to meet you, Agathe," Brida said, but she was thinking about what Rissi had told her. *If you want to know the truth about who you are and where you come from, look in a broken Temple.*

Could Rissi have meant a Temple here?

"Agathe, who did you think I was? What am I supposed to remember?"

But before she could respond, the smoke dwindled, puffed, and then disappeared. An expectant hush settled over the square. People shuffled their feet, coughed, and blew their noses, but no one spoke.

A cloud of red burst from the chimney and cheers erupted from some in the crowd.

Brida's stomach flipped. *No!* she wanted to wail.

"I knew they'd find the poor fool guilty," Agathe said. "I tried to warn him he was getting too careless, but he refused to listen. It's a bloody shame. He was a good man. One of the best." Sighing, she shook her head. "Justice shouldn't have a price, but the queen pays for the Council's expensive manors and fancy horses, so . . ." She spread her hands with a wry twist of her mouth, sadness in her eyes.

Then, abruptly leaning forward, she clutched Brida's hand. "Listen, you seem like a sweet girl," she murmured, "no matter who you are. So I'll give you a word of advice. I don't know what business got you tangled up with *him*"— she tilted her chin toward the queen's Huntsman, who was talking to the guard again—"and I don't *want* to know, but if I were you, I'd lose myself in town while I still had the chance. I'd head straight for the old Temple, due north. You'll find sanctuary there, and . . ." She squinted, pursed her lips. "If you *are* who I thought, if you've just forgotten . . . well, could be you'll find what you need to know there, too."

She straightened, shoved her pie in her mouth, and ambled away without looking back.

Confusion twisted Brida's belly. So there *was* a Temple here. But what did Agathe think she knew about Brida's past? They'd never met before. . . .

Brida watched Agathe slip through a gap between a couple of men and disappear, until a roar from the crowd dragged her attention back to the citadel.

A bell clanged as the wooden doors swung open. The guards stepped aside, saluting smartly. For a heartbeat the crowd held its breath, and then a line of men in long white robes marched out.

"The Council of Wisemen," someone said behind Brida. But where were the women? And this Council didn't seem complete without a Voice, to record their decisions, hold their memories, and tell their stories to the people.

Guards followed, dragging a sobbing man dressed in rags.

"This man, Mason Bolder, has been found guilty of the crime of treason. He did knowingly and deliberately break Queen's Law by telling malicious and false stories. He did knowingly and deliberately break Queen's Law by keeping pigeons and sending illicit wingnotes. Given the nature of his crimes and the risk they present to the peace and prosperity of Fenwood Reach, Queen Moira's realm, we, the Council of Wisemen of Edgewood, do sentence him to death by hanging. Penalty will be carried out immediately. If any wish to have last words with the condemned, they may approach and form a line."

Brida desperately wanted to speak to him, to ask if he knew Mother Magdi. To ask if he was really a priest. But if she drew attention to herself, she risked Magdi's safety as well. Tears filled her eyes and spilled down her cheeks. She clenched her fists, rocking back and forth on the balls of her feet. What could she do? What *should* she do?

As if sensing she was on the edge of a reckless impulse,

one of the Hounds growled and brushed her knee with his tail, freezing her in place.

No one stepped forward, so the councilman rang the bell again and motioned to a man in a red cloak. "It is time for you to administer justice," he announced.

The condemned man suddenly straightened his shoulders and sucked in a breath. "Where crops fail, thistles grow!" he cried.

"Silence!" The man in red—the executioner—took Mason roughly by the arm and tossed a black hood over his head. The bell sounded again as faint whispers rustled through the crowd, repeating Mason's strange words. The entire procession prepared to march toward the gallows.

Tears burned Brida's eyes. *This* was the real crime.

Just then the Huntsman threw out an arm and called, "Halt in the name of Moira, Queen of Crows!" A startled silence fell as every head turned to stare at him.

For one soaring second relief swept through Brida. The Huntsman was going to save this man.

"I have a more fitting punishment than death," he said, something dark echoing behind his words.

Brida went cold.

The councilmen exchanged glances. "Yes?" one finally said.

The Huntsman beckoned, so the executioner pulled his captive closer. "Better that he live in service to the queen to make amends for his crime rather than dying uselessly." He tossed something to the executioner, but Brida couldn't tell what it was.

The executioner caught it, turned it over in his hands.

Now Brida could see that it was a collar of some sort, with steel thorns. *Oh, no.*

The executioner lifted the black hood off Mason's head and buckled the collar around his neck. For one startled breath, glittering sparks enveloped him and Brida felt his magic. He *was* a priest! But then the collar seemed to snuff out his power.

The condemned man screamed.

The people nearest him stumbled backward and some fled the square entirely. Brida could only watch in horror as the man's jaws stretched, his face deformed. Still screaming, he fell to the ground. His arms and legs began shifting. Hair sprouted along his face, down his neck, over his limbs. . . .

He was turning into a dog. No, into a Hound.

Brida folded, knees buckling. She'd known there was something not entirely natural about them from the beginning, but to think that they were *men* . . .

The old woman's whispered advice rang in her ears. *If I were you, I'd lose myself in town while I still had the chance. Head for the Temple.*

Without thinking, Brida leaped to her feet and ran.

PART THREE

SISTERS

SEVENTEEN

The Narrows

THE HOUNDS WERE still harnessed to the dogsled and the Huntsman was preoccupied with Mason, but Brida knew it wouldn't take long for them to notice her absence. She needed to be as far away and as well hidden as possible by the time they started hunting her.

She tried not to think about the way the pack had torn into the rabbits and licked blood off their muzzles.

She tried not to think about twiggy creatures crawling out of tree trunks or bone monsters bursting from the ground. She wasn't in the woods anymore—she was in a busy town crowded with people, and maybe she had a fair chance at escape this time.

Brida ducked past a man carrying a heavy satchel and dodged a woman pushing a barrow. A throng of people hurried away from the square, too shocked by what they had seen to speak above low, frightened murmurs. Someone muttered, "The thing about thistles is that if you cut one down, more will grow from the roots." His neighbor hushed him, grabbing his elbow to draw him away as Brida wondered what he meant.

She slipped through a group of girls roughly her age and let the crowd push her past the gallows, across a cobbled street, and around a corner. Heart galloping like a horse, she risked a glance over her shoulder but couldn't glimpse the Huntsman or his Hounds.

Elbowing her way out of the crush of people, she ran down a side street lined with small shops and pressed herself into a deserted doorway. Panic fluttered in her chest and her knees wobbled.

Slow down and think, she told herself. *Hounds have noses. They can follow scent and trace you. You can't outrun them for long. But if you can make it to the broken Temple, you might be able to hide until they lose interest.*

Both Rissi and Agathe had hinted at the answers the Temple might hold, the sanctuary it might offer.

All she had to do was find it. *Due north*, Agathe had said . . . but which way was north?

Brida craned her neck, standing on her toes as she studied the sky. Too many buildings cluttered her view and she couldn't tell which direction she needed to head in.

"Psssssst," someone hissed from the mouth of a nearby alley. Brida startled, and then saw a thin boy with shaggy hair the color of hickory bark and dark eyes that tilted up at the corners like questions. His wrists and ankles hung too far out of his clothes, but his shirt and trousers were clean.

A badge on his chest depicted a symbol she didn't recognize, a swirled line that looked almost like a flame.

"Psssst," he whispered again more urgently, beckoning to her.

She darted into the alley and he grabbed her hand.

"Hey!" she cried, but he put a finger to his lips and shook his head. Swallowing her protest—whoever this skinny boy was, he couldn't be any more dangerous than the Huntsman's Hounds—she ran along beside him as he led her through a maze of crooked streets and shadows.

Edgewood was larger than Brida would have guessed. And once the boy took her away from the cobbled streets and stone buildings of the city's center, it grew more crowded and confusing. Buildings leaned toward each other across gaps so narrow she banged her elbows on the walls more than once, and she lost any possible sense of direction.

Half expecting to hear the barking of Hounds any moment, she clung to the boy's hand and prayed they wouldn't get caught before finding refuge.

Brida's breath rasped and her muscles burned by the time they reached an iron gate closed with a heavy lock. The boy dropped her hand.

Panic buzzed in her ears. She was trapped.

But he eased around a pile of rubble, brushed aside a stained piece of fabric, and disappeared.

Brida stared after him, baffled.

A moment later he reappeared, cobwebs in his hair and

a smudge of dust across his sharp cheeks. "You coming, or what?"

"I—I can't. There's a man with a pack of Hounds. . . ."

"The Huntsman," he said, a grim look on his pinched face.

"Yes. Well, he's . . . he was supposed to take me to the queen, only I ran. He'll come looking for me, and I don't want you to get hurt when his Hounds trace me here. Can you tell me how to find the old Temple? Please? A woman named Agathe said—"

He nodded. "We can take you right to it. But first, you need to help Hush. Hurry!"

"There's no time. The pack will follow my trail and—"

He gave a snort and tilted his head. "You got the magic. Why can't you just trick the Hounds? Make 'em think you ran one way, when really you hid here? And then make a spell to cover up your smell." He shrugged like it was a simple thing.

"How did you know I could do magic?"

"Saw you in the square. Some people have a certain look . . . I dunno, a glow or somethin' . . . around 'em and then I know they can do stuff." He shrugged. "Yours is different from most I've seen, but I reckon it's 'cause you in't from here, are you?"

Brida didn't know how to answer him. How was he able to sense magic? Did he have the ability himself?

As if guessing her thoughts, he shook his head. "Nope.

Been tested, but I can't work magic. I just know when others can. Now come on! Hush needs you."

This skinny boy knew more about magic than she did.

Sighing, Brida closed her eyes and tried to concentrate. A faint breeze, smelling of moss and dirt and old stone, dust and mildew, cooled her face.

Gently calling strands of magic, Brida lifted the scents off her own skin—horse sweat, crushed grass, dew-damp wool, herbs, the lemon-and-rose-scented soap she and Magdi made—and twisted them into an invisible ball. Tossing this to the wind, she imagined sending it on a winding path far, far from town. Then she took the mossy smell the breeze had carried to her and wove it around herself like a cloak. *Please let this work*.

She opened her eyes to find the boy studying her.

"There," he said, with some satisfaction. "Told you. Now let's go!"

Brida hesitated. Was this a trick? A trap? Should she try to find the Temple on her own?

But if he had mischief in mind, why would he have helped her hide from the Hounds? And he'd said someone needed help. . . .

Gathering her resolve, she followed him into a tunnel concealed by the filthy curtain. The passage twisted twice and sloped down into what looked like an abandoned cellar. Piles of half-rotten crates lay in the corners, and one wall was obscured by shelves filled with unmarked boxes and bottles.

"Where are we?" Brida whispered.

The boy laughed. "You don't have to whisper no more. Who's gonna hear?"

Brida cleared her throat. "Then where are we?"

"Home." He spread his arms wide.

"And . . . who are you?"

"I'm Bones, but we can fuss about introductions later. Come on! Hush and Bear are upstairs." He took off, scampering like a jackrabbit.

Brida dusted her hands on her hips, climbing up a creaking flight of broken stairs to an upper loft. Straw mattresses lay along two walls, with a trunk of ragged clothes in one corner.

A stout boy with skin like sun-warmed maple and dark curls leaped to his feet. "Get out!" he shouted, preparing to charge Brida like a bull.

"Stop! No, Bear, she's fine. She's magic," Bones cried, holding up a hand.

The boy called Bear—he was certainly fierce enough for the name, and taller than Brida—skidded to a stop. "You sure?"

Bones nodded. "Yep. Saw it all the way across the square."

"She in't gonna tell somebody we're here, is she?" Bear asked, eyes still peering suspiciously at Brida from under angry brows.

"She don't want nobody to know she's here, either. And Hush needs her help."

Bear's face immediately softened. "She's getting worse."

Now Brida noticed a girl lying beneath a flimsy blanket on one of the mattresses. Her face was pale, lips cracked and peeling. Shadows darkened the skin beneath her fluttering eyelids and her hands plucked restlessly at wrinkles in the blanket.

"What happened?" Brida asked softly. "How long has she been sick like this?"

The two boys exchanged wary glances, and then Bear said, "She hasn't really been well since the fire, but three days ago she got too tired to get out of bed."

"The fire?"

Bones answered. "Yep. Burned half the Narrows in one night."

"The Narrows?"

Bones snorted and waved his arms. "The Narrows. What we ran through on the way. This is as far inside the Narrows as you can get and still be in town. No one comes here much anymore. Bad luck, they say, but in't the worst already come?"

Don't say that! It can always get worse, Brida almost said, but there was little enough hope in this broken-down building. What good would it do to crush the last seed?

"How long ago was the fire?" The buildings she'd seen were so decrepit she couldn't tell what was char or rot.

The boys frowned at each other.

"Hmmm." Bear counted on his fingers. "Two moons ago, I think? Or maybe three."

"And how old are you?"

"What difference does that make?" Bear scowled again.

"Just curious." Brida shrugged. "I'm twelve. Almost thirteen."

Bones slapped a hand on his chest. "I'm thirteen winters, Bear is sixteen."

Bear ignored them, studying the girl on the bed again. With one hand he gently smoothed the blanket beside her.

Brida's heart twisted and a lump of tears rose in the back of her throat. She had to swallow twice before she could ask, "And Hush? How old is she?"

Bones spread his hands, shrugged.

After a moment, Bear glanced over his shoulder and caught her questioning gaze. "Dunno," he finally admitted. "'Bout our age."

"How did you three meet?" It was just a casual question, but Bear and Bones exchanged a long look. Brida sensed a silent conversation stretching in the air between them and wished she hadn't asked.

Oh, brambles. How does Mother Magdi always know what to say?

"Never mind. It doesn't matter. Oh, and my name is Brida." She approached the bed and gently laid a hand on the girl's burning forehead, trying not to wince at the heat.

"What happened to Mason?" she heard Bear ask. It sounded as if he'd known the priest and her curiosity sparked.

Bones answered, "Smoke was red."

"Blood and rusty iron!" Bear cursed. "He was a good man. I don't know who can fill his place."

"He wasn't hanged, at least. Huntsman took him for a Hound."

Brida moved her hand to Hush's chest, felt the breath struggling to rise beneath her palm and the uncertain rhythm of a weak heartbeat. Even through the fabric, the girl's fever flamed so high Brida half expected to see her skin blister.

"That's hardly better!" Bear protested.

"He's still alive."

"Suppose that's something," Bear agreed after a moment. And then he added, "Where crops fail, thistles grow." Bones repeated the phrase.

Glancing over her shoulder, Brida was about to ask what they meant, how they'd known the condemned priest, but Hush let out a feeble gasp and thrashed her legs.

"Can you tell what's wrong with her?" Bear demanded, lifting a limp strand of Hush's hair as Brida tried to soothe her.

Brida examined Hush's arms and legs, seeing no signs of rash or pox, no injuries or open sores. "I'm not sure yet. Was she hurt in the fire?"

The boys shifted uncomfortably. Finally Bones said, "Must've been, but she don't talk so it's hard to say for sure."

"She doesn't talk?"

"Nope," Bones told her. "But mostly we know what she's thinking anyway. Least, we did until she got too sick."

"Have either of you been sick?"

"No. Not a bit."

"Has she eaten anything bad? Or been around anyone else who was sick?"

Bear shook his head. "Nope. We all eat the same. Dunno what happened to her."

"Unless . . ." Bones rubbed his arms and took a breath. In a dark voice he said, "Could be a hex."

— EIGHTEEN —

Hex

"A HEX?" THE thought was enough to shake Brida's composure. Hexes had to be cast from dark magic, and they were very rare. "Who would wish to harm her?" Brida said it lightly, as if to reassure the boys that this was nothing but a fever that would soon break. After all, that was the most likely explanation. . . .

She didn't expect their reaction.

Bear leaned across the bed and grabbed Brida by the wrist. His eyes had gone wild and a flicker of fear sizzled through her body. He was so much bigger and stronger than her.

"The queen," he said.

"Why would the queen—"

A shadow darted across the small window on the far wall, accompanied by the flap of wings. The watery pane of glass had a crack in the bottom corner and was so covered in dust it barely let in a dim glow, but Bones flung himself toward it. Pressing his nose against the dirty window, he stared at the sky for a long, breathless moment.

"Not a Crow. Just a dove," he finally said.

"A white dove?" Brida asked, and then realized she was being witless. Of course it wouldn't be *her* dove, so far from Oak Hollow.

Hush sucked in a rattle of air and Bones flew back to her bedside, standing beside Bear. "Can't you help her?"

"I'll try, but . . . I'm not a hedgewitch." *And I'll probably never be a hedgewitch.* "I'm just an apprentice, and . . . I'm not a very good one. I'll do everything I can for your friend, but I can't promise it will be enough."

The confession tasted bitter on Brida's tongue, but she owed them the truth.

Bear's muscular shoulders hunched as if he'd been hit and he turned away, but Bones smiled. "You got strong magic. You can do this."

Brida didn't share his confidence, but she'd endangered these boys the instant she followed Bones from the alley. The least she could do was try to save the girl they cared about.

Pressing her folded hands to her stomach, she took a few slow breaths to calm and clear her mind. She needed to remember everything Magdi had taught her. If she made a mistake now, she might not get a second chance to help Hush.

"Bones, can you find me yarrow, grated gingerroot, and

peppermint leaves?" These formed the foundation for most remedies and were commonly stocked with spices, but Brida couldn't risk wandering around the market looking for a shop with the Huntsman and his Hounds out there.

"I'll go," Bear said, rising and lumbering toward the door.

Brida grabbed the small purse of coins Mother Magdi had insisted she carry and tried to hold it out to him, but he thrust his hands in his pockets.

"I don't need your money. I can get the herbs myself."

If he was half as quick as Bones had been, she had no doubt he could snatch whatever he wanted and disappear before he was noticed—even given his stature. But she didn't want to try a healing spell with stolen ingredients.

The thought must have crossed her face because he gave her a scornful look.

"Don't need to pinch, either. I'm a smith's apprentice. I got my own coin." Still frowning, he marched to the door and disappeared.

With a sigh, Brida dropped her money back in her pocket and turned to Bones. "I also need a kettle of water. You'll have to heat it to boiling, and find me a clean cup. Will you do that?"

He darted to a wooden chest with rusty hinges and started rummaging through cast-iron pots and cracked stoneware bowls.

Brida returned her attention to Hush. Doubt settled

in the pit of her stomach like a millstone. How could she heal an illness this serious when she couldn't even pass the Greenleaf exams?

She needed Mother Magdi. Magdi would take one look at Hush and know precisely what ailed her. Magdi would know exactly what herbs to use and how to blend the necessary magic.

Unfortunately, Brida was Hush's only hope. She had a feeling it was going to take all her strength and skill. She just prayed she had enough to give.

Bones returned with a kettle and a chipped cup. "These work?"

"They'll do."

"There's a hearth in the other room, but I gotta fetch water from the well outside."

"Thank you," she told him.

While he dashed downstairs, Brida spread her hands just above Hush's body and closed her eyes. She tried to remember how she and Mother Magdi had worked together to heal Dev's injuries. Could she do the same thing by herself?

Letting her mind go still and quiet, she called magic to her fingers and probed, carefully, through the heat rising from Hush's fevered skin. She tried to send cooling energy from her hands, but the pale girl wheezed and turned her head restlessly from side to side.

"Easy, child," Brida said, practicing the voice Mother Magdi would have used, though it felt false coming from her own mouth. Hush was no more a child than she was, but nothing else sounded right, either.

She was terrible at this.

Letting her palms drift over Hush's slender frame, Brida tried again to send cool relief on gentle waves of magic, but the girl's fever continued to burn.

Maybe she really was hexed.

Fear slithered down Brida's neck and coiled at the base of her spine. She knew even less about removing hexes than she did about healing.

Bones clattered back into the room just then, a smear of soot along his brow and a damp stain on the hem of his faded shirt. The scent of ash and mud followed him. "Got the fire started in the other room and the water on to boil. What else?"

"Thank you. Can you find some rags we can use—"

He didn't wait to hear the rest before racing away.

Hush's eyes had just fluttered open when Bear arrived a few moments later, carrying a small canvas satchel. He took one look at the bed and all but threw the satchel at Brida.

"Hush!" he cried. "You're awake!"

Her cracked lips parted, but a heartbeat later her eyes drifted closed again.

Bear knelt at her side, tucking his chin to his chest. Tears gleamed on his lashes.

Bones returned with several mostly clean linen strips. "These work?"

"Those are perfect. Thank you. Will you help me by the fire?"

He nodded uncertainly and led the way to a room that could have been called a kitchen in better days. A brick hearth occupied one wall, a small fire burning cheerfully in the very center. Bones had hooked the kettle over it and a wisp of steam rose from the spout.

Brida opened the satchel Bear had brought and discovered not just the basic herbs she'd asked for but others as well. Shame stung her cheeks as she poked a finger in and stirred the dried leaves and stems.

She could smell peppermint, and the grated gingerroot was easy enough to identify, but . . . these pale blue petals. Were they chicory or coolbright or something she'd already forgotten? And these strips of bark . . . willow? And was this slippery elm? She thought she could tell the yarrow, but how could she be sure?

She needed to ask Bear, but he'd bowed his head over Hush and Brida couldn't make herself disturb him.

Maybe she could just listen to the magic. *Please don't fail me now,* she begged.

Concentrating on a whisper of air and the faint tingle in her fingers, Brida took some of the herbs and crushed them into the chipped cup, then poured boiling water over them.

"These should steep until the water changes color," she explained to Bones, "and then I need you to strain the petals and leaves out. While you fix the tea, I'm going to make a poultice to draw the heat out of Hush's skin."

He furrowed his brow but nodded, bending down to study the cup.

Brida took the rest of the ingredients and knotted them in one of the linen strips, then dropped the bundle in the hot water for a moment. She used a thread of magic to rapidly cool the poultice and hurried back to Hush, laying it across her forehead.

Bones followed a few moments later with the cup of herbal tea.

"She has to wake long enough to drink this," Brida told the boys. "Can you help me raise her head?"

Using another strand of magic, Brida infused the herbal tea with healing energy, with strength and optimism.

As Bear and Bones gently prodded Hush awake and lifted her to a sitting position, Brida held the cup to her lips. "Hush, sweetling, I need you to take a few slow sips. This will help you feel better." *I hope. Great Mother, please let it be so.*

The girl blinked dazed, glassy eyes at Brida, but her lips parted slightly. Brida tipped the cup just enough to let a trickle of the healing tea touch her mouth.

Hush swallowed and a grimace of pain crossed her delicate features.

"Very good. Now try another," Brida encouraged.

Hush took another tiny sip, and then another.

Hope lit Brida's heart. Maybe this wasn't quite as dire

as she'd feared. Hadn't Mother Magdi always said that children attracted fevers like honey drew flies? And most of them bounced back quickly after a dose of remedy.

But then Hush's body stiffened, her eyes widened, and she collapsed on the bed—knocking the cup out of Brida's hand.

"Hush!" Bear cried, wrapping his arms around her and trying to wake her again.

Bones shook his head. "It's not sickness. Told you she was hexed."

His words were arrows, puncturing hope.

NINETEEN

Wind Magic

FOR A MOMENT, panic held Brida paralyzed as the girl on the bed struggled to breathe. Had she made a mistake with the herbal tea, given Hush something toxic by accident?

"Help her!" Bear cried, replacing the poultice on Hush's brow and stroking her cheek.

I don't know how! Brida almost shrieked, but she swallowed the scream and tried not to choke.

Bones picked up the pieces of the broken cup and found a scrap of rag to mop the spilled tea. He nodded to Brida, a quick little gesture that somehow said *I trust you. You can do this.*

She leaned over the bed, casting her senses over the girl and fervently hoping she hadn't made things worse with her fumbled hedgemagic.

With frayed strands of power, Brida felt Hush's feeble pulse, counted the uneven beats of her heart. Sending her senses deeper, straining until sweat beaded on her upper lip and her muscles quivered with tension, Brida tried to follow the paths of illness through Hush's body. The girl hadn't been poisoned—on purpose or otherwise—but she didn't seem to have any sort of fever Brida had encountered before, either.

Then, as Brida's arms and legs trembled with exhaustion and her vision started to blur, she glimpsed a faint shadow buried deep within Hush's tissues.

The instant she sensed it, the shadow slipped away—but it wasn't quick enough. Brida had seen it.

Bones was right. Hush *had* been hexed, and whoever had done it used a power darker and stronger than Brida had ever encountered.

Brida's knees wobbled and she sank to the floor, panting as if she'd just run a league.

The boys watched her, wary and expectant.

"Well," she finally said, gulping air, "it *is* a hex."

Bones shrugged, unsurprised, but Bear groaned and hid his face in his hands.

"Are you sure no one else can help? Bear, what about the woman who sold you the herbs? She obviously knows healing. She probably has more experience than I do and if she could take a look—"

"She already did," Bear grunted. "She's a good healer, but she don't have magic."

Brida sighed. "Then I'll try to lift it myself, but I can't make any promises. I've never attempted anything like this before." She'd never even *seen* a true hex until now.

"What do you need us to do?" Bones asked.

"Hold her hands. Let her hear your voices, so she knows the way back to the land of the living if her spirit gets lost."

Bear made a strangled sound and clutched one of Hush's hands as if he might drown without it.

Bones stood on the other side of the bed, grabbing Hush's other hand.

Magdi would have given the boys gentle words of encouragement and comfort, but Brida didn't have time to fish for the right things to say.

Hush was fading fast.

Closing her eyes, Brida called up strands of magic—and immediately knew they weren't going to be strong enough.

Magdi's the healer. I can't do this alone.

The boys murmured softly at Hush's bedside, begging her to stay with them, to wake and recover.

Brida had healed the injured Hound near the boneyard by herself, but this was a *girl* under a terrible hex.

Think! Brida told herself. *You're running out of time!*

A rising wind rattled around the building, distracting her as it banged loose boards and whistled through gaps in the cracked walls. It howled through the shadowed alleys of the Narrows outside and roared around the peeling shingled rooftops of abandoned buildings. It grew louder, drowning out the boys' voices.

For a moment, Brida was afraid the white stormhorse

was being chased through the city. But this wind didn't feel like that wild rush of elemental magic.

Still, it gave her an idea.

Brida let magic rise beneath her skin and used it to call the wind. In her mind, it was like trying to hold a galloping horse with a single thread. Wind was, by its very nature, fickle and capricious. But she was desperate.

Weaving strands of magic through the wind's currents, Brida tied the wind to the building like one of the ribbon kites children launched on the first day of spring. She felt it whip around, fighting the restraint—and then, like an unruly horse suddenly yielding, it settled.

Brida clenched her teeth in concentration and slowly teased out one wisp of wind at a time. She worked instinctively, braiding strands of magic with the wind and then weaving each one through Hush's body as lightly as a whisper, as soft as a breath.

The magic wind currents flowed beneath Hush's skin, through her blood, around her bones. The hex shadow was strong . . . but it could not withstand the rush of wind. It weakened beneath the onslaught, fraying and thinning like a flag in a storm until it finally gave way.

Threads of darkness seeped out of the girl's pale skin and vanished in the beams of rich afternoon sunlight spilling through the hazy window.

The wind sang in Brida's ears, poured through her body, and tore free with a sound like a river crashing over rocks.

The building shuddered and, in a brittle silver explosion, two of the windows shattered. Shards of glass spun in a cyclone near the walls until Brida mustered the strength to force the wind back outside where it finally dissipated, leaving the ground dusted with broken glass.

Hush's eyes fluttered open.

"Whoa," Bones breathed, face lit with awe. "Brida, you did it!"

Bear was giddy with relief to see Hush awake and lucid. He helped her sit up, patting her hands as Bones crouched beside the bed. The boys started chattering so fast their voices tumbled over each other.

Brida slumped to the floor like a Harvest Feast puppet with the strings cut as her magic flickered out. She was too exhausted to feel triumph, too worried to celebrate. She'd never worked with so much power before, had never attempted such a complex spellweave by herself.

Holding the wind the way she'd done could have had disastrous consequences, but she hadn't seen any other option. Bones had said hardly anyone came this far into the Narrows, right? Hopefully no one would notice and any wind damage would be minor.

Watching the boys fuss over Hush lifted her spirits. This time she'd done something right. She'd found a way to use her own magic and—

Brida sucked in a sharp breath. *Her own magic.* She'd called the wind and it answered.

What if . . . could it be . . . she had *wind* magic?

Puzzle pieces clicked into place. Though Brida knew hedgemagic might draw from the power of the wind, she'd never seen Mother Magdi work with wind this way. She thought about the dandelion that had first revealed her ability. Magdi had assumed the blooming indicated hedgemagic, but what if the real trick had been the wind blowing away the seeds?

And Brida's link to the wind might explain her connection to the white stormhorse, too.

Maybe I'm a terrible hedgewitch's apprentice because I'm supposed to be a Windwitch instead! The thought filled her heart with a bubble of glee. Maybe she wasn't a failure at all—maybe she just had a different talent!

And then the joyful bubble popped. She plucked the baggy, torn, and mud-stained knees of her leggings and brushed at the dried leaves and bits of brambles caught in the hem of her filthy tunic. Her mouth twisted wryly.

Who was she kidding?

Windwitches were rare. *Very* rare. So rare that Mother Magdi had a book with all their names listed—and over the centuries, the list didn't take up two full pages.

What made her think that she—small, scared, and clumsy—could actually be the next Windwitch? There wasn't anything special about her. After all, her own parents hadn't wanted to keep her.

Wishful thinking, that's all.

Still . . . it felt good to know she could use her magic to help people, even if she had to figure out her own way to do it. Maybe, after she escaped the Huntsman and had a chance to talk to Mother Magdi and the other hedgewitches, she would understand her talents better.

Or maybe everything would make sense once she saw the Temple.

Hush caught Brida's eye and smiled. With a graceful gesture, she indicated that the boys should fall quiet. Then, silently, she beckoned.

Brida took a breath and struggled to stand. From the corner of her eye she saw Hush's fingers weave a pattern in the air and a moment later Bear was at Brida's elbow, helping her to her feet.

"Go ahead, lean on me," he told her. She didn't want him to see how terribly weak she felt, but when her knees trembled she had to grab his arm.

Bear guided her closer to Hush's bedside. The girl rose, placing both her hands on Brida's cheeks. Her thumbs traced Brida's eyebrows, the line of her jaw. She glanced at Bones, who nodded and said quietly, "I know. I saw it, too."

Before Brida could ask for an explanation, Hush stepped back, hands flying as she drew figures with her fingers.

Bear translated. "Hush says she's sorry she can't speak, but she wants you to know how grateful she is for your help.

239

There's something you gotta see, but first we need to barricade the windows and then . . . we eat."

Hush frowned at him, gesturing more emphatically. Clearly that wasn't quite what she'd said.

"I'm sorry." Brida walked to the broken windows, gingerly brushing the battered wooden frames. "I didn't mean to lose control like that. It was just too much to hold. . . ."

"Don't apologize!" Bones cried. "You saved Hush!" He was already dragging a splintered board to the wall, propping it in place.

Brida chewed her lip. "It appears so. And I'm sorry to be a bother, but I really do need to find the Temple. Could you just tell me how to get there?"

"I told you we'll take you," Bones promised. "Soon as we're done."

Bear said, "Speaking of the Temple, Hush, we have some terrible news. Mason Bolder was caught and . . ." He shook his head and lumbered around the abandoned rooms, salvaging crooked doors and wooden planks. "I can't believe that Council of Corruption condemned him."

Bones nodded. "But he wasn't hanged. Huntsman took him."

Hush frowned and said something with her hands, but the boys didn't translate out loud and Brida didn't want to pry. How did these three know an exiled priest?

Together the two boys managed to scavenge a handful

of rusted nails. They hammered the boards over the gaping windows while Brida helped Hush change her clothes in another room.

"There. Now we go eat!" Bear said, rapping his knuckles against the wood as the girls returned.

Hush's forehead puckered and she whipped a series of gestures at him.

Bear shook his head. "You're both weak as kittens and the market will be closing soon. We'll find food first, and then you can show her the Temple."

Brida's curiosity battled the hunger pangs knotting her stomach. What did Hush know of the Temple?

Before anyone could respond, a large crow launched itself at the single remaining window. Its sharp beak sent a fracture spider-webbing across the grimy glass, and then another crow thunked against the window. Two more hit the just-nailed planks with a noisy flurry of beating wings and harsh cries.

Brida flinched and backed away nervously.

She wasn't the only one.

Bear wrapped an arm around Hush and started to lead her from the room while Bones stared out the window, eyes wide and horrified.

The wind has agitated them. The wind . . . or her magic.

Brida cast her senses out, hoping to calm them. Only, they didn't seem like crows at all. She felt nothing but darkness and sorrow, fear, anger, and hate. They had to be Crows.

Bones grabbed Brida's elbow and tugged her to the door. "Come *on*."

"We can't go out there! There are too many!" Brida gasped.

Bones gave her arm a sharp yank. "If we stay, they'll break through. Come on, we know a way."

But it was too late. An earsplitting *crawwwwwk!* shivered the air as a Crow burst into the room, dragging pieces of broken window glass with her wings and feet.

"Blood and ashes!" Bear swore, plunging toward the wall. While he wrestled a spare board into place, blocking the opening, Bones chased the bird around the room. With a wild lunge, he snatched the blanket from Hush's cot and flung it over the Crow.

Tumbling to the floor, the Crow thrashed and croaked and scrabbled around beneath the covering.

Bones grabbed the furious bird in both hands.

"Stop! What are you doing?" Brida cried.

"What do you think? Wringing its miserable little neck before it flies back to the queen."

"You *can't*." Brida was horrified.

"But it's a queen's *Crow*," Bear said.

"And Crows are filthy spies," Bones added.

Brida remembered the Crows she and Magdi had hidden from in the valley. She swallowed a lump of fear so dry her throat clicked and she nearly choked. "But we can't just kill her!"

Hush grabbed Bones by the wrist and when she had his attention, she spoke to him with her hands. Glancing at Bear once or twice for a translation, he reluctantly nodded and left the bird in a squawking heap on the floor, running into another room.

"Hush told him to find a basket or barrel. We'll put the Crow inside and leave. By the time she escapes, we'll be long gone and no harm will be done," Bear said.

Brida could tell he wasn't convinced. "I'm sorry," she said again, knowing it wasn't enough. "Maybe when I leave I can draw them away and you can stay—"

"Nah," Bear said in his gruff voice. "They've come before. You're not the only one they're looking for."

Brida was relieved he didn't blame her for bringing their notice with her magic, but who else were they seeking?

TWENTY

The Second Feather

ONCE THE CROW was contained, the boys accompanied Hush and Brida out of the tunnel beneath the old building and through an alley partially blocked by rubble. They ducked under a crooked doorway and wove between crumbling walls, clambering over broken bricks and ivy-choked stones as they worked their way deep into a maze of forgotten places.

More Crows circled overhead, harsh croaks echoing off the ruins, but they didn't seem to notice the ragged group clumsily scrambling away.

Bear helped Hush through the first rough patches, but released from the hex's hold she seemed to gain strength by the second. Soon she was all but skipping ahead. Every few paces she'd pause to glance over her shoulder, beckoning them onward.

Brida struggled to keep up with the others. Lifting the hex from Hush had left her hollowed out, but hunger was a strong motivator.

When the commotion of the Crows had faded, Hush jumped off a broken pillar and turned slightly. She led them through what had once been a garden and then down another alley. They began circling back the way they'd come, keeping to the shadows so no birds could spot them.

The air cooled and took on the ripe hue of a dying afternoon, and Hush urged them to go faster.

Brida panted, lungs burning and muscles protesting. The second time she stumbled, Bear grabbed her by one hand and Bones the other, and they held her upright as they pushed her to hurry.

Just as Brida started to think she'd never make it, they slipped around the corner of a stone building and rushed down a clean, wide street. Two more turns and they'd reached the market.

Brida leaned against the back of a wooden stall, trying to catch her breath as tiny purple and gold sparks burst at the edges of her vision. She was exhausted, ravenously hungry, and suddenly too afraid to move. "I can't," she gasped, pressing a hand to her stomach. "If the Huntsman and his Hounds find me—"

"Use your magic to hide yourself again," Bones suggested.

"Too drained. Once I've recovered some energy, maybe, but . . ." She shook her head.

"Wait here, then. I'll take a quick look." He darted away, disappearing between one blink and the next.

Bear hunched beside her, concern softening his gruff face. "I'll bring you a cup of water. Hang on." He lumbered toward one end of the market, waving and exchanging greetings here and there.

As Hush patted her shoulder, Brida let her gaze wander the side of the market she could see. A few vendors—a woman selling hanks of dyed wool, a man with polished knife blades, someone with bits of lace and ribbon—were already packing their wares and folding up their tents. But there were still more things to buy than Brida had ever seen in one place before. Baskets woven in different shapes and designs, stoneware and crockery in colored glazes, copper pots, tin ladles, bone needles . . . She stared in astonishment.

Bear returned a moment later with two hollow gourds of water balanced carefully in his calloused hands. He handed one to Brida and one to Hush.

Brida sipped the water gratefully. It was cool and slightly sweet.

Bear had just offered to refill the gourd for her when Bones jogged back to them, a grin lighting his face. "The Huntsman and his pack went through South Gate some time ago. Goodman Mercer said he was chasing after *storm-horses*! Can you believe that? It's not like Mercer to tell fairy stories, but he swears the Huntsman left and that's all that matters."

"Stormhorses aren't real," Bear huffed. "Are you sure the Huntsman's gone?"

"For now, yes."

"They are," Brida said quietly.

"What?" Both boys looked at her in surprise, but Hush nodded.

"The stormhorses. They're real. I've seen them. The queen—"

"Quiet!" Bones and Bear cried. "Don't call her attention!"

Brida glanced at the sky reflexively. She didn't see any Crows . . . yet. Lowering her chin, she whispered, "The Huntsman has three so far, but he's after the last two. I was trying to help them when he caught me."

"For true?" Bones asked, eyes wide. "What do you think she wants with them?"

Bear scowled. "Nothing good."

Just then, Brida's stomach rumbled and she pressed her fists against her belly.

Bear rubbed his chin. "We need to find food before the market closes."

She hesitated. "Why don't you go on ahead while I wait here? I don't want to draw attention. I have some coins—"

Hush twisted her lips and arched her brow in an ominous expression. Flashing a series of quick gestures with her hands, she waited for Bear to translate.

"Hush says we go together. We'll be safer in a group."

Brida let herself be persuaded. The truth was, she already liked Bear, Bones, and Hush, despite their secrets, and didn't relish the thought of being left behind.

As they slipped down one of the market aisles, Brida found herself studying the people she passed more than the things displayed for sale. She noticed the pinch of hunger in their sallow, sunken cheeks and dim eyes, and by the seventh or eighth tent she realized they'd already been through half the market without finding a single stall selling food.

The din surrounding her slowly sorted itself into distinct voices, snippets of conversation, random comments.

"Snow in midsummer," one woman muttered to her companion. "I haven't had fresh berries in two years, and my apple trees are next to dead. The queen is killing Fenwood Reach!"

"Quiet!" her friend hissed, grabbing her sleeve. "Herself might hear you."

Both women cast their eyes to the sky, and Brida's blood turned cold and thick.

She was so distracted she didn't realize the others had stopped walking until she ran into Bear's broad back.

"These are barely fit for pig slop," he was saying to a gnarled old man. The table in front of them held a sparse collection of wrinkled apples, musty turnips, and dried grapes. "I'll give you five bits for the lot."

The man's face puckered. "Son, I'd love to give it to you. Looks like you and your friends could use a bite. But this is the last I have, and how will I buy seed or supplies come spring if I haven't got the coin? It's five bits an apple, three for a scoop of raisins, and two for a turnip. That's the best I can offer."

Bear growled and hunched his shoulders, leaning down when Bones plucked at his sleeve. There was a murmured argument, and then she heard Bear say, "I *can't*. I spent most of my coins at the healer's."

Before Brida could offer to pay, a woman in a striped shawl elbowed past them and dropped a clinking purse on the table. "I'll take it all," she said.

At the next food stall, a man with bruised eyes sold hot potatoes wrapped in scraps of old paper and round loaves of course bread.

Brida laid a hand on Bear's arm. "Let me." She fished in her pocket, withdrawing half a dozen copper and tin coins.

As she was about to ask for bread and potatoes, a man lurched to the table and slammed a fist down.

"What game are you playing, pond scum?" he shouted. He thrust a potato in the seller's face. The inside was darkened with rot.

"I—I didn't know. They looked fine, I swear!"

"I want my money back, or I'll call the guardsmen over and have you arrested for a cheat."

"Here! Please, I'm sorry. I didn't know!" The seller held out three iron bits and the angry customer snatched them with a scowl, stomping off.

Brida exchanged a look with Bear. The potatoes looked appetizing, steaming slightly in their paper wrappers. Salt crystals glistened on their skins. But if the insides were no good . . .

"We'll take four bread rounds, please," she said, handing over her coins.

"Like to try potatoes? They're still warm from the fire."

When Brida shook her head, he sighed. "They're last year's, it's true, but what else have we got?"

Bear gathered up the bread and they turned away, finding a quiet corner to eat.

Brida's stomach growled as she took the first bite. The bread was coarse and tough to chew, but it was better than nothing.

Bear watched her swallow and then scowled at his own piece of bread. "No wheat. Rain and hail kept battering the crops, so now we have to make do with animal feed."

"Barley and millet aren't just for animals." Bones tore a bite off his round.

Hush held her bread in the crook of one arm and gestured with her hands. "Taste like it, though," Bear translated aloud, and grinned.

Brida choked on a laugh. A heartbeat later she was wiping tears from her eyes.

She hadn't realized just how fortunate her village had been. They'd suffered from the uneven seasons, it was true—winter freezes that lasted too long, summer heat that split the ground—but no one had gone hungry. Unlike the starving refugees who'd wandered into the valley, people in Oak Hollow had found ways to manage.

She thought about the apples in Magdi's garden, the berries and nuts. She recalled the long hours Magdi was often gone, the exhaustion traced in lines along her face.

In addition to healing hurts and helping people with remedies and charms, Mother Magdi had spent years shielding Brida, protecting Oak Hollow and the surrounding valley.

Brida just hadn't thought about how much effort that took, what it must have cost.

Or how powerful Mother Magdi must *really* be.

"What's it like where you live?" Bones asked, as if following the direction of her thoughts.

Brida stared at the bread in her hands, picking off a tiny bit and placing it in her mouth to give herself time to find words. She finally said, "Small and peaceful."

"Who do you live with?"

Unshed tears clogged her throat. "I was left with a hedgewitch when I was a baby," she admitted. Reluctant to say more, she asked, "And what about you? What's your story?"

After a moment, Bones said, "My da was a music

teacher in secret. Ma kept a printing press hidden in her kitchen pantry. She was trying to save all the books that the queen—"

"Quiet!" Bear snarled.

Bones lowered his voice. "Ma tried to save all the books that *she* wanted burned, only she got caught. My sisters were in the house when the guards came, but I was out at the market. I saw the smoke—" His voice broke. "Next thing I knew, they were all gone." He wiped his eyes with a sleeve.

What could Brida say after that? It was too ugly, too raw, too wrong for a simple *I'm sorry*.

"Someday she will pay for all the pain she has caused," Brida said, surprised to discover she truly meant it.

Bear gave a fierce nod as he swallowed a bite of bread. "That's what my da always said. We lived on a farm west of the Narrows. Gran was a hedgewitch. Ma helped sometimes, even though she didn't have much magic knack herself."

He studied his hands, jaw working, and then continued. "Things were tough. The cycle of seasons started to go wrong. Some years rain turned our fields to bogs and nothing but moss and duckweed would grow. Other years summer lasted so long the ground cracked and everything scorched.

"Farms all around started to fail, and then the guards came looking for food. They stole whatever we still had and whipped us for not working hard enough." Bear's mouth twisted bitterly. "As if we weren't working our skins off already.

"Gran tried to use hedgemagic, but she said it felt like the power had run as dry as the well in our south field. She and Ma went to the castle to consult with *Herself*."

Brida forgot the bread she held, listening as Bear lowered his voice even further.

"I don't know what happened, but that was the last time I saw Gran or Ma."

Bear tore off a bite of bread with his teeth and chewed as though he could swallow his words. When he resumed speaking, his lips twisted on his story's sour taste. "Da waited for them to come back. He waited and waited, and then he headed to the castle to find them. The next day, the guards came. They—"

He choked, turned away, and finally mumbled, "Anyway, I was the only one who survived. A neighbor brought me to Edgewood in his cart, and I met Bones."

"And we found Hush, and here we are," Bones said, patting Bear on the back.

Brida wanted to ask about Hush's story, too, but was reluctant to pry further. They'd been through dark times and she didn't want to peel the scabs off raw wounds any worse than she already had. If Hush wanted to share, she would listen . . . but when Brida glanced at the other girl, Hush looked away.

They finished eating in silence after that.

Brida swallowed the last dry bite and dusted the crumbs from her fingers. She was still weak and hungry, but at least she wasn't on the verge of collapse.

If these three could endure without complaining, so could she.

Bear shoved away from the wall he'd been leaning against. "Come on. Let's see what else we can find."

Two tents away a woman and her husband were just folding up a cloth and stacking empty baskets. "Oh, dear," she said when she saw them. "You're too late. The last lot of pigeons sold a moment ago. I'll have rat or squirrel tomorrow, if you come early."

Brida pressed her lips together and tried not to shudder.

They walked on, reaching the edge of the market without finding anything else to eat. More people packed their wares and prepared to leave, and the sun slipped lower in the sky.

"Getting late. We'll try again tomorrow," Bear said.

Brida rubbed her nose. "You promised to show me the way to the Temple. I'm sorry to insist, but it's important."

Hush tugged at Bear's sleeve and wove a series of urgent gestures with her fingers, glancing pointedly at Brida and then passing a hand along her face.

"Are you sure it can't wait until the morning?" Bear asked Hush in a low voice. "Brida looks done in and it's a long way."

Again the gestures, with a hint of impatience.

"Good point." Raising his eyes, Bear said, "We'll go right now, if you're up for it. Probably safer to spend the night there than in our quarters anyway. Mason keeps—*kept*—supplies there for anyone who needs a refuge."

Brida nodded eagerly. "Thank you."

Bones scratched his chin, glanced around. "Better hurry. Can't be out in the Narrows after dark," he explained to Brida.

She was about to ask why they stayed in the Narrows if it was so dangerous, but a *crawwk!* froze her tongue. Was it an ordinary crow calling farewell to the sun, or one of the queen's Crows crying a threat?

They didn't wait to find out.

Bear took Hush's hand and Bones grabbed Brida's wrist and they ran from the market, dodging down a side street and slipping back into the shadows.

Just before they rounded the corner, a taunting Crow's cry filled Brida's ears and something whisper soft touched the back of her neck. Cold shivers drizzled down her spine and for a single sharp-edged heartbeat her body felt like it was cracking open, folding inward, spinning backward.

She knew that sensation.

Brida gasped and slapped a hand against her neck. When she drew her fingers away, they were stained black with a familiar glittering soot.

A second Crow feather. The queen had found her again.

TWENTY-ONE

A Broken Temple

TENSION THRUMMED IN Brida's body. The last time she'd been touched by a Crow feather, the Huntsman had called her *feathermarked* and captured her. What would happen now that she'd been marked again?

"Wait!" she cried. "A feather landed on me!"

Hush turned back, face white and pinched with worry. But then her eyes softened and her lips curved in a smile. She said something with her hands and Bear hurried to translate.

"It was just an ordinary bird feather. If it had been a Crow feather, you would have transformed into a Crow and been compelled to fly to the queen."

"No, you don't understand. It happened once before, the same way. A black feather that turned to glittering soot or sand when it touched me."

Hush considered this, then her fingers started whipping words quicker than Bear could speak them. "That's not the way the feathermark usually works, but it's possible her power doesn't affect you. In any case, we need to hurry. Come on! It's nearly dark!"

Brida followed as fast as she could, but fear nipped her heels. She knew it had been a Crow feather, even though they'd been so careful to avoid notice. She just wasn't sure why she'd been feathermarked *twice*. Did Queen Moira know she'd escaped the Huntsman? What could the queen want with her, anyway?

Hopefully she never had to find out.

To distract herself, she asked, "Why can't we be out after dark? If the Narrows is full of thieves and troublemakers, why do you stay there?"

Maybe they have no choice, she realized, and bit her lip.

But Bear didn't sound offended when he answered, "Thieves and troublemakers? Nah, we're the only troublemakers. Whole place has mostly been abandoned since the fire. Sometimes people spend a night or two in the Temple, but that's about it."

Brida sighed, shoulders loosening. "Then there's nothing to fear in the dark. I know all the night-charms for owls, starhawks, foxes, wolves, coyotes, nightcats. . . . They won't hurt you."

The litany reassured her and she spoke with increasing confidence.

Bear snorted. "It in't any natural creatures that prowl the Narrows after dark. I reckon even wolves and nightcats would avoid them things."

A twist of terror made Brida stumble and she scraped her elbow on the rough edge of a stone wall when she caught her balance. "What things?" More bone monsters? Tree creatures?

"Bad things, called up by the queen's sorcery. Even she's afraid of them now, and won't come near the Narrows. That's why *we* stay," Bones answered, taking the lead.

"What *things*?" Brida repeated, a tremble in her voice. What could be so bad it frightened the queen?

"You don't want to know," Bear said, hurrying her along.

They passed a row of tall buildings looming over the road with steeply pitched tile roofs and unfriendly doors. Lights flickered in the gaps between heavy curtains, but as the daylight leaked from the sky an oppressive silence filtered through the shadows.

Where were the neighborly conversations exchanged on front porches? Where were the children walking dogs or playing hoops in the alleys?

Brida shivered and crossed her arms over her chest.

Suddenly, an eerie howl climbed through the quiet of early evening and ripped through the stillness.

A Hound.

Brida tripped and skinned her knees on the cobblestones before Bear gripped her arm and hauled her back to her feet. "I thought you said they'd all gone!" he cried, glaring at Bones.

"Goodman Mercer swore they had!"

"Well, one must have been left behind. Or else they've returned," Bear said grimly. "Let's go!"

"Brida can just"—Bones waved his hand vaguely—"send her scent away again. Only this time," he added to her, "maybe you should do the same for us, too."

Brida sucked in a breath and tried to call her magic, but she was still worn out from removing Hush's hex and both hunger and fear had sapped her strength. Clenching her fists, she concentrated on gathering their scents—sweat and soap, dust, herbs and bread and stale tea, iron and leather— and replacing them with the fragrance of the dying day, with the smells of hearth fires and cooking, cooling stone, and all the things they'd seen in the market. Her magic fizzled like a wet ember, though, no matter how hard she strained.

"I can't," she admitted breathlessly. The feathermark had once again suppressed her magic. How long might the effects last?

"We're just a few blocks from the Temple. We'll be safe there if we hurry," Bear said.

But as they turned a corner Brida heard the click of nails on cobbles and a low growl sent echoes off the stone. A massive Hound lurked near the mouth of the nearest alley, nose sniffing the air.

He spotted them at the same instant and threw back his head to howl.

"Run!" Brida screamed.

Bear and Hush veered right, she and Bones left.

Stumbling, panting, fighting the urge to look behind her, she followed Bones down a filthy gutter full of refuse and murky water and then through a desolate square with a cracked fountain.

The Hound followed too fast for them to shake him, bounding after them on massive paws.

"This way!" Bones cried, ducking through a curtained doorway and weaving past startled faces huddled around a small cast-iron stove.

"Wait!" Brida protested, skidding on a frayed carpet and plunging through another doorway, back into the open air.

Bones ignored her, racing up a set of stairs to a flat rooftop and then leaping a gap to the next. Brida followed as fast as she could, exhaustion threatening to swallow her.

Pausing for a heartbeat, Bones cupped his hands and blew a long whistle. It was answered a few paces ahead and to their left.

"Come on!" he urged, clattering down a rickety wooden ladder and across what appeared to be a stable yard for carriage horses. They slopped through dirty straw and manure, ran past a surprised groom, and raced back down a wide road.

Drunken laughter and loud voices poured from the building on the corner—a tavern, Brida guessed—and Bones slowed as they approached.

Hush and Bear rushed past the opposite corner, meeting

them with relieved grins—until another howl melted the smiles from their faces.

They took off again, running until Bear cried, "Here it is!" He lurched to a stop and pointed at a wrought-iron gate opening into another maze of alleys and dim passages.

Bones took the lead, cutting through a ditch and heading toward an ivy-covered corner. Glancing over his shoulder with a finger pressed to his lips, he crouched low and crept through the hedge at the base of the stone wall.

Hush went next, Brida followed, and Bear brought up the rear.

They stumbled along a dank passage draped with dusty cobwebs, down a flight of uneven stone steps, and right to a massive wooden gate. An iron lock forbade entry, but Bones whipped two thin pieces of metal from his pocket and slipped them into the keyhole. With a practiced flick of his wrist, the lock clicked and he straightened, wearing a satisfied grin. He shoved the gate open and waved a hand, urging them all inside.

"The Hounds can't follow us," he said. "It's still sanctified ground, even if the queen thinks she destroyed the Temple. We're protected here."

As soon as Brida stepped through, the feathermark dissolved in a tingling rush of sweet relief. She found herself standing in an abandoned courtyard filled with crumpled drifts of dried leaves and scraps of paper. A cracked marble statue of a woman holding a baby in her arms stared for-lornly at them.

She looked like the drawings Brida sometimes found in Mother Magdi's collection of contraband books.

The Great Mother.

Hush grabbed Brida by the hand and tugged her past darkened arches and empty courtyards, through cracked cloisters. Long indigo shadows crept across the stone, pooling in the corners.

Speeding up, Hush ducked under a collapsed archway. Glossy green and white vines hung like lace from the chipped stone and the air smelled of damp earth, dust, and crushed leaves.

They had to crawl, at one point, through a gap in the fallen masonry, only to emerge in a space barely high enough for Brida to stand without hunching.

Hush backed into a narrow crevice and motioned for Brida to go ahead.

"Hush says there's something inside you gotta see. We tried to tell her it could wait until morning, but she insisted. Go on," Bones said behind her.

Brida took a deep breath and eased forward slightly. She stepped through a doorway and the echoes of her footfalls gave the impression of a vast, vaulted space holding the scent-memory of incense and candle wax.

When her eyes adjusted to the dim gray light, she noticed a row of columns—some leaning, some broken—stretching off to her right. To her left, a handful of arches obscured smaller openings. Debris blocked some of them, and the ceiling seemed to have collapsed up ahead.

But a pale shape practically glowed beneath one of the arches. Strange energy drifted along Brida's skin and hummed in her bones. After a moment she recognized it as a residue of white magic, drawing her toward the gleaming figure.

Brida's footsteps fell too loudly and she cringed. This was a place for silence, for serene contemplation. Breaking the stillness felt like profaning something sacred, so she walked on tiptoes. . . .

Until she realized what she was seeing, and froze.

In the alcove below the arch stood a woman carved from marble, the stubs of old candles still stuck to the stone base at her feet. She wore a long gown hemmed with stars and a diadem with a crescent moon cupped between her brows.

Brida took a slow, deep breath and thought about Rissi and white magic, about the lessons Mother Magdi had taught her. About each village's Voice weaving stories in secret patterns of beads and knotted strings. About the things they weren't supposed to tell, of times *before*. About sacred circles and the worship of the Great Mother, about soaring stone Temples built for the gods and goddesses and kept by priests and priestesses until the Queen of Crows drove them out.

Brida knew what this statue was meant to represent: a

priestess of the Great Mother before she became *mother*, when she was still *maiden*. This priestess must have been someone special, someone worthy of recognition and respect, for her to have been immortalized in stone. The candles at her feet signified the petitions of desperate pilgrims praying for intercession.

Yes, Brida knew all this from conversations she'd had with Mother Magdi late at night, when the world outside their cottage was quiet and sleeping.

What she *didn't* know, couldn't guess, was why the statue wore a face so like her own.

"Brida?" The low voice sent echoes around the vaulted chamber and startled Brida from her reverie.

She had no idea how long she'd been kneeling before the statue, gazing at that too-familiar face, but a cramp in the arch of her foot and a throbbing ache in her knees told her she'd spent too much time on the hard floor. She pressed herself upright, stretching the kinks from her back and legs.

At first she'd tried to talk herself out of the truth in front of her eyes. *You don't own a silver looking glass. All you've seen is your reflection in still water, and how reliable can that be? You're tired and wrung out and imagining things, that's all.*

The more she studied the statue, though, the stronger the resemblance seemed. The face was older than hers, with a firmer chin and higher cheekbones. But the nose, the angle of the eyes, the curve of the lips . . . those were all hers.

She stared so long the face almost seemed to move.

Rissi had told her that she'd find the truth about herself in a broken Temple, but what did this marble priestess say about her? What did Agathe, the old woman at the trial outside the citadel, think she could remember?

What did Hush want Brida to see so desperately she risked Crows and Hounds to bring her here?

"Brida?" a muffled voice called again.

Bear, Bones, and Hush scrambled in a moment later.

"Are you all right?" Bones asked her.

Brida nodded, but her eyes slid sideways to the marble figure.

Hush stepped up beside her and took her hand.

"Who is this?" What Brida wanted to ask was, *Do you know why I look like her?*

None of them acted surprised at the resemblance, and then she remembered Bones saying, "I saw it, too."

She turned to Hush. "What does it mean?"

Hush stood on her toes, stretching up to brush the statue's cheek with her fingertips. Then she tapped Brida's cheek.

"Yes, I know I look like her. But *why?*"

Hush gently led her around the pillar and into another arched grotto.

At first it appeared empty, but then Brida noticed the dim glint of color on the walls. Walking closer, she discovered a series of tiled mosaics. Each section seemed to tell a story.

Hush pointed to the first, motioning Brida forward.

Brida had regained enough strength to breathe in her palm and summon her blue glow-globe. It flooded the space with pale, watery light.

The first mosaic panel depicted three young girls, tangled hair flowing behind them like tattered banners—silver blond, dark chestnut, and raven black—as they approached a crone poised on the edge of a cliff. Eagle wings stretched behind her.

Brida recognized it as an illustration from the story the Voice had told on the Day of Remembering.

It showed three sisters on the Veiled Cliffs, the moment before one cut her hair and tried to bind the Windwitch. Before the Windwitch transformed herself into an eagle and flew away.

It was the last day the wheel of seasons turned the way it was meant to, without spinning sideways or backward, too slow or too fast—though no one knew it at the time.

The next panel showed a young woman, hair woven in braids beneath a crown of rosebuds and ribbons. She wore a simple white gown with flowers embroidered around the hem, and she carried a slender willow wand decked with streamers and tiny golden bells. A thicket of trees stood in one corner, a man waiting among their trunks. A golden crown glinted on his head and bonfires glowed along the hills in the distance.

This looked like the traditional Beltane celebrations

Brida had heard about. Though Queen Moira had outlawed them, some towns still practiced the old ways in secret to welcome the spring.

A young maiden was selected to represent the spirit of the land, the soul of the Great Mother. She chose a young man to be her consort, and in a sacred ritual they blessed the land with continued fertility for the coming year. Children born of such unions were believed to be good luck.

Brida leaned forward, holding her glowing globe of breath-light closer to the surface of colored tiles.

The maiden in this panel looked like the white marble figure in the other alcove.

She looked like Brida.

Slow shivers chased across Brida's skin as she moved along the wall, studying the mosaic. There was a blank space here, an odd break in the progression of the mural. The edges of the panels to either side were rough and chiseled, as if someone had removed part of the image.

As if someone sought to hide a piece of the story.

The last panel showed a woman in a cloak of gleaming, iridescent black crow feathers and a silver winged crown. She ascended the polished steps of a stone dais, preparing to take her throne. Her eyes were cold and triumphant, her chin set in fierce determination.

Wait . . . this must be . . . Moira, Queen of the Crows. But then . . .

Brida let her light wink out.

Moira and two sisters. A truth she couldn't quite wrap her head around thrummed in her skull.

Hush took her by the hand again carefully, and led her out of the alcove.

The boys hung back, guarding the entrance as Brida and Hush made their way across the aisle, through the broken columns, past a long-dry fountain, and down a curving flight of steps that forced Brida to summon her ball of light again.

At the bottom of the stairs, Hush pushed open a door and led the way through what appeared to be a cluttered storage room. Rotting crates, old barrels, and a number of canvas-wrapped shapes lay in random piles. Several stout chests were scattered among baskets of moldering linens and brittle beeswax candles. The musty air made Brida sneeze.

Near the back of the room, Hush paused in front of a large rectangular object covered in a faded, dusty velvet drape. Glancing over her shoulder to make certain Brida was paying attention, she swiftly pulled the fabric aside to reveal another mosaic panel.

The missing section from upstairs.

Brida's breath hissed between her teeth as she saw the secret.

This panel showed a woman riding in the back of a cart pulled by a small brown donkey. She wore a white cloak embroidered with the triple moon—one waxing, one full, one waning—in silver: the symbol of a priestess, indicating sacred magic.

In her arms she held a baby swaddled in gray cloth, but misery was etched on her face.

On the right side of the image, a woman wearing a cloak of crow feathers and rage in her expression held a bolt of jagged black lightning in one fist, aiming it at the priestess.

And in the background, a woman in a cloak with a wide green band and three leaves on the chest stood with her arms outstretched, as if waiting to receive the baby.

Brida leaned closer, knowing even as she did so that it wasn't just a shadow or trick of the light.

The woman in the hedgewitch's cloak had a tiny mark beneath her right eye, identical to the scar on Mother Magdi's face.

And that meant . . .

Brida's hand shook, her blue glow-globe wavering.

Magdi and Moira were sisters, and . . .

Brida pointed to the priestess in the cart. The woman with Brida's face. "Her name?" she whispered.

Hush drew her finger through the dust along the edge of the frame.

Maigin, she wrote. *Your mother.*

TWENTY-TWO

Three Sisters

A LOW, EERIE wail reverberated through the cracked walls, but Brida was too shocked to react.

My mother's name was Maigin. She repeated it to herself, tasting the shape of the word. *Maigin. Mother.*

Magdi is my aunt. Queen Moira is my aunt.

The Queen of Crows was her *aunt*.

Brida stared at the scene drawn in tiny colored tiles, trying to make sense of it. Why hadn't Mother Magdi—*Aunt Mother Magdi,* a voice in the back of her mind shrilled wildly—ever told her?

That black lightning bolt in Moira's hand . . .

And then she started to understand.

Mother Magdi had said her most important responsibility was keeping Brida safe. That there was information she needed to share, but knowing it was dangerous.

Magdi had protected her. *Hidden* her.

Until Brida looked in a scrying bowl and the Queen of Crows herself looked back.

Brida pressed her fists against her eyes, sickness churning in her stomach. What had she done?

Maybe the queen hadn't gotten a good look. It had all happened so fast . . . maybe all she saw was a girl with magic peeking where she shouldn't have been.

Hush prodded her lightly in the small of her back, urging her up the stairs and back to the main level.

Brida let herself be pushed along, numbness spreading through her limbs. At least the Huntsman hadn't taken her to the castle. She couldn't imagine what the queen might have done. . . .

Bones had risked the queen's rage to save Brida's life, putting him and Bear and Hush in danger.

By the time she and Hush reached the boys, she was trembling.

Bear draped an arm around her, helping her to a seat on a pile of moth-eaten wool carpets. Bones plopped to the ground beside her, wrapping his skinny arms around knobby knees as he regarded her with worry.

Hush knelt gracefully and began speaking with her hands, hardly waiting for Bear to translate. "My mother and yours were priestesses here, in the Temple of the Crescent Moon. You and I were both Beltane babes."

Brida forced herself to breathe. Just as Rissi had promised, she was finally getting answers.

It just wasn't the story she had expected.

Before Hush and Bear could continue, a cry sounded

outside the walls and Brida flinched.

Bones patted her shoulder. "They can't get in here. We told you. It's sacred ground, even if it in't a Temple any longer."

Bear said, "It's a safe place to spend the night. We've done it before. Now let Hush tell what she knows."

Brida sucked air through her teeth and knotted her hands in her lap. She couldn't let fear distract her from the truth. "I'm listening," she croaked after a moment, the words clawing past the raw lump in her throat.

Hush wove more words with her hands and Bear translated. "You've heard about the threat of civil war if Lady Melianna didn't have an heir to hold her family's province, her desperate wish for a baby, and the three feathers cast by the Windwitch? You know of her three daughters born within moments of each other?"

"I've heard pieces. . . ."

"You know the old fireside tales saying that three girls, born on the same day in the same town, are all likely to wield strong powers?"

Brida nodded.

"Well, your mother, Maigin, was the morning child. She demonstrated talent for sacred magic the first time she was taken to the Temple of the Crescent Moon. She could remember every song, every . . ." Bear paused, scratched his chin, and tilted his head to the side. "Wait, what does that mean?"

Hush repeated the flicker of her fingers, then slowed down each gesture.

"Invo—oh! Invocation. Sorry. Your hands were moving too fast. Anyway, so Maigin could remember every invocation, incantation, and ritual nearly perfectly after hearing it only once. Even as a small girl she was wise beyond her years. People said she heard the whisper of the Great Mother. She knew things before they happened, could read the patterns of a person's choices in the lines of their palm.

"Magdi, the child of midday sun, showed a . . . Slow down! An . . . *aptitude* for green hedgemagic. She could coax an oak from an acorn faster than a squirrel could eat one, and seemed to know by instinct where any herb or wildflower could be found.

"Moira, though, was different. No one could deny that the night daughter was clever, but cleverness and wisdom are not the same thing. She had strong power, too, but not the practical kind that Magdi worked nor the sacred kind that Maigin studied. Even from the beginning it was something . . . darker.

"People started noticing . . . troubling incidents . . . around the manor: stones falling, ovens catching fire. Injuries that couldn't easily be explained. The cooks left. The maids left. And Magdi was left with a scar below her eye."

Brida caught her breath. "Moira did that?"

"Could've been an accident—we all know children collect bumps and bruises as easily as marbles—but Moira had been seen outside Magdi's room scarcely a moment before her window shattered."

Brida hugged her knees to her chest.

"When the sisters were nine, Lady Melianna took them to the top of the Veiled Cliffs to have their destinies read like every woman in that region of Fenwood Reach had done since memory began.

"Moira, however, wasn't interested in fate. She wanted more power—to control the elements, the magic of the seasons. She cut her hair and threw a binding spell, but the last Windwitch turned herself into an eagle and flew away. Lady Melianna forbade the sisters to speak of it. When they climbed down from the cliffs and returned to the old manor at Idlewild, she simply said the girls were destined to be remembered.

"A fortnight later, when the weaver and her daughter climbed the cliffs, they were greeted only by a soaring eagle's shadow. When the baker's wife and her daughter climbed the cliffs, they saw the same thing. And so did the next girls. And the next.

"There were rumors, then, about what had happened. And yet, despite the talk, no one was especially concerned. Everyone knew magic was a tricky thing, not to be trusted. Who could tell the ways of witches? Perhaps the Windwitch had simply grown tired of all the tangled hair.

"Maybe that winter came a little sooner than expected, and maybe the snow lay a little thicker. Maybe the ice snapped sharper and the wolves crept closer than usual, but every season carries its own surprise."

Bones shifted his weight and cracked his neck, but he listened as closely as Brida did.

"In time, though, the weather definitely began to shift. So slowly at first it seemed only a matter of . . ."

Bear frowned. "Wait, what's that mean?"

Hush repeated the movement of her hand, slow and deliberate. Then she added a flurry of other gestures and he nodded.

"Right. At first it was only a matter of curiosity. Something the old ones gnawed over as they sat in their rockers by the fire. But eventually things got so bad no one could deny that something had changed. The rhythm of the seasons had been broken, and there was no Windwitch to set it right again.

"Meanwhile, the lady's three daughters grew into great beauties, each in her own way. Maigin was pale as dawn light, with hair like spun silver and clear blue-sky eyes. Magdi was warm and golden, copper skin and chestnut hair and eyes the color of rich earth or tree bark. Moira's beauty, though striking, was stark and cold. Midnight hair, rose-red lips, and eyes as green as forest moss or pine shadows.

"As the girls grew, so did their abilities. Maigin was welcomed as the first new initiate to the Temple of the Crescent Moon in more than a generation. She learned to use her sacred magic to read the patterns of the stars, shift the tides of conflict, predict the rise and fall of king- and queendoms, and call on the blessings of the Great Mother and the Sky Father.

"Meanwhile, Magdi's hedgemagic drew seekers from across the realm. Her charms and remedies were stronger than those of any other hedgewitch, before she'd seen her eighteenth summer. She healed wounds, birthed babies, and brought luck and love to those who asked for help.

"But Moira . . . she was the quiet sister, the watchful one. She stayed in Idlewild after their mother died, but she wasn't content to be a lady. What no one knew, then, was that her powers fed off ambition, jealousy, greed, and anger—and she was growing stronger than anybody could have imagined."

A dank chill rose from the old stones. Hush shivered and Bear said, "Bones, grab the firewood Mason hid behind the altar. Go on. You've already heard this story, and it will only get colder before morning."

Bones opened his mouth as if to argue, but goose bumps pebbled his skin where his sleeves didn't quite cover his wrists. He jumped to his feet and hurried into the shadows.

Hush and Bear kept weaving the story together. "Things went on like this for a while . . . until King Malcolm sickened and a terrible drought sucked the life from the land."

Bones returned with an armful of dead branches, half-rotten boards, dried twigs, and the broken leg of a

276

bench. He dropped it with a clatter and disappeared again, presumably to gather more.

"Though the people had celebrated the spring festival of Beltane for generations—with colored eggs, ribbon kites, and rabbit races—it had been a long while since a priestess had been chosen as the Maiden Spirit, the heart of the moon and representative of the goddess. But this year, facing such terrible difficulty . . . the priestesses in the Temple of the Crescent Moon knew the ritual required something extra."

A thump and a muffled curse interrupted, and a moment later Bones came back with more wood. "Stubbed my toe." He scowled. "And I can't find the fire starter. Where's the flint?"

"Let me," Brida offered, carefully arranging the wood in a cone-shaped pile far enough away to avoid danger from flying sparks, but close enough to offer warmth. "Right here? Inside?"

"It's already been destroyed by the queen and her guards." Bear spread his hands. "Why not?"

"Very well . . ." Brida called a tiny wisp of magic, sending it into the dry wood until she felt it catch. A curl of smoke rose from the center of the pile, wavered, then steadied. A small yellow flame leaped from one of the branches and spread until a cheery blaze crackled.

All four of them held their hands toward the fire, relishing the warmth.

After a moment, Hush rubbed her palms together and resumed shaping her story.

Bear cleared his throat, scratched the side of his nose, and spoke for her. "They chose Maigin as the Maiden Spirit, thinking that her youth, beauty, and strong sacred magic would bring greater blessings to the—is that word *parched*? To the parched land.

"And because the king was ailing, his advisers sent his son, the handsome Prince Andri, to act as the Sun Lord, the spirit of the hunt, to bring not just fertility but healing and strength to both the land and the king—if the Maiden priestess agreed.

"Now, Maigin was nervous about what was to come, though she'd been well prepared and was willing. But after Moira saw the handsome prince, she was not content to sit outside the Beltane circle and watch her sister perform the sacred ceremonies.

"She stormed inside the Temple, demanding that the prince be allowed to name his own Spring Consort. She had convinced herself that, given a choice, he would pick her.

"The priestesses resisted—at first. After all, Moira had not studied the sacred magic. She hadn't earned her initiation and the right to wear the triple moon insignia. And besides, ritual tradition dictated that the Consort was selected by the Maiden and not the other way around. Maigin was the Maiden. The choice should have been hers.

"No one knows quite what happened then, what threats

278

or spells Moira wielded, but the next day the priestesses yielded to her demands. Prince Andri, Spring Consort, would choose his Maiden.

"And he chose Maigin. Moira flew into a rage. There were other young men who would have been happy to leap the sacred bonfires with her, to dance past midnight and wake in her arms, but Moira would have none if she couldn't have the prince.

"You were conceived that night, as was I. You were your mother's first Beltane baby, and I was mine's last. Nine months later, the Temple of the Crescent Moon welcomed us. We were supposed to grow and learn together within its walls, as was traditional. We might have been initiates ourselves.

"The drought might have relented, washed away by the magic of a mother's birth blood. The land might have recovered, healed by the power of new life. The Windwitch might have returned. But Moira's anger had seethed in the dark, where no one guessed what she was doing.

"She had discovered sorcery."

TWENTY-THREE

Princess of High Rock

AS IF CONJURED by the word *sorcery*, a series of skittering noises dimly penetrated the walls of the old temple.

Brida held her breath, listening to the scratching and scuffling. "What *is* that?"

Bear grunted and tossed another dry branch on the fire. Sparks swirled above them, cooling flecks of rising ash. "Mostly rats," he finally said. "Stray cats. Other things."

A scream pierced the temple's stillness and Brida lurched to her feet. Someone was out there. In the dark. Someone who might need help.

Clutching frayed shreds of courage, she staggered toward the temple entrance, prepared to—

Bear grabbed her arm and yanked her backward. "What are you *doing*?" he hissed.

"You can't go out!" Bones cried.

"Someone's out there!"

"That's not a someone. That's a some*thing*." Bear tugged

her to the fire and all but shoved her back onto the pile of carpets.

Brida's throat clicked on marbles of cold fear when she swallowed. "What do you mean?"

Bones flung another stick on the fire. "Revenants," he said. A burst of embers punctuated the word.

"The undead?" Brida shook her head. "There's no such thing. When a spirit passes from the realms of the living, the body that held it dies." Sometimes the spirit might be restless, it was true, but she wasn't going to say that when the three faces blinking at her across the flames were pale with fright already.

Besides, restless spirits were mostly harmless. A bit of salt and sage, maybe a pinch of lavender, and they'd find their peace. She'd seen Mother Magdi do it.

But Hush's hands flashed in the shadows, spinning silent words. Her eyes were grim, lips pressed tight.

"In the natural order of things, yes, the body dies. But the queen's magic has upset the balance. She knows she's losing her hold. The weaker she feels, the firmer she clenches her fist and the darker the magic she wields. That magic is like a poison. Or a plague. It spreads, pooling in forgotten places."

"She's not the rightful queen. The land knows it, and the people know it, too. Most are just afraid to admit it," Bones said.

"What do you mean, she's not the rightful queen?" Brida asked.

Bones cast a sideways look at Brida, an expression she couldn't read.

"Go on, Hush. Tell her the rest, unless your arms are getting tired?" Bear brushed her shoulder lightly.

Hush ran a hand through her hair, rubbed a spot on her cheek, and smiled. She patted his leg, then told him something with her hands.

Whatever it was, he blushed and wouldn't speak it aloud. He waited for her next gestures before resuming the story.

"Prince Andri stayed with Maigin during her pregnancy, and soon he announced his desire to wed her.

"The Temple of the Crescent Moon was reluctant to grant a blessing. It wasn't customary for a priestess to marry—especially not her first Beltane consort—though it wasn't forbidden. But he was the prince, and he was kind, and Maigin had grown to love him."

"Besides, the Temple knew a wedding would strengthen their bond to the throne," Bones added.

"Yes," Bear agreed and Hush nodded. "It seemed a good thing all around and the people rejoiced."

"Everyone except Moira," Bones interrupted.

"Do you want to tell it, then?" Bear growled. "Or will you hold your peace and let me and Hush do it?"

Bones pinched his lips shut and folded his arms.

"Three moons before you were born, Maigin and the

prince spoke their love oaths and exchanged silver rings beneath a bower of pink and white roses. The whole kingdom celebrated. Delegates even came from across the Five Realms to offer gifts of glass, silk, spice, and perfume.

"Only Moira was absent from all the festivities."

Brida scooted closer to the fire, stretching her arms and legs toward the crackling heat. A chill crept through her bones to gnaw at her heart, and the warmth of the flames did nothing to dispel it.

"The prince moved into Maigin's chambers to wait for the delivery of her Beltane baby—you—while she completed the last stages of her training. Then they planned to move to King Malcolm's castle on High Rock, near the Temple of the Seas.

"Magdi, meanwhile, embarked on a tour of the entire realm, accompanied by three royal botanists, a naturalist, and two elderly hedgewitches in order to improve her already considerable skills with green magic. It was a valuable chance to discover the different plants and animals across Fenwood Reach, an opportunity to collect rare specimens to use in her hedgemagic. She'd been reluctant to leave Maigin, but the priestesses promised to look after their own and insisted Magdi make the most of her journeys. She would only be gone for a moon or two, after all, and so the sisters parted.

"As the days passed, Maigin's happiness grew . . . but so did Moira's jealousy. When old King Malcolm died, Maigin and Prince Andri would govern the land. Moira couldn't stand to see that happen. She was tired of sharing everything with two sisters, tired of standing in their shadows. Idlewild wasn't enough. She'd learned to do things with magic that no one else had even attempted, and she believed that gave her a better right to rule.

"She had a plan, and she was willing to use her dark sorcery to see that it came to pass."

The clawing noises outside the Temple walls grew louder. Brida shivered, teeth chattering and muscles cramping as she tried to ignore the horror she couldn't bear to imagine.

Revenants, accidentally created by the contaminating effects of Queen Moira's wicked powers.

"You need to hear all of it," Bones said, moving closer and wrapping an old blanket around her shoulders. "Ignore the revenants—they can't cross sacred ground. We're safe here, I promise."

Brida gave him a wobbly smile, wishing she could believe it.

Hush's hands flew faster and Bear's words rushed as he tried to keep up. "When Magdi returned, sunburned and mud spattered and brimming with powerful new knowledge, she realized that Moira was plotting against their sister. Magdi wasn't certain what shape the threat would take, so she wove protection spells for Maigin and binding spells against Moira. She hoped her green hedgemagic would somehow stand against the dark force of sorcery.

"As the time of your birth drew closer, Moira made her move. She put a spell on the old king, forcing him to marry her. Then she gave Maigin's prince a beautiful robe of emerald velvet with a border of black crow feathers. It would've been rude to refuse, so he thanked her and slipped the robe around his shoulders. He died three hours later—cursed or poisoned, though no one could prove it—and left the old king without an heir.

"Maigin was heartbroken—and terrified that her sister might try to harm her baby next. Might try to harm *you*. The only person she knew with enough power to resist Moira was Magdi, so she asked for Magdi's promise to watch over you, to raise you, to keep you safe if anything happened to her. And Magdi agreed."

Tears burned Brida's eyes. Every time Dev and his friends had called her a stray, a foundling, a lost baby no one wanted, her heart had broken a little bit more.

But they were wrong. She'd been loved. She was *still* loved.

Hush's hands kept moving. Bear cleared his throat and continued translating. "The night of your birth, the old king died. To be fair, he'd been ailing for some time, so who's to say whether it was nature's clock or Moira's spells? But with his death, Moira claimed the crown.

"Maigin begged the Great Mother for justice. She sang the sacred prayers for protection and strength, and she asked Magdi and the priestesses of the Temple to help her perform a ritual of banishing to eliminate Moira's danger.

"But Moira was prepared. She had a ritual of her own ready, and she used her sorcery to turn the banishing back upon the circle of priestesses. Some of them went mad. Some simply lost their breath and died. The others . . ."

Bear waited for Hush to finish her thought. She twisted her fingers together and quirked her lips as if looking for the words she wanted, but after a moment she settled on a few simple gestures and Bear said, "They were turned to shadows and the Temple was broken."

"Shadows? Like the revenants?" Brida whispered.

Hush shook her head and responded with her hands. "Shadows like moon-moths," Bear translated. "Gone when the sunlight hit them."

"Oh, no . . ."

"But their spirits are the reason this ground is protected," Bones added.

Hush's fingers flickered. "Meanwhile, Moira was discovering that claiming a crown is not the same as keeping it. No one trusted her. No one *liked* her.

"But the people of High Rock had loved Andri, and if he loved Maigin they were ready to love her, too. They'd heard stories of Maigin's grace and beauty, her wisdom and kindness. A queen who was also a high priestess, a queen who knew the sacred spellsongs? She would be good for the realm, they knew.

"A Council of Lords was called, and with the support of the Temple of the Seas, they voted to withdraw Moira's crown and give it to Maigin instead, recognizing her royal right through marriage to Andri. You were named royal heir, Princess of High Rock, and a company of guards was sent to escort you and your mother safely to the castle.

"Once again, Maigin had been chosen over Moira, but Moira would never let her have the crown.

"You were three days old when Magdi hid you and your mother in a sanctuary deep in the wood. For nearly a fortnight, Maigin nursed you and regained her strength, waiting for her guards to come.

"But Moira was stronger even than they guessed. When the royal guards arrived and tried to seize her crown, Moira turned them into Hounds, forcing them to obey her orders. She sent Crows winging across the realm to spy for her. To punish the people of High Rock for choosing her sister over her, Moira destroyed the castle and the Temple of the Seas, scouring High Rock until nothing was left but bare stone.

"She moved to Rookery Point, built a castle, and made it the new capital city of Fenwood Reach. At first, people tried to resist, but her punishments were so cruel, her power so terrifying, that eventually they were forced to recognize her stolen rule.

"It didn't take Queen Moira's Crow spies long to find Magdi's sanctuary. Maigin sacrificed herself to shield you, and Magdi carried you away to keep you hidden. We never knew where, but my mother said she believed one day you would come back.

"And here you are."

A silence broken only by the snap and hiss of the fire settled over them. The scraping noises outside had stopped sometime during the story and chill darkness pressed against the wavering circle of firelight.

Bones stared at her with bright eyes. "Hush heard the Great Mother in her dreams, saying change would come with the return of a long-lost girl. But *I* found you. I could tell there was something special about you when I saw you in the square." He beamed, though Brida was too stricken to smile back.

Her chest ached as if she'd run too far too fast, or sucked in air too cold to breathe. As if she'd been kicked in the ribs by a horse. She pressed a hand to the pain and forced herself to breathe slowly, deeply.

"So, she's dead then," Brida whispered, mostly to herself. Tasting the loss.

Hush's hands flashed and Bear cast a sharp look at her, surprised. Then he cleared his throat and said, "Everyone believes so."

Brida's chin jerked up. "What?"

"Magdi deflected the killing blow with the assistance of one surviving priestess—my mother. Your mother survived the attack."

Curtains of black sparks swept across Brida's vision

and the world sloshed around her as her mind struggled to process what she'd been told. She pressed her hands to her head. *My mother is alive.* "But where is she?"

"Hiding in disguise until the queen's power is broken. That's all my mother said. I'm sorry—I wish I knew more."

Brida tried to swallow the sorrow in her throat but sobs spilled out anyway. She wrapped her arms across her chest, shaking helplessly as tears blurred her vision.

Magdi had let her believe, all this time, that she was a foundling. And though Magdi had offered love and comfort, the weight of that lie had pressed grief and loneliness deep inside Brida's bones. Even if it had been for her protection, the loss *hurt* and anger rushed through the wound in her heart like blood.

How could Magdi have hid something so important for so long? How could she have *lied*?

Rissi had told Brida not to be mad at Mother Magdi when she discovered the secret of her past. Rissi had known—or at least guessed.

Brida frowned, letting her anger spill away. No—Magdi had done what she thought was best. This wasn't her fault— it was Moira's.

Queen Moira had taken too much from too many. She *had* to be stopped, but if Mother Magdi and all the priestesses and all the other hedgewitches had already failed, what else could be done?

What could Brida do?

Bones leaned against her, rubbing her back. Hush and Bear moved in to hold her, a circle of unexpected friends.

At least she didn't have to face the truth alone.

"What happened to *your* mother?" Brida asked Hush, after she'd caught her breath and wiped her eyes.

Hush glanced at Bear, and then at Bones. A tiny frown weighed the corners of her lips, but she sighed and raised her hands once more.

Brida immediately regretted the question, realizing it might be a painful memory or a secret Hush wanted to keep. "I'm sorry. I didn't mean to pry. If you'd rather not talk about it, I understand."

Hush tipped her chin and raised one shoulder, as if to say she didn't mind. She resumed speaking with her hands, more slowly now.

Bear watched her face as much as he watched her hands, translating carefully. "My mother, Roana of Eastbrook, grew up with the three sisters and felt sorry for Moira before she knew what Moira was capable of. When Moira destroyed the Temple of the Crescent Moon, my mother—by design or accident—was the only priestess who survived.

"Before Magdi went into hiding with you, she asked my mother to stay close to Moira, to keep an eye on her and send occasional wingnotes by messenger pigeon. My mother agreed to do the best she could.

"She became one of the queen's most favored ladies-in-waiting. I spent my days in the kitchen with the servant children, but I spent my nights in my mother's rooms, in a luxurious apartment near the queen.

"My mother secretly taught me as many sacred songs and rituals as she could. I had a spark of sacred magic, you see—nothing as strong as Maigin's, but enough to make things happen. We kept it hidden, a harmless game between us. Then one day the queen caught my mother sending a message to Magdi's secret circle of hedgewitches. She . . ."

Hush pressed her hands to her face and tears spilled from her eyes. Bear wrapped her in a hug, smoothing her hair and murmuring in her ear.

After a moment, she straightened up, gave Bear a watery smile, and flicked her hands. "She killed my mother and sent a serpent made of smoke to steal my voice so I wouldn't sing the sacred spells ever again. I ran away, finding work here in Edgewood as a weaver's apprentice.

"She didn't know I survived. I met Bear and Bones, and we managed on our own until I grew careless and a Crow saw me. . . .

"That hex would have killed me if you hadn't come along." Hush reached out to touch Brida's wrist, and smiled.

"Thank you, Princess," Bear translated for her.

TWENTY-FOUR

Thistles and Revenants

BRIDA JERKED HER head at that word. *Princess*.

She wasn't a princess. She was just a girl learning how to use her magic and generally making a muddle of it. She wasn't even certain what sort of magic hers was. It didn't seem to be green like Mother Magdi's. Maybe it was white, like her mother's?

Was she meant to be a priestess?

Brida thought about the way the wind had answered her summons, but then a horrible new possibility occurred to her.

If she was the niece of a wicked queen, was there a chance she might have black magic, too? What if her power was sorcery?

No. It can't be. I want to help people, not control them. I want to free the stormhorses, not use them. I'm nothing like the queen. I refuse to be!

I can't let her catch me.

Casting about for something solid to anchor her spinning

thoughts, Brida asked, "How can we stop her?"

For a moment they stared at each other around the fire, flames reflected in their eyes. A bit of sap hissed and popped, a piece of charred wood collapsed.

"Well," Bones finally said, "whispers spread no matter how hard the queen tries to silence 'em." With a mischievous grin, he added, "I mean, I should know. I'm one that spreads 'em."

"I don't understand."

He tapped the flame-shaped badge on his chest. "I'm a messenger, aren't I? Folks are used to seeing me run here and there and near about, so a few words in the right ears . . ."

"What good are whispers and rumors against the Queen of Crows?" Brida asked, a twist of bitterness pinching her mouth.

Hush's fingers flashed and Bear translated, "Words have power."

"Yes," Brida conceded, "but the queen has *sorcery*. Her guards have *weapons*."

Bear interrupted, "Words can be weapons, too. People say Queen Moira stole the crown, and look what it brought. Frost kills spring blooms, drought kills summer crops, and fruit on the branch rots overnight. We're starving. Last year there were riots when the granaries ran empty and people tried to raid the palace gardens. Moira may be a sorceress and a queen, but she can't stop the things people think in the quiet of their own heads. People know she's to blame for the broken seasons and the dying crops."

"And where crops fail, thistles grow," Bones added fiercely.

"What does that phrase mean?" Brida asked. "I heard it in the square during the trial."

Bear and Bones exchanged a long look. "It's just an expression," Bear said.

Hush smacked him in the chest, tipping her chin toward Brida. *Tell her*, Brida thought her lips said.

Bear hesitated, and then he asked, "What do you know about thistles?"

Confused, Brida answered, "Well, milk thistle is good for digestive complaints and liver ailments, and blessed thistle can be used for—"

"Wrong question, Bear." Bones chuckled.

Bear huffed, "Thistles are weeds, right? Prickly and invasive. They choke out other plants and thrive on poor ground."

"Yes, but that doesn't mean they aren't useful." Although Brida had to admit her least favorite chore was digging thistles out of the pasture. It felt strange to defend them after all the hours she'd spent cursing their existence.

But Bear slapped a hand on his thigh and exclaimed, "Exactly!"

Brida blinked at him. She still wasn't sure what he meant.

Bones shook his head and grinned at Hush. "He does

better when *you* give him the words, eh?" Hush smiled back and patted Bear's knee.

"Listen," Bones said. Tendrils of smoke from the fire curled around him as he leaned forward. "For years and years no one could do anything against the queen. Like you said, she's got guards and spies and dark sorcery. But she concentrated on her own power and forgot to pay attention to what her people needed."

"And if you take too much from the land, it goes barren," Bear interjected.

Bones continued, "One by one, people started to defy the queen. Like thorns in her side, understand? In small, secret ways at first. Maybe they hid books or taught music or shared memories of what Fenwood Reach used to be. Maybe they traveled to other lands, looking for help. Her guards tried to enforce the rules, tried to make people obedient and loyal. But the harder the queen squeezed, the more determined we became. Anger spreads and resistance grows, just like thistles."

Brida caught her breath. "And you're the messenger. . . . That phrase is a code of some kind, isn't it? You started a resistance movement. A rebellion!"

"Mason Bolder started it. He contacted a few hedge-witches and started coordinating plans. I just helped spread the word."

"The Circle of Thistles!" Brida exclaimed. Mother Magdi must have been involved from the start.

"Food riots were only the beginning," Bear growled. "Soon we'll be strong enough to pull Queen Moira from the throne. There are more of us than she has guards." His eyes glinted as he looked from the fire toward Brida.

A pit opened in Brida's chest and threatened to swallow her heart. She'd seen a monster made of bone burst from the broken earth. She'd seen a creature of twigs crawl from a cleft in a tree trunk and watched a man—Mason Bolder, who thought he could stand against the queen—turned to a Hound by a leather collar. What chance did her friends have against Moira? The Queen of Crows was wicked and powerful and . . .

"She has stormhorses," Brida gasped.

The fire crackled in the sudden silence. Bones stirred the embers, laying another stick on top. Bear shifted his weight, opened his mouth as if to say something, and then swallowed.

Brida understood. It was hard enough to believe that elemental stormhorses of legend were *real*. How could they wrap their minds around the queen capturing a herd?

"But how did she even find the stormhorses? I thought they were a fairy story, a myth," Bones said.

"I don't know," Brida admitted. Magdi had told the Council of Wisdoms about a summoning spell she'd sensed. Was it Moira's? It must have been some strong, strange magic to draw creatures like the stormhorses to Fenwood Reach.

Bear drummed his fingers on his knees and scowled. "What do you reckon she intends to do with them?"

"Whatever her plans are, I'm afraid your thistles won't be strong enough to survive the stormhorses," Brida said miserably. "I felt their magic. It's wild and reckless and . . ." She shook her head. "It's dangerous." It was also gloriously beautiful, but Brida couldn't forget the destruction in Walnut Creektown.

Hush spoke with her hands. "Maybe Moira figures the power of the stormhorses will be enough to silence the protests, crush any rebellions."

"People still won't believe she's the rightful queen," Bones said.

"She doesn't have to be the rightful queen if no one can stand against her," Bear translated for Hush.

Bones fidgeted with his badge. "Maybe she plans to use the stormhorses to control the seasons."

Brida's ears buzzed with a swarm of sharp, stinging thoughts. The hunger in the market, the desperation of people with nothing left to lose . . . *Was* it possible the stormhorses could help? Not if they were controlled by a woman who would kill for a crown, but . . .

Without the Windwitch, something *had* to bring things back in balance.

But she'd seen the wreckage in their wake. Too much weather magic was just as devastating as not enough. And Mother Magdi had been very clear that the magic of the stormhorses was not for them to use. "If Queen Moira can access that kind of elemental power," Brida warned quietly, "it's hard to say what she might be capable of."

Bear said, "Then we need to make sure she can't."

Brida nodded. "Somehow I must get word to Mother Magdi. We'll find a way to free the stormhorses." She rubbed a hand across her face. "And then we'll figure out the rest."

Bear stood and stretched. "It's about time Magdi came back to Rookery Point, anyway. She has to see what her sister is doing. We could use her help."

Guilt kicked Brida in the stomach and she wrapped her arms around her knees. Mother Magdi had worked so hard to protect the valley towns. . . . Brida had seen refugees and had known—distantly—that other places weren't so fortunate, but she hadn't truly understood the danger of their daily lives. "I'm sorry," she murmured, gazing blearily into the fire.

Hush frowned at Bear and he shrugged. "What? I know Magdi was just trying to keep Brida safe, but Brida's here now, too, right? If only Mason hadn't been caught. He could have sent a wingnote."

Brida raised her head. "Where are his birds?"

Bones shook his head. "The guards took all his pigeons and destroyed the coop. We'll have to find some other way of contacting Magdi."

Hush spoke with her hands and Bear repeated, "That's a problem for the morning. We need sleep." He yawned. "And

I've got to be up early. Master Smith will expect me to stoke the forge."

After everything that had happened, everything she had learned, Brida was desperate to see Mother Magdi again. But she couldn't argue with the need for rest. She helped Hush bank the fire, piling bits of broken stone around it to keep the embers safely contained. They arranged the dusty remnants of carpets and curtains in a circle of makeshift bedrolls and listened to the silence pressing against the Temple's darkness.

Hush was the first to drift into sleep, Brida guessed by the slow, steady rhythm of her breaths. Bones was next, curled on his side and softly snuffling.

"Brida?" Bear whispered, so quietly she assumed she'd only imagined it. Then he repeated her name. "Brida?"

"Yes, Bear? What's wrong?"

"I just wanted to say thank you. For . . . Hush, and everything."

"I'm the one who should be thanking you. You all saved me from the Huntsman, and gave me the truth of who I am. You—"

A light snore told her that Bear had fallen asleep, too.

Brida closed her eyes and tried to relax, but she couldn't let go of the worries gnawing at her. She tried taking slow, deep breaths, but the musty air clogged her nose. *Home* smelled like horsehair and saddle leather and Magdi's soap—not cold stone, forgotten candle wax, and moth-eaten fabric. She missed the warm, earthy comfort of cedar and straw thatch, herbs and apples, roses and clover.

She twisted on her side. *You will need all your energy and wits tomorrow*, she told herself. *You need to sleep!*

But she still couldn't settle in.

She hadn't given Burdock his evening brushing, or tossed him his hay, or pressed her cheek against his neck to whisper good night. Where was he right now? Was he safe? And what about Nettle, and the chickens, and the cats, and the dove?

A sudden wind screamed past the Temple walls and an answering surge of magic blew through Brida's body. *The stormhorses.*

This might be her chance to help them.

Brida leaped to her feet as wind poured through cracks in the masonry, the gaps in the old arches and windows, the splintered timbers and broken doors. It gusted around the vaulted space, sending cyclones of dust and debris and still-warm ash spinning in the corners.

She couldn't rein it in—it was a rush of power and panic, fear and fury.

The white mare.

Without pausing to think, Brida flung herself toward the vine-draped entrance of the Temple. She *had* to help the stormhorses. She had to keep their magic out of the queen's grasp, otherwise her friends' rebellion would be crushed before it finished taking root.

"Brida! Wait! You can't go out there!" Bear shouted, but the roar of magic in her ears was so loud she barely heard him.

She plunged outside, whipping her head back and forth as she ran to the end of the alley, trying to sense which direction the stormhorses were galloping. If she could just—

The wind died as abruptly as it had risen, taking the surge of Brida's magic with it. She sank to her knees, chilled and shaken.

She understood immediately what had happened. The Huntsman had captured the last two stormhorses.

Queen Moira had the entire herd.

Gulping air, Brida stared up at a sky swirled with glittering stars. *Which way?*

If she could just calm her heartbeat and slow her breathing enough, maybe she could sense the thread of magic affinity that bound her to the white stormhorse, follow it to the captive herd . . .

A pebble clattered in the shadows behind her. To her right, something scuffed the ground. Ahead of her, a whisper of movement, the soft hiss of something racing past . . .

The back of Brida's neck prickled and magic shivered a warning across her skin. She rose to her feet, spun in a circle.

A pale shape shuffled around the corner while another drifted into a pool of shadows.

Revenants.

She turned and sprinted back toward the Temple entrance. Bear and Bones hung out of the doorway, frantically beckoning her. "Run!" Bear shouted. "Faster!"

She was one stride from safety when a rotting figure with a ruined face loomed out of the night murk ahead of her, blocking her way. Brida screamed and lurched backward, nearly shoving herself into the grip of another one of the creatures. A third shambled toward her from the mouth of a collapsed building.

She conjured a blue glow-globe in her palm and held it above her head, hoping the light would frighten the figures away.

All it did was show her in stark detail how terrified she should be.

Their faces leered at her, flesh falling away from too-sharp cheekbones while dull, cloudy eyes rolled in sunken sockets. Shriveled lips peeled back from rotting teeth and wisps of hair barely clung to scalps so mottled they looked like mossy boulders.

"Don't let them touch you!" Bones yelled. "Their touch is death!"

Bear had grabbed an ax—a massive thing, with a polished wooden haft and a gleaming edge—and stepped over the threshold of the sacred boundary.

The closest revenant made a sound like a hiss and moved toward him.

With a ferocious swing, Bear hacked the revenant's head

off and it dissolved into a sickly mist. Turning to the next, he shifted his grip on the haft and prepared to swing again. "Hurry!" he called.

Hush and Bones grabbed Brida by the arms and hauled her back inside the Temple.

"What were you thinking?" Bear growled, plunging after them. "You could've been killed!"

"The stormhorses," she panted. "The last two stormhorses. The Huntsman caught them."

"And what did you think you'd accomplish by running out there?" Bear scowled. "You can't help anyone if you let yourself get hurt!"

Brida hung her head. She *hadn't* been thinking. She'd been reckless and impulsive, just as Mother Magdi would've said.

And it could have cost her friends their lives, too.

"Brambles and thorns," she muttered. "I am a walking menace. Everything I do is a mistake."

Hush led her back to her pallet beside the fire—now dying in a scatter of weak embers and charred wood chips. Bones set about stacking fresh kindling while Hush and Bear held a hasty conversation too low for Brida to hear.

"I am so sorry," she said miserably. "I just . . . The stormhorses. I *felt*—"

"Hush says there's no need to apologize. We are all unhurt, and that is what matters," Bear said gruffly.

Bones tossed a branch on the pile of glowing coals he'd

scraped together and blew on it, coaxing a bright flame back to life. "There," he said, rocking back on his heels and dusting his hands. "That'll last a while. Back to sleep now, eh?"

Brida groaned. "Sleep?"

"We'll talk more in the morning," said Bear.

Brida lay down and listened to them drop into dreams one by one, but the fire had dwindled to a red glow before she finally closed her eyes and followed them.

TWENTY-FIVE

The Third Feather

BRIDA AWOKE TO a crick in her neck and the taste of ash in her mouth. The fire had gone out and she was cold. Blinking sleep from her eyes, she sat up and tugged her cloak closer. A gray morning light filtered into the old Temple, glittering off dust motes hanging in the air.

Hush stirred sleepily in a pile of old blankets beside Brida. It was hard to guess how sick she'd been just the day before.

Hard to imagine how long ago yesterday could seem.

Brida thought about the queen's spies, about the hex and the magic she'd used to lift it. What would Moira do if she knew who Brida actually was?

Just then Hush opened her eyes and smiled. Brida couldn't help smiling back.

Maybe fate had a reason to draw her and Hush together: two Beltane daughters, in the Temple of the Crescent Moon where their mothers had worshipped the Great Mother of All.

Bear stirred, groaned, and mumbled, "Forgot how bloody uncomfortable it is in here."

Hush grinned and flickered a response back with her fingers. By the arch of her brow and the dimple in her cheek, Brida could tell she was teasing him.

"I know, I know," he grumbled. "I'd be a lot more uncomfortable if I'd awoken to the feel of a Hound's teeth or one of the queen's Crows flapping in my face. But still. Someday I'd like to sleep in a proper house again."

Brida cleared her throat. Plucked the frayed edge of the drape she'd used as a blanket. "Um, you could . . . you all could come with me, maybe, back to Oak Hollow? Mother Magdi would love to meet you. And, Bear, if you like working a forge I know Goodman Smith would be happy for—"

He stared at her with a strange expression on his face. She flushed and looked away, cursing herself for being foolish. Why had she assumed they would even want to leave? They barely knew her.

She just wanted to know they'd be safe.

"Never mind," she said, ears burning. "It was only an idea."

"Nah, it's just you're a prin— Wait. Where's Bones?"

Brida glanced to the pile of rugs beside her and froze when she realized Bones wasn't curled up inside them. "Bones?" she shouted.

"Eh?" He scampered in, holding a small paper parcel. "What's wrong?"

"You scared the sap out of me! Where were you?" Brida cried.

"Woke up early and decided to scavenge us some break-fast. See?" He unwrapped the parcel proudly, displaying a handful of wrinkled crab apples, dried berries, a small round of goat cheese, and a loaf of hard bread. "But the best part is . . ."

With a flourish, he produced a waxed paper twist that held a small piece of honeycomb.

"Bones, you are brilliant!" Bear thumped him on the back. "I'll fetch some water."

Hush slipped from her blankets and stood, beckoning to Brida. Hoping Hush would show her where to relieve her bladder, Brida hastily rose and followed.

Hush led the way to a makeshift latrine behind the Temple. After they'd finished, instead of turning back the way they'd come, she took Brida to a sandy courtyard par-tially obscured by thick climbing vines and a thorny hedge.

Hush held a finger to her lips and grabbed a stick. Kneel-ing, she smoothed a flat space in the sand with the side of her hand and then used the sharp end of the stick to write: *My voice?*

"You want me to restore it," Brida murmured.

Hush nodded emphatically and wrote: *Please*.

"I can't make any promises, other than to try my best."

Thank you, Hush wrote, eyes shining.

"Don't thank me yet. I don't know if I can do it." Brida

didn't even know where to begin.

Hush rose and tossed her head as if to prove her unconcern, but Brida grabbed her arm. "I am serious," she said. "This is a great risk. I don't know what could happen if I make a mistake."

Hush shook her head and smoothed the patch of sand. *I need my voice to sing.*

"The spellsongs."

Nodding, Hush erased the words and wrote: *Our magics together. Free the horses. Find your mother.*

Brida chewed her lip. She'd felt the power of the spellweave she and Mother Magdi had wrought with Rissi and knew that blending magics could have a far stronger impact than working with one alone. Maybe she and Hush really could—

Hush tapped her foot and Brida looked down, seeing more words. *Then we face Moira.*

Hush swiped the sand clear and wrote in large, firm letters: *PLEASE. I NEED MY VOICE.*

"Girls? What's taking so long? We're ready to eat!" Bear called. He jogged around the corner and stopped when he saw the words in the sand.

"No," he said, helping Hush to her feet. "It's not safe." He practically tugged her back inside the Temple. "Come on. Bones has got the food spread."

She yanked her arm away and turned back to Brida. *Please,* she mouthed.

"It's too dangerous." Bear scowled at both of them.

Yes. For the queen, Hush mouthed.

Brida studied her. "You understand the risk?"

Hush nodded, eyes fierce as a warhawk's.

"Then I'll try."

"If you restore her voice," Bear said, "the queen will be even more determined to silence her forever."

"The queen hasn't exactly left her in peace as it is, though, has she? You know words hold power, Bear. We were talking about it last night! Even ordinary words, even ones that can't build spells or carry invocations or start revolutions. It's not right to keep that from her. She deserves to speak."

"She *can* speak. She *does* speak. We're the ones that just need to understand better."

Brida said, "That's true. And you do a wonderful job of translating. But she'll still need you even if you aren't her voice anymore. If there's a chance I can give her back the power to speak out loud, for herself, don't you think I need to try? It's what she wants."

Hush reached up, pressed her hands against his cheeks and held his gaze. *My choice*, she mouthed.

He sighed and looked away. "I'm just worried."

"Me, too," Brida admitted. "But I owe her the attempt."

They returned to find Bones tearing off pieces of bread. "Did you get lost out there?" he quipped, but Bear just grunted.

Brida gratefully took the piece of bread he offered.

"The crab apples are a bit puckerish, but if you eat them with cheese and honey they taste pretty good," Bones said, pouring dried berries and crab apples in her palm.

"Thank you," she said, mouth already full.

Brida was still licking crumbs from her fingers, pondering Hush's voice and the stormhorses, when Bear stood and said, "I've gotta run to the smithy to light the forge fires. Stay here until I get back. I'll let you know what I find out about the Huntsman."

He adjusted his cloak and tucked his ax into a belt loop. Hush gave him a quick hug before he hurried off.

Bones wiped his hands on his pants. "I asked around some this morning, but everyone laughed when I mentioned stormhorses. Told me to go back to my nursery and listen to my stories there. I couldn't find anyone who might have spotted them yesterday—or if they did, they wouldn't admit it." Frowning, he said, "If the Huntsman took the stormhorses back to the queen's stables at Rookery Point, it might be impossible to free them."

Brida rose and paced a lopsided circle around the remains of last night's fire. "We *have* to find the herd. They're the embodiments of elemental energies. Rain, snow, sun, wind, and thunder—can you *imagine* what the queen might do with that much power?"

Hush leaped in front of her. With a fierce scowl, she mouthed, *my voice!* and pointed to her throat.

"I know. I promised I'd try, but we have to hurry. I still need to send word to Mother Magdi someway, and I'm afraid we're running out of time."

While Bones swept up the cold ashes and gathered up the blankets, rugs, and moth-eaten drapes they'd used as bedding, Hush and Brida ducked into one of the small arched spaces.

Sunbeams sliced through cracks in the stone, sending slanting rays of dust-glittered light across the floor. Hush sat down and crossed her legs, an expectant look on her face.

But Brida wasn't sure how to begin. Lifting the hex had been difficult enough. How could she return a voice?

She reached for hedgemagic out of habit but immediately knew she wouldn't be able to make it work for this. She simply didn't have the necessary skill.

Maybe she could try to wield sacred magic—white magic—like her mother. After all, Rissi and Agathe had sent her to the broken Temple to explore the mysteries of her past, but what if there was another truth to discover?

"Hush," she whispered, "can you help me work white magic? Do you know the words of a spellsong that might—"

But Hush was already shaking her head. She mouthed, *Not your magic.*

"My mother—"

Doesn't work like that.

Brida sighed. She knew that magical ability wasn't a legacy to be inherited like land or titles, that even though magical tendencies might run in families, there was no way to predict who would have the talent or how it would manifest. But she'd hoped sacred magic might be a connection with her mother.

Well, if she couldn't use white magic and if her green magic wasn't strong enough to restore Hush's voice, the only chance she had was to call the wind again. If she could.

Spreading her fingertips until they prickled—like the static crackle of cold, dry air or the tingle of blood after the hand has fallen asleep—she spun wisps of energy and tried to summon the wind.

Nothing happened.

Raising her arms, she focused her will and strained to catch a breath of air, a wisp of breeze, *anything.*

All she succeeded in doing was lifting a single strand of hair off the back of her neck.

It had been so easy, so instinctive, when she used the wind to banish the hex on Hush. She couldn't understand why it wasn't working now.

Maybe if she could sense the stormhorses, she could somehow use her link with the white mare to draw the wind back to her. . . .

She closed her eyes and *stretched* her mind, but all she felt was a muffled absence. A blank expanse where she'd expected to feel the rush and tingle of wild magic.

What was wrong with her? Surely she should have recovered her strength by now. . . .

Had one of the revenants touched her last night? Had it killed her magic? Was it the feathermark again?

Suffocating panic sucked the air from her lungs.

Breathe. Think. Maybe the stormhorses are too far away. Maybe the silver rope the Huntsman used to catch them or the silver halters the queen forces them to wear severed the magic connection, but you can still use the natural wind. You just need to try outside.

"I can't feel my magic in here," she admitted to Hush. "We need to step outside the Temple."

Bones had finished clearing away their little camp and was tucking a small knife into a hidden sheath, not paying attention to them.

Chewing her lip, Brida stepped from the Temple's shadows into oppressive heat and stillness. The silence was so heavy it squeezed a dull ache from her temples. It was almost like the ominous moment before a storm breaks, though the sky was cloudless.

Dread slid down her skin like the beads of sweat already dampening her tunic. Everything felt *wrong*.

Bones had said the dying priestesses had sanctified the Temple grounds, but how far did that protection extend? He said the revenants couldn't enter, but could they somehow break the barrier?

Brida trudged farther from the Temple ruins, clambering across a pile of rubble near the back of the building. Hush followed, anxiously twisting her hands as Brida cast her senses through the air, seeking a whisper of wind. But her breath seemed to tangle in her chest until it was a tight knot between her ribs. Gasping, she collapsed as if her bones had suddenly grown too heavy to support their own weight. Fear blurred her vision.

What was happening?

Desperate now, she gritted her teeth and clawed for any strands of energy she could reach—sunlight, dew, solid earth. But they slipped from her grasp as color leached from the ground, as the sun seemed to dim and the earth trembled. At the edge of her awareness the white mare and the herd of stormhorses screamed.

It took Brida a long, panting moment to understand.

She was too late. The queen controlled the stormhorses and had already found a way to tap their energies.

Struggling for breath, Brida became aware of a vague thrumming in the ground. A heartbeat later the triumphant call of a Crow split the air, followed by a burst of barking.

The Huntsman and his Hounds had found her.

"Go back inside!" she yelled over her shoulder at Hush. "Stay with Bones!"

Desperate magic rose in her blood, then sputtered and died before she could weave a defense.

She'd failed the stormhorses. She'd failed Hush. She'd failed her mother.

The Hounds burst into a rubble-strewn courtyard just outside the Temple grounds, dragging the Huntsman's wheeled dogsled to a screeching halt. He leaped out, face a thundercloud of fury.

Brida considered fleeing back inside the Temple, but what sanctuary could it offer now? She was already trapped, and she needed to keep her friends safe.

One of the Hounds growled and the Huntsman called, "Come now, little mouse. The Hounds are hungry and I can't promise they won't treat your friends like their next meal."

"Brida don't—" Bones started to say, dashing from the Temple shadows, but another Hound snarled and stepped closer.

"Let's not have any trouble," the Huntsman said.

He didn't want to hurt her, Brida knew. But he would, if he had to.

Bones thrust a hand in his pocket—reaching for his knife, Brida assumed—but Hush laid a hand on his arm.

The Huntsman said, "If you come willingly, I'll forget I ever saw your friends here."

Before Brida could react, the Crow gave a loud cry. A black feather fell like a scrap of night sky and landed on her shoulder.

TWENTY-SIX

Crow Wings

A BURST OF black and scarlet pain blinded Brida. She tried to scream a warning to Hush and Bones, but the breath rattled in her throat and her tongue couldn't find the shape or taste of words.

The ache intensified, folding her body along lines she couldn't have imagined. Her muscles stretched, tore, shrank and re-formed as liquid agony surged along her veins and blazed across her skin. Her bones bent or broke or simply melted away, but she hurt too badly to care.

And then the pain vanished, like a flame suddenly doused.

Air rushed back into Brida's lungs and her heart thumped, lurching into a rhythm no longer familiar to her. What had happened?

She opened her eyes.

Blinked. Blinked again.

Tried to shake her head.

The world tilted oddly, and everything loomed too large

above her. She saw colors she couldn't name, layers and layers of color, with sharp edges and crisp corners as if the air had turned to glass.

Sounds assaulted her in a dizzying rush: the whisper of a mouse's claws in a gap between the Temple's cracked stones, the scurry of beetles beneath the grass, the rustle of worms through the earth, and the flutter of a moth's wings somewhere out of sight.

She breathed in and drowned in a sea of mingled scent: the sweet tang of green growth, the dry must of ancient stone, the rich warmth of dried wood, and the smells of old smoke and cold ash.

The salt tang of sweat and fear, the smell of herbs and soap.

Hush and Bones.

As her thoughts snapped back into focus, Brida cast her eyes around desperately for her friends.

There. Staring at her with twin expressions of grief and shock.

Staring *down* at her.

Struggling to raise herself, to stand and walk, Brida found herself flailing—

Wings. *Wings.*

She hopped and fluttered helplessly in the middle of her discarded clothing as understanding slowly dawned. Her consciousness wove its way through this new shape, in and around hollow bones and gloss-black feathers.

Brida had been turned into a Crow.

She tried to cry out, tried to yell for Hush and Bones to *run*, but when she opened her mouth—her beak!—the only sound that emerged was a harsh and ugly croak.

"Crawwwwk!" Run. Hide!

Brida needed to get away. She spread her wings and tried to launch herself into the air, but her mind couldn't comprehend her new form and all she succeeded in doing was flopping uselessly on the ground.

Trying again, she fanned her tail feathers, raised her wings, and prepared to leap—only to have a small metal cage slammed around her as Bones cried, "No!"

A calloused hand shoved her inside and latched a little door shut. She was caught.

Brida fluttered and squawked in a panic, but the Huntsman prodded her through the narrow bars of the cage. "Be still," he warned.

She nipped his finger and he gave the cage a shake. "I mean it. Don't agitate the Hounds."

Then he bent down and picked up an eagle feather on the ground. He twisted it in his fingers, tilted his head to the sky, then glanced at Brida before dropping it again.

Sighing heavily, he said, "The queen has her horses. If you'd just stayed hidden . . ."

He rattled the cage and she stumbled, knocking a wing against the side. She glared at him, but he studied her with sharp intensity. "Your magic has called the attention of every Crow in the queen's realm. She's desperate to meet you. Not a mouse any longer, hmm?"

Feathers ruffled, she snapped at him.

"Please understand, I had no choice." He whistled shrilly, the sound piercing Brida's skull.

She cowered in the wire cage, hating her vulnerability and helplessness.

But when the pack of Hounds answered his call, loping toward him with their mouths gaping and their tongues licking frothy saliva from their muzzles, Brida suddenly appreciated the meager protection the cage offered.

Especially when one of the Hounds growled and snapped at her. As he lunged, she caught the iron-copper smell of fresh blood and the rank stench of rotten meat gusting from his crooked teeth.

The Huntsman kicked at him. "Bones and ashes! Unless you want to learn what happens to Hounds that can't be trained, you'd best follow the rules."

The Hound cowered and licked his muzzle, but hate flared in his eyes and Brida knew he couldn't be trusted.

What happens to Hounds that can't be trained? she wondered, and then decided she didn't want to know.

Brida's cage was loaded on the dogsled and piled with furs, canvas sacks, and the tunic, leggings, and boots she'd been wearing.

The Huntsman shouted a command and the Hounds took off, racing out of Edgewood and—Brida assumed—toward the capital city.

She could barely see out of her cage and after a while she gave up trying. Tucking her head beneath her wing, she closed her eyes and tried to conserve strength and energy. She had a feeling she would need both before much longer.

She must have dozed because when she next opened her eyes the quality of light had shifted. Rich amber beams slanted beneath the pile of wool and fur on top of her cage and dazzled her sight.

Brida sipped the air and wondered if she could still work spells.

She tried to stir a little magic, just a whisper, but the effort left her sick and dazed. Though she could *feel* the power in her bones, a muffled heaviness held it down.

She tried to talk herself out of panic.

Mother Magdi and the Circle of Thistles couldn't be that far behind. Hopefully Bones would bring them word of her capture.

In the meantime, Brida would learn everything she could about the queen's plans. Maybe the information she collected could help the resistance.

Unless, of course, the queen killed her first.

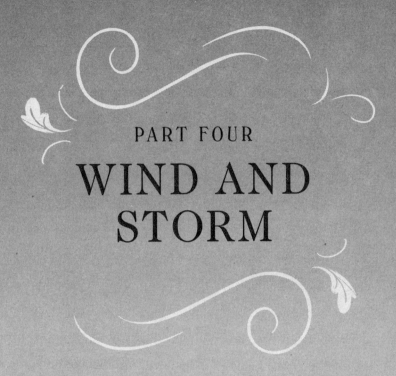

PART FOUR

WIND AND STORM

TWENTY-SEVEN

Queen of Crows

BRIDA'S FIRST IMPRESSION of Rookery Point, the capital city, was stink and sound and shadow.

The sun had slipped past the point of high noon by the time the Huntsman steered his dogsled through the massive wooden gates guarding the main road into the castle complex and then beneath the heavy iron portcullis protecting the inner courtyard.

He jumped down from the back of the dogsled where he'd been riding and two sullen-faced boys with sunken cheeks immediately ran up, bowing their heads. They took the harnesses off the Hounds and led them to a long, low building Brida assumed held the kennels.

As terrifying as some of the Hounds were, the thought of men forced to live as dogs sickened her.

Of course, she was a girl in a birdcage, which was no better.

The Huntsman lifted her cage from the sled and tilted his head to stare at her. "Listen, I just need you to know that this isn't—I mean, I never meant to—"

"Bring this to your rooms, my lord?" a man in black livery called, hefting a travel-stained and weather-worn satchel.

The Huntsman sighed and gestured acknowledgment as he strode toward the palace doors, leaving Brida blinking in confusion.

She tried to look around, but every time the Huntsman jostled the cage it started swinging, making it hard to focus on details. All she caught was a blurred, dizzy sense of soaring gray stone and dark iron.

And then she was being carried down a long corridor dimly lit by smoking torches; past a row of grim banners depicting battle and blood; through a vast open hall; and up a narrow, curving staircase. Servants in black hurried past, heads down and eyes averted. Guards stood at attention, faces blank.

Brida's entire body vibrated in fear.

The Huntsman reached a door carved with strange symbols, feathers, and fangs. He pounded it with his fist, and a moment later a stiff guard with a black feathered plume on his helm opened it. Seeing the Huntsman, he saluted and stepped aside, announcing, "The Huntsman is here, Your Majesty."

"He may enter," a silken voice announced.

The Huntsman marched through the door, Brida's cage swaying queasily in his grip.

The same woman Brida had seen in her scrying bowl

days—a lifetime!—ago rose from the velvet couch she'd been reclining on and gracefully adjusted her satin gown. The fabric was an indigo so dark it looked nearly black until she moved, and then flashes of blue streaked the skirt.

Moira, Queen of Crows. Brida's aunt.

She wasn't wearing her feathered cloak, but three black feathers had been clipped in the coils of her dark hair, blending in so perfectly a casual observer might not notice they were there. Her green eyes were cold as pine frost and there was something stern in the set of her lips.

The Huntsman knelt clumsily, knocking Brida's cage against the smooth marble floor.

The queen stepped forward. Brida felt the weight of Moira's gaze and fluffed her feathers uncomfortably.

"So," the queen finally said. "What is her power?"

The Huntsman shifted but did not rise. "I'm sorry, Your Majesty?"

"Her *power*. What can she do?"

"I . . . I do not know, Your Majesty. She's just a girl. Your feather found her, so I brought her with me."

The queen clicked her tongue. "Just a girl? And yet she managed to escape you and all your Hounds. I sensed magic in Edgewood I have not felt in many, many years. So. Tell me again. What power does this girl have that she could so cleverly evade my keenest Crows, my best hunter, and a pack of my specially trained Hounds? She must have *some* skill . . . or else you've become so lazy and lax in your attention that you just let her wander away. In which case . . . what use would you be to me then?"

Brida saw the sudden beads of sweat that sprang to his brow, saw the tremor of his lips and the twitch of the muscles in his jaw.

"She's quick, Your Majesty," he said. "I do not know enough of magic to say, but I do know she's clever and quick."

"Hmm." The queen turned away, pacing to the window at the back of the room and then spinning toward them again. She crooked a finger, allowing the Huntsman to stand though he kept his head bowed.

Brida held herself still, relieved the queen didn't seem to know who she was yet and desperately hoping she could keep it that way.

"Quick and clever I can use, that's certain," Queen Moira said. "But I can't understand how she managed to avoid the binding of the feathermark. . . . It has never taken three feathers. Never." Her voice was low, as if she spoke mostly to herself.

She snapped her fingers and the Huntsman handed her the cage.

Brida bobbed her head and spread her tail feathers for balance as the queen raised the cage to her face.

Moira leaned close, her breath smelling of wine and roses and something bitter as she said, "Why did it take three feathers to turn you into a Crow, I wonder?"

Brida clicked her beak. *I don't know. But now I am one, so you can just ignore me. . . .* At least until she could figure out how to fly away and turn herself back into a girl.

With a wave of her elegant hand the queen said to the Huntsman, "You have Hounds to tend. You are dismissed."

He bowed and hurried out without meeting Brida's gaze.

The queen tapped her lips with one perfect nail and smiled slowly. "Let us see what we're dealing with, shall we?"

She flung open the cage door and grasped Brida in a strong hand. Brida desperately flapped her wings, but with one quick motion the queen plucked a feather from her tail and blew on it, letting it drift to the ground. At the same instant, she opened her hand and dropped Brida.

For one blinding moment, Brida fell. She expected the shock of impact, the crush of fragile bones, and threw her wings wide in panic, fluttering helplessly. But instead of rising, she grew heavier.

When the pain came, it wasn't what she'd expected.

It pierced her body, striking sparks of agony along her bones until she couldn't breathe. She was being stretched and twisted and torn apart, and all she could think was, *This isn't how I'm supposed to die!*

"Breathe, girl. Breathe," the queen said.

Brida gulped air and the pain evaporated.

She opened her eyes, blinking past the shimmer of involuntary tears, and discovered she was back in her true shape, standing on shaking legs and wrapped in a flimsy black dress. The abrupt rush of relief, however, was quickly replaced by the realization that the queen could see her face.

Moira, Queen of Crows, would know exactly who and what Brida was.

Brida shivered—partly from the chill, but mostly from fear—and dropped a curtsy, keeping her chin tucked and eyes down.

Silence thickened, an invisible fog reaching clammy fingers down Brida's throat to steal her words.

After a long moment, the queen pressed a fingertip beneath Brida's chin and lifted her face, turning it from side to side as her venomous green eyes traced Brida's features.

She recognizes me.

"So," Moira murmured. "My Crows told me they had found a girl with strong magic. You're the one I saw in the scrying bowl, aren't you? What is your name?" Sharpening her voice, she added, "And do not lie to me, for I shall know if you do."

Mother Magdi had given Brida lessons in building mind-shields and protecting her secrets.

Be as honest as possible, the hedgewitch had instructed, *but hold what you must close to your heart. Fool the inquisitor with illusions and imaginary memories. If you are focused enough, they will never see the deception, for who is to say which thoughts are real and which are false but you?*

Did the queen know who Brida really was? Or was she just trying to decipher how much Brida already knew? Either way, the uncertainty felt like standing on the edge of a precipice while the ground heaved beneath her feet.

"My name is Brida," she admitted. A dark whisper brushed the edges of her mind, seeking the lie.

"And where are you from?"

Again that feather-light touch, that shadowy intrusion. But Brida couldn't speak the truth, because if she named Oak Hollow, the haven Mother Magdi had worked so hard to build would be destroyed.

So she gambled. She built an image in her mind of a small, secluded town surrounded by rocks and pine trees and said, "Pine Bluff."

"What is your mother's name?"

"I do not know for certain," Brida said, filling her voice with all the regret and insecurity she used to feel when thinking of her missing mother. She layered it with remembered taunts, Dev's endless songs and cruel tricks. All the times she'd been called a foundling, a lost child, a stray.

"Ahhh," the queen breathed, though Brida couldn't tell what she was thinking. "Someone took you in, then?"

"Yes. And made me an apprentice."

"Who?"

"The Millers," Brida lied, making up an imaginary couple. But her mind spun memories of the bakery, warm and fragrant with the scents of sugar, cinnamon, honey, and yeast. She pictured the baker's hands covered in flour, apron strings tied in a neat knot.

"You're a baker's apprentice?"

"Not a very good one, I'm afraid."

"Hmm. Well, perhaps you need better instruction. Would you like to work in my kitchens?"

Brida answered with as much enthusiasm as she could muster, "Oh, yes! That would be lovely! But I would not want to disappoint you. . . . Goody Miller said I wasn't fit to feed the chickens."

The queen regarded her with cool appraisal. "I suspect your true talents simply weren't recognized. Is there a hedgewitch in your town?"

"Oh, yes! She keeps jars of leeches on shelves in her pantry and a bowl of eggs to crack in water when someone is ill. She can see what's wrong with them by the shape the yolk takes! It's like magic."

Brida wrapped her response in earnest enthusiasm, concentrating on gossip she'd heard of old Goody Luckitt from Springbrook Junction, west of the valley, who called herself a hedgewitch though she had even less magic than a blackfly. The best that could be said of Goody Luckitt's remedies was that they were largely harmless.

The queen turned away, pacing back to the window.

Brida's tongue tingled with the effort of blending half-truths and outright lies, but she couldn't relax her guard yet. The queen's sharp interest kept her alert.

"Were you tested for magical abilities?"

Brida could answer this one honestly. "No," she said. She never had been—Mother Magdi had always been sure

Brida possessed the talent. She'd skipped directly to her Greenleaf exams—which she had failed. Twice.

"And is there a Temple in your town? A priestess?"

This, too, Brida could answer with the truth. "No, Your Majesty. The Temples were closed long before I was born, I think. We celebrate the Eight Sacred Days, and we have a special place in the woods for important ceremonies like handfastings and so on. But mostly folks are too busy to concern themselves with religious matters. I heard there was an old priestess once many years ago, but when she died there was no one to take her place." She carefully concealed any hint of Rissi in her mind.

"Have you ever wanted to see a Temple?"

"Why would I, Your Majesty? I was told they were dangerous places." What was Queen Moira trying to ferret out with these sharp-fanged questions?

"Smart girl. And now . . . I'd like you to indulge my curiosity for a moment."

"Certainly, Your Majesty," Brida answered in a cheerful voice, but her stomach rolled uneasily. The queen was setting a trap, she was sure, but what form it might take she couldn't guess.

"Come with me."

The queen swept from the room, collecting a wake of servants and guards as she proceeded down a gleaming onyx corridor. Oil lanterns hung from wrought-iron sconces in the shape of tree branches, but so much sunlight poured from glass panes set into the ceiling that they were unlit.

As they passed a set of wide wooden doors covered in carvings of feathers, an old man with stubbled cheeks and a scar trailing the length of his neck burst into the hall and sketched a hasty bow. "Your Majesty, the missing Crow has returned."

"Ah! Very good. Let us see what she knows." Beckoning Brida forward, the queen threw open the heavy doors, releasing a cacophony of croaks and calls that abruptly fell silent.

Brida's ears were left ringing in the sudden quiet and her stomach spun like a leaf in the wind.

The queen led her inside a vast chamber with a vaulted ceiling. Straw covered the floor and the walls were bare stone, with niches cut at regular intervals. Iron hooks protruded from each niche, holding suspended cages.

Most of the cages contained gleaming black Crows. They shifted their weight from foot to foot, the stench of fear thick.

Sickness seeped up the back of Brida's throat.

"My Rookery," Queen Moira murmured to her, the words hard as iron.

Near the center of the room stood a small scarred table and on its surface a bedraggled Crow hunched as if in pain. Scraps of faded cloth were tangled around one foot.

Oh, no. Brida recognized the fabric and knew this was the Crow that had burst through the window after she lifted the hex on Hush.

Raising her head, the Crow fixed a dazed eye on Brida's face.

She recognizes me. What if she tells the queen everything I've done?

Brida swallowed a lump of misery as the queen stalked to the table and lifted the exhausted Crow. Cradling her in both hands, Queen Moira said, "What do you have to say?" Then she tossed the bird into the air, plucking a feather from her tail at the same instant.

The Crow shrieked, a sound like the squeal of rusty iron against stone or the splintering of dry wood. It flayed Brida's nerves and she clenched her teeth.

A black cloud, glittering like starlight on a dark pond, swirled around the Crow. It circled faster and faster until Brida couldn't even see the bird anymore—and then a pale shape emerged from the cloak of shadows.

A trembling girl stood before them in a flimsy black tunic, auburn hair swinging past her lowered face in a curtain. She crossed her arms over her chest and shuddered as the sparkling black dust evaporated.

Bear and Bones had nearly broken the neck of a *girl*.

Brida almost retched.

Bloodied scrapes marked the girl's ankles, and when the queen raised her chin with a slender finger Brida saw more cuts along her cheeks. She'd injured herself on the broken glass.

"What happened? What did you see?" Queen Moira demanded.

The girl's gaze fluttered to Brida and then down.

Please . . . Brida couldn't even finish the thought. Fear drummed so loudly in her ears she could barely hear the girl's shaking voice.

If she ran now, how far could she get before the queen's guards subdued her? Hopelessness numbed her muscles.

"I sensed the magic residue in the Narrows, just as you suspected, Your Majesty. But I saw no sign of the one who had cast the spell. While I was investigating, a couple of gutter boys grabbed me and threw me in a barrel. I escaped before they could wring my neck." Her voice broke and she coughed.

"The other Crows mentioned two girls with the boys?"

"I'm sorry, Majesty. I was in a barrel and saw nothing."

"You did well to escape. You may spend the next three days in your human shape. See Mistress Crofter for salve to put on those scrapes."

The girl bowed her head, but when the queen had turned away her eyes flickered to meet Brida's gaze.

Brida nodded to her, a quick acknowledgment of the risk she knew the girl had taken, a gesture of gratitude.

Maybe she had an ally in the castle. Maybe together they could find their way out.

"Come, Brida," the queen called, already gliding from the room.

TWENTY-EIGHT

The Apothecarium

BRIDA'S LEGS TREMBLED as she followed. What would happen to her now?

At a fork in the corridor, the queen dismissed all her attendants and ushered Brida along a private hall. "Tell me," she said, "where my Huntsman first found you."

When Brida swallowed, it felt like choking on ash and feathers. She didn't want the queen to know she'd been following the stormhorses, didn't want to say anything that might lead back to Mother Magdi or her friends.

She raised her chin, smoothed her face, and spun a lie. "I was on my way to see a dear friend. She could be my sister, we're that close. And she's getting ready to speak her love oaths in a fortnight, only she hasn't got a ma, either, so I've been helping her with all the linens and things she needs for her bridal trunk. Goody Miller said I could have the time off, and she even gave me my own sewing kit with new needles and everything," she chattered glibly.

"Only then I heard a terrible howling and barking, and

suddenly a pack of the most ferocious hounds I'd ever seen surrounded me, snarling and snapping. . . . A crow flew overhead, I remember, and a feather landed on my hand. The Huntsman saw it and said I had to come see you."

"And didn't you *want* to come to the castle? Isn't it an honor to be summoned before your queen?" The words were as cold and sharp as winter ice, and as dangerous.

"Oh, I did!" Brida said breathlessly. "And it *is*." She dropped a curtsy, as proper as she could make it. "I only ran when we got to Edgewood and I saw that man turn into a Hound, and he looked so fearsome, and I just . . . I just panicked. All I could think of was getting away from those big teeth."

"I can understand why that would frighten you."

"Yes! I didn't even think. I just fled until I found an abandoned building and then I hid."

"And who helped you? Surely you didn't spend a night alone and afraid."

Brida saw the trap and dodged the question. "Who would have helped a stranger like me? Who could I have trusted?"

"And are you glad to see me now?"

"Oh, for certain, Your Majesty! Only it's all still a bit of a shock, isn't it? I mean, I was supposed to be embroidering daisy chains on kitchen towels and now I'm walking with the queen!"

"Fate has a way of surprising us, doesn't it?" The queen

paused before a heavy wooden door with bronze hinges and a carved border of leaves, ferns, and wildflowers twining along the edges. "I'd like to show you my apothecarium," she said. "But before we step inside, I have just one more question."

Brida nodded, fighting to keep her face blankly eager the way she imagined the girl she'd invented would look. *Daisy chains on towels?* It was the best she could come up with.

"Tell me, Brida . . . how did you learn to scry while working in a bakery?"

For one perilous second Brida lost all her words and could only blink. And then she coughed, cleared her throat, and said, "Scrying?"

"I saw you in the bowl. I want to know how."

"I thought you looked familiar, but I wasn't expecting to see the queen in my mixing bowl, was I?"

"Who taught you?"

Brida clasped her hands and put a contrite mask on her face. This was an easy half-truth to tell. "It's only a trick I learned one day when I was scrubbing pots. I was tired and just letting my mind wander while I swirled the water about, and then I saw one of the neighbors taking his cart to market like I was peeking through a window. After that I did it every now and then when I got bored. I didn't mean any harm by it, I swear."

The queen's eyes scanned her face, and then she nodded.

"Well, Brida, I believe I found you for a reason. You have an unusual ability, and I can teach you things you would never dare to dream. Come, let me show you my apothecarium."

Brida had expected the queen's apothecarium to feel like Mother Magdi's green room, filled with the sun-sweet tang of dried herbs and humming with the warmth of deep earth magic. But as soon as the queen opened the door, a seething energy poured out—something dark and strange, cold and creeping. It wrapped Brida in a buzzing haze that made her teeth ache.

It felt like trouble.

She hesitated at the door, but the queen urged her inside with a firm hand at her back. She had no choice but to enter.

Where are you, Mother Magdi? Why didn't you warn me that the queen was your sister? What am I supposed to do?

Sturdy wooden shelves lined two walls, displaying an extensive assortment of glass bottles and jars. Like the ones in Magdi's cottage, these bore written labels and contained various seeds, petals, crushed leaves, dried stems, powders, and distilled essences. A mortar and pestle waited on a table near the far wall beside a cauldron and a wooden spoon. Melted candle wax had cooled in colored puddles along the table's surface and burn marks scarred one end.

"What do you think? It's taken me many years to build my collection. You'll find herb specimens here that no one else could find, from the farthest reaches of the known world. Spices traded from across the great sand deserts, and sap from the frost forests near the frozen north."

Hush said she poisoned Prince Andri. If she poisoned my father, does she mean to poison me, too?

Brida swallowed the sick feeling sloshing in her stomach and tried to look suitably impressed. "Truly, I've never seen such a variety."

Stepping lightly toward the table, the queen said, "Since you're here, would you please find me the vervain? It will be in one of those." She pointed to a row of wicker baskets along a lower shelf. They were filled with dried bundles of leaves and stems, but there were no labels.

Brida bit her bottom lip. If she identified the vervain, would the queen know she lied about who she was? If she didn't, would the queen punish her for disobedience?

It felt like a game she couldn't win.

She glanced at the baskets, hands trembling. She knew vervain, had memorized its magical properties and healing uses. She knew where it grew and when to harvest the leaves for greatest potency . . . but she couldn't recognize it. All the herbs in the baskets looked the same to her: faded greenish-brown, dry and crumbly.

"Go on. I just need a pinch or two." The queen turned back to the cauldron on her table, picked up the spoon.

Heart hammering, Brida stammered, "I am sorry, Your Majesty, but I do not know which is the vervain. We don't bake with it, and I don't see a label on any of the baskets."

The queen glanced up. "Oh? Well, never mind then. Fetch me the book from the chest beneath the window."

Relieved that the queen didn't seem angry or disappointed, Brida turned to obey. But as she approached a heavy wooden chest bound with brass and leather, a flickering light along the floor snagged her attention.

A violent red-and-purple glow traced strange shapes in the air at ankle height, and something about their design told her she did not want to step over any of them. The symbols writhed like snakes or salamanders, ominous and predatory.

Noticing her sudden stillness, the queen looked over at her. "Is there a problem?"

Brida twisted her hands. "I . . ." What could she say? *I see glowing shapes and I am afraid to walk through them?*

The queen laughed.

As Brida gaped at her, she clapped twice and the twisting symbols disappeared. "Ah! I thought I sensed strong potential in you, just as my Crows said. I was not wrong, though it's clear you have no hedgemagic."

"I . . . Wait, what?"

"Come along." Queen Moira swept from the room, forcing Brida to jog in order to keep up. "You must be hungry. It's nearly dinner, and we can speak over the meal."

She crooked a finger at one of the girls waiting near the end of the corridor. "Ninn will show you to your room and help you dress, then take you to the dining hall. You shall sit at my table. I have a surprise for you."

Ninn was silent until they were well out of earshot of the queen. "You passed her test then, eh?" she finally murmured.

Brida stammered, "Test?"

Pausing near a dim stairwell, the girl hiked up her black skirts to reveal a livid mark around her ankle. "I haven't got the magic, but I do what I'm told so she lets me stay a girl rather than a bird." She dropped her hem and continued walking.

"So . . . if you don't have any magical abilities, why are you here?" Brida asked, fumbling for words that wouldn't sound insulting.

"Why did I get myself turned into a Crow in the first place, you mean?" Ninn gave a sharp, sour laugh, lips twisting as if she'd sucked a lemon slice.

"A piece of bad luck, that was. Apparently, one of my younger sisters has the talent. And I'm the one that used to mind them, so. I didn't think nothing of the feather when I saw it spinning through the air—I just caught it to show my sisters. Next thing I knew, I was flapping myself toward the castle just as fast as the wind and my wings could carry me. Didn't have a choice about it, neither. I tried turning back for home, only I couldn't."

Ninn gave her lemon-pucker laugh again. "And wasn't she surprised to find a Crow like me, who couldn't tell magic from a belch in the wind?"

Brida found herself grinning back at Ninn. "What happened then?"

"Well, the queen realized her Crow scouts—the ones supposed to find girls like you—had made a mistake. She sent them back out for whichever of my sisters actually has the magic instead of me, but my ma happened to see me poof into a bird. Apparently she packed everybody up and moved away, and far as I know none of the Crows has found 'em yet."

"But the queen won't let you go?"

The girl shrugged. "Where would I go? Ma's up and left, and who wants to hire a girl marked as the queen's own?" She kicked her foot out from under her hem, flashing those strange marks again. "Anyway, it's not so bad as long as you do what the queen wants."

"What about the other girls?"

"You mean the ones that are still Crows?"

Brida nodded.

"Well, some of them are being punished for different reasons," she said, turning down a side corridor and lowering her voice. "And some of them are good at picking up magic in other girls, so the queen keeps them as scouts."

Ninn glanced at Brida with something like pity in her eyes. "Every now and then she finds a girl like you, with strong magic. She'll keep you as an apprentice."

Unless she kills me first, Brida thought, wondering what surprise the queen intended for her at dinner.

Ninn showed Brida to a small set of rooms near the top of a tower at one corner of the palace. The door opened into a sitting room with a faded couch in front of a fireplace. A tiny writing desk stood in one corner and an archway led into the bedroom.

Brida eyed the narrow bed draped in gray curtains, a chest of drawers, a tall wooden wardrobe, and a tarnished mirror hanging above a china washstand and basin. It all looked clean and comfortable enough, but a cage was still a cage.

Ninn pointed out a narrow door. "Toilet's in there. Mark of the queen's favor—you get your own privy closet. If you need to use it, I'll lay out your clothes for dinner."

As Brida watched Ninn open the wardrobe and rustle through hanging gowns in shimmering colors, she wished she had been left as a Crow—it might be safer than dinner with the queen.

TWENTY-NINE

Spell Glyphs

AFTER BRIDA HAD washed with cool water and soap that smelled of moss and spiceflower, she was given a white gown trimmed in silver scrolled embroidery at the hem and neckline. A wide ribbon belt cinched her waist.

She smoothed her hands across the rich silken fabric and twitched when the full skirt swished around her legs. It was a far cry from her usual shabby tunic and leggings and it felt like wearing someone else's skin.

Ninn put her hands on her hips and tipped her head. "Pity your hair's so short," she lamented, "else I could braid it up fancy."

For the first time in her life Brida found herself worrying about how she looked as she glanced at herself in the mirror.

She'd been teased by Dev and his lackwit friends, but somehow she'd never thought to question her *appearance*. She kept her hair chin-length because it was easy and didn't tangle too much in the wind. She wore a tunic and leggings because she could hop on her pony and ride whenever she wanted.

She had so many reasons to feel inadequate—how she looked just hadn't counted among them. Now she chewed her lip and wondered what people saw when they regarded her.

And she wondered why that should matter.

But it *did* matter, didn't it? Not because of whether she looked the part Moira expected her to play—whatever that might be—but because she had her mother's eyes, chin, nose. . . . Were there people here who had known Maigin, other than the queen? Did anyone remember her?

Hush had said Maigin was still alive, somewhere—just in disguise. Was she nearby? Would she and Brida ever manage to find each other?

In the end, Ninn simply dried Brida's hair with a rough cloth and then brushed it until it shone before sliding a silver headband behind her ears with a white rose clipped to one side. "That will have to do. At least your complexion is lovely—those freckles are charming. Now hurry—the queen hates to be kept waiting."

Cramming her feet into satin slippers that felt too insubstantial to be called shoes—oh, she missed her soft leather boots!—Brida hurried after Ninn, trying not to trip over her skirts.

By the time they reached the doors of the dining hall, Brida's stomach was too knotted with nerves to be hungry.

She balked at the doors like Burdock when he didn't want to walk into the barn.

Ninn pressed a hand against the small of her back and all but shoved her in.

A man in a black vest announced, "The queen's guest: Brida of Pine Bluff."

Heads turned to stare, eyes landing on her like stinging wasps.

From a table on a dais at the far end of the room, Queen Moira stood and spread her arms in welcome. "Come, join me." Her voice rang like a bell.

A warning bell.

Brida forced her trembling legs to carry her past the tables of whispering faces, down the length of the room, and up onto the dais. She curtsied to the queen and was shown to a seat at the queen's right hand.

As she was about to sit, however, the queen took her by the hand and announced, "I am delighted to present to you my long lost niece and heir, the Princess Brida Corwinus, fostered these many years and returned to us at last."

The silence was so loud it almost hummed in Brida's ears. Her knees wobbled.

The queen had called her *niece*, and *princess*. The queen had recognized her, just as she feared.

She opened her mouth to deny it, but the words powdered like stale crumbs before she could speak them. After all, what could she say? Her own face told the truth.

If the queen intended to kill her, Brida just hoped it wouldn't hurt. She hoped Burdock wouldn't miss her too much and that her friends would stay safe.

Tears gathered behind her lashes and she blinked them away.

I'm sorry, Mother Magdi.

But Queen Moira wore a wide, triumphant smile. "I trust that you will make her feel welcome. There will be ample opportunity for you all to get to know her in the days to come, and a formal ceremony soon. Now, please, enjoy your meal!"

She squeezed Brida's fingers and indicated that she should sit. "You, too, child. You'll feel better after you've eaten."

Dazed, Brida practically collapsed into her chair. A servant immediately stepped forward to offer a goblet of chilled water scented with lemon and rose, while another draped a white linen cloth on her lap.

Brida thanked them and then saw by the queen's face that she should have remained silent. The others in the room pretended the servants were invisible, but Brida couldn't help offering a grateful smile in return for a bowl of creamy pumpkin soup and a plate of roasted turnips and greens. She declined the baked chicken and the stewed venison, the thinly sliced ham and the pigeon pie, however.

"A wise idea," the queen murmured. "Rich food must be tasted gradually, else it may upset the digestion and we have much to discuss."

Brida almost said she didn't eat meat, then wondered if this was another test. She couldn't risk saying anything that might put Mother Magdi in danger.

The weight of secrets sank in her stomach.

"This must seem so strange and sudden to you," Moira said, crooking a finger at a servant. When he hurried over, she said, "Fetch the stuffed mushrooms and herbed rice for the princess."

Brida almost protested—she didn't want to be an inconvenience, and she'd lost her appetite anyway—but the queen's expression was so cool and forbidding she couldn't summon the courage to speak.

"You are probably filled with questions. I'm sorry we didn't have the chance for a longer private conversation this afternoon. All you need to know, child, is that I've been looking for you for a very long time."

The servant returned with a tray for Brida, bowing low as he placed two dishes on the table before her. He darted away without ever glancing at her face.

"Try the rice. It will settle your stomach," Moira said.

A flicker of unease danced in Brida's belly. What sort of herbs were in it? Yet with the queen staring so pointedly at her, and the itchy weight of all the eyes following her every move, she had no choice but to take a tiny bite.

Surely the queen wouldn't poison her *now*, before the entire court, after publicly introducing her?

Brida swallowed and it felt like forcing pebbles down her throat.

"Yes, my dearest Brida. I have been looking for you for a *very* long time. In fact, I'd almost given up hope that you were still alive, until I saw your face through your . . . *mixing bowl*, was it?" She gave a short, harsh laugh.

"And even then I hardly dared to believe. . . . I convinced myself I'd been mistaken, since I caught only the briefest glimpse. But there can be no doubt now. You are the very image of your mother."

Brida set down her fork. What did Queen Moira intend to do with her?

Moira sipped her wine, splashing a couple of drops on the table when she set her goblet down. "You would have been too young to remember, but I am your mother's sister," she said, tracing a smoothly manicured nail through the spill. "She was a priestess in the Temple of the Crescent Moon."

Brida blinked, her surprise unfeigned. She hadn't expected the queen to offer the truth so openly.

"Did you know *I* closed all the Temples?"

How was Brida supposed to answer? She took a sip of water, watching the queen warily over the rim of her goblet.

But Moira didn't wait for her response. "It's true. And it's because of your mother." She dragged her finger back and forth through the wine, drawing some sort of pattern.

Brida's eyes followed the design, the hum of voices in the hall blurring. She was *so* tired. It was hard to focus on the queen's words, even though she knew she must.

"She had strong magic—oh, yes, you would have been so proud of your mother!—but she was too meek, too gentle, to control it," the queen continued, still tracing symbols in the spilled wine.

"One night she accidentally conjured a nightrider and he breathed his darkness into her mind, unbeknownst to us. In the months that followed, he used his wicked influence to shape her actions, to corrupt her rituals, to drag her spirit into the realm of shadows though her body walked the earth. The nightrider used your mother to turn the Temple of the Crescent Moon to darkness and evil."

That couldn't be true! Could it? Brida shook her head, dazed.

The mingled smell of wine and herbs and perfume, candle wax and silver polish, roasted meat and woodsmoke clogged her breath. She couldn't think straight. When she glanced away from the queen, she saw a sea of pale faces and staring eyes and open mouths.

A nightrider. A *demon*.

Magdi had warned her about the dangers of sorcery and spirit summoning, but she'd never told Brida that her own *mother* might have tangled with such powers. Of course, she'd never spoken to Brida about her mother at all.

Had Hush been wrong? Or was she caught in demon magics, too?

Brida's head spun.

Moira laid a hand on her arm. Brida's muscles quivered beneath that cool touch, her eyes drawn back to the strange pattern the queen had made in the wine on the table.

"I didn't want to believe it, either," she said softly. "For too long I ignored the signs, pretended I couldn't see what was happening. But when she became pregnant with you, I could no longer deny the truth. I knew that you were in danger, so when the demon took your mother, I arranged for you to—"

The door at the end of the hall burst open and a gust of wind swirled in. It blew through the room, snuffing out candles and tossing skirts.

It rippled across the table on the dais, smearing the symbols written in wine.

Brida rubbed her face, the queen's last words floating in her ears as everyone else's attention flew to the messenger who had appeared so suddenly.

The torn hem of his cloak was mud-stained and dirt smudged his forehead when he yanked off his cap to bow, but Brida was distracted by a white dove circling the sky behind him, framed in the open door.

"Your Majesty," he said. "I apologize for the interruption, but I have urgent news."

The queen clicked her tongue. "We shall continue our

conversation tomorrow, Brida. I imagine you are exhausted. When you have finished eating, Ninn will show you to your proper quarters." She swept down the dais toward the messenger.

Brida's eyes followed the dove, her thoughts slowly clearing. *No.* The queen was wrong. Brida knew in her bones that her mother was kind, and wise, and good. She would swear it by bud, bloom, and branch.

The dove flew away, and Brida glanced back at the smear of wine on the table.

Those symbols . . .

She suddenly guessed what they were. Spell glyphs. *Sorcery.*

The queen had lied to her, and had tried to use dark magic to make Brida believe it.

— THIRTY —

Circle of Thistles

THAT NIGHT, BRIDA couldn't sleep.

Ninn had taken her to a different suite of rooms near the queen's, richly furnished and lavishly decorated. A carved wooden bed piled high with a goose-down mattress and soft blankets beckoned her weary body, while a fire crackled comfortably in the stone fireplace. But the queen's lies had jangled her nerves and she couldn't settle.

Her teeth ached with the taste of magic, and the hum of distant power seethed in her blood. Was the queen working a spell?

The entire castle seemed saturated with traces of Queen Moira's dark magic.

Brida paced the floor, head throbbing. It could just be the stress of the strange situation she'd found herself in, but a buzzing sense of something *wrong* grew stronger.

Images of the bone monster that had attacked Dev, the twiggy tree-creature that had clutched at her in the woods, and the revenants near the broken Temple of the Crescent

Moon haunted her. Queen Moira's sorcery was like a toxin infecting the realm, waking nightmares. And now, with all the power of the stormhorses in her grasp, what terror would she wreak next?

Brida walked to the window and pressed her forehead against the cool glass. She stared into the moon-silvered night. Her rooms were near the top of a tower and below her she could just make out a patchwork grid of stone-walled courtyards and gardens. Flickering torches cast eerie shadows in the corners and danced across a cluster of buildings huddled near the castle. One must be a smithy—the ring of hammer on anvil echoed loudly enough for her to hear even up here.

She still couldn't quite believe that the stormhorses were trapped somewhere nearby. She was *this close* to a herd of legends. It was as if she'd stumbled into one of the Voice's stories.

But she needed to find the stormhorses and free them—for their own sake and the safety of everyone in the realm. And this might be her best chance.

Was the queen keeping them in the castle stables? Could Brida get there without being seen?

A gust of wind moaned past the window, igniting her urgency.

She flung a cloak around her shoulders and shoved her feet into the closest shoes she could find. They weren't boots, sadly, but at least this pair had leather soles and a buckled strap to keep them from slipping off her feet as she ran down the stairs.

Keeping to the shadows, she raced along empty corridors. She didn't know where she was going; she just followed the drumming impulse in her blood.

As she neared the main hall of the palace, the sharp sound of synchronized marching feet stopped her. Pressing herself into a dark corner, she held her breath and hoped the guards wouldn't come too close. After a tense moment, their heavy boots moved past her and out of earshot.

She crept down a crossing hallway, then caught a murmur of voices and flattened herself against the wall near a gilded door left ever so slightly ajar.

"They call themselves the Circle of Thistles," a man was saying.

Brida's ears pricked. The hedgewitches helping the resistance . . . Curiosity compelled her closer and she sidled nearer the door, holding her breath.

"How many?" the queen snarled.

"I'm not certain, but your sister seems to be the leader."
Magdi.

There was a sharp thump, like something thrown in anger. "Where are they? What are their plans?"

"They can't be more than a few leagues away, Your Majesty, but we haven't had any luck infiltrating the group. I can't say what they intend to do. Have your Crows—"

"The Circle of Thistles has woven some sort of ward

spell. The Crows can't get close enough to be of any use." Rapid footsteps swept toward the door and then away, as if the queen paced the chamber.

"What would you have me do, Your Majesty?"

"Take a company of guards and the Huntsman's Hounds. Track the Circle down and bring me every stubborn, stupid hedgewitch so I can erase them once and for all. I should have done this years ago. I'm tired of their meddling and I refuse to let them interfere with my plans any longer. If they're so fascinated by my stormhorses, they can experience the power of the herd for themselves." The guard's response was lost beneath the ripple of her cruel laughter.

Dizziness sloshed through Brida and she staggered away. At the end of the corridor she leaned against a pillar to catch her balance and her breath, knowing that the smart thing to do would be to hurry back to bed where she belonged and also knowing that she couldn't do it.

Mother Magdi was in danger. *All* the hedgewitches were, and without them Brida didn't think the thistle rebellion could survive.

Her friends, everyone she cared about, would die.

Brida chewed her lip. She had to warn Mother Magdi and the Circle of Thistles, but the likelihood of finding them in the dark before the guards or the Hounds did was a weak gamble. Unless . . . what if she scried?

Mother Magdi would be furious with her for taking the risk, Brida knew. Moira had already seen her through the veil of scrying once, and if she caught Brida doing it again the price could be her magic or her life. But the thought of hiding in safety while Magdi and the hedgewitches faced desperate danger twisted Brida's stomach.

She couldn't keep wearing the queen's fancy clothes and eating the queen's fancy food and sleeping in the queen's fancy rooms without doing something to help the people she loved.

Maybe if she was quick enough, careful enough, she could connect with Mother Magdi before the Queen of Crows even noticed.

Maybe a little distance from the castle would conceal what she was about to do.

Gulping air and beginning to shiver, Brida rushed down a side hallway that ended in a narrow door. A guard sat beside it, chin tucked to his chest and breath rattling in his throat as he slumbered.

Clenching her teeth, she crept past the guard and laid a cautious hand on the door. It swung open soundlessly.

Brida darted through, discovering a weedy, haphazard garden enclosed in a low fence. Pausing beneath an overgrown arbor covered in creeping vines, she tried to catch her breath. She had to find a fountain or a pool, some still puddle of clear water. There must be one somewhere in the castle gardens, but she needed a secluded spot that might offer some protection from notice.

Heart hammering, Brida hurried along the crooked,

uneven path into a labyrinth of thorny hedges. She was afraid to conjure her blue glow-globe in case it drew attention, but then, it wasn't really necessary. Despite casting the world in stark black and silver shadow, the moon offered just enough light to see.

She threaded her way through the labyrinth, disappointed there was no fountain in the center, and ducked out of a gate. A trail of crushed rock gleamed in the moonlight until it dwindled under a copse of heavy-limbed trees.

A Hound howled in the distance. Had he found the hedgewitches already? She ran as fast as she dared, letting the pull of the wind guide her past a ragged herb garden and a bed of dying roses. *Take me to water,* she begged, thinking of the way she'd found the creek near the Huntsman's camp days ago.

Wind whispered in her ear, drawing her down a fork in the path toward a grove of willows. Echoes of baying Hounds chased her into the trees and a sob rose like a thundercloud in her throat.

If she was too late, all was lost.

But there beneath the willows was a small spring-fed pool, gleaming in a pale shaft of moonlight. Brida flung herself to her knees on the mossy bank and stared at the glinting silver surface of the water. There was no time to count to three, no time to wait. She had to *see.*

Emptying her mind, she strained for a glimpse of Mother Magdi and prayed she wouldn't encounter Moira or one of her Crows instead. She poured her magic into the pool as dark mist clouded her vision. Suddenly, she was enveloped in stinging pain that prickled her skin and burned like . . . like falling into a patch of thistles.

The harder she tried to connect, the worse the sensation became until she was practically grinding her teeth in agony.

She rocked back on her heels and let the night air cool her flushed and sweating skin. Queen Moira had said something about the Circle of Thistles casting a ward spell. . . . Was this it?

Relief slowly calmed her racing heart as she considered Mother Magdi's power. Magdi had protected Oak Hollow and all the towns of the valley for so many years. . . . Brida shouldn't have worried about her shielding abilities.

But then another Hound howled and a wind gust shook the willow branches, and Brida remembered the way the blight by Maple Hill had broken Magdi's protective charms. Mother Magdi was the strongest hedgewitch Brida had ever met, but Queen Moira was a sorceress with magic so destructive it could poison the very land itself.

And Moira planned to use the stormhorses against the Circle.

Brida leaped to her feet. She was afraid Magdi's ward spell would only last so long. The best way she could help now was to free the stormhorses and give the hedgewitches a fighting chance against Moira's power.

She spun around, trying to recalibrate her sense of direction. Which way were the royal stables?

A breath of wind so faint she thought she imagined it at first carried the echo of a horse's anxious whinny and Brida raced to follow it. She ran through shadows, straining her ears for the sound of guards, terrified she'd be caught by the Queen of Crows.

A shed loomed out of the darkness and she stumbled to a stop, legs burning and breath rasping. She crouched low and strained her ears for any suspicious noises.

This didn't look like the royal stables she had expected to find. Built of weathered boards and cedar shingles, it looked more like a gardener's toolshed than a barn for magical horses. But the wind sang at her back, urging her forward as if to promise this was no mistake.

Brida crept closer, balancing her weight on her toes to avoid snapping twigs or rustling fallen leaves. A strange magic suffused the air.

The wind spun around her and she heard horses chewing hay, switching their tails, stomping their hooves. . . .

She knew she was pushing her luck, but the longer she hesitated, the greater the chance she might get caught. Whispering a prayer to the Great Mother, she darted forward and shoved both wooden doors.

They creaked but did not budge. Calling a tiny spark of magic to her hand, she sent her awareness through the cracks in the doors until she sensed a barred lock. A quick twist and a flick with the magic, and the doors swung slowly open—just wide enough for her to slip inside.

The atmosphere of magic inside the shed was so intense Brida leaned against the wall to catch her breath.

The air smelled of hay, oats, and horses, but it held the sharp tang of something deep and wild. A warm glow filled the makeshift barn and at first she believed it was a lantern carelessly left lit, but a closer look revealed the golden palomino giving off a nimbus of light. Swirls of energy spun dust motes in twisting ribbons, while glittering showers of snowflakes or raindrops occasionally burst from the ceiling.

If seeing the stormhorses from a distance had been overwhelming, seeing them up close was something else again. The sheer power radiating from them—the experience was intoxicating.

For a long moment, Brida simply stared, swaying on her feet. The horses stared back, nostrils flaring and tails swishing. She let out a breath of awe, and their ears swiveled to catch the sound.

The blue roan pawed the floor of her stall, and the black stallion kicked the wall boards. "Quiet, now," Brida murmured, "else someone will hear and come to see what's wrong."

The white mare nickered, soft and low. She tossed her head and a gust of wind ruffled Brida's hair. It carried pain and fear and sorrow, and something in Brida's blood rose to meet it.

Stepping closer, Brida noticed the silver halters. The queen had woven a spell into each one, sorcery strong enough to bind and control the stormhorses—dark power that burned the edges of Brida's consciousness and clearly caused the horses intense pain as it cut into their delicate skin. But even so, the intense energy of the stormhorses was barely contained. The air nearly crackled with it.

She reached for the spotted bay mare in the nearest stall, eyes blurring with tears at the sight of a creature so wondrous held captive and hurting.

"I'm going to help you," Brida whispered, stroking the mare's velvet neck.

I'm petting a stormhorse, she thought, giddy bubbles of disbelief rising in her chest. But the mare's misery, confusion, and anger soured in her own throat.

Sliding her palm toward the mare's ears, Brida reached for the slender silver halter. The instant her fingers touched it, a streak of searing agony sizzled through her skin. Choking on a scream she knew she must keep silent, Brida stumbled backward, clutching her hand to her chest.

There was a sudden sharp click, like the twist of a latch, and a hollow creak.

Behind her, the door opened and a man's voice said, "What have you done?"

— THIRTY-ONE —

Unexpected Allies

BRIDA FROZE, CRADLING her injured hand close to her body. It was too late to hide. Her thoughts scattered like rabbits under the shadow of a hawk, frantically seeking some excuse or explanation that might lead to safety.

"What were you *thinking*?" the man demanded.

Brida knew his voice. She slowly turned to face him, palms damp and chest tight with fear.

He stood in the doorway, a black silhouette against the moonlit darkness. Lifting a lantern in one hand, though its tiny flame was quickly swallowed in the light from the golden mare, he strode inside. A long color-shifting cloak— this one woven in night hues, black and gray and midnight blue—swirled about his ankles, making him flicker in and out of visibility. He slammed the doors closed.

The Huntsman.

Desperation and determination flared in Brida's heart and blazed through her body, fueled by the fear and anger of the stormhorses. Here was the man responsible for their capture. Here was the man who had inflicted such pain upon them.

And she would not let him stop her.

"I'm going to free them," she said. Drawing magic from the wind outside, from the starlight and the woods and the silver dew, from the power in her own blood, and even from the horses themselves, Brida held so much magic it spilled from her hands in crackling ribbons of color.

"Wait, mouse—"

Brida wrestled more energy than she'd ever felt before, trying to weave a spell that would release the halters and—

"I can't let you do that, as much as I might wish," the Huntsman said sadly.

A glint of silver glimpsed from the corner of her eyes distracted her. An instant later she felt the sting of a lash around her wrist. The burst of pain drove the air from her lungs and knocked her to her knees as her magic poured away in a rush.

For a heartbeat or two, all Brida could do was stare in shock at the silver whipcord wrapped around her arm, her magic suddenly beyond her grasp. She gritted her teeth and tried to yank her arm free, but the pain only bit worse. "Let me *go*!" she snapped.

"I will, I promise. But you're lucky I came out here to check on them myself. The stable lads have orders to kill intruders on sight, and your status as princess won't protect you."

Brida tossed her head. *Next time I'll take more care to be invisible, then*, she thought.

As if reading her thoughts, he said, "Things aren't that simple."

Voice softening, he came closer and loosened the whiplash without entirely releasing it. "I need you to pay close attention." He pulled a charm on a long leather cord from beneath his shirt and waited for Brida's reaction. It was a dried thistle bound in colored thread, with two glass beads and a feather knotted around it. Something made by a hedgewitch for love and protection.

"Where did you get that?"

"My wife, Nera, has been a thorn in the queen's side for some time now. . . . She's a member of the Circle of Thistles."

Brida sucked in a breath and he nodded. "So you've heard of them, then."

"Nera?" Brida repeated, but the name wasn't familiar to her. Still, if his wife was in the Circle of Thistles, that meant she knew Mother Magdi. . . .

Hope battled horror. But how could she trust the Huntsman? He'd already caught her twice, and she'd heard the queen's guard mention efforts to infiltrate the Circle. What if the Huntsman or his wife were part of those efforts? Would he betray Mother Magdi to her sister?

She backed away, gaze darting from the stormhorses to the door as she weighed her options.

He sighed. "Listen, I didn't know who you were when I found you, and then it was too late. But now . . . I'll do what I can to help. I've been given a message: 'the Circle tightens.' We can't act too quickly or the whole thing will unravel, you see?"

Was he lying?

Her breath turned to stones in her chest. "Where are your Hounds?" she asked.

"In the kennels," he said, frowning.

"No." Brida shook her head. "I overheard the queen speaking with one of the guards. She knows about the Circle of Thistles. She ordered him to take the Hounds to find the Circle and . . ." Her throat closed on the words, but she made herself spit them out anyway. "She plans to use the stormhorses to . . . *erase them all.* That's what she said. If I don't let these horses go, Nera and the others won't have a chance."

He stumbled back a step, alarm pinching his brows. "What? No—that's not possible!"

"They also talked about trying to infiltrate the Circle." She pinned him with an accusing stare.

"She promised that if I did as she asked, she would keep my family safe. She said—" He paced by the door, cloak swirling in his agitation. "Wait . . . You can't possibly think *I* am the infiltrator!"

Brida snorted, tipping her chin at the whiplash still coiled loosely around one of her wrists. "Well, you've captured me twice, chased down my friends, imprisoned the stormhorses, and turned an innocent man into one of the queen's wicked Hounds. I don't know what to think of you, but I don't trust you."

His jaw clenched as if he'd suddenly been slapped in the face, and then he noticed that she'd eased closer to the stalls. Before she could reach for the nearest mare's halter, he yanked the whiplash tight again and tugged her away.

Panting with pain, tears blurring her eyes, Brida hung her head. Soft lips nuzzled her shoulder as the white mare stretched her neck over her stall door, blowing softly in Brida's face.

"Whose side are you on? If we don't free the stormhorses, the queen will use their magic against the hedgewitches! She'll drain all their power and then she'll be too strong to defeat," Brida said.

"Don't you think I *want* to? But my son—you've already met him. Bowen. He's one of her Hounds."

Brida flinched in surprise. Bowen was the name of the Hound she'd healed by the boneyard. Bowen was his *son*?

"Until he's out of harm's way, I have to act the part of her loyal Huntsman. Can't you understand?" He scrubbed a hand over his face. "I'm only doing what I must to keep my family safe! I can't openly defy her yet, but I'm trying to help!"

"What about everyone else's family?" she snapped back.

He looked away. "It doesn't matter. The halters are like

this whip." He flicked his other hand, gave a quick jerk of his wrist, and the lash unwound. "They're magic—the kind of magic we can't fight. You know what happens when you touch them. No one but the queen herself can release the stormhorses, and she won't unless we have the means to force her."

Brida rubbed the mark left on her skin but otherwise remained still. "Is the Circle nearby?" Maybe there was still a chance she could warn Magdi even though her scrying hadn't worked.

"Closer than you suspect. I'll get a message to Nera tonight and when the time is right, we will make the queen pay for what she's done. But now I need to get you back to the castle before anyone notices you are gone. Come on—if the queen has sent my Hounds on a hunt, someone will be looking for me. We must hurry." He held out a hand and, when she refused to take it, sighed. "Whatever you might think of me, I *am* on your side."

Brida cast a longing look at the stormhorses and tears burned her eyes. *I* will *set you free*, she promised them silently.

Before leading Brida back to the castle, the Huntsman dug a small glass jar of ointment from a trunk in the back of the makeshift barn. "We can't let the queen see those burns on your fingers or she'll know immediately what you tried to do. Here . . ." He gently smoothed something cool and floral scented on her hand.

Brida sniffed, guessing the ingredients. Lavender, rose, aloe . . . Mother Magdi mixed a similar salve for the baker and the blacksmith. "Thank you," she said grudgingly. After all, her injuries were his fault.

As they walked, she asked softly, "These aren't the castle stables, are they? Why would she keep the stormhorses here? Everyone knows she has them—it's not a secret."

He chewed the end of his beard before answering. "Ah, mouse, I think it may be that she's half scared of them. Even with those halters, they're hardly under her control. And all that power, that energy . . . it isn't meant to be contained."

Brida turned her palm up, staring at skin that had been seared a livid red before the burn cream had soothed it. "Does the queen want me dead, like my mother?" she whispered.

"I don't think so. Not yet, anyway. Though she didn't call you princess out of family love, she knows her position has weakened. I think she hopes naming an heir will show people she has a legacy to protect. Still, you must be careful—the moment she perceives you as a threat, she won't hesitate to kill."

He patted her shoulder. "But the Circle won't be long now. Where crops fail, thistles grow. The time for change is at hand. Quiet now—we're getting close."

Brida chewed the inside of her cheek to keep silent. She felt something bigger than she'd dared to imagine unspooling around her in the darkness, and all she could catch was a glimpse now and then, an occasional hint.

The Huntsman took Brida across a sagging wooden bridge. The creek below was only a thin ribbon in the starlight, but rapid, frothing water gurgled beneath their feet. This wasn't the way she'd come, but when she opened her mouth to ask he laid a finger against his lips and shook his head.

In a breathless hush, she followed him up a path and through a clearing surrounded by heavy spruces and pines. She stumbled more than once until the Huntsman took her by the elbow. His feet seemed to know the way even through the shadows.

At one point he paused, head tilted as he listened. Bats skimmed the tree canopy and small creatures—mice or voles, most likely—rustled in the underbrush, but otherwise silence pressed the sound of Brida's own heartbeat against her ears.

After a moment, the Huntsman gave a gentle tug and they continued walking, more slowly and carefully than before.

A voice somewhere off to the left asked a question and received the answer: "All clear." Footsteps clicked away, a tidy little rhythm against the flagstones.

The Huntsman stopped. Waited, and waited, and waited . . .

Brida's nerves screamed.

And then he pulled her forward so quickly she nearly fell. Half lifting, half tugging her along, he rushed through the trees, around the corner of the stone wall enclosing the queen's private courtyard and garden, past the edge of the royal stables, and through a small door.

Brida found herself back inside the castle, at the end of a corridor lit at long intervals by dim lanterns. "Servants quarters," he breathed in her ear. "Run as quick as you can to the stairway, go up three flights and take the first door on the right. At the end of that hall, you'll see two closed doors side by side. Knock on the left twice, then twice on the right. No more, no less. Someone will return you to your room. Quickly now, and quiet!" He gave her a little shove in the small of the back before vanishing in a swirl of his color-shifting cloak as he hurried outside.

Balancing lightly on the balls of her feet, Brida ran soundlessly up the stairs and to the set of doors described by the Huntsman. Knocking as instructed, she chewed her lip until one of the doors swung open. A thin arm shot out, grabbed her, and yanked her through.

Brida was too surprised to make a sound. Ninn stood before her. "This way," she said, and then gave a start. Cheeks flushing, she dipped a curtsy. "Forgive me, princess."

Brida shook her head. She didn't feel like a princess, and she certainly didn't want to be treated like one. "I don't know the way back to my rooms, and I—I don't want . . ."

Ninn nodded and laid a finger by her lips. "I understand, and I willna say a word about it. Come along, then." With another quick curtsy she led the way through a corridor so close Brida had to tuck her elbows to her sides and duck her head.

It ended in a small room filled with shelves of linens, drapes, and cakes of laundry soap. A door near the back opened into another narrow passage, and this one took them into a wide hall.

She leaned forward and whispered in Brida's ear, "Your door is the last on this side. See it, by the torch?" And she fled without another word.

Brida ran lightly down the hall and was about to open her door when a flicker of movement at the far end of the corridor snagged her attention. A slender figure, oddly familiar, stood just outside a spill of light from one of the oil lanterns. Brida blinked and rubbed her eyes. Was she seeing things, conjuring images of her friends out of loneliness and worry?

But the girl gave a little wave and vanished around the corner.

She was real, and Brida had recognized her.

Hush was in the castle.

A Certain Pony

BRIDA AWOKE SORE and sleepy. After her midnight ramble, she'd spent hours wrestling nightmares in her twisted blankets. Her dreams had been filled with flames and flooding, snowstorms and spinning winds. She'd been haunted by girls with wings and men with the faces of snarling dogs; and when she finally clawed her way to the surface of morning, her head throbbed and her muscles ached.

Ninn bustled about, quietly laying out garments and ribbon. When she realized Brida was awake, she smiled and said, "Good morning, Princess."

Brida coughed and swung her legs out of bed. "I'm only me. Brida." She waited for the other girl to mention her nighttime wandering and tried to come up with a credible explanation.

But Ninn just said, "Well, the queen has asked that you attend her this morning, so hurry and wash. There's breakfast for you on the table by the window, and then I'll help you dress."

Brida wasn't hungry, but it was such a strange luxury to have someone else fetch her food that she hated to appear ungrateful. She plucked a berry from a pretty dish, nibbled some cheese, and crumbled the edges of a honey-glazed bun, but every time she swallowed she thought of the hungry faces she'd seen in the market, the withered orchards and barren fields she'd heard described around Edgewood.

She thought of Hush, Bones, and Bear. She'd been convinced that she had seen Hush last night, but in the harsh glare of daylight filtering through the castle windows it was easy to believe she had imagined it.

She also considered Mother Magdi and the Circle of Thistles as questions hummed like bees in her head. What were the hedgewitches planning? Were they still safe? Would they get word to her somehow?

Could the Huntsman be trusted, despite the hold the queen had over his son?

Brida was on her way to the queen's audience chamber, dressed in a pigeon-gray gown with black lace trim, when the queen herself appeared. Hastily bobbing a curtsy and fumbling with the slick, unfamiliar skirts, Brida flushed.

"Follow me, child" was all Moira said, so Brida let herself get swept up in the current of servants, ladies, and guards trailing after the queen.

They spilled from the castle and spread in a loose semi-circle in the outer courtyard. Someone half shoved, half guided Brida to a spot beside the queen.

Two men appeared, leading a small pony between them.

Brida, confused and distracted, wasn't paying close attention. She was too busy wondering what she was doing in this crowd of fancy people.

"Your Majesty, I thought the princess needed a mount, and I found just the pony," the Huntsman announced in a ringing voice, stepping forward.

Startled, Brida turned her gaze on them—and almost betrayed herself with a giddy burst of giggles. The pony, looking thoroughly annoyed by his new saddle and beaded bridle, was Burdock. Though his mane was neatly braided, his tail gleamed like a silk ribbon, and his hooves were polished jet-black, there was no mistaking that bay coat, the two white socks on his back legs, the whorl of hair just to the right of his forehead, the little snip of white just above his upper lip. He was unusually clean and polished, but he was definitely Brida's own clever pony.

And then she took a closer look at the man holding Burdock by the reins—because he wasn't a man at all. She recognized Bear's broad shoulders, warm maple skin, and dark curls.

"Your Majesty," Bear said, "if it would please you and the princess, may I present this pony as a gift? He is sturdy, loyal, and strong." Bending low, forehead nearly touching his knees, he bowed and waited for her response.

Please, please, please say yes! Brida thought, afraid to

breathe or move or smile for fear the queen might read the truth in her face.

Burdock caught her eye and wrinkled his nose, as if to say, *Look what they've put me through, just for your sake!* But then he flicked his ears and licked his lips and she knew he was as glad to see her as she was to see him.

The queen held out her hand and, after someone hissed to Brida, "Take it!" Brida laid her fingers in that smooth, elegant palm. Together, Queen Moira and Brida approached Burdock and his temporary groom.

Releasing her hand, the queen asked Brida, "What do you think, little highness? Would you like him for your own?"

Hardly daring to speak above a whisper, Brida murmured, "Oh, yes, Your Majesty, I would be most grateful."

"Do you know how to ride?"

"Not properly," she answered, and it was mostly true. She'd never ridden in a lady's saddle before, or asked Burdock for showy gaits and fancy movement. They'd just enjoyed each other's company, rambling all over the countryside.

"Well, then you shall have to learn! In addition to lessons with me, you will report to the stable so that Huntsman Darius may assign someone to begin teaching you."

Brida curtsied. "Thank you, Your Majesty."

Queen Moira smiled and tapped her finger against her lips as she studied Brida's face. "I know how excited you must be. You may spend the morning getting acquainted with your new pony, and then report to my apothecarium after the midday meal."

Brida bowed her head, but the queen had already turned back toward the castle.

Still, Brida waited until the heavy doors closed behind the last of the retinue before flinging her arms around Burdock's neck. "I missed you so much! How did you come to be here?"

With her cheek still pressed to Burdock's sleek coat, Brida glanced at the Huntsman and Bear and said, "*Thank you*. How did you find him? How did you *know*?" But even as the words left her mouth she guessed the answer.

Mother Magdi.

Straightening so fast she startled Burdock, Brida blurted, "Wait! Where is she? Is she here?"

If Mother Magdi were here, Queen Moira would kill her.

Brida knew this in her bones as surely as she knew the stormhorses were in pain or that trees craved sunlight and still earth or that Burdock would do anything for a handful of fresh, sweet clover. And the truth of it scared her to shivers.

The Huntsman laid a finger across his lips and she gulped, gaze flying to the sky in case there were Crows nearby to overhear.

Relieved to find the sky clear, she stroked Burdock's

nose and scratched under his forelock the way she knew he liked. Flapping his lips in a goofy grin, Burdock pressed his head into her hand and nickered.

"You have no idea how glad I am to see you," she told him.

"Let's show him into the barn, shall we?" the Huntsman suggested. "You can settle him in his stall."

Holding Burdock's reins lightly in her palm so she wouldn't jerk on his mouth, Brida carefully led him across the courtyard and toward the stable. He jigged and pranced behind her, sensing her mood.

At the stable doors he balked, pulling back.

"Come on," Brida said, with a gentle tug. "Follow me."

When he tossed his head, she caught the bridle by the noseband and looked him in the eye. "Burdock, if you don't behave, the queen will send you away, and I might never find you again!" Her voice cracked and she had to swallow a bitter lump of sudden tears in the back of her throat.

Burdock huffed in her face, rubbing his nose against her cheek and snuffling her hair. With a long sigh as if to say, *All right, fine then!* he marched into the dim stable and halted in the middle of a neatly swept aisle.

Brida grinned, guessing his thoughts. This was no dusty barn full of hay and goats. No, this was a horse palace, all gleaming wood and sweet-smelling sawdust shavings in each stall. Rows of fancy horses, proud necks arched, glanced at the small pony standing in their midst.

Burdock stepped closer to Brida, nudging her thigh with his nose.

Rubbing circles on his neck, she said, "I know how you feel. I don't really belong here, either, but it won't be forever."

At least . . . she *hoped* it wouldn't.

An empty stall near the end of the aisle was open and waiting, so Brida led Burdock toward it. When they were only a few feet away, the Huntsman said, "I couldn't keep your friends away."

Two heads peeked out: Bones and Hush.

So she hadn't imagined Hush last night!

Brida dropped Burdock's reins in a loop around his neck and ran to them. They hugged and patted one another's shoulders as if to be sure they were all real and in one piece.

"It is so good to see you," Brida murmured. "But it's not safe here!"

"We know," Bear said, joining them. "We aren't staying. But Hush knows secret ways into the castle, and we've started helping someone important to you." He raised his brows significantly.

"You mean Mother M—"

"Don't speak her name!" the Huntsman interrupted. He had removed Burdock's saddle and was giving the pony a brisk rubdown, ignoring Burdock's annoyed stomps. Pausing in his grooming to hold out the charm he'd shown Brida earlier, he gave it a slight shake. "This isn't strong enough to shield your words from the queen's sharpest interest, and that name is certain to draw her attention like nectar does a wasp."

Brida winced in apology and twisted her fingers together. "What happens now?" she whispered.

Hush reached over and clasped her hand.

Brida squeezed Hush's fingers. "I'm so sorry I didn't give you back your voice."

Hush flipped her other hand over and back, and Brida didn't need Bear's translation to understand she meant that it didn't matter. But it *did* matter, and Brida murmured in her ear, "If you come to my rooms tonight, I'll see what we can do."

"We were so worried about you," Bear said.

A lump swelled in Brida's throat. "And I worried about all of you. I'm *still* worried. The queen is dangerous, and she knows about the Circle of Thistles."

Suddenly, a bell rang across the courtyard and Burdock shifted uneasily in the aisle.

The Huntsman said, "Time for the midday meal. Brida, you'll have to tell your friends farewell for now." He finished brushing Burdock and let the pony trot toward her.

Bear handed her a folded note and stepped out of the stall with Hush and Bones. "Until later, then," he said, giving her a rough hug as he passed.

Bones wrapped his thin arms around her, too, and

whispered, "Watch out for yourself, hear me?" and then Hush kissed her cheek.

Brida took Burdock into the stall. As he buried his face in a pile of hay, she smoothed the note open and read: *Stay strong, stay silent, and stay safe. I am near. If you need me, Burdock knows how to find me. With love, M.*

The ink faded as soon as her eyes traced each word, but she clutched the crumpled paper and brushed sudden tears away with the back of her sleeve.

"Hurry, lass, or the queen will be angry with both of us," the Huntsman called.

Brida sniffed and gave Burdock a watery smile. No matter what the queen had planned, she wasn't alone. She was surrounded by love.

THIRTY-THREE

Black Magic

BRIDA REPORTED TO the apothecarium as soon as she'd finished choking down her midday meal of stewed apples and an oatcake. She'd been too nervous to eat much, but she tried to smile and act as if nothing bothered her. After all, she had to play the part of a girl suddenly elevated to princess. People were watching her, weighing her words, studying her face—she had to live up to their expectations.

Which would be so much easier if she knew what those expectations were.

She tried making idle conversation with the girl in black who led her to the queen's apothecarium, but the girl wouldn't—or couldn't—speak. Hurrying the rest of the way in silence, Brida attempted to still her galloping thoughts.

Queen Moira greeted her at the door. "Do you like your new pony?"

"Yes, Your Majesty, very much," Brida told her.

"Please, call me Aunt Moira unless we're in public. We must get to know one another without the bother of titles, don't you think? We've lost so much time already."

"Yes, Your—yes, Aunt Moira."

"Very good. I am having riding clothes made up so that you can begin lessons with whomever Huntsman Darius assigns tomorrow morning. Your afternoons shall be spent here, with me."

Brida hoped the queen couldn't guess the glow in her heart from the promise of riding Burdock again.

"Now, what do you know of magic?" the queen asked.

Was this a trick question? Brida twisted her fingers together behind her back and said, "Not much, Your—Aunt Moira."

"Do you know how many types of magic there are?"

"Well, there's hedgemagic."

"Yes, and . . . ?"

Brida chewed the inside of her lip. She couldn't risk saying anything that might rouse the queen's suspicions, especially if Mother Magdi was nearby.

"I don't know," she said, putting her pretend role as baker's apprentice on like a disguise. "Not much magic involved in mixing dough and baking bread, is there?"

The queen smiled. "Well, in addition to learning how to be a proper princess, you will also learn how to use your magical talents—which I expect will be quite impressive."

Brida shifted nervously. "I'm not so sure about that."

"First lesson: types of magic. Hedgemagic is the most common, and also perhaps the weakest. Most hedgewitches are simply skilled gardeners. Healers and midwives may be hedgewitches, though magic isn't necessary if they've taken time to study the uses of medicinal plants. Knowledge and wisdom are often safer and more effective than simple magic. It's too easy for ignorant people to fall into superstition."

Nodding to show she was listening—though she disagreed—Brida waited for the queen to continue.

"The second type is sacred magic. This was your mother's magic. I mentioned she was a priestess nearby?"

"Yes," Brida croaked, mouth so dry her voice cracked.

"This is the traditional magic of the Temples. The priests and priestesses used it in rituals for the good of the land. Until your mother conjured a nightrider . . ." She waved an elegant hand. "Well, we've already spoken about her grave mistake and what it cost this realm."

An ember of anger ignited in Brida's chest and she had to swallow the furious words burning her mouth. She remembered the queen's story during last night's banquet, the lies Moira told with a magic charm drawn in spilled wine. Brida fought to keep her face smooth. Moira had to believe the lie spell had worked or she might see Brida as a threat.

Hold your tongue. Be patient.

The queen beckoned Brida closer and pointed to a low worktable. Three black candles in pewter candlesticks stood in the center, with a bird's skull—a crow's?—resting on the left and a bowl of water on the right. Intricate patterns of geometric shapes had been drawn in chalk, and around the edges of every figure were symbols from a language Brida had never seen before.

As she stared at the lines, a dull ache bloomed between her eyes and she blinked to clear the pain.

"The third type of magic is called sorcery, or shadow magic. I discovered it myself." Moira picked up the bird skull and stroked it with one hand. "It is the power of transformation, of illusion, of secrets. The power of knowledge that comes from deciphering the hidden wisdom the universe conceals."

Brida's stomach gave a wobble. Knowledge was well and good . . . but if the universe kept secrets, perhaps it was for good reason.

The queen held out the skull, offering it to Brida. "And I will share with you all that I have learned, so that after I am turned to dust you will have the power to continue my works."

Clenching her fists, Brida stared at the empty eye sockets of the small white skull. Brambles and thorns, she didn't *want* to learn what the queen knew.

But Moira frowned and thrust the skull at her.

Brida forced herself to uncurl her fingers and take it. She saw now, up close, more geometric shapes and patterns etched into the bone with precise detail. The skull radiated echoes of fear and pain and death, darkness and deep cold. Her hand shook with the urge to throw the thing as far away from her as she could.

The queen paced a circle around her, arms folded. She tapped one hand against her elbow, as if drumming out the rhythm of her thoughts. "There is another sort of magic," she said after a minute. "Or there was. Windmagic. But it is very, very rare. A Windwitch can call the weather elements, weave storms, spin seasons, read breezes, and balance tides. Once, I met—"

The loud, harsh cry of a crow issued suddenly from the skull in Brida's hand. She was so startled she screamed and jerked her hand away.

The skull fell—and was caught in midair by Queen Moira. She laughed at Brida's shock. "I should have warned you it might do that. But look! Watch this."

Setting the crow skull carefully down on the table, she pointed to a symbol inlaid in the floor, the design rendered in some dark metal that contrasted sharply with the polished wooden planks.

Moira started to hum a series of discordant notes that jarred Brida's bones and made her ears ring. The symbol on the floor turned silver, and then, as the queen began to chant words Brida couldn't understand, it took on a pale blue glow. The queen's chant sped up, each strange syllable striking the air like a warning chime. The glow brightened, flaring purple, red, then orange until it looked as if a living flame writhed along the floor.

Brida stepped back, dread gnawing cold hollows through her body.

In the corners of the room, shadows emerged. One by one, wisps of darkness slunk along the walls and puddled on the floor. Oozing, sliding, spilling through the room until they surrounded Brida.

Trembling with fear, she considered fleeing. Once she reached Burdock, they could—

The queen grabbed her by the arm. "Watch," she commanded.

The shadows melted together and started spinning, a cyclone barely contained within the room. Brida shook as the darkness gathered force and shape, drawn to the symbol on the floor. When it looked as if the shadows might swallow the orange glow, they burst in a shower of crow feathers that flew to the outer edges of the apothecarium and hung suspended in a circle at eye level.

A watery sphere now appeared above the symbol, a floating bubble containing drifting shapes and colors. It was almost like . . .

A scrying bowl.

Brida leaned forward, straining her eyes. Sure enough, the faint swirls clarified until she realized she was looking at a small girl in a ragged dress and stained apron. A long braid hung down her back. It took Brida a second to understand that the girl was running away.

The queen laughed. "The ones who run always possess the strongest talents." Plucking a feather from the circle around them, she cast it at the sphere and it was sucked inside.

Startled, Brida saw the feather catch in the girl's braid and, an instant later, the girl's body contorted horribly as she transformed into a Crow.

Brida's stomach heaved and she had to look away.

A heartbeat later the Crow flew from the bubble in the center of the room and landed with a croak on the queen's outstretched hand. The circle of suspended feathers fell to the floor in a rush of black sand that turned to smoke and disappeared.

Queen Moira rang a silver bell and then turned to Brida with the Crow balanced miserably in her palm. "Don't look so horrified, little highness! She'll have a good and useful life here in the castle. What future could she anticipate in her village? Herding geese? Slopping pigs? I've given her the gift of flight. I've given her freedom from worry—she'll be fed, clothed, and sheltered as long as she provides faithful service."

Brida could barely tear her eyes away from the dejected Crow now fluttering helplessly on the queen's arm. But there was another reason for her dismay.

The queen's magic didn't work the way magic was supposed to.

Brida had been taught that the energy in the world existed in a state of flux, flowing from one thing to another while remaining balanced and harmonious. When she drew magic power from the elements around her, it was to direct it elsewhere. She couldn't create or destroy energy, she just borrowed it. Shifted it around.

She used the power in her own blood and bones to shape it, so she could feel the moment when she might be drawing too much. And Mother Magdi had taught her how to give back, how to complete the circle. It was one of the most fundamental lessons of hedgemagic: you gave thanks to the Great Mother when you harvested a plant, and you tended the new life growing in your garden. The cycle gave magic its strength.

When Brida worked with the wind, she felt the currents of energy echoed in her own body and sensed the balance of magic.

But the queen's spell . . . Moira had drawn more power than Brida thought was possible, but when she sent it into the symbol on the floor, it had been . . . consumed. Brida had waited to feel the magic rebalance itself.

Instead, she felt . . . drained.

She'd experienced something like this before, when she and Mother Magdi tried to heal the blight at Maple Hill. The aftereffects of the queen's sorcery had left the land sickened, haunted by evil shadows. Brida's own energy was swallowed by the void.

Queen Moira's magic was like a ravenous hunger. Was this why she sought girls with magical potential? Was she somehow fueling her spells with their power?

Brida remembered Mother Magdi saying that the queen would use whatever magic she could find, but she hadn't fully grasped how far Moira would go. With the power of the stormhorses at her disposal, and a circle of hedgewitches in her sights, the queen could steal enough magic to break the world.

Brida needed to know more about Queen Moira's sorcery so the Circle of Thistles could defend themselves and defeat her. And tonight Brida would make another attempt at releasing the stormhorses. Hopefully the Huntsman wouldn't expect her to try again so soon.

She glanced up to find Moira studying her with narrowed green eyes, the new Crow still flapping her wings in panic. Brida pasted on a weak smile. "Your powers are unimaginable. I am sure she recognizes the honor."

The queen's response was interrupted by a knock on the door. "Enter," she called.

The Huntsman swept in, green and gray and blue day-colored cloak swirling. He held a cage in his hand, studiously ignoring Brida.

Queen Moira thrust the Crow at him. "Reward the scouts who found her, and see that she gets settled in. I'll test her aptitudes tomorrow."

"Yes, Your Majesty," he said, bowing low.

The Huntsman opened the cage door and shoved the frightened Crow inside. Her eyes went glassy with fear and Brida's heart twisted. "I'll send you an update this evening, Your Majesty," he said, and carried the Crow out.

Brida wished she knew the girl's name.

When I free the stormhorses, I'll find a way to free you, too. I'll find a way to free all of us, she promised.

Queen Moira brushed her hands together. "Where were we? Ah, yes, the different types of magic. So. Sorcery, sometimes called black magic, uses symbols to draw and direct the power of each spell. These special symbols are called glyphs, and each one has its own unique purpose. A simple spell may use one or two glyphs, while more complex workings combine them in precise ways. Does this make sense?"

"Yes, Your Majest—Aunt Moira."

The queen smiled at her. "You're a smart girl, and I sense a great depth of power in you. I don't think it will take you long to learn how to write your own spells. But the first step is memorizing the base glyphs: the four elemental symbols for earth, air, fire, and water; the two for breath and body; and the two for binding and breaking. You'll find paper and charcoal pencils on the table there in the corner and a scroll of these glyphs. I want you to practice copying each one and—"

There was another knock on the door and for a moment Brida almost smiled, thinking about Magdi's cottage in Oak Hollow and the constant interruptions from the townsfolk needing help. She missed all of them—well, maybe not Dev, but certainly the rest—and hoped they were managing well enough without Mother Magdi.

Moira snapped, "Enter."

One of the queen's guards stood in the doorway with a slender man in travel-stained clothes. A smudge of dirt—or was it a bruise?—darkened one cheek and a long tear slashed the knee of his riding breeches. His bare head looked windblown and Brida wondered where he'd lost his cap.

A Crow flew in behind them, perching on the queen's shoulder. It croaked in her ear and she frowned.

"Your Majesty," the guard said, bowing, "this man arrived with a disturbing report." He glanced at Brida, and added, "We may have to deal with some . . . *thistles*."

Brida fought to keep her face blank, though a surge of fear swept through her.

"My Crow tells me they were last seen a league from Edgewood. Where were your patrols? Where were the Hounds?"

The guard cleared his throat. "Uh, searching for—"

She waved a hand. "Never mind. I shall deal with it."

The queen tapped a finger against her lips. "Princess, please take your lesson materials to your rooms and practice your copying there this afternoon. We shall meet again tomorrow."

"Yes, Your Majesty." Echoing the queen's formality, Brida sketched a curtsy and hurried to the table to gather paper and pencils. But as the queen left with her Crow, followed by the guard and the disheveled man, Brida's stomach dropped like a stone.

On a wooden counter behind the table, she saw a woven wreath of shining horsehair. Different strands created a blend of color: white, black, buttercream . . . and by the hum of magic she sensed, Brida knew it came from the stormhorses' tails.

She glanced toward the door. She was alone, and the queen was preoccupied. What if . . .

Brida eased forward, paused, then took another step. Her pulse fluttered in the hollow of her throat like a trapped moth. All she had to do was stretch her arm, reach out her fingertips, and grab the woven circle. . . . If she could get it to Mother Magdi somehow, the hedgewitches could hide it, use it, destroy it—*anything* to keep it from Queen Moira.

Her hands shook. The queen would know Brida had stolen it and her fury would be terrible. Could Brida pretend she'd just been fascinated by the different colors of horsehair, could she play innocent and convince the queen she hadn't meant to lose it?

Or would the queen kill Brida as she had tried to kill her mother, Maigin? As she'd killed Brida's father?

Brida yanked back her arm—and then her resolve firmed. There were too many lives at stake. Until she could manage to free the stormhorses, she *had* to keep their power out of the queen's grasp. This was a start.

Trembling, she reached out once more. But just before she could snatch the strange wreath, an ominous hiss filled the air.

Startled, Brida's gaze flew to the corner of the apothecarium. Something shifted, solidified . . . and slithered toward her.

A snake of smoke and shadow.

She gasped and jerked away, but another hiss spun her sideways as more shadows behind her began to coil along the floor. Were these like the snakes that had stolen Hush's voice?

Of course the queen wouldn't leave her magic workroom unprotected—Brida should have known. Clutching her paper and pencils to her chest, Brida ran from the room, barely slipping past the hissing snakes.

She would just have to watch for another opportunity, and hope it didn't come too late.

— THIRTY-FOUR —

Wind and Blood

BRIDA EYED THE scroll of glyphs she'd spread across her writing desk. They were simple things—just lines, really. Copying them would be like learning to write her letters or practicing runes.

She didn't *want* to learn the queen's sorcery, though. Just the thought of it chilled her blood. But what if it was the only power that could defeat Moira? What if she could use it to help Mother Magdi and the hedgewitches?

An ache gathered in Brida's forehead and she pressed her fists to her eyes. Should she at least try?

Magic hummed a warning in her fingers as she grabbed a charcoal pencil and set the tip against the paper. She hesitated, remembering the times she'd followed threads of magic and wisps of power in Mother Magdi's green room. She'd always trusted her magic to show her what was necessary, had often felt the kiss of wind tugging her along.

This, on the other hand . . . there was nothing about these glyphs that felt trustworthy.

Taking a breath, Brida traced the first line for the glyph of air and her hand immediately cramped. A slosh of sickness churned through her stomach and she dropped the pencil as a rush of wind swept the room. At first she assumed it came from the glyph, but as it swirled around her she realized the gust fluttered the scroll as if trying to blow it away.

She flexed her hands and let the scroll roll back up, concealing the disturbing symbols. The wind sighed, softened, hushed.

She shoved the scroll of glyphs away.

Right now, the wind—and everything inside her—said that the queen's glyphs were not for her to use. And she trusted her own power and intuition far more than she trusted the Queen of Crows.

Rising to pace, Brida thought about the way the magic inside her breath, bones, and blood called to the magic in the wind and how the magic in the wind called her, too. She considered the threads of magic she could sift from air, the way each strand tingled in her fingers or buzzed across her skin. Maybe she couldn't be a Windwitch—they were rare, and strong, and special—but the wind had helped her more than once. Somehow her power was connected to it.

She would cling to that knowledge rather than learn to work dark sorcery.

She just had to figure out how she could use the wind as a weapon against Queen Moira. Could she use it to free the stormhorses?

Her restless feet carried her to the open window and she leaned out as a new horizon of possibilities opened before her. An eagle soared in wide, sweeping circles above the hills to the north and Brida followed it with her gaze, wondering if the wind would answer her call again.

Just as she was preparing to reach with her senses, the eagle she'd been watching suddenly dove with a piercing scream and Crows flew up to meet it.

What was happening?

Craning her neck, Brida peered down at the maze of courtyards and ragged gardens below. A group of men and women in homespun tunics and wool dresses burst into view, brandishing pitchforks, old swords, and bows. The eagle swooped above them, tearing at the Crows that tried to attack. Dim sounds of shouting reached her ears as a cluster of the queen's guards ran to meet them, shields and swords shining in the sunlight.

It was a bad time for a food riot, she thought—and then she spotted other groups clashing behind the stone walls near the smithy and in one of the gardens.

Straining her eyes, she glimpsed spots of purple on the homespun vests, jackets, aprons, or cloaks of the people confronting the guards, and dread dropped like a stone through her chest.

The resistance—but they were moving too soon! She hadn't freed the stormhorses or done anything to weaken the queen, and now Moira's power would overwhelm them all.

Brida tore off her fancy princess gown and flung on her old tunic and leggings. She rummaged in the bottom of the chest at the end of her bed until she found her boots, then crammed her feet inside the soft, familiar leather. She rushed out of her room—and ran smack into a contingent of the queen's guards.

The one with black feathers edging his surcoat—the captain, she assumed—grabbed her by the arms and marched her along with them. "We've been ordered to take you somewhere safe and secure," he said in a voice like gravel.

Brida spun and twisted, trying to yank her arms out of his grip. He tightened his hands until her skin bruised. "Let me go!" she cried. "I need to check my pony!"

"He'll be fine. Quit acting like a child and have some dignity," he growled. "You're the princess and the queen wants you protected."

Heat stung Brida's cheeks and she stopped struggling. Throwing her chin up and straightening her shoulders, she asked, "Why? What's going on?"

There was a stir among the accompanying guards, but all he said was "Trouble."

"Then I must join Queen Moira. My *aunt*. I am sure her power is more than adequate defense."

He grunted but did not change pace or direction, hauling Brida down a spiral flight of stairs, through branching corridors, and down more stairs.

"Are you taking me to the dungeons?" she asked in disbelief.

"A safe room."

"No! I insist you return me to my chambers or bring me to the queen. At once!"

"I'm under orders."

Not caring what he thought of her, Brida twisted around and tried to kick his shins. He simply heaved her over his shoulder and continued walking until they reached a narrow door with an iron grille. One of the guards kicked it open. The captain hefted her off his shoulder and shoved her inside.

"Oh, I nearly forgot. The queen wants you to wear this." He clasped a thin silver bracelet around her wrist. "And she needs a lock of your hair." He snipped a few strands and slammed the door shut.

Brida heard the click of the lock and the stomp of their heavy boots leaving, and yelled, "Let me out of here!"

A tremble ran through her body when she glanced at the bracelet. It was fashioned from the same silver substance as the halters on the stormhorses, and it made her skin burn. She desperately tried to claw it off, but there was no visible clasp and it fit too tightly to slip over her hand.

Brida sucked in a deep breath and clenched her teeth. She would *not* let the queen take her magic. But when she tried to summon her power, the bracelet turned to white flame along her arm and she cried out in agony.

She hammered on the door, shouting until her throat was burned raw. She had to get out, had to help her friends before it was too late.

Slumping on the floor, she twisted and pulled at the bracelet. Despair howled in the corners of her mind and she begged the Great Mother for help.

And then something rattled at the door. There was a click, a scrape, and the door swung open slowly.

Brida sprang forward, teeth bared and tears spilling down her cheeks. She was prepared to hit and kick her way out, if that's what she had to—

She slid to a halt as Rissi and Hush peered in. Brida flung her arms around them. "How did you know I was down here?"

Rissi grinned and Hush pointed to the floor.

Confused, Brida followed her finger and noticed a patch of coiled shadow near the base of the wall. With a faint rasping noise, it began to move—slithering and straightening until she was staring directly in the face of the iridescent snake Rissi had called Mystery.

There was no time for wonder. Hush grabbed her hand and mouthed *Hurry!*

Hush led the way down the hall and back up the twisting stairs, Rissi bringing up the rear. Together they ran through the castle corridors, the snake moving swift as water to patrol the way beside them. "But how did you get here?

Did Mother Magdi bring you?" Brida asked Rissi, panting as they raced through the servants' quarters.

"Actually," Rissi answered, "a priest named Mason Bolder did."

"Mason Bolder?" Brida glanced at Hush, who nodded.

"He knew my mother, you see. He sent me a wingnote mentioning that another daughter of the Temple was in trouble. The queen had put a hex on her, he'd heard, and he was worried. He wondered if I could help. I mentioned the note to Mother Magdi as soon as I received it, but by then she was already trying to find you."

They slipped down a back staircase and followed Hush through a hidden passage so small they had to crawl. Rissi lowered her voice to a soft murmur. "Mother Magdi sent me on ahead, and Mystery decided to accompany me. We were headed for the Temple of the Crescent Moon—or what's left of it—when we met Bones. Apparently, he recognized my magic."

The great snake raised her head and licked the air with her forked tongue. Scenting guards, she led the three girls through an empty suite of rooms, past a gallery of faded paintings, and into a darkened corridor.

"Anyway, Bones explained what happened to Mason and told me you'd been turned into a Crow. But he also said that you'd already lifted the hex on Hush. Now all you have to do is give her back her voice and together we can help the Circle and the resistance."

Brida struggled to keep up, the bracelet on her arm already draining her strength. She twisted her wrist and said, "I can't with this thing on. But you have white magic. Here—we can hide in this closet while you work your spells. Mystery and I can keep watch."

Rissi shook her head. "I already tried, but I don't know the right spellsongs and I'm not strong enough to work without them."

"Then lead me to Mother Magdi. As soon as she gets this bracelet off, we can restore Hush's voice."

"I'm going to try, but the hedgewitches are with the resistance. I don't know if we'll be able to reach her." Rissi frowned.

Weapons, Hush mouthed, waiting for them near the end of the corridor. She pantomimed a bow and arrow before racing down the hall with Rissi, peering into storerooms. Brida followed, throwing open doors until she found a mostly empty armory. Dull swords too heavy for her to lift were stacked in an untidy pile beside dented shields, broken spears, and . . . There! A small bow and a cracked quiver holding a handful of crooked arrows.

It wasn't much, but it was something. Grabbing it, she skirted the walls of the room and stumbled across a wooden crate of old daggers in leather sheathes. The blades were rusted and pitted, but the knives were small enough to fit in her palm and sharp enough to hurt. From her earliest memories Mother Magdi had taught her to do no harm, to save lives rather than take them. But the situation was desperate and she didn't know what else to do. Hands shaking, she gathered a couple of the daggers and raced out of the room.

"Here!" she called, breathless. "Found some!"

Hush's eyes lit up when she saw the bow and she gestured eagerly. When Brida handed it over, she cradled the bow in her arm, testing the string. The quiver of pitiful arrows raised her brows, but she took them with a smile and raised her chin, indicating they should hurry on.

Brida handed the daggers to Rissi, fighting the impulse to wipe her hands. Rissi took all but one. "You'd better keep it," she said. "I'm afraid it won't be much use in a raging battle, but at least you'll have *some* defense."

Brida closed her trembling fingers around the hilt, hating the cool, slick weight of it.

She hoped she wouldn't have to use it.

Hush slowed as they approached a side door leading to the kitchen gardens and the back edge of the stable yard. A muffled commotion outside dully penetrated the thick stone walls of the castle.

Mystery lifted herself in shining coils, hissing ominously.

"Maybe you two should just wait here. I'll take a look, see if I can catch Mother Magdi's attention, and bring her close," Rissi said.

Hush frowned and shook her head. *I won't hide*, she mouthed fiercely, easing the door open.

"Careful!" Rissi cried as Mystery slithered through first,

and then the girls stepped outside. The door slammed closed and they were swallowed by a rush of noise and chaos.

Weapons clashed, men shouted, a woman screamed. Crows filled the sky with a storm of feathers and furious cries. They circled and swooped, beaks and talons aiming for faces as they dove away from the great eagle Brida had seen from her window. Packs of Hounds stalked the castle grounds, snarling with muzzles already bloodied.

Brida clutched her dagger in a hand gone numb. They had walked into a tempest of hate and anger, and for a shocked second it disoriented her.

People were *dying*.

Rissi yelled as a Crow hurtled toward her, but a blast of magic sent the bird tumbling from the air. "Do you see Mother Magdi?" she called.

Brida peered through the chaos, wincing at the crumpled figures lying still, the wounded people crawling away. Crimson puddles stained the stones, and for a moment she swayed as dizzy horror swept gray curtains across her vision.

They had to stop this before more lives were lost.

Straightening her shoulders, she hurried forward, gaze fixed on the cluster of women standing behind a broken section of garden wall on the other side of the courtyard. The green leaves of the hedgewitch's emblem were clearly visible on their cloaks, and they all wore thistles pinned to their collars. She didn't see Mother Magdi among them, but perhaps they could remove her bracelet so she could be useful.

Swords clashed against pitchforks, knives spun through the air. The hedgewitches hurled spells and charms like weapons, knocking arrows from the sky before they found their marks, protecting as many people as their magic could reach.

But it wasn't enough.

More guards spilled from a gate and rushed into the courtyard. The hedgewitches shifted their focus, sending spellweaves to block their advance.

Brida noticed Bear fighting beside a group of farmers and laborers, his ax sweeping deadly arcs through the queen's guards. Hush must have seen him at the same moment. She ran toward him, an arrow already nocked and bow drawn.

A Hound suddenly spotted Brida and snarled. Hackles raised, he plunged toward her.

"Get back!" she shouted, knowing that not all the Hounds were innocent like Bowen and Mason but also aware that they had once been men. "You don't have to fight for her! Join us and we can free you!"

But he snarled and she saw the hatred blazing in his eyes, the gleam of his teeth. She scrambled backward, raising her dagger even though she knew it wasn't enough to stop him. The small blade would barely scratch his hide.

Behind her Rissi sang a spell to slow him down, turn him aside. But his hunger for violence was too strong.

He growled and took a leap.

Brida tried to run, but the entire castle grounds had

become a bloody battlefield and two more Hounds had locked their gazes on her.

"Stop!" she screamed. "You don't have to do this!"

The Huntsman heard and turned to her, face grim and gaunt. Deep lines of worry and regret made him look as if he'd aged a decade overnight. "Leave her alone!" he hollered, but he had lost control of his pack and one of the Hounds snapped at his arm. "To me!" he yelled again. "At ease!"

But the Hounds were battle crazed and had forgotten whatever allegiance they may have had to the Huntsman. He threw himself in front of Brida, plunging a knife in the chest of the attacking Hound with a grimace. The Hound collapsed on his side, tongue lolling from his mouth as the life left his body. The air shimmered around him and a moment later a man lay on the ground.

"Get back in the castle!" the Huntsman called to Brida, but she couldn't cower inside while so many were fighting for their lives.

Rissi tapped Brida's shoulder. "Look! Mother Magdi!" She pointed.

Magdi darted behind a couple of farmers pummeling a guard with shovels and hung a charm of wood, feathers, and ivy on a stone protruding from the courtyard wall. Brida saw her slip away, hanging another charm a few feet farther on.

Rissi ran to help, but before Brida could follow, one

of the queen's guards recognized her. "Hey! What are you doing out here?" he demanded, grabbing her by the arm and yanking her back toward the castle doors.

Brida tried to pull free, but his hand gripped her so tightly she felt the press of his ragged nails through her sleeve. "Let me go!"

He beckoned to two other guards. "The princess!" he shouted.

"No! Leave me!" Fighting the pain of the queen's bracelet, Brida desperately tried again to draw threads of magic, but the strands were spiderweb flimsy and dissolved in ragged tatters before she could do anything with them.

The effort left her sick and shaking. Her wrist burned so badly she could barely move her arm.

Just then, Rissi's voice climbed above the clamor of the battle, each note a haunting chime as she sang a spell. Brida looked over her shoulder in time to see Mother Magdi signal the other hedgewitches, and together they wove green magic with Rissi's white. The charms Magdi had hung around the castle grounds activated with a hum that buzzed in Brida's teeth and bones, and around the courtyard guards dropped weapons from senseless fingers.

"Where crops fail, thistles grow!" The rebels yelled, cheering as the guards staggered dizzily.

Brida lurched away from the guard holding her and ran toward Magdi. Joy lit her heart. Mother Magdi was *here* and she was safe and the guards were overcome. The hedgewitches would remove Brida's bracelet and restore Hush's voice. They would punish the queen for her evil and heal those who'd been wounded and free the stormhorses and—

Bones skidded into the courtyard, face white. "She's coming!" he cried.

A shadow suddenly fell across the courtyard and Brida glanced up in dread. The sky was clear, but even as she scanned the cloudless blue expanse the color drained away, leaving it dull gray.

The ground heaved and her gaze snapped back to the courtyard. Color leached from the world around her, darkening the stones and blurring the edge of shadows. One of the Hounds started to whine as a tremor rippled through the flagstones and opened fissures in the ground.

Queen Moira strode into the courtyard, indigo-black skirts swirling. She carried a flaming brand that burned purple, and when she drew glyphs in the air they floated in glowing shapes. The symbols she traced sucked life, energy, *magic* from the world.

Brida tried to take a breath and panicked when she couldn't force enough air into lungs flattened by the queen's ravenous sorcery.

The hedgewitches stumbled, and even Magdi looked shaken as their charms decayed before their eyes. Crumbled bits of wood and ivy drifted down.

Then, from the broken ground, snakes emerged. Dozens

of them—mottled, diseased, eyes like clouded glass. They writhed and twisted, hissed and spat. And they were clearly attracted to magic. Their pale, dust-covered tongues flickered as they slithered toward Rissi, Mother Magdi, and the hedgewitches.

The Circle retreated, struggling to cast new spellweaves that only dissolved in the strange energy void Queen Moira had wrought.

Brida lurched forward, determined to reach Magdi and Rissi, but a crack opened in the ground beside her and a snake slipped out. It opened its mouth, needle fangs glinting in the odd, dull light as it fixed her in a glazed stare.

Then Mystery was there, somehow even larger and more magnificent than before. She raised herself up, swaying slightly. With a long hiss like the escaping whisper of a secret, she began to shed. As patches of her shining scales flaked and peeled off, the pieces of discarded skin dissolved—bringing color back to the ground they touched.

Mystery hissed again and, faster than Brida could blink, whipped around the other snakes—consuming them one by one.

Each one she swallowed seemed to swell her size until she towered above the stunned people staring at her. She glittered in the daylight. And then, tongue darting from her lips, she plunged into the ground and was gone.

There was a low rumble and the earth rolled—and then a burst of color and magic poured across the courtyard.

The great snake had healed some of the damage Moira had done, and hope filled Brida like a cool breeze.

But Moira was only getting started.

She drew another series of flaming glyphs in the air and raised a braided twist of shining horsehair. Brida recognized it with a dawning sense of horror.

The queen was going to use the power of the storm-horses, just as Brida had feared.

A sudden thunderclap reverberated around the castle grounds and when the last echoes rolled away, the ground became a sea of dirt and stone underfoot, heaving and toss-ing like the ocean. A silent scream filled Brida's head as the bracelet she wore turned to scorching ice on her wrist, and then she felt a *pulling* sensation and the queen began to draw away her magic.

It was like being turned inside out and Brida collapsed, retching.

Around her, Crows fell from the sky with keening cries as the queen dragged away whatever magic they'd possessed.

The hedgewitches were beyond Moira's reach—she had no way to control them—but the power void she created weakened them as well. Hush struggled toward Rissi and Magdi, but the knot of hedgewitches couldn't stand against Moira's sorcery.

And she wasn't done yet. She raised the horsehair wreath in one hand and drew more glyphs with the other, and the sky turned bruise black. Livid clouds boiled up, tongues of blue lightning licking the sudden darkness.

"I am your *queen*!" she roared. "How dare you defy me? Do you not see my power?"

In the strange indigo gloaming, Brida saw shadows pool around the castle courtyard. Oozing and slinking, slipping and twisting, they coalesced—growing fangs and claws, horns and spikes, tentacles and tails.

A man wailed as one of the shadows fastened itself to his leg. The color leached from his skin, and then he sagged as his life drained away. All that was left was a faded gray husk.

Panic burst like a toxic bubble and people scrambled to flee Moira's wicked shadows.

But she had turned her attention to the hedgewitches. "Circle of Thistles," she sneered. "Well, it's past time I dealt with the weeds in Fenwood Reach."

"Sister!" Magdi cried. "It's not too late! Surrender the power you've stolen and join us. Together we can heal the damage and—"

"Surrender?" Moira shrieked. "This power is *mine*."

"You've broken the sacred oaths, Sister. But if we work as one, blending our magic—"

"I won't step aside just so you can steal my queendom!"

Moira's eyes fell on Brida. "Princess," she beckoned.

Brida backed away and rage twisted the queen's face. "Bring her to me!" she ordered the Huntsman and two Hounds.

The Huntsman hesitated, but the Hounds plunged toward Brida. She sensed Mother Magdi cast a spellweave to stop them, but the queen's glyphs simply consumed Magdi's magic.

From the corner of her eye, Brida saw a third hound leap to intercept them. She thought she recognized his eyes . . . Bowen.

The Hounds crashed by her legs, wrestling and snapping. Brida tried to run, but the bracelet had drained all her energy and all she could do was scramble clumsily.

Sharp, burning pain pierced her ankle as one of the Hounds fastened his jaws around her leg. The other ripped a gaping wound across Bowen's shoulder and leaped for her arm, tearing her skin as she tried to shove him off.

Arrows whistled through the air to strike the attacking Hounds as the battle between the resistance and the queen's forces resumed. The hedgewitches desperately wove defenses against Moira and her shadows, but she controlled the power of the stormhorses.

Brida had been granted a brief respite, but the cost was too high to bear.

Badly wounded, struggling to breathe, Bowen collapsed beside her. The Huntsman threw himself down, hand stroking the Hound's head. Sobs racked his body. "Oh, my son," he moaned. "I have failed."

The breath rattled in Bowen's chest and pink froth

bubbled at his lips. His sides heaved, but he managed to thump his tail once.

"Nera!" the Huntsman cried. One of the hedgewitches screamed and began to run, but a ring of shadows hemmed her in.

And then Brida felt something . . . shift . . . inside her body. A faint chime sounded, the clink of metal on stone.

She looked down in shock. The queen's bracelet had fallen from her blood-slicked arm.

Blood. *Her blood*.

Hedgewitches didn't use bloodmagic—it was the unspoken magic. But Queen Moira clearly had . . . and Brida shared her aunt's blood.

Shutting out the screams and clashing shouts, Brida clawed whispers of wind from the queen's spinning storm and used her magic to carefully stitch Bowen's gashes closed. She channeled healing power deep within his bones and muscles, working as quickly as she could.

She would never be the healer Mother Magdi was, but she had gotten stronger. Within seconds, he was back on his feet and giving her a silly wolfish grin. Grinning back, she reached to ruffle his ears and a slick of her blood dripped onto the wide leather collar around his neck.

A strange twinge buzzed beneath her skin as the collar sprang open. A wash of color immediately enveloped the Hound, swirling around him until it was all Brida could see.

The Huntsman clasped her by the arm. "What—" he started to say, and then the beastly shape of the Hound fell away and a thin young man in faded clothes stood before them.

"You've saved him!" the Huntsman said, tears pouring from his eyes.

"Twice!" Bowen grinned, exultant. "Thank you, Princess."

"I'm no princess," Brida said. "But I know how to free the stormhorses."

THIRTY-FIVE

The White Dove

BRIDA RAN TOWARD the royal stables, dodging not just guards and shadows but even castle servants, who saw their chance to overthrow the queen and wasted no time in targeting the girl they thought was a princess.

"I'm on your side!" Brida shouted. "I'm going to stop the queen!" But no one listened, so she covered her head with her arms and pushed her body harder, instinctively spinning a shield out of the wind.

She had to hurry—while Bear and Bones and the Huntsman fought the guards, Mother Magdi, Rissi, and Hush battled Moira's storm and shadows with the Circle of Thistles. But they couldn't withstand Moira's power for long. Not when she still drew on the magic of the stormhorses.

Brida found the stable yard in shambles. A goat knocked over a wheelbarrow full of manure and kicked a groom in the shin when he tried to throw a rope around her neck. Then she jumped over a hitching post and ran beneath a panicked horse's belly, bleating in glee as the horse reared and dragged his groom out of the way.

A surprised laugh bubbled in Brida's chest. "Nettle? What in the green world are you doing here? Let me guess . . . Mother Magdi left and you just followed?" The goat tossed her head and bleated again, kicking up her heels and darting off to do more mischief.

While some of the grooms tried to calm the horses, others tried to steal them. For a heartbeat, Brida was afraid someone may have hurt Burdock—he would never allow himself to be taken—but when she called his name he kicked his stall door down and galloped toward her.

Without bothering to saddle him, she grabbed his mane with both hands and flung herself onto his back. "Keep up the good work!" she called to Nettle. Then twining her fingers in Burdock's thick mane, she wrapped her legs around his barrel, leaned forward, and told him to *run*.

They shot out of the stable yard and raced past the castle gardens. "Follow the wind, Burdock!" she urged.

He whinnied and tossed his head, stretching his neck out as his hooves skimmed the ground. Plunging past snarling Hounds, he jumped a stone wall, tucking his knees to his chest to clear it. He galloped down a hill and splashed through a swift creek, then raced through the trees.

Burdock was fast, as far as ponies go, but now the wind seemed to lift and carry him. The ground beneath his drumming hooves blurred and it was all Brida could do to hang on as he ducked and twisted around massive tree trunks.

And then, up ahead, she spotted the secret barn. It would have been hard to miss—streaks of forked lightning split the sky overhead, gusts of wind rattled the trees and shook the timbers, and snowflakes danced in glittering clouds around it. As Brida slowed Burdock to a trot, furious, frightened whinnies echoed from inside.

Burdock whinnied back and lurched to a stop outside the barn door.

The queen's silver halters might allow her to draw on their power, but the stormhorses fought Moira's hold with all the strength of their fury. Their elemental magic was rapidly becoming unstable—and even more dangerous.

Brida slid off Burdock's back, leg muscles cramping from the wild ride. Half-afraid, she tugged open the door and entered the barn.

Shadows pooled along the dusty aisle, feeding off the energy of the stormhorses. They resisted as valiantly as they could. Sweat foamed on their necks and flanks, and breath roared through their flared nostrils.

Brida hurried to the first stall. The roan horse squealed but did not back away when Brida reached for her halter.

The pain in Brida's arm had dulled to a steady ache and her blood had started to dry, but she scratched the scabbed bite with her fingernails until a fresh line of red bloomed. She felt a quick sting as she grabbed the halter with her blood-smeared hand, but then the silver cheek piece dissolved and the roan horse was free. A burst of rain cooled

Brida's flushed face when she opened the stall door to let the horse out.

On to the bay with white spots, and then to the black thunder stallion. Then to the golden palomino.

Queen Moira's writhing shadows clung to Brida's ankles now, sapping her strength. Sparks fizzed at the edges of her vision but only one halter was left. . . .

A roar burst through the open barn door and a spinning cyclone of feathers and black sand appeared. A dull silver glow filled the center, widening into a spherical opening.

Queen Moira stepped out, a cloak of crow feathers falling from her shoulders.

Hush and Magdi stumbled through a moment later, bruised and bloodied.

"I gave you *everything*," Moira snarled at Brida, striding down the aisle with the horsehair wreath in her hands. "I made you a *princess*. I offered to teach you my secrets, to share my power. You would have been a daughter to me, one day ruling my realm. And yet here you are. A traitor. I should have guessed you were as bad as your mother."

The shadows climbed Brida's legs, leaching away her energy. She could barely stand, but she reached a trembling hand toward the last silver halter and closed her blood-stained fingers around it. With a light chime, it too dissolved and the white mare was free.

Instead of running to join her herd, the white mare— the wind horse—whinnied and pawed the ground. She advanced, stomping and snorting, and the shadows retreated like an ebbing tide before the rush of her magic.

Brida gulped air, slowly straightening as the white mare's power fed her own windmagic. "I would *never* have been your daughter," she said. "And the stormhorses aren't yours to hold."

The white mare reared and lunged for the queen, but Moira turned to smoke and feathers before the horse reached her. The mare raced through the door, but the queen reappeared a heartbeat later with a cruel laugh. "They won't get far," she said, shaking the circle of braided horsehair.

Magdi hurriedly wove a charm to bind the queen, but even without the halters holding the stormhorses captive, the wreath in Moira's possession gave her a connection to their elemental power. Tenuous as it was, Magdi wasn't strong enough to overcome it and subdue her sister.

They had to get that horsehair wreath away from the queen, but first . . . Brida had promised Hush her voice, and she had an idea.

Drawing in as much magic as she could hold, threads of the stormhorses' power inexplicably fueling her strength, Brida wove Hush's voice back from the wind, the sound of rain, the song of birds, the plink of ice.

Hush opened her mouth as the magic poured in, and she sang.

Her voice was a soft and wispy thing, at first, but Moira flung her away with a look of rage. As Hush's song strengthened, the queen's shadows weakened.

"That's it! Together now!" Magdi cried, grasping Hush's hand.

Brida wove windmagic through Hush's song, calling on the bitter chill of mountain gusts and the fiery breath of desert storms, the salt spray and fury of ocean tempests and the crisp tang of fall breezes.

Magdi added a spellweave of hedgemagic, ripe with the promise of green growing things and built with the sturdiness of oak and stone.

Moira's eyes narrowed and her cheeks paled, but she could still call on the power of the stormhorses and all her black sorcery. Cursing, she spread her arms. A dark cloud like soot and cinders swirled around her. It spun faster and faster until she was completely obscured. When it suddenly collapsed, in her place there stood a massive Crow clutching the horsehair circlet.

Magdi lunged to catch her, but Moira launched into the air and flew from the barn.

Brida ran outside—and into a maelstrom.

The stormhorses had tasted escape, but so long as Moira held strands of their hair they were not truly free. They raged against that bond, racing in circles before the barn. Lightning struck the ground again and again, throwing chunks of dirt and clods of grass into scorched, sizzling air. Rain poured from the sky in silver curtains that gusted sideways in the white mare's wind, obscuring Brida's vision and soaking her to the skin in seconds. Chill blasts of snow-laden air sent ribbons of frost ghosting along the ground and Brida's teeth chattered.

The horses galloped faster and faster in a circle, their elemental energies tangling in a storm unlike anything Brida had ever imagined.

The barn shook with the force of it, strips of wood peeling away in the onslaught of wind and rain. A lightning strike hit the roof in an explosion of splinters, and curls of smoke rose from the charred black mark.

Hush was thrown back, slammed against the doors of the barn. She opened her mouth to sing a calming spell, but her words were swallowed by the storm.

Magdi had no better luck. The bruised and battered hedgewitch was knocked to her knees, but she kept her face tilted to the sky as she searched for Moira.

But the magic in Brida's blood rose to meet the magic in the wind and weather, filling her with a rush of wild elation. Though the storm's gusts whipped her hair and tore at her clothes, she marched to the center of the stormhorses. With every circle the herd galloped around her, more power poured inside her skin until she felt as if her heart were made of sky.

Burdock pinned his ears and lowered his head, neck straining against the force of the magic tempest as he tried to forge a path closer to Brida. Buffeted by the wind and rain, flinching from the crackling lightning bolts, he finally gave up and backed away, whinnying forlornly as he stood guard near Hush and Magdi.

Brida tipped her chin up and spotted Moira in her Crow form, circling overhead, weaving in and out of cloud wisps beyond the wind currents. In the midst of the chaos, Brida felt a rippling moment of perfect clarity.

Her windmagic linked her to the stormhorses more surely than any silver halters or strands of stolen hair could do, because she was bound to them by natural affinity, by awe and wonder and respect.

Together, they would defeat the Queen of Crows. They were the only ones who could.

"Now!" Brida cried, and pointed. The black thunder horse reared and pawed the air, sending bolts of lightning crashing through the clouds, but Moira dodged them.

"She's beyond our reach!" Magdi cried.

Brida closed her eyes and wrapped herself in wind and rain, sun and snow, the crash of thunder. She felt the rush of the storm in her own blood, roaring in her ears and drumming in her chest. She was filled with it. She was *part* of it.

When another lightning streak flashed from the black stallion's hooves, she flung up her hands, catching the bolt in the wind and throwing it with perfect aim.

The lightning struck Moira's chest with a purple sizzle and she fell from the sky, spinning dizzily but unable to right herself.

She fell, and fell, and fell.

The stormhorses slowed to a canter, then a trot. And then they stopped to watch her descent, the fury of the elements calming at last.

Black feathers and sour, glittering magic burst—leaving the queen's crumpled form lying on a carpet of leaves and moss, still clutching a ragged circle of horsehair.

Brida snatched the wreath up and ran to the white mare, offering it on her open palms. But the mare only nuzzled her, whiskers brushing her cheek like the lightest dawn breeze. The others came to blow their farewells in her face, nudging her shoulders and hands with their velvet noses. With a glad whinny, the white mare tossed her head and led her herd in a swift gallop—back to their own realm, however far it might be.

Brida stroked the shining hair in her hands, still feeling tingles of the stormhorses' magic.

Burdock trotted to her, ears flat and lips pinched anxiously. Brida laid an arm over his neck and kissed his face. "You were so brave," she told him.

Magdi rose and approached her fallen sister, a white dove fluttering cautiously from the trees to land on her shoulder.

Brida followed, leaning over the broken queen. Regret and sorrow left her chest hollow. Moira had done terrible things, but she was still Brida's aunt.

Magdi stood beside Brida, wrapping her in a hug as they watched the light of life seep out of Moira's eyes and her body go still. "Can we heal her?" Brida murmured.

"Some things can't be healed, dear one. It is for the Great Mother to decide what happens next." She rubbed a hand across her face. "Ah, Sister. I tried to tell you what would happen if you let jealousy and hate take root. If only you'd been satisfied with your own white magic, instead of grasping for ever more power and letting the darkness corrupt you."

With a flick of her wrist, she sent grasses surging up like a blanket to cover the queen. Wildflowers emerged and bloomed, and a sapling took root. As Brida watched, it grew and thickened and spread until a massive oak stood where the queen had been lying only moments before.

The wind danced in the tree's branches, and Brida could swear it called her name.

Mother Magdi must have heard it, too, for she said, "I suspected you had talents yet to be discovered. My dearest niece, you will be a marvelous Windwitch."

"No, I . . . I can't. I mean, maybe I can call windmagic, but Windwitches are rare and special and—"

"Brida, *so are you*."

Suddenly, the giant eagle landed before Brida, tilted her head to one side, and fixed her golden eyes on Brida's face. Though a couple of her feathers had been rumpled in her skirmishes with the Crows, she was beautiful.

Understanding slowly dawned. "Wait . . . Are you . . . are you the Windwitch?" Brida murmured in awe.

Once upon a time I was. But I have spent far too long hiding in the mountains. Now I am too old to take my human shape, she said in Brida's mind, her thoughts carried by gentle wisps of wind. *Join me before I must go. There are things you should know.*

"Join you? But I—"

Have you not guessed why it took the queen three feathers to turn you into a Crow? It was because your spirit had already chosen its own shape . . . that of the eagle, sovereign of the skies. Trust the wind, trust yourself, and trust me. Come, now, fly with me!

Doubt glued Brida's feet to the ground. She could do tricks with her windmagic, yes. She could blow a ball of glowing light into her palm, locate things, hide her trail. She could use windmagic to heal injuries—though not as well as Magdi could with hedgemagic—and she'd even learned to lift a hex. But turning herself into a bird?

"You can do it, Brida," Mother Magdi said. Hush nodded encouragement. The white dove flapped her wings and warbled.

A thread of wind tied itself into Brida's hair and tugged, insistent.

Brida closed her eyes and let the air currents ripple across her skin. She took a deep breath—and then, suddenly, she was made of wind and clouds and bright sun. Her skin prickled and shivered, tingled and buzzed, as feathers sprouted. Her bones turned to air, twisting and folding until she lost any sense of shape or form.

It wasn't at all painful. Just . . . strange.

And then she opened her eyes and let out a surprised cry—an eagle's cry.

She could see *everything* in sharp-edged detail, rendered in vivid colors she'd never even imagined. She spotted an ant crawling on a blade of grass several paces away, a snail peeking from beneath a pebble at the edge of a tiny puddle. Tilting her head, her eyes traced the veins in every leaf on every tree around them.

She could practically see the wind itself.

This is far better than being a captive Crow! Brida exulted.

Fly! the Windwitch urged, chuckling.

Brida spread wings wider than a tall man's arms and beat the air, lifting off the ground with several powerful strokes.

Warm drifts of wind stroked her belly, lifting her higher. She screamed in triumph and joy, soaring effortlessly as the Windwitch circled nearby.

Down below, Burdock whinnied and kicked up his heels, galloping in the shadow of the two giant eagles. A small white dove fluttered above him.

Angling her tail feathers to refine her course, Brida streaked through the sky. She sped away from the castle and the smoking ruins of the battle, skimmed the forest, hearing the song of the wind in the leaves. Small birds hid in the dappled shadows, and timid deer peeped at her from beneath the boughs. A fox slipped through the underbrush, dislodging a cloud of flies and gnats.

Then her massive wings carried her over a rolling meadow. Grass rippled beneath her, a green ocean teeming with bugs, mice, moles, and rabbits. *What do you see? What does the wind tell you?* the Windwitch murmured in her mind.

Brida cast her senses out, paying closer attention.

Now she saw the damage the queen had wrought. There were patches of disease in the meadow, swathes of dead brown grass, blackened wildflowers, weeds, and bare dirt. Some of the trees in the forest clung to faded leaves or rust-colored pine needles, and some bore weeping scabs across their trunks. Vines choked out fragile ferns and tiny wildflowers. Unpredictable seasons had disrupted the normal cycles of fruit, nut, and acorn production, and many of the birds and squirrels she spotted were slowly starving.

We're too late! It's all dying. She screamed her rage into the sky.

No, we're not! The Windwitch called back. *What does the wind say?*

Brida climbed a draft higher, and then higher, and still higher until all she saw were clouds. She couldn't bear the sight of such widespread destruction, of impending death.

But the wind whistled in her ears, whispered in her mind.

It told her of a warm, gentle, cleansing rain rolling slowly along the horizon. It promised soothing warmth, and mild nights. It sang of balance returning, of eggs hatching and fawns taking their first wobbling steps. Of foxes hiding kits in safe, dark dens and rabbits nursing their young in cozy nests. It carried scents of budding flowers and flowing sap, of new leaves unfurling and old leaves being shed.

The wind told her that the land could heal. That it was, already, beginning to recover.

Brida plunged through the clouds, swooping down to the Windwitch. *The wind says things will get better.*

They will. They are already, but you must work with the hedgewitches, the priestesses, and the priests to repair the damage and prevent further harm. You, brave girl, will be the next Windwitch. You will learn as I did—listen to the wind itself, and it will teach you all you need to know. But if you need me, call on the wind and I will hear.

They circled slowly lower, gliding on sinking currents.

Where will you go? Why can't you stay? Brida asked.

I will follow the stormhorses beyond the edge of the Five Realms, to the Shadowlands of the Silver Fae. It is where I belong now, the Windwitch answered.

Will they be back?

I cannot say. But they have blessed you with an echo of their power, the ring of their braided hair. You will be the most powerful Windwitch the Five Realms has ever seen.

They landed on a rocky outcrop overlooking a glittering ribbon of swift-flowing water as Burdock, sweat damp and blowing, galloped toward them, accompanied by the white dove. Magdi and Hush rode up a few minutes later on Velvet.

You have done well, little wind-sister. Perhaps we'll meet again someday. And with a last wild cry, the Windwitch-eagle leaped into the air and soared away.

The white dove spread her wings and sang a trilling warble of farewell.

Brida closed her eyes and shook off her feathers, dropping her eagle form as easily as if it were a cloak. When she opened them again, the world seemed so much softer and duller, but the faces of her friends—her *family*—were clear and that mattered more than anything.

Mother Magdi extended her arm, letting the dove perch on her wrist. "Brida, dear heart, in an effort to protect you, I have kept too many secrets for far too long. This dove . . . she is one of them."

"I don't understand."

"Moira tried to kill your mother when you were just a tiny babe. She did not succeed—but the only way I could save Maigin was to seize Moira's spell and convert it into one that would disguise your mother's form rather than end her life."

"Do you mean . . . are you saying . . . that dove is *my mother*?"

The white dove cooed and bobbed her head, and Brida remembered all the moments she'd spotted a white dove in the woods around Magdi's cottage. "But I tried to befriend her and she never—"

"She was afraid of getting too close. Afraid Moira would find you both. But she's been keeping an eye on you, all these years."

"Mother?" Brida whispered, tasting the shape of the word. "But then why haven't you restored her human shape?"

Magdi's brows puckered with regret. "I may be a strong hedgewitch, but the energy that fueled Moira's killing spell was greater than any magic I could call now. I'm afraid this disguise is beyond my abilities to remove."

Hush clapped her hands together. "I know the sacred spellsong to change her back, but my magic is rusty from long disuse. If we weave ours together again, though—"

"Yes!" Brida cried.

"This evening then, under the full moon," Hush said. "With Rissi to help."

Burdock whinnied and rubbed his chin on Brida's chest. They all returned to the castle together, the dove perched on Brida's shoulder to coo love in her ear.

That evening, as a full moon floated above the castle, Hush and Rissi clasped hands. Together they sang notes as clear as dewdrops in a soaring melody, pure and bright as starlight. Brida spun threads of wind along the waves of their voices, and Magdi wove a magic net of spider silk and tiny crystal beads she placed around the dove.

As the sacred song climbed moonbeams and filled the night, a pearl-colored mist swirled slowly around the white dove's form. It spread, and brightened, and filled the net of spider silk until the song had ended. Then in a flash of silver light a woman stood in place of the dove, wearing a pale beaded gown and swaying unsteadily.

"It has been too long since last I walked as a woman," she said, tracing a hand along her thigh.

Brida ran to her, flinging her arms around her mother as broken sobs shook her body.

"Brida, my daughter," Maigin murmured, smoothing a hand over Brida's hair. "I am so proud of you."

She beckoned Magdi, clutching her sister in a fierce hug. "Thank you for keeping her safe. For hiding us until the time was right." She pulled back, holding them at arm's length and smiling through her tears. "The three of us have a great deal of catching up to do."

THIRTY-SIX

Windwitch

IT TOOK TIME to clean the mess at the castle.

Most of the Hounds were killed in the rebellion, including Mason the priest, who died defending Bear and Bones. But Brida returned the survivors to their human form and Mother Magdi dispensed justice. Those who refused to abide by the laws of the land were exiled. The others—innocent of any crime worse than crossing the queen—were awarded medals for bravery and given jobs repairing the damage to the castle and the capital city.

The Crows also recovered their human figures, but Mother Magdi, at Brida's suggestion, made them feather amulets that would allow them to shape-shift at will.

"Flying is the ultimate escape," Brida said, "and after what the queen did to them, after she stole their magic and used it for her own ends, don't you think they deserve to revel in their freedom whenever they wish?" Hunting crows would be outlawed in case someone with a strong arm and a slingshot might accidentally bring down someone's daughter or wife or mother.

There were memorials to hold for those who'd lost their lives and plans to make, then, in the days that followed. Hush was determined to rebuild the Temple of the Crescent Moon and Bones eagerly threw himself into the work. He proved to have a knack for architectural design, and his ability to sense magic potential meant the Temple already had a number of future initiates. They also planned to add a school and a home for children without parents.

Maigin decided to build a new Temple of the Winds on the Veiled Cliffs at the northern end of the valley and sent wagons of lumber and stone rolling along the road, promising to meet her work crew there soon.

Rissi was invited to stay at either Temple, but after consulting with Mystery she decided to return to her own sacred grotto once she'd learned all the spellsongs and sacred chants Maigin could teach her.

Half the people in Rookery Point wanted to name Brida their queen and continue on as they had before, because hadn't she been Moira's niece and designated successor? But the other half didn't want anything to do with her for the same reason.

It made her sad to think how many years they had suffered under the Queen of Crows. She wanted them to know she was different, that she could help. But they didn't seem to care about Brida the girl—all they saw was the symbol of a crown she'd never wanted and the shadow of her aunt's feathers.

In the end, it didn't matter. She was a Windwitch, not a queen. It would be several years before she came into her full strength, Mother Magdi explained, but she had good instincts and the wind liked her.

Already people swore they felt a change in the weather.

More hedgewitches came out of hiding and started forming a Council of Wisdoms for Rookery Point and a new one for Edgewood. Nera, the Huntsman's wife, had several women and men in mind. They could govern without a queen.

Most important, perhaps, the people of the capital asked Bear to be their Voice, to begin recording and remembering their stories. After gentle prodding from Hush he agreed.

Together she and Bear would teach a language of hands and facial expressions to those who couldn't hear or speak so they could share the stories, too.

Stories have power, after all, and memories shape the future.

The hedgewitches from the Circle of Thistles gradually scattered back to their own villages and homes, carrying new stories with them.

Brida, Maigin, and Mother Magdi prepared to do the same, packing saddlebags for the long ride back to the valley. Burdock and Nettle were just as ready to leave Rookery

Point—now called Eagle Point, in honor of Brida.

But Brida was worried. "Mother Magdi, if you still need my help when you get back to Oak Hollow I can stay with you a few days a week and live in the Temple the rest of the time."

"Ah, child, you're sweet to think of it. But you will be much too busy practicing your windmagic to continue assisting me with hedgemagic, and your rightful place is with your mother in the Temple of the Winds. But I will enjoy your company anytime just the same," Magdi patted her shoulder.

"Who will be your apprentice, then?"

"Take Dev," Maigin suggested, wrapping beeswax candles and crystals in cloth as she packed them in a trunk.

"Dev?" Brida spluttered. "You can't be serious! He's a butcher and a bully."

"The boy is afraid of blood, and his father shames him for it," Maigin said gently.

Brida swallowed the insults she'd been stringing together and blinked. Afraid of blood? Was his bullying a way to prove his courage, then? To make himself feel big and brave?

She shook her head. "Doesn't matter. He's cruel. And he knows nothing about healing or birthing or potions or anything!"

"No, he doesn't. But I believe he might have magic. And I watched him in the woods many an afternoon. He keeps a secret garden in a clearing, with hives for bees. He has a love for flowers, and cares for the only collection of wild orchids I've ever seen in the valley. Maybe he can't deliver babes or mend broken bones, but he'll tend your garden, Magdi, and your animals. It will be good for the boy."

Brida caught her breath. All those times she'd seen him in the woods, she'd thought he was following her just to give her grief. But if he was protecting his secret . . .

Magdi tapped her chin with a finger. "You may be on to something, Sister."

Brida sighed. "If he gives you any trouble, though, I'm going to turn him into a toad."

The wind spun flower petals around her feet and Burdock tossed his head with a snort. From somewhere far in the distance, Brida heard the cry of an eagle and the thunder of galloping hooves.

She raised her hand in farewell, letting strands of wind-magic sift between her fingers.

The flowing breeze felt like hope and she couldn't wait to see what stories it might carry next.

Acknowledgments

Writing these pages is, if I'm being honest, almost harder than writing the actual book because words can't hold the depth of my gratitude or the sheer volume of luck and privilege and astonishment I feel at being able to share it with you. So many people had a hand in turning my ink-and-paper imaginary world into a book—it would be impossible to thank every single one. If you've ever said a kind word about my writing, offered your enthusiasm, or cheered me on at all, please know that your support and encouragement kept me going and made this possible. If you are holding this book in your hands, I thank you.

That said, this book could not have existed without the hard work and help of the following people, and I owe them special thanks:

Sarah Landis, my absolutely brilliant dream agent— thank you so much for taking a chance on me and Brida. I can't imagine a better advocate and there's just no way to adequately express my appreciation for everything you've done. Thank you for making me an author. I can't wait to see what happens next!

Alice Jerman, my incredible editor—thank you for asking thoughtful questions and sharing keen insights, for encouraging me to peel back layers I barely even knew existed in order to bring Brida's story into sharper focus. Thank you for loving this story like I do and turning it into something special. Working with you has been a complete joy.

Clare Vaughn, editorial assistant—thank you for your hard work and kind enthusiasm. You sent me an email when I tackled my first edits talking about how much you enjoyed this story and it was exactly the boost of courage I needed. I'll never forget it.

To Cathleen McAllister for the gorgeous artwork and Gemma Roman for the absolutely perfect lettering, and to Alice Wang and Alison Donalty for designing an utterly stunning cover—you have my endless, dazzled gratitude. Thank you all so much for wrapping my story in something so lovely and magical—it literally brought me to tears when I first saw it, and I'm still in awe.

Martha Schwartz, copy editor, and Jon Howard, production editor—thank you for your careful reading and sharp eyes, for polishing each page and turning my manuscript into a real book. You've transformed a dream into something tangible, and I'm so grateful.

And thanks to *everyone* at HarperCollins Children's

Books involved in publishing, producing, or promoting this book. I am so honored to be one of your authors and so grateful for this opportunity.

Warm thanks also to all my #TeamLandis agency siblings (in no particular order): Erin A. Craig, Jess Rubinkowski, Meredith Tate, Lyudmyla Hoffman, Julie Abe, Emily Lloyd-Jones, Elizabeth Unseth, Jennie Brown, Ron Walters, Amanda Jasper, Elisabeth Funk, Leah Johnson, Shelby Mahurin, and Isabel Ibañez (and anyone else I've missed or who signs before this goes to print!)—thank you for answering my stupid questions, keeping my secrets, and sharing your experiences. You are all so talented and creative—I can't believe I'm lucky enough to be part of your group.

Carrie Jones—thank you so much for leading the first Write Submit Support class at the Writing Barn. Your feedback on the beginning section opened my eyes to new possibilities and changed the way I think about engaging with characters. Your gentle, friendly encouragement gave me the motivation to query—if it hadn't been for you, this would likely still be a file on my desktop. Thank you for everything! (And thanks as well to Bethany Hegedus, my classmates, and everyone at the Writing Barn who made the class possible.)

Sarah Prineas and Dorothy Winsor—thank you for welcoming me to WisCon years ago and reading my first attempts at fiction without telling me I was wasting my time. You made me feel like this might someday be within reach, and I'll never stop being grateful.

Meghan Scott Molin—thanks for cheering me on since the LJ days. Your faith that I would one day be published kept me going when I'd started to lose my own.

Kelly Jones and Edith Hope Bishop—I owe you huge hugs and a virtual tea party in gratitude for the unfailing support and sisterhood, shared wisdom, and evening chats. Thank you for the feedback and the friendship. You've been with me since the beginning and all I can say is that the path would have been so much darker and lonelier and more discouraging if you hadn't been there to light the way.

Dr. Amy Davis and the staff at Crossing Back to Health—thank you for literally saving my life. When I first came to you, I was desperately ill and horribly frustrated. Your willingness to listen and your unique approach to medicine gave me the answers I needed and set me back on the path to health. I wrote the first draft of this book during the worst year of my life and wasn't sure I would survive to write another story, but I'm still here and I feel better than ever thanks to you.

To all the members of Scribes Tribe: Candace, Amy, Meghan, Mary H, Deborah, and Mary S—thank you for your comments on the first few chapters. Your eagerness to hear what might happen next gave me the confidence to keep writing. I am so grateful for your support and friendship.

To Abby, Chris, Roxanne, Nancy, and everyone at CMB—thank you for taking such good care of my horses and for letting me indulge my barn kid fantasies. It took 40+ years, but it was worth the wait! And Abby, I can't thank you enough for everything you've done. Riding lessons with you are the best sort of barn therapy sessions. Somehow, all the times you've talked me through fear, insecurity, or anxiety in the saddle ended up growing my courage for all sorts of challenges in life. Thank you for being my trainer, riding instructor, counselor, and friend.

Alice and Steve—I'm so grateful for my new bathroom and doors! Thank you so very much for giving up your summer to work on my house so that I could spend mine writing. Your generosity and hard work mean so much to me. And I promise I'll never ask you to set a new tub again.

To my parents, Paula and Dan—thank you for raising me with a library card, bookshelves, and a flashlight. Thanks for reading my first folded-paper-and-crayon-sketch "books" and for always being my biggest cheerleaders. And to my siblings: Rebecca, Emily, and Tom—thanks for letting me exercise my imagination with make-believe games in the yard, and for all the support now. Love and hugs to all of you!

Finally, and perhaps most important, thanks to my husband and children for *everything*. Taryn, thanks for brainstorming with me over tea and cookies, for late-night book talks, and for the battle scene. I owe you for that one!

Alec, thanks for lending a hand whenever necessary and making me laugh so hard I cry. Thanks for being excited even if books aren't your thing. I am so proud of both of you and can't wait to see where your own life stories lead you.

Andy, *thank you* is too small to tell you what you mean to me or how grateful I am for the life we've built. Your love has shaped my world: wide skies and a red barn, horses and cats, pickup trucks and farm dogs and muddy boots. Bonfires and rodeos. Children and laughter and two decades (so far) of adventure. You've encouraged my ambitions, supported my dreams, and believed in me even when I lost faith in myself. I'm so excited to see what the next chapter holds for us. I love you. And also, Tractors Are Good.

Read on for a sneak peek at
a new magical adventure

— ONE —

Broken

LARK MAIREN BALLED her fists and pushed her body faster, stumbling over pebbles in the path and ridges left by tree roots. She plunged through ferns and tangles of bittersweet vine, racing toward the waymarker at the edge of her family's property—the last place she'd seen her brother, Galin.

Melting frost glittered on the grass and soaked the toes of her leather boots as she panted clouds of mist in the chilly morning air, but the ache in her lungs and legs was nothing compared to the pain in her heart. *He'll be there. He has to be there.*

Distant voices called back and forth while thundering hoofbeats drummed echoes from the ground. Search parties followed her in a wide sweep, since she was the only one who had watched the Wild Hunt ride past this stretch of the border. They hoped to find a hint, a clue that could explain why Galin hadn't returned with the other Hunters at dawn.

Had he been thrown from his shadowbred horse? Was he lying injured somewhere?

By the time Lark reached the granite-and-moonstone waymarker indicating the boundary of the Fae realm, her parents were already riding to meet her. "Any sign of him?" she called, but Da shook his head.

She bent forward, bracing her hands on her thighs to catch her breath as disappointment and exertion left her gasping. Last night the wind had smelled of smoke and apples, cinnamon and salted caramel, and the deep green musk of Fae magic. This morning it carried the sour scent of worry and the salt-tang of sorrow.

As she wheezed, her parents argued quietly about how to proceed, their horses catching their nerves and fidgeting anxiously this close to the border.

"Lark, tell us again exactly what you saw," Ma said. Ma— River Mairen, Horsemaven of the Borderlands and five-time Hunter—nudged Legacy, her gleaming black shadowbred mare, closer while Da hunched awkwardly in the saddle of a neighbor's massive bay plow horse. He'd ridden the Wild Hunt once as a young man, Lark knew, but he was a tailor and a dressmaker now. The magic shadowbred horses—part mortal, part Fae—that his wife's family had been breeding and training for generations made him nervous.

They made Lark nervous too, which was why she

preferred to run to the waymarker on her own two feet. Even if that meant she was now too winded to speak.

"Lark?" Da asked.

She had hoped—had let herself *believe*—that no matter what trouble Galin might have found, he would somehow make his way back to this marker to wait for her.

But if he could have made it this far, he would have returned all the way home, wouldn't he?

"Where are you, Galin? What happened?" she murmured.

"Lark, we need to hear every detail you remember," Ma urged. "Perhaps there's a clue we've missed."

Lark had snuck out the night before to watch the stampede of human and Fae Hunters, never expecting to witness her brother's last ride. Guilt and sorrow stuck in her throat like day-old oat bran mush.

"First there was a rush of wind," she said, frowning at a single red toadstool near the base of the waymarker. "Then the pale glow of the White Stag bounding along the border, guiding the Hunters, and the rumble of hooves galloping after him." The image was burned in Lark's mind: a full moon casting silver-rimmed shadows, the surging tide of black shadowbred horses breathing sparkling mist from flared nostrils, racing hounds baying in full song, birds filling the night sky, Fae Hunters in cloaks woven of spiderwebs and starlight. . . .

And the lead rider, wearing a flame-bright crimson

cloak, a golden vest, and a circlet of blazing autumn leaves upon his head. The Harvest King in all his glory, looking right at her.

Lark recalled shrinking back, afraid of getting in trouble. She should have been tucked safely in bed beneath a quilt embroidered with protective sigils and lucky symbols—Wild Hunt nights were full of magic and chaos, even for those who weren't Hunters—but curiosity had tugged her outside.

Her sister, Sage, was riding the Hunt along with Galin that night, and Lark had wanted to see them both. So she slipped from her house and skimmed up the path, past the stable, around the orchard, through the woods, and here to the closest waymarker.

She never expected the Harvest King himself to notice her. Fear curled her toes against the cold ground, but he'd smiled kindly and raised a hand in greeting.

In that moment of distraction, a tangle of brambles and thorns burst from the ground beneath him. Lark now told her parents how vines as thick as her arms erupted like snakes, wriggling and twisting around the legs of the king's magnificent shadowbred. Finger-long thorns ripped into the horse's sleek black coat, raking trails of red-and-silver blood. The shadowbred shrieked and turned to smoke, throwing the Harvest King from his back.

"I screamed," Lark admitted. "And then suddenly Galin was there, riding up on Whimsy. He leaned over, reached out, and gripped the king's hand. Galin pulled the Harvest King up behind his saddle and they raced past the brambles."

"Who else did you see? How did the other Fae react?" Da asked, worry puckering his brow.

"There was a beautiful Fae riding beside Galin, with shining sun-gold hair. She smiled at him when he rescued the king, but I lost sight of them as they rounded the curve of the hills. Sage followed a few minutes later, so I waved to her and ran back to the house. That's all I know. Do you think Galin is still with the king? Maybe he'll be celebrated as a hero and escorted back with honors! We should go see if—"

But it was clear from her parents' expressions that they didn't share her excitement.

"All the other Hunters returned as expected," Da mused. "No major injuries . . . I can't understand why Galin wasn't with them."

"He's always been a courteous boy. Perhaps he stayed a bit longer to offer comfort after the loss of the king's shadow-bred, though I don't see any thorns or brambles now," Ma said, gaze sweeping the ground.

Lark sighed. "No . . . that's the strange thing. As soon as Galin and the king rode out of sight, the vines withered to dust and blew away. Oh!" She suddenly remembered. "I saw something tumble from the king's vest pocket when he fell. I don't know what it was . . . something round and silver." It had smashed in a scatter of tiny pieces while thistles clawed through grass and leaf loam, stretching toward the king. She paced a circle around the waymarker. Perhaps some pieces remained?

"Probably a mirror. The Fae are vain," Ma said dismissively, snapping Lark's attention back to the discussion at hand.

"I bet you're right," Da murmured. "Maybe he simply didn't have time to return to the barn with the other Hunters before the Faevoring ceremony. He's probably in the square at this very moment, and here we are in a panic for no reason." He forced a chuckle and gathered his reins.

Ma nodded but didn't call off the search. "Sage and the rest of the Hunters should be there for the Faevoring now. Go see if Galin is with them." She hesitated before adding, "Just in case he's not, Legacy and I will ride farther along the border. There's a tricky stretch between the waymarker at Hawkridge and the one at Crestview, and if he tried to ride that far with the king behind him . . . Well, I just want to make sure he wasn't thrown and injured. If there was a problem we can't afford to waste any daylight."

Lark glanced reflexively at the sky, even though she knew it was early yet. They still had most of a day to search for Galin if he didn't turn up at the Faevoring ceremony.

However, if they didn't find him by moonrise the border would close. And Galin wouldn't be able to make his way back.

"Galin could still return in the spring when the border

opens for the Mayfair Hunt, couldn't he? If he's somehow been trapped in the Fae realm, surely the May Queen would let him return then?" Lark asked, fretting aloud.

Da bent from the saddle to lay a warm hand on top of her head. "There's always hope—and right now I'm hoping he's waiting for his Faevor with your sister and the other Hunters."

But his lips were pinched in a grim line and Lark's spirits sank like stones in a puddle. Galin *had* to be in the square, otherwise she knew the odds weren't on his side. If he didn't return by moonrise, he'd be stuck in the Fae realm until spring. That would be six moonturns of eating Fae food and drinking Fae water and breathing Fae magic.

By then he might be forever changed. And she had never heard of anyone returning after getting caught on the wrong side of the border.

A worse thought occurred to her, sharp and stinging as a nettle scratch. The brambles hadn't suddenly appeared by accident. What if the Fae king was attacked on purpose? The Twilight Court might be even more dangerous than usual. No place for a mortal.

Still, if anyone had a chance it would be her brother. He'd been brave enough and strong enough to save the Harvest King, so he was brave enough and strong enough to come back too.

He had to be.

"If you find Galin or hear word of him, send a message

through the scouts. I'll check in as soon as I can." Ma sighed and twitched the reins. "In the meantime, Lark, I need you to hurry home straightaway. Take care of the shadowbreds who've returned from the Hunt and wait for us there."

Lark nodded, chewing her lip.

"And watch the road, do you hear me?" Da urged.

"I will," Lark promised. *Watch the road* was code for *Be wary of the Fae.* "You too."

"Luck of the winds!" Ma said, and then she spun Legacy toward the south and cantered away.

"I'm heading to the square, but if you need anything Sarai will be looking in," Da said. "I'll be back as soon as I can." And he rode off too.

After watching him go, Lark pressed a hand against the worry squirming through her belly and turned for home, until a strange croak coming from the fall-faded grass caught her attention.

Surely it wouldn't be a wildkin—not the morning after a Wild Hunt.

Everyone knew the Fae couldn't be trusted, but there were *rules*. Treaties. Traditions . . .

And the most important tradition was the twice-yearly ritual of the Wild Hunt, meant to preserve the balance of power and protect the Borderlands from rogue wildkin magic.

The safest time in the Borderlands was the morning after a Hunt, when any mischievous wildkin had been chased back to the Fae realm where they belonged and the simmering chaos of Fae magic had been temporarily quieted.

Only . . . something had gone wrong on this Hunt and Galin hadn't returned. He was the first Hunter to disappear since the Accords had been signed generations ago, since Mairen Horsemavens had started raising shadowbreds and training riders.

Lark couldn't decide if that was comforting—because then surely Galin would be all right?—or terrifying, because if he wasn't in the square as they hoped, what would it mean? What else could have gone wrong?

The sound came again: a desperate gurgle and a scuffle.

Fear slithered through Lark and she clenched her teeth, tensing her muscles to run. If there was something Fae hiding in that grass she wanted nothing to do with it. But then she saw the tentative flap of a black wing and suddenly realized what she was hearing.

She carefully parted the long stems to find a raven, clearly injured and blinking up at her.

"Ohhh," she breathed, kneeling beside the wounded bird. "You poor thing."

Some of his ink-slick feathers were rumpled, and a small trickle of crimson blood drew a jagged line down his chest. He seemed to gasp for air through his open beak.

"Did you get hurt in the Wild Hunt?" she murmured. Ravens didn't typically fly in the dark, preferring to roost until morning instead. But last night she'd seen a storm of ravens—as well as hawks, owls, bats, vultures, magpies, jays, and gulls—soaring above the galloping shadowbreds and their riders. Perhaps this bird had been wounded in all the commotion.

He blinked one bright eye and clicked his beak. Cautiously, Lark stroked a finger along his wings. One definitely appeared broken.

She hesitated, glancing at the pine and oak trees casting shadows over the waymarker. Although she didn't sense a tingle of magic around this raven, he clearly had *some* connection to the Fae or he wouldn't have been flying on a Wild Hunt night. And that might make him dangerous.

The raven let out a hoarse croak that sounded eerily like *Help!*

Lark couldn't just leave him on the ground. These woods were home to red foxes, prowling cats, brown bears, and even an occasional hunting pack of wolves. A vulnerable raven might be eaten before she even made it home.

Besides, she had a knack for fixing broken things so maybe she could at least offer aid.

"I'm afraid I'll have to jostle you a bit," she told him, "but I'll bring you somewhere safe and I'll try to help you heal." She might not know much about mending wings, but she could ask Netty Greenwillow, the local healer, for advice. At the very least, she could provide food and water away from predators.

Scooting closer, she reached her hands beneath his body to scoop him into a soft pouch made by raising the edge of her blue tunic. As she did, something nicked her finger and she let out a surprised yelp.

Startled, the raven thrashed his good wing and paddled his feet. Worried he would hurt himself worse, she quickly nudged him into her tunic and wrapped the fabric around him. Before she straightened, however, she spotted the sharp rim of a thin circle in the matted grass beneath the bird. A bead of her blood still gleamed on the tarnished surface, oozing slowly into the silver as she studied it.

What was it? It was too large to be a coin. . . .

Was this what she had seen tumble from the king's pocket? It didn't look like a mirror, as Ma had assumed, but in the dirt it was hard to tell.

The raven shifted and clicked his beak. Impulsively, Lark pinched the metal disk—careful not to cut her fingertips on the sliver-thin edge this time—and thrust it into her pocket before hefting the bird in her arms and climbing to her feet.

She hurried home, the back of her neck prickling as though she were being watched the whole way.

She tried to distract herself from worry by imagining what magical Faevors her sister and brother might be awarded for completing the Hunt. Surely Galin's would be something special, since he'd helped the Harvest King?

When he got home, she would help Da fix a special meal to celebrate.

The raven croaked and Lark told him, "Everything will work out. You'll see." But she was trying to convince herself.